BLATANT DESTINY

Adventures of a Victorian Soldier - Book 3

M. J. TWOMEY

Warning

This book is a work of fiction. The scenes with actual people from these historic events are fictional. The place names used reflect names used in the nineteenth century.

CHAPTER ONE

April 9, 1860, Baltimore, County Cork, Ireland

It had been three years since he smelled gunpowder and wet his saber, three years since he'd killed a man, and three years since he helped to topple a tyrant. Life as a country squire in the southwest of Ireland was much simpler. Samuel Kingston swayed into the wind on the clifftop and scanned the craggy islands beyond the sea boiling in Baltimore Bay. What a view; what a beautiful place he'd chosen for his home. He was a fortunate man—even more fortunate to be alive.

Far below him, a fishing boat hurtled out of Baltimore harbor with her reefed sails taut. Seven miles away on the horizon, long and angular in profile against the wolf-gray sea, a steamship crept west around Fastnet Rock, a black rock thrusting out of the Celtic Sea like a broken tower. Sail disappearing for steam, portending the past bidding farewell to the present, just as Samuel now eschewed his bloody bygone days.

He lowered his battered spyglass. He'd sailed for leisure with Padraig many times since they'd returned from Nicaragua early in eighty-seven, and experience warned him the black clouds stacking the sullen sky promised foul weather, as did the bright-barked birches sawing in the blustery west wind around the manor. What sailor wouldn't already have run for a harbor in conditions like these? He lifted his lens again. He knew most of the fishermen in Baltimore, but the craft was too distant to recognize the helmsman or the two figures laying nets on the deck. He skimmed the lens back to the steamship, creaming the whitecaps, with smoke from her twin funnels smudging the dreary sky. Bound for New York, no doubt.

"Samuel."

He tapped the spyglass shut. He'd been to New York twice on his way to Nicaragua, and each trip had brought little but sadness.

"Padraig's here." Sofia beckoned him from the manor's courtyard. She still wore her tweed hacking jacket and the riding breeches that scandalized everybody in West Cork.

Chuckling, he pocketed his tube and headed back. It wasn't only his Nicaraguan wife's riding astride that shocked local society, it was their marriage. He was Protestant; she was Catholic and of a different race.

He swiped a hand through his windswept hair. To hell with them. The Kingstons were no strangers to controversy, a reputation founded in Father's outbursts against the Anglo-Irish landowners who'd caused thousands to die in the famine. The persistent rumor that Samuel had slain Louis Greenfell, the Fifth Earl of Baltimore, in Nicaragua hadn't endeared him to the gentry either, although Greenfell had bloody well deserved it after kidnapping Father and forcing Samuel to fight for William Walker. As a leader of the filibusters, the infamous American adventurers who traveled to Latin America to capture land, Walker had seized the Nicaraguan presidency and promptly brought back slavery, a practice Samuel despised even more than the British class system.

Sofia met him halfway across the rolled and manicured lawn, her honey-colored cheeks still flushed from her ride. She puckered her red lips to kiss him, smelling of apple-scented perfume, fresh sweat, and horses. "He's with John in the family dining room."

They'd only eaten in the formal dining room twice since occupying the new manor a year ago. All that money wasted on fashionable decor: a gas chandelier, heavy tapestries, a long table and black walnut chairs imported from France, and matching sideboards loaded with china, silver, and crystal. Still, they'd liberated a fortune in gold from William Walker, gold sent by the Earl of Baltimore and other greedy aristocrats keen to purchase a piece of Walker's slavery state. No reason they shouldn't spend it. He had plenty left, even after purchasing vast tracts of land around Baltimore.

The clatter of ash and the aroma of burning coal greeted them in the dining room. On his knees, warding off four-year-old John's clumsy strikes with a wooden saber, Padraig Kerr reminded Samuel of Padraig's father, a veteran of the Peninsular Wars who'd trained both of them to fight. Like Jerry, Padraig was above average height with a broad torso, pea-green eyes, and an untamable tangle of blond hair (though Jerry's was now waning).

"Look, Father," John squealed, bouncing from foot to foot. "Uncle Padraig brought me a birthday present. Someday I'll fight with the Seventeenth Lancers as you did."

"Your birthday's not until June, darling." Sofia disarmed the child deftly. "I think your uncle brought those toys for himself."

"Ah, Mama, eso no es justo."

"I don't want my baby going off to war. Do you want some Cossack to scar your nose like Padraig's?"

"*Sí!*" John touched his nose and screwed up his face, and the adults laughed.

"Don't think I didn't notice your Spanish, John." Samuel tousled his son's wavy black hair. "Remember, we only speak English at home."

"Uncle Padraig started it. He always speaks Spanish. You and Mama, too. I hear you."

Samuel chuckled and took out his tobacco. The frustration of living in a family that spoke two languages. "Yes, but we're not falling behind in English. You are. Do you want to be the only Corkman with a strange accent?"

John made a face. "I'm not a Corkman, I'm an Irishman."

Padraig whooped, making John jump, and thumped the boy's shoulder. "Good man. And never say you're British."

"You're not turning him into a Fenian rebel, are you?" Samuel offered Padraig his tobacco and paper.

Sofia swept the tobacco from his grasp. "Now Samuel, I asked you not to smoke around the children. Make do with snuff, and you can smoke in the library after we eat."

Padraig rubbed the purple scar across his nose, an injury from their ill-fated charge with the Light Brigade four years ago. Samuel shook his head to clear the memory as he pulled out Father's snuffbox.

"You shouldn't carry that around." Padraig placed his wooden sword on an overstuffed, leather chair. "You'd be distraught if you lost it. Carry another."

Samuel stroked the engraving on the gold box, the Kingston family crest, a knight's helmet above a rampant lion. "It was Father's favorite, may God rest his soul. I go nowhere without it." He offered the snuff to Padraig.

"John, run and see if your baby sister's awake," Sofia said. "I'm sure Padraig would love to see Maria."

"Ahh, Mother, she's only a baby. I want—"

"Don't you 'ahh, Mother' me, young man." Sofia switched to Spanish. "Really, Padraig. You mustn't put ideas of the army in his head. He's going to be a landowner like his Uncle Jason ... like his father finally is."

Samuel's mother had died giving birth to him, and María Kerr, Padraig's Spanish mother, had raised Samuel. Both men spoke Spanish fluently, a skill that served them well during Nicaragua's Filibuster War.

Samuel drifted to the bar cart. "He must learn to defend himself. You of all people know that, darling. Drink, Padraig?"

"Whiskey, please." Padraig rose from the red Persian rug and moved to the fireplace. "You're not too shabby with a carbine yourself, Sofia, as I recall."

She blew on her hands to warm them and joined him at the fire. "I don't know why Kitty lit the fires so late. Move over. You're hogging the heat with your backside stuck to the fireplace like a Bandon Town Protestant."

Firelight danced in the crystal glass Samuel handed to Padraig. He passed a glass of red wine to Sofia and pinched her playfully. "You've become as coarse as Mickey Óg. What has become of Colonel Valle's innocent daughter?"

It was a jest. Sofia was active in the Catholic church and helped old Father Mulcahy with the school he'd founded years ago at Springbough, the family estate close by in Clonakilty. She shared their Catholics tenants' disdain for the ruling class; that Samuel himself was Protestant hadn't tempered that. He understood her point. Though Anglo-Irish aristocrats controlled the country, most of them did little to protect the downtrodden peasant class who had few civil liberties, especially when it came to land rights and a franchise to vote. And to think he'd once thought having a title the most important thing in the world.

"Innocent? Colonel Valle's daughter is just plain rude." Padraig sniffed. "Calling me a Protestant—downright insulting."

"Well, you never show up at mass. Don't think your mother doesn't notice." Sofia poked her tongue out at him.

Samuel's lungs expanded. God, he loved this woman. He lifted his glass toward Padraig. "When you've been drinking all night, it's hard to fast and even harder to rise for mass the next day."

"I'll repent when I'm closer to dying." Padraig threw back his whiskey. "Sure, isn't that what confession's for? Anyway, I'm safe with all the indulgences Mam has offered to save my soul, enough to free every sinner in the county from purgatory"

Sofia stopped swirling the wine in her glass. "I remember a few times when death didn't seem far at all. You should go to mass."

"Don't worry." Padraig placed his glass on the mantle, picked up a brass poker, and stirred the fire. "There'll be no more wars for me. Steamboats are my future. I'll have the biggest fishing fleet in Ireland."

There was a knock on the open door, and Mickey Óg Spillane popped his head inside. He was as thin as a cadaver, as tall as Samuel at over six feet, with an old face, though he was only twenty-seven, the same age as Samuel and Padraig. He was the son of a cottier over at Springbough, the Kingston family estate where all three men had grown up, and Mickey had moved from Springbough to work as a laborer at the new manor, Las Peñitas. When all three had been boys, he'd trailed Samuel and Padraig everywhere. Mickey was far from bright, but he was loyal, and they were fond of him.

Mickey twisted his battered cap in his hand. "Beggin' your pardon, ma'am, but Cook mentioned you were looking for me."

"Oh yes, Mickey, thank you. It's about the croquet hoops." Sofia's amber eyes twinkled. "Didn't I ask you to place the hoops on the east lawn?"

Mickey bobbed his head. "Yes, mistress, you did. But sure, it made no sense to pound those metal hoops into dat beautiful lawn, so I made the crochet or whatever you call it closer to the Trag Beach cliff instead." He regarded Sofia and Samuel with a satisfied grin. "Clever, no?"

Padraig spluttered and spilled the whiskey he was pouring at the bar cart, and Samuel dipped his chin to hide a smile.

Sofia didn't blink. "Do you know what croquet is?"

"Dat newfangled knitting that Cook started doing. Bloody clever, really, because you only need one needle, so if you lose one of yer pair, you can keep going." He scratched his temple. "Come to think of it, I don't see what it has to do with dem hoops I was hammerin' in by the cliffs."

"Unless you're knitting a bloody big jumper." Padraig skipped behind Mickey and tickled him just as he had done when they were boys.

Sofia flashed Padraig a glare but spoke patiently to Mickey. "It's croquet, Mickey, not crochet. And thank you for considering my lawn, but a ball won't roll on the rocky ground and tuffets over there. Why don't you put the hoops where I suggested, please, and let me worry about the holes."

"Roight, ma'am. I see, ma'am, the ball has to roll." Mickey beamed as if she'd given him a prize. "I'll do dat right away, ma'am."

He stood there so long that Samuel wondered if he was waiting for Sofia to pet him. It wouldn't have surprised him; everyone on the estate worshipped her. "Thank you, Mickey. That'll be all."

"Roight, Master Samuel, I'll be off now."

Padraig took a sip of whiskey as Mickey left. "Our Mickey's not the sharpest saber in the armory, is he?"

"I can think of a few dumb things you've said too." Samuel moved to the bay window, where the steamship was now a smudge on the horizon. "That steamship got me thinking about Father, lying somewhere in the Nicaraguan jungle. I need to bring him home. He deserves to lie in peace with the rest of our ancestors. There are four generations of Kingstons in the grave-yard at Springbough. He's the only one missing."

Sofia joined him at the window. "You tried, darling. Emanuel Chavez combed that place and never found Father's body. An unmarked grave in the jungle, its's like searching for a coin buried on the seashore."

He placed his arms behind his back and gripped one wrist. "But I swore I'd bring him home. It's my fault he died there. If only I hadn't fought that blasted duel. It started the entire chain of disasters. Perhaps I—"

"Now, don't start on about that again." Padraig threw up his hand. "You were fifteen, and William Greenfell forced you into it."

He sensed Sofia drawing close, and she slipped a hand around his shoulders. "If you hadn't fought that duel, the Greenfells would never have compelled you to fight in Nicaragua, and you'd never have met me."

He softened at her optimism. "You're right, darling. I'm only saying that someday, I should search for him."

"I'll bet they buried him close to Greenfell's hacienda, where his underlings made us dig our own graves before trying to murder us." Padraig's fair face darkened.

"But someday." Sofia stared west toward the windswept cliff, a faraway look in her amber eyes. "And I could see Filipe again. I often wonder if he's truly all right. He writes he is, but that's a large hacienda to operate. And he's so young."

Samuel pictured her rambunctious brother. *Sofia in Trousers*, Padraig had once called him. "He's nineteen now, a man. And Chavez and the veterans of our old Euronica company will look after him."

"Twenty of the hardest pathfinders who ever lifted muskets." Padraig moved the play sword aside and winked at Sofia as he sat on the armchair. "I trained them myself. He'll be fine."

Samuel turned from the window and raised an eyebrow. "*You* trained them? As I recall, you didn't want the role of sergeant major and made me play the mean instructor."

"Well, they were the worst collection of miscreants ever conscripted into an army." Padraig beamed fondly. "Thieves, poachers, and worse."

"Don't forget the defrocked priest," Sofia added.

"A priest who could track and kill like an Indian," Samuel corrected. He missed the men who'd fought beside them too. Unlike his time in the Seventeenth Lancers, where the army had forbidden officers from fraternizing with enlisted men, Samuel had eaten with the Euronicas, camped with them, and even stolen ammunition with them when William Walker had refused to arm the native troops.

"Chavez *is* an Indian." Padraig uncurled a cigarette paper. "And now he's living with a nun."

Boots clattered in the hallway and Mickey Óg ran into the room, breathless. "They're in trouble. The hoops . . . I was—"

"The hoops are in trouble," Padraig cried teasingly. "Oh dear, what—"

"The boat, sir. Out in the sound."

Padraig sprang to his feet. "Who's out today? I kept my boats in the harbor. A storm is coming."

Samuel darted to the door. "I saw a fishing boat head out a while ago. Let's see."

All four of them strode across the green lawn. The roar of the tide as it raced out of Lough Hyne increased at the cliff's edge. In the ocean far below, close to where Samuel saw it earlier, the fishing boat shivered in the rolling waves. She had lost her mast, her gaff and sails were in the water, and a tangle of ropes and rigging littered her deck.

Padraig took a step back. "That's Finn Collins' *Oisín*. We must do something."

Samuel had never spoken to Collins, but he knew Padraig had crewed with him on the *Oisín* as a boy. "What can we do from here?"

"Here? Nothing." Padraig threw up a hand to shade his eyes and surveyed the sullen sky. "But we can get my boat and rescue him."

"It'll take too long to fire the boiler and make steam." Samuel had picked up some knowledge of steam engines in their travels through Nicaragua.

"Not today." Padraig faced into the wind as if gauging its strength. "Martin and I were working on the *San Juan* this morning, and we fired up the boiler. I left him searching for a leak, so he'll still have steam pressure. Come on."

Thank God he'd sailed frequently with Padraig these past

three years and had become an experienced sailor. He would need all his skill this day.

The fishing boats were tied up two and three vessels deep at Baltimore's tiny pier, with their halyards flogging in the wind, bucking on the waves. The rasps of their hulls grinding together made Samuel wince as he dismounted.

Padraig's two steamboats were easy to spot by their bright red funnels. He'd named them the *San Carlos* and the *San Juan*, after the riverboats on the San Juan River in Nicaragua. *Sure, didn't that place make us rich?* he'd asked Samuel. *This'll help me remember it.* Samuel had silently disagreed, preferring to forget much that had happened in Central America.

Padraig rubbed his hands together at the sight of smoke puffing from the *San Juan*'s funnel. "There you go, still flames in the firebox. I never doubted you, Martin, old boy. Right, let's get her underway."

Samuel passed Belle's reins to the stable boy who'd accompanied them. "Take the horses home, Brian, and watch for us from the cliff. When we sail back to harbor, bring them back." He glanced uneasily at the six-foot waves storming through the bay and swallowed. *If* they came back from the sea. He wasn't as comfortable as Padraig on the ocean. Padraig had helped on Finn Collins's boat while Samuel was at boarding school and was a seasoned sailor. The wind tugged at them, smelling of salt and fish, rattling the rigging of the boats around them.

He followed Padraig aboard the *San Carlos*, scrambling over nets and flailing his arms for balance. As he jumped across to the *San Juan*, the gleam of a round copper helmet on the *San Carlos* caught his attention, and he almost fell as he landed on the deck. He spun around and saw a tall chest with a brass wheel attached to either side of it. Was that an air pump? Padraig recently said he was going to start diving, but Samuel dismissed it as another wild notion.

"Is that a diving ..." Samuel shut up. Now was not the time to distract Padraig. Not when lives were at risk. Nevertheless, he'd have a word with his friend later and convince him to stop his daft diving plan.

Padraig cupped his hands around his mouth. "Martin, are you there? Martin?"

A surging wave lifted the vessels and shot a fountain of spray up between their hulls, soaking both men. Samuel lost his balance and fell to his knees.

Martin O'Sullivan, skipper of the *San Juan*, popped up from the companionway. The moon-faced old salt was far shorter than Padraig and had a belly as round as a cannon ball. He wiped his grease-stained face with a soiled rag. "Didn't expect you back. Sure, I'm finished. Fixed the leak in the feed line to the boiler and all."

"Good, because we need her now. Finn Collins is in trouble off Sherkin Island."

Martin stuffed the rag in his pocket. "Serves him bloody right. Told him there was a blow coming, and the wretch laughed. His father would roll over in his grave if he saw him. He taught him better. Now we've to stick our necks out to save the old goat. Fortunately, there's fire in the box. We'll have steam enough in a jiffy." He lifted his nose and sniffed the wind like a dog. "But the weather will get worse before it's better."

"We must chance it. Finn's always been good to me." Padraig moved to untie the bow line from the cleat. "Is your boy below?"

"Yes. But hold your horses till we get some steam up."

The sea poured over the *San Juan*'s prow as she plowed out of the harbor forty minutes later with the shrouds on her mast twanging as she rolled and plunged. Samuel clung to the cockpit coaming in a borrowed oilskin, with his forearm up to shield his eyes from the spray dashing over the bow. The icy water ran down his collar, making him shiver. The deck vibrated, and the engine snorted each time the bow burrowed into a trough and threw the propeller clear out of the water. His stomach churned. Thank God they hadn't eaten lunch. He didn't need Padraig teasing him for vomiting on the work-scarred deck. Martin's youngster, Peter, accustomed to the jarring movement, toiled below decks, where it stank of smoke and hot grease.

Sherkin Island's pier was a half mile off the bow as they steamed south when Samuel spotted Collins's *Oisín* wallowing in the sound between the island and the stubby peninsula. It was three cables away, so low in the water it often disappeared into the troughs. The spars and sails were overboard, streaming a web of ropes and rigging that held the hull's stern to the wind so the waves struck the boat beam on. Two men clung to the jagged stump of the mast while another gripped the tiller hard over to port.

"There. Do you see her?" Samuel bellowed into the wind.

The crew at the mast's stump waved frantically and shouted.

"I've got her." Padraig took the wheel. "Martin, take Samuel forward and prepare a heaving line."

Martin hesitated, chewing the inside of his cheek.

Padraig jammed the brass engine order telegraph to the right. "You're the skipper, but this is my boat. We've still got a chance before Finn's on the rocks."

Samuel lurched to the starboard side and grabbed the gunwale railing as the deck vibrated harder and the screw churned to maximum revolutions. Waves reared over the side and showered him, and his arms wrenched in their sockets as he clung on.

"One hand for the boat and one for the work," Padraig bellowed above the chaos. "Hold on at all times."

Hold on? Hell, Samuel had no intention of releasing his grip. But he had to, because Martin was thrusting the end of a coiled rope into his hand.

"Tow rope line. Belay this bitter end on that cleat there, Mr. Kingston. I'll bend the other end onto a messenger line."

"Hang more fenders on the starboard side." Padraig jabbed a finger at the canvas pads hanging from the opposite side of the boat, which were used to stop the pier wall or boat moored alongside from scratching the hull. "Take them from the port gunwale."

The *San Juan* was narrow, but the pitching deck made it seem fifteen yards wide. Samuel wasn't going over there; the *San Juan* would have to take her scratches. He clung to the gunwale.

Martin crawled across the bucking craft, untied the fenders from the port side and draped them over the opposite rail.

Fifteen minutes later, *Oisín* was fifteen yards away, wallowing low in the water, listing to port.

"Is it hopeless?" Samuel would have been happier charging a hundred Cossacks.

The wind whipped off Padraig's flat cap, and it landed aft at the transom.

The rain plastered his blond hair back from his broad forehead as he wrestled the wheel. "I'm not leaving them out here." His voice was barely audible above the engine's growl and the waves thumping the hull.

"If anyone can do it, your man can," Martin reassured Samuel. "He's a born sailor."

Padraig moved the engine order telegraph back, and seconds later, the *San Juan* slowed. He coaxed her upwind of the *Oisín* and signaled Peter in the engine room to stop the screw churning. They stalled, rocking alarmingly but sheltering the smaller boat in their lee.

The wind pushed the *San Juan* toward the fishing boat. The fishermen's pleas overcame the wind, and blood poured from a gash in one man's head. One fisherman released his grip on the mast's stump and lurched to the gunwale.

Martin heaved the messenger line high, and the wind snatched it, pushing it over the side of the crippled boat. It landed three feet aft of the fisherman, who dove on it.

Samuel released his held breath. "He's got it."

"Make sure the rope runs free when he pulls it." Martin began feeding line over the side.

A wave surged across the *Oisín*, rushing knee deep over her deck and almost sweeping the fisherman off his feet. The *San Juan* was ten feet from the fishing boat now, and Padraig's face was pale as he hovered a hand over the engine order telegraph. If a wave hurled them onto the sinking boat, their hull would cave in. The heavy rope tugged and ran through Samuel's hands, the prickly hemp heating his palms. A second fisherman crawled down to help his mate, and together they hauled the line across. Waves exploded over their heads, and the wind buffeted them, flogging their oilskins around their knees. The helmsman—it had to be Finn Collins—staggered to the mast and helped the injured man over to where the other clung to the side in the boat's waist. He pumped his fist in the air and cheered when the thicker rope came aboard.

Padraig levered the engine order telegraph to starboard, the engine chugged faster, and the *San Juan* labored ahead. "Take up the slack."

Samuel stood shoulder to shoulder with Martin and hauled on the rope. It was like trying to move a mountain. The spiky hemp sawed in his hands, burning his palms. The *San Juan* chugged closer to the sinking boat, nervous as a virgin mare before a stallion. In interminable minutes that seemed like hours, Padraig maneuvered the *San Juan* forward and astern, slackening the line that Samuel and Martin hauled in until Samuel's hands were blistered and his muscles ached.

Even as Samuel had nothing left to give, a wave lifted the *San Juan* and slammed her down beside the *Oisín* in a fountain of spray.

"God bless, lads, you made it." Finn pushed the injured youth across toward Martin as Samuel belayed the line on a cleat.

Martin dragged the youth over the side by the scruff of his neck. "Christ, Finn, but you're the lucky man. And who's this? Bridie Ahern's lad, is it?"

The youth flopped facedown on the deck. "B-blessed Virgin, we're s-saved."

Martin scoffed and helped a second crewman aboard. "'Tis Padraig Kerr you should thank, Raymond. Nobody else would've been crazy enough to come after you today, not even the Blessed Virgin. We can't save your boat, Finn."

"I know. Rescuing us is enough." Collins tapped the shoulder of the waterlogged fisherman beside him. "You're next, Terry."

Collins jumped across to the *San Carlos* last. When he landed beside Terry on deck, Padraig rammed the engine order telegraph over, and Martin cut the rope tied to the *Oisín* with a single blow of a hand axe. The engine growled, and the *San Carlos* surged away from the sinking boat.

Samuel almost heard Collins's bones creak as he slumped on the wet deck. "I never thought I'd be happy to see one of these infernal steam machines." He was an old man, with a scanty white beard covering his long chin and sharp eyes in his leathered face.

Something rasped along the *San Juan*'s hull, and her stern jinked hard to port as she jarred to a halt, pitching Samuel off balance. The wheel spun wildly, and Padraig cursed as the spokes slapped his hands. Heart pounding, Samuel grabbed the stern rail and peered over the transom. Hooked under the *San Juan*, a rope streaming from the fishing boat was slackening and tautening as the waves rolled under the stern.

Hard-soled shoes beat the deck, and Padraig arrived beside Samuel. "The devil's luck, it's wrapped around the rudder. We must cut it free before it rips the steering off. If it's wrapped around the screw, the *Oisín* could drag us under when she sinks." He stooped to untie his shoelaces.

The steamboat yawed and pitched in the wild Celtic Sea swells. The water would be freezing, but Samuel was a far stronger swimmer than Padraig.

"I'm the better choice." He peeled off his oilskin and shivered in the April wind.

Padraig grabbed him by the arm. "You won't know what to do."

"Cut that bloody rope, isn't it?" Samuel unbuttoned his shirt. "I managed fine when I slashed that revenue cutter's steering lines back in New York."

"Fair enough."

"I need a sharp knife."

Tools rattled in a nearby locker, and Padraig pulled out a sheathed knife. "This has a serrated edge. It'll saw through faster. Hurry, we don't have much time."

Samuel stripped off his trousers and stood shaking as Padraig threaded a piece of rope through the loop in the knife's sheath.

Collins let out a breath. "Christ, Mr. Kingston, those scars on your shoulder and leg . . . Got them in the war, did you?"

Samuel ignored him and tied the knife around his waist while Padraig dropped a rope ladder from the entry port. Spray squirted three feet into the air, and the hull groaned each time the stern thumped on a wave. If he thought about what he was doing too long, he mightn't plunge in at all.

He scratched his stomach on the transom as he slipped into the seething sea. As he sank in the freezing ocean and dropped his jaw in shock, saltwater gushed into his mouth—acrid, icy cold churning down his throat—it sparked paralyzing spasms, choking him, locking his windpipe so he could not breathe. Eyes squeezed shut, he flailed in the waves, coughing violently, fighting for air. His gullet opened, the wheezing subsided, and he panted in shallow breaths. He had to settle down, to take control. His breathing steadied, but panic lurked a heartbeat away.

"On your left," Padraig hollered, "three feet away. No, not that way—behind you. Hurry."

As a wave heaved Samuel upward, he forced his eyes open, wincing as the saltwater stung them. The rope was there, flecked with tar and taut as an ash lance. He gulped salty, stinging air, kicked his legs, and grabbed hold of the scratchy hemp before bowing his head to meet the next wave. His ears popped as it swallowed him, but he clung to the rope, his shoulder muscles creaking painfully.

Surfacing again, he took a deep breath and wrapped his leg around the bucking line. It hummed like a bowstring as the *San Juan* rocked and juddered five feet away, and the spikey hemp gnawed at his shin and ankle as he began slicing it with his blade. His head was underwater, he couldn't see, and his hands were numb from the cold, but he still felt pain when he cut a finger. Plunging up and down in the water, he dared not open his mouth, and the pressure to breathe built like steam in a boiler. His arms ached, and the twanging movement and lack of air disoriented him. He must continue cutting—nothing but severing this line mattered if he wanted to live, if any of them were to survive. White spots spun before his eyes, and his head reeled. All that mattered was cutting that cursed rope, and he kept on sawing the blade.

His lungs clamped, involuntarily driving bubbles of air from his lips. His eyes flew open even as the tar-flecked hemp unraveled and parted. It lashed him as it whipped away into the watery gloom. Pain shot, hot as fire, up his side, and he dropped the knife. He flailed and broke the surface, sucking air into his burning lungs, his heart pounding and blood coursing in his ears. *Settle down, breathe steadily. Control yourself or you'll drown.* He trod water, forcing his breath to gentle while the waves tossed him like flotsam with the boundless power of the ocean.

When he opened his eyes, the *San Juan* was twenty feet away, pitching on the waves. Padraig was shouting and beckoning wildly, but all he could hear was the grinding, seething surf. He swam hand over hand, pitching up and down, his heavy legs dragging him under, his teeth chattering. Padraig wouldn't engage the screw for fear of chopping him to pieces. It was up to Samuel.

He was numb from cold, and his muscles were screaming. He wearily kicked his legs, threw an arm forward, and dragged it back as he flung the other arm ahead. This was getting him nowhere. He craned around, grabbed another breath on the crest of a wave, and shot out a weary arm—a feeble stroke. He'd nothing left.

He began to sink, flailing as pressure stung his eardrums. His arm snagged a rope, and he opened his eyes. A messenger line from the *San Juan*.

Energy jolted through him, and he clawed the line closer. He wound his arms around the rope and clung to it as another wave surged upward. The line went taut and yanked him forward. At the peak of the wave, he glimpsed two blurred figures on the boat reaching for him.

His stomach threshed. He was saved.

At the transom, he grabbed the greasy rope ladder and coughed to clear his aching lungs. He lacked the strength to climb. His scrabbling feet grazed the barnacles clinging to the hull, and the stinging pain on his bare soles made him wheeze.

Boots clattered on the deck above him, and hands clutched him beneath the armpits.

"We have you, lad, fair play to you," Martin wheezed as they dragged him inboard and deposited him in a quaking heap on the deck. "The *Oisín's* gone down. If 'twasn't for you, she'd have taken the lot of us with her."

Samuel sagged on the deck, reassured by the changing beat of the engine and the smoke and embers vomiting from the funnel into the sullen sky. Padraig removed a white-knuckled hand from the wheel, twisted around, and smiled. Despite the raging weather, the fishermen closed around Samuel to clasp his shoulder and pat his back, and he did his best to return their silent thanks with an energy he did not feel as Padraig creaked his head from side to side, as if grinding out the tension. *Oisín's* crew had been lucky. Only a skilled sailor could have managed this rescue.

Several feet away, Old Finn sat with his back against the gunwale. He fixed Samuel with his bloodshot blue eyes. "Nasty day. Are you too wet to light a smoke?"

CHAPTER TWO

"'With us, there can be no choice; honor and duty call on us to pursue the path we have entered, and we dare not be deaf to the appeal. By the bones of the moldering dead at Masaya, at Rivas, and at Granada, I adjure you never to abandon the cause of Nicaragua. Let it be your waking and your sleeping thought to devise means for a return to the land whence we were unjustly brought. And, if we be but true to ourselves, all will yet end well.'" Parker French looked up from the manuscript. "A fine rallying call, General. Your account of the Central American campaign ends with the promise of a new beginning."

William Walker took a deep breath of humid air thick with the stench of New Orlean's French Quarter sewers. It had been a great idea to write in the third person, like Julius Caesar's account of his Gallic Wars; it sounded unbiased. This would enhance his reputation and bring volunteers flocking to his lone star banner when he returned to seize all Central America. He tugged at his black cravat and glanced out the arched window. Shutters thrown open, and not a gust of wind stirred the clammy New Orleans heat. "President. Call me President. I'm the elected president of Nicaragua. Tell me, will the public greet this account sympathetically?"

French sucked in his cheeks. "To be honest, General—Mr. President—you portray some of our former comrades as unreliable. They won't be happy about that." French claimed to be the same age as Walker, thirty-four, but his smooth skin and high cheekbones made him look much younger.

Walker snatched the book from French's hand. Because of his limited resources, he'd trusted too many liars, braggarts, and fools, the likes of Domingo de Goicuria, Louis Schlessinger, Henry Titus—and of course, Parker H. French, but he wouldn't mention that. He needed French for an unsavory task. The snake would be ideal for destroying the turncoat, Samuel Kingston. "The account must be authentic. And I spoke no ill of you. I never mentioned that you swindled settlers on the Oregon Trail or joined with Mexican brigands to rob some of those same settlers when they discovered your deceit. Had I known that history, I would never have sent you to Washington as my ambassador. Frankly, you embarrassed me."

Dealing with a crook like French was hot work on a hotter evening. Walker rose from the overstuffed armchair and moved to the window. Perhaps he'd catch a puff of fresh air. But there was nary a breath up Royal Street; the still air was tainted with the stench of urine and stale booze. The clocks had barely struck eight but revelers were inebriated already, staggering from bar to bar on the narrow street, catcalling prostitutes or brawling over the price of a drink.

French's close-set eyes widened, and he rushed to defend himself. "That's unfair, sir. I've stood beside you through the worst of it. When others—"

"I don't need the world's approval to carve out an empire in Central America."

A knock sounded on the door, and Joe Czarnowski walked in. "Telegram, Mr. President. From New York."

Walker's skin prickled as he took the paper from Czarnowski. He'd forbidden his agents to put anything in writing unless it was urgent. He ripped it open.

. . .

NEW YORK

April 10, 1860

Contributions for trade mission are slow. Anticipate sufficient for initial journey but will need substantial funds to keep mission active. Urgent that you source alternative funds.

Frank Anderson

Walker ripped the card into pieces. His last venture in Nicaragua had made the investors nervous, and the lily-livered scoundrels wanted to sit on the fence until he handed them the nation. Crying shame the Earl of Lucan and his cronies had backed away as well, but they were terrified Samuel Kingston would publish the Baltimore papers, proof of the Anglo lords' involvement in his plans to abolish the slavery ban in Nicaragua. Damned Kingston. And if the interfering Irishman hadn't stolen his gold—

Czarnowski coughed and tugged at his braided queue. "Will there be a reply, sir?"

"No, damn it, that'll be all." Walker dismissed Czarnowski with a jerky wave. It was no matter; the plan in motion would take care of it all. Kingston was the key, but far too clever. He needed careful plans to capture him. "Back off, French, give me room to think."

French sidled back toward the window, mopping his sweating neck with a bandanna. He was a weasel, but he was the right man for this job. He'd claimed to have lost his left arm in the Mexican War, but he'd also claimed to have been a lawyer in California.

"I'm willing to offer you a hacienda in Nicaragua," Walker said, "if you help me capture Samuel Kingston."

"Kingston." French smoothed the empty sleeve of his impeccably pressed frock coat. "He's a tough one. I was lucky to escape with my life the last time we clashed. Why him?"

"I'd control Nicaragua now if it weren't for his interference. First, he stole a fortune in gold—my war chest—then he helped the Costa Ricans cut my supply line. Without access to volunteers and supplies, it was only a matter of time before the Central American allies defeated us." It would be different this time; he would ally with General Cabañas and his Honduran rebels. "You were with de Burg when he buried Kingston's father, were you not?"

French bit his lip and hesitated. Walker tapped his foot. The bastard was weighing his options, seeking the best advantage.

French made eye contact. "You assigned me to work with de Burg, but—"

"So you know where the body is?" He didn't have time for games. He was late for a meeting to review evidence with Maloney.

"Yes, yes, I do. What of it?"

"Colonel Valle's son has searched everywhere in San Juan del Sur, including de Burg's old estate, for the body." Walker dabbed his sweating forehead with a neatly folded handkerchief. "I hear Kingston wants to bury his father in Ireland. If we can lead young Valle to the remains—anonymously, of course—Kingston will come for it. When he does, you'll capture him and force him to return my gold." If he didn't get his hands on Kingston first himself. But French didn't need to know that part.

"It's almost five years since he took your gold. What makes you think he still has it?"

"He purchased a vast estate in Ireland. He must have money still, but if he doesn't, he can mortgage his land to ransom his freedom. But once he pays . . ." Walker's throat throbbed. "Once he pays that ransom, I'll kill him for ruining my plans."

French raised his hand. "Hold on there, General. This isn't my fight, and Kingston's in Ireland now. Why not have your Irish associates deal with him?"

"They dare not act against him." Walker glowered at French. This was his fault, and he should fix it. "I ordered you to make sure de Burg delivered the gold to my barracks, and you let Kingston take it—and you're the only survivor of his attack. So what really happened?"

"It's as I've explained, sir. He and thirty of his savages ambushed us on the road. I fought my way free and escaped when the rest of the men fell."

The liar. Walker ground his teeth. He'd visited the ambush site the following day and seen the tracks of five attackers, not thirty. He swatted the air as if it would sweep French's lies away. Still, he had to tread lightly; he needed the oaf. "Whatever. In the end, you let Kingston take my gold, and now you must retrieve it. As I said, I'll give you the Valle hacienda if you capture Kingston."

French whistled appreciatively. "All of it? What exactly must I do?"

Loud voices floated through the open windows; more people were about in the street. He should have chosen a hotel on the edge of town. "I've two hundred volunteers training outside the city, and as soon as I beat this charge, we're sailing for Greytown. I want you to go ahead to Nicaragua and find Colonel Ivan Garcia, the director of the Chinandega Department. He's still loyal to me, and he'll help you spread word of the grave's location. Once Filipe Valle hears of it, I'm certain he'll send men to find old Kingston's bones." Finally he'd pay Kingston back. Walker's throat was dry, and he picked up the glass of water. "All you need do is wait for Kingston to show up."

"All? Kingston's dangerous. I can't take him without help."

"Don't worry, you'll be reinforced before he arrives."

"And the Valle estate? You'll really give it to me?"

"Capture Kingston and it's yours."

"Slaver," yelled somebody in the street, and a bottle flew through the open window and shattered on the parquet floor.

A rock clattered against a shutter, and Walker flinched. He hurried to the desk and picked up his revolver.

"Come out, you tyrant," a woman screamed shrilly.

French's face glistened with sweat as he produced his own pistol. "Who are they?"

"Abolitionists. They've been agitating since my trial began. Don't worry—"

A rap on the door interrupted him. "President Walker, we need to leave now before these wretches block us in."

Walker rammed the revolver into the holster at his waist and snorted impatiently. Maloney should've wrapped up this case by now, but like a typical lawyer, he was dragging it out. He should've defended himself. God, he was sick of America. Even the South was going soft. "Let's go, then."

The sound of scuffles and angry voices rose from the street.

"Go home, Yank, and leave Mr. Walker in peace. This is the South, and you ain't telling us what to do."

"Damnation, you're unpopular." French tugged at the collar of his shirt.

"Blasted darkie-lovers." This voice was slurred. "Three cheers for President Walker."

French smirked. "And popular."

"Shut up. I have to leave." Walker crammed on his black felt hat and strode to the door. "Get down to Nicaragua and deal with Kingston."

In the hall, Joe Czarnowski surrounded him with four rifle-toting guards. "Twenty of them out there fixin' to stir up trouble, Mr. President, and about the same number of your supporters."

"We'll head directly for Maloney's chambers." Walker descended two steps at a time. "If they block us, knock some heads."

The low snarl of voices outside grew louder as they approached the stained-glass front door. Czarnowski threw it open to a sea of sweaty, twisted faces and snarling mouths.

"There's Walker. Murderer!"

"Slaver."

"Go get 'em, Walker! You should be our president here, not in Nicaragua."

This spectacle had gone on for days, and Czarnowski clearly knew Walker's supporters from his detractors. He hammered the butt of his rifle into a stout man's gut, toppling him against those behind him. The other guards followed his lead, punching a gap through the cheering and jeering factions.

Walker followed behind them, smacking his bone-dry lips. Maloney had better haul up his breeches and squash these charges. This scene was getting tiresome.

CHAPTER THREE

"I don't see what business I have with your family solicitor and Ireland's solicitor general. Why would they ask you to invite me?" Padraig pushed the green velvet drapes farther back and peered out the large bay window of Las Peñitas's well-appointed sitting room. "I'm no good at mixing with these highbrow muckety-mucks. Chester Inwood's the other visitor, you said? He has an estate in North Cork, right? I heard about him. He treats his tenants well by all accounts."

"Your father says so. I don't know why they're coming, but it's a chance to ask Rickard Deasy about his proposed land act. I need to know if he got my letters and included my suggestions." Samuel rose from the green silk sofa as the butler padded into the room. "It's all right, Peadar. I'll take care of the drinks. Want a whiskey, Padraig?"

"I'm awake, am I not? Whiskey, of course." Padraig fiddled with the window latch.

Peadar fussed with his navy livery. "Are you certain, Master Kingston? I know how you like your whiskey."

"Neat. He takes it neat, Peadar. I should know, I was his orderly for years." The window sash creaked as Padraig lifted it, and the spring breeze rustled the lace curtains, filling the room with the smell of fresh-cut grass and salty ocean. "That's better, it's awfully close in here."

"He was a hopeless orderly, Peadar; he seldom lifted a finger." Samuel popped the stopper from the crystal decanter on the bar cart.

"So you can thank me for training him, Peadar. I'll have a double, Samuel."

Peadar wiggled his bushy gray eyebrows. "Then I'll leave you to it, sirs."

"That must be them now." Padraig pressed his scarred nose against the glass. "Fine pair of blacks hauling Mr. Inwood's coach. Or should I say his lordship? I never know with you landowners."

"It's Mister Inwood. Many of the landowners have no titles." Samuel pushed the stopper back in the decanter. "I suppose we better wait until they get here, or they might think us rude."

"Public school boys, always worried what people will think. Pour my blooming whiskey, for goodness sake." Padraig stooped and stuck his head out the window. "My, aren't your visitors afternoonified? Toffs dressed to the nines to impress the master of Las Peñitas."

Samuel had to smile. Who was Padraig to talk? He was wearing an expensively tailored waistcoat and tight checker-patterned pants in the latest London fashion. It was a wonder he hadn't split them. "Listen to the kettle calling the pot smoky and wearing those ridiculous gas-pipes. Stop gawking out the window as if you've never seen a carriage. Sit down, for God's sake."

There was something familiar about one of the two men Peadar ushered in with Peter Norton. Around Samuel's age, the stocky man had a wine-colored birthmark on his forehead partially hidden beneath dusty blond curls.

"Samuel, what a pleasure." Norton approached with zeal that belied his years. "Thank you for meeting us."

"Of course, Mister Norton." Samuel shook the gnarled hand.

"I must confess I'm eager to hear what this mysterious meeting's about."

"You may know Chester Inwood. Chester has an estate outside Middleton."

Inwood shook Samuel's hand. "We met once in Cork, at Reverend Welby's funeral. At Saint Anne's in Shandon."

Welby's rigid opposition to Samuel's marriage had not endeared the former pastor at the local church in Kilgariffe to him. Not like Reverend Mills, the incumbent, who treated everyone as Christians regardless of where they worshipped. Samuel had only attended Welby's funeral at Jason's insistence. "I thought I knew you, Mr. Inwood. Welcome."

The third visitor had a patrician air; he was lean with receding hair and a jutting chin, more striking than handsome. All the same, there was something attractive about his engaging smile, the reassuring grip of his hand, and the amiable tone of voice. "Rickard Deasy from Enniskean."

It took much control not to shuffle back. Rickard Deasy, Member of parliament for County Cork and solicitor general for Ireland stood in his sitting room. "Welcome, Mr. Deasy. I mean . . . or should I say Your Honor?"

Deasy laughed easily. "Rickard. Please call me, Rickard, Captain."

Captain had been Samuel's rank in Nicaragua, under William Walker in the Democrat army, but few people in Ireland even knew he'd fought in Central America; it was not something he was proud of. How much did the solicitor general know about him? Who had told him?

Samuel angled his chin away to hide his reddening face and touched one of the overstuffed wingback chairs arranged around the marble fireplace. "Please, call me Samuel. Why don't you take a seat? A drink perhaps? Whiskey? Wine? A gin?"

"Sorry I'm late, gentlemen. One of the tenants stopped by for my advice." Sofia whisked into the room, stunning in a powder-blue floor-skimming dress fitted over a bodice that emphasized her slim waist. Samuel savored the unmistakable scent of apple perfume, it was so her.

She had obviously impressed Inwood; whose jaw dropped while his gray-blue eyes widened.

Deasy, the suave politician, stepped forward to greet her. "Mrs. Kingston, I presume? Thank you for receiving us."

After they sat and exchanged the customary pleasantries, Deasy took out his pipe and tobacco while Peadar poured drinks. "I'll cut to the chase, gentlemen. I've reviewed your careers and found them remarkable. You fought valiantly for the Crown overseas, but I find it even more remarkable that you helped topple that filibuster, William Walker in Central America."

Samuel's hand halted the glass he was passing to Padraig, who jerked his head back. How the hell had Deasy discovered th—

"Don't blame old Norton here, he kept your affairs private, as any solicitor should." Deasy used a penknife to tamp the tobacco in his pipe. "I have access to intelligence from all over the world in my position. But we're not here to talk about that. We're here because you two are a good example of what Ireland must become. Irishman and Anglo-Irishman, Protestant and Catholic, working together to promote a greater good. Now we want you to help us promote a better Ireland. Samuel, like your father, you've have been loud in your defense of tenant rights. I received your letters."

"What rights?" Samuel ran a hand through his hair to bridle his frustration. "Tenants live in one-room stone shacks with earthen floors, no chimney for a fire to warm them; not even a window. The little food they can keep after paying rent is inadequate and monotonous. They have no security of tenure, and landlords can toss them out at will." Samuel found he had moved to the edge of his chair. He flushed and slumped back beside Sofia. "Sorry, I—"

It was Inman who now sat forward, and he offered a small smile. "No, not at all. I quite understand. But you're not the only

Anglo-Irishman who feels that way. We want to change this inequity. Rickard has included your suggestions in the new legislation and now he's steering it through parliament."

Samuel took a deep sip of whiskey, and it burned his throat. He shouldn't have let his passion sweep him away. Deasy had acted on his ideas. "The Landlord and Tenant Law Amendment Act. Thank you, sir. I'm grateful." He raised his glass toward Deasy, who scraped a match with his thumb.

The politician touched the spluttering lucifer to the bowl of his pipe and puffed out a cloud of smoke. "This law will help these people immensely. It abolishes any feudal rents paid by labor to a landlord and makes contract law the basis for tenancies. It protects tenants. Nobody can be evicted at a whim anymore."

"And it provides that all leases of over twelve months must be evidenced in writing to be enforced as you suggested." Inwood set his glass on the walnut coffee table and rubbed his hands together.

Samuel scanned their animated faces. These men cared.

Padraig huffed and pulled his tobacco from his pocket. "You'll never get parliament to pass that act. Too many Anglo-Irish conservatives will block you. It's not in their interest to give anything to tenants, to Catholics."

Deasy gestured with his smoking pipe, and the sweet scent reminded Samuel of Father. "No, Padraig. Don't think this is about religion. It's about wealth and power. Anglo-Irish Prot—"

"We want to rectify this wrong, as do many of the landowners I know. They're—" Inwood flushed. "Sorry, Rickard, I didn't mean to interrupt you."

Deasy waved him on with a flourish. "No, carry on."

"Many of us want to improve our tenants lives. We're doing that on our own estates, and we want to make it law." Inwood glanced at the door before lowering his voice. "You'd be surprised how many Anglo-Irish patriots want Ireland to have its own parliament again."

"Fat chance of that." Padraig spread a cigarette paper on the coffee table. "Back in 1800, the Anglo-Irish of the Protestant Ascendancy controlled the Irish parliament and consented to its extinction when they voted for the Union. Of course, they were well rewarded with pensions, peerages, and—"

"Now that's not strictly true, Padraig." Inwood paused. "I did it again. Interrupted. Sorry."

Inwood's politeness or his passion seemed to disarmed Padraig or perhaps, like Samuel, he had remembered there were Anglo-Irish patriots. Some, like Wolf Tone and Robert Emmett, had even died for Ireland.

Padraig waved his hand. "I admire your enthusiasm. Carry on."

"I was going to say that the Catholic hierarchy was strongly in favor of the Union back then, hoping for rapid emancipation and the rights of Catholics to sit as MPs."

"And, to be fair, they might have been right." Samuel peeled a cigarette paper from Padraig's packet. Anglo-Irishmen helped O'Connell push the emancipation act through parliament."

"Even Palmerston supported the Catholic Emancipation Act," Chester said.

Padraig threw down his box of lucifers without lighting his cigarette. "Palmerston! Don't talk to me about that churl. He was the worst of the absentee landlords back in the famine. Worse than bloody Lucan. Didn't he evict two thousand tenants when they couldn't pay their rent, and them all starving. How the hell could they pay with the spuds rotting in—"

"Calm down, Padraig." Sofia's face flushed. "Please lower your tone. What will little John think of you if he hears this shouting?"

China rattled as Peadar halted at the door with a tray of cups, saucers, and silver, his eyebrows shooting up his forehead. Ann, the young parlor maid, almost dropped a silver tray stacked with sandwiches as she bumped into him and yelped.

"Look, you terrified Ann." Sofia pulled a face at Padraig. "Come in, Peadar. Ann. You know Padraig doesn't bite."

Padraig could be such a hothead, and these men seemed genuine. If anything were to change in Ireland, it would require the Irish and the Anglo-Irish to work together. The new liberal party had formed a government the year before with the third Viscount Palmerston, Henry John Temple, an Anglo-Irishman, as prime minister. Was it possible this alliance of disgruntled Whigs, free trade supporting Peelites, and reformist Radicals would do more for Ireland? Deasy's land act hinted they might.

Unbidden, Inwood fetched a side table and helped Ann set down the tray as Peadar passed out cups and saucers. "Padraig, I understand your concerns. But consider this: Palmerston is far from perfect, but he's better than the conservatives. We must work with what we have."

Padraig's breathing slowed, and he lit his cigarette, saying nothing.

"Shall I pour the tea, Mrs. Kingston? Help your young lady here?" Inwood hovered a hand over the teapot.

"Thank you, Mr. Inwood. Very kind of you." Sofia exchanged glances with Samuel.

He studied Inwood anew. A man volunteering to bitch the pot; he seemed a perfect gentleman.

"This brings us to the reason for our visit." Inwood finished pouring Sofia's tea. "I understand your concerns, Padraig, but perhaps you can help. To further our political agenda, we need more liberals elected to parliament. We'd like one of you to stand for a Cork County parliament seat."

Padraig dropped his ham sandwich on his lap. Samuel's skin tingled, and his thoughts fuzzed.

"Me run for the British parliament? I think that whiskey went to your head, sir." Padraig picked up the sandwich and huffed. "Escúchalo a él. Not a chance, I won't be seen dead in the British parliament. Nest of vipers. The Anglo-Irish members are not inclined to help the poor here."

Deasy tugged at his dark-colored cravat, Norton squirmed in his seat, and Inwood bit his lip, all staring at Padraig as if struggling to understand his Spanish.

"Padraig has pressing business concerns and feels he has no time for politics." Samuel's translation was far more diplomatic than it was accurate.

"I understand." Inwood picked a sandwich from the plate offered by Sofia. "Thank you, Mrs. Kingston. And how about you, Samuel? Would you consider running for office? We need more Anglo-Irish patriots on the inside, working to free Ireland from the close control of the British parliament." His voice trailed off as Deasy shifted in the chair beside him.

Deasy's eyes flicked to the door and back to Samuel. "Confidentially, our final objective is reestablishment of an Irish parliament; a contentious goal best approached softly. This win with the new land act is a beginning. Your family is popular with the middle class in West Cork, you'd find a lot of support if you ran."

A seat in the British parliament beside men like Lord Paget and Palmerston, this was an outrageous idea. Samuel brushed crumbs off his frock coat.

"I implore you not to dismiss this out of hand." Deasy's dark eyes fixed sharply on Samuel. "I admit it's hard to focus parliament on Irish affairs with all the distractions from other parts of the far-flung empire, but we must try. You—we may dislike Palmerston, but he's mellowed on the Irish question, though the rhetoric of militant Irish Americans still gives him sleepless nights. He can be swayed, especially if all factions from this island work together: Irishman, Anglo-Irishman, liberal and conservative."

Samuel glanced at Sofia. What did she think?

"It's not about religion." Sofia's cup rattled as she placed it and the saucer on the side table. "It's about wealth and power. We had a civil war in Nicaragua, Catholic against Catholic; it was about land, power, and wealth."

"The Anglo-Irish have all the land. They stole it from us." Padraig jabbed his jaw out, challenging them.

"The Kingstons have owned this land well over a hundred years, Padraig." Samuel knew it was a complicated, thorny subject. "We've invested everything in it. Who exactly should we return it to? While pondering that question, should Norman descendants return their land in England to the descendants of the Anglo-Saxons? Should the Anglos in their turn surrender their land to the descendants of the original Britons whose country they invaded? Where will it end?"

Deasy had fired up his pipe again, and he puffed a cloud of blue smoke into the air. "That would be difficult. But perhaps we can find an equitable way to share the land, a buyback or something. My family are brewers, and the people buy the booze. I jest, of course. But whatever we think of Palmerston, we must find a way to work with him. More hard times lie ahead for small holders and cottiers if nothing changes. The Americans are flooding Europe with cheap corn, and that is driving down earnings here."

Inwood blew out a long breath. "Dear God, I hope you are wrong, Rickard. What with taxes, expenses, and poor grain prices, it's already a challenge preserving my property intact and maintaining good relations with the tenants."

This was a chance to make a difference, to litigate for tenant rights, land rights, and possibly Ireland's independence. But to enter the snake pit of politics . . . Samuel bit the inside of his cheek.

Deasy saw him glance at Sofia and clasped his hands. "It's a big ask, I know, and we've imposed on you enough already. Why don't you think about it? Talk it over. You can let us know. Thank you for the refreshments."

Norton creaked to his feet. "Thank you, Mrs. Kingston, Samuel, Mr. Kerr. It's a beautiful spring day, I'm sure you want to enjoy it."

After seeing their guests to their carriage, Samuel found Padraig tucking into the plate of largely untouched sandwiches.

"For sure I'd cop a mouse for telling off one of those English Tories, if I was in Westminster." Padraig looked up. "So you'll be the next member of parliament from these parts then?"

Samuel dropped onto the sofa beside Sofia. "Not likely. I don't have the patience."

Sofia craned around, and her golden eyes flashed at him. "Well, don't go on complaining about the state of the country then, not if you're unwilling to change it."

Padraig swallowed his bite of sandwich. "Sofia's right. You might help if you—"

"You say. Yet you rejected the offer without hesitation." China clinked as Samuel stacked the plates of nibbled sandwiches on the tray.

"I'm only saying." Padraig threw up his hands. "You know I haven't the temperament for politics."

"Sleep on it, darling." Sofia smoothed her dress. "It's a gorgeous day. Let's take a ride and enjoy the weather. Would you like to come, Padraig?"

"I wish, but I can't live the life of a country squire. I've work to do on the boats." Padraig winked at Samuel and grabbed another sandwich as he rose.

Rickard Deasy, one of the most powerful men in Ireland, wanted him to seek election. Samuel frowned as he helped Brian saddle Belle. He didn't need the hassle. Nobody would vote for him anyway. He stroked the mare's neck, and the spikey hair tickled his hand as she shivered. "Will you vote in the next election, Brian?"

"I'll be old enough, sir, but I lack the income to qualify for a franchise. But even if I had the right, why would I bother? I don't know any of these politicians, so how could I them pick one?"

But Brian knew Samuel, many locals did. If he could only be sure he'd make a difference. He frowned and shuffled over to fetch Goldie's bridle. No, he was just being foolish.

CHAPTER FOUR

Two weeks later, the ocean air, smelling of salt and seaweed, invigorated Samuel as he reined Belle in at Lough Hyne's old stone quay. Seagulls wheeled in the blue sky, hurling high-pitched cries over the restless Celtic Sea. It was more like summer than mid-May, with the glassy lake a blaze of color, reflecting the yellow gorse and purple bracken and spring leaves flourishing on the hillside. Red admiral butterflies floated over the wildflowers on red-banded wings, birds chirped their thanks for the sunshine, and the tidal race sang as water rushed from the lake back to the Celtic Sea.

"Whoa, Belle." It was time to tell Sofia he'd decided not to run for parliament. It would probably disappoint her, as she hoped he'd fight for change in Ireland, but he couldn't impose the friction of a political campaign on his young family.

Sofia stopped her chestnut mare beside him and rested a hand on the pommel of her saddle as the wind fanned a long strand of hair that had escaped her wide-brimmed hat. "It's so peaceful. It sobers me that this is where it all started."

He released a heavy sigh. "It was a long time ago."

"To think you were only fifteen! How did you find the courage to fight a duel against such an infamous duelist?"

The tips of his ears flushed. "I was immature and stupid."

"Not stupid, I—"

"I tried to stop William Greenfell from murdering his tenant in cold blood as his men evicted that poor family, and he challenged me when I knocked him down. I should've walked away, but I didn't. I was too angry."

"You couldn't have known."

"It sparked a vendetta that caused Father's death."

She edged Goldie closer and touched his arm. "He would have died anyway. He had a bad heart."

He tipped his face up to the crisp blue sky. "I know, but at least he would have died here and not as a captive in Nicaragua."

"You're not still blaming yourself for that?"

He shook his head. "I did for a while, as you know. Now I understand it was all Louis Greenfell's fault."

"Well, you paid him back in sabers for that." Sofia petted Goldie's neck. "So you've made up your mind not to stand for election?"

He fingered the buckle on the reins. He wanted to change things, yes. But their lives had finally settled down. The threat of William Walker and the rogue lords who'd aligned with the filibuster no longer loomed over them, and why would he risk more hassle? He bit his lip. He wanted to help the working people, but any election brought controversy and animosity. Political opponents would highlight his mixed marriage and drag the family through the dirt to discredit him. He broke eye contact with her. "No, no, it's best I don't."

She nudged Goldie against Belle, forcing him to look at her. "That's fine. You know I support you whatever you decide."

She took that easier than he expected. He kissed her lips. "Thank you, darling. That means a lot."

"Ha! There goes my chance to meet the queen." She wheeled her mare. "Let's get back to see Maria before she goes to bed. By the way, I thought you were going to talk Padraig out of using that diving contraption. The town is buzzing about his antics in the harbor. I heard he was underwater at the pier for over an hour."

If only it was that simple, but with Padraig, things were seldom simple. "I tried, but you know how he is."

"Yes. Bullheaded." Sofia laughed and crammed her slouch hat down farther as she heeled Goldie ahead.

Samuel nudged Belle to follow Sofia. "Worse, he's going to dive an old wreck off Sherkin Island as soon as the weather's better."

"If God had meant us to swim under water, he'd have given us gills. I better not catch you in that hideous thingummy of Padraig's." Sofia coaxed her mare into a trot.

Fat chance of him ever risking that.

As they followed the lake and rode east onto the narrow road to Las Peñitas. A tall rider trotted toward them, his outline familiar.

Samuel squinted. "That's Jason. I wasn't expecting him, were you?"

"No. I wonder what brings him here." She heeled her mare into a canter.

Samuel's older brother was tall like Samuel, but he had narrow shoulders and a pale complexion whereas Samuel was broad and dark. And those were far from the only differences between them. Samuel was the adventurous type, but Jason was a peaceful man, content to manage Springbough, the estate in Clonakilty that had been in the Kingston family for generations.

Jason waved his bowler hat and called a greeting. "They told me I'd find you here. I've got a letter from Nicaragua."

Sofia yelped. "Filipe. He never bothers to write, no matter how I beg him. Oh, I hope nothing's the matter." She halted her mare beside Jason and hugged him.

It was no surprise to Samuel that Filipe hadn't written; few nineteen-year-old boys bothered to lift a pen. He'd hated writing when he was Filipe's age. Sofia was worrying over nothing.

Samuel shook Jason's hand warmly, and Sofia reached out for

the letter.

Jason passed it to Samuel instead. "He addressed it to you. Strange."

Samuel barked a laugh. "He must want something. But he sent it to Springbough Manor. Didn't you tell him we moved?"

"No matter how many times I tell him, he keeps using your old address ... Boys." Sofia tapped her finger on the reins. "Boys and men."

Samuel rolled his eyes at Jason, broke the seal, and handed her the letter. He recognized his place in the pecking order. "See what my dear wife thinks of us, Jason? In his defense, the only time Filipe visited Ireland, he stayed at Springbough. It's all he remembers. So what does he say? I hope—"

"Shush, darling." She handed the letter back to him. "Read it."

My dear Samuel,

I trust this letter finds you all well. How are my nephew and niece doing? I can't believe I've not met little Maria Elizabeth yet.

Right now my sister's probably scolding you because I never write, but this letter is for you, dear brother-in-law. I want to be the first to tell you we've found your father's mortal remains. It was Chavez, actually. He didn't want to disappoint you, so he never ceased searching, and recently we heard a rumor that a white man was buried near the old Greenfell hacienda. Well, your Euronicas searched and found him, and now he's here in Chinandega.

Knowing your affection for family, I'm certain you'll want to bring him home. Until then, Don Kingston is welcome here as our honored guest. With William Walker gone, it's safe enough—only the usual corrupt bureaucrats about, some more aggressive than others.

Please give my love to my sister, and I hope to see you both soon.
Saludos,
Filipe

· · ·

"They found Father's remains. It was Chavez, bless his heart." Samuel glanced at Sofia. Would she let him go?

Jason's mouth dropped open.

"I can't believe it. Filipe has Father's remains." Samuel's skin prickled. They must've been so close to Father's mortal remains when Greenfell's men made them dig their own graves three years ago. If only he could bring him home, a space awaited him next to Mother in the family crypt at Springbough. Father should be with his ancestors.

"It's bothered you all this time, but now Filipe has found him," Sofia said.

"It would mean facing—"

"But his death wasn't your fault."

"I've accepted that." He folded the letter. He needed time to consider such a long trip before he brought it up again. "But where are our manners? Jason, thank you for bringing Filipe's letter. We're on our way back to Las Peñitas for supper. You must join us. Sofia found a splendid wine in Cork, and I want you to try it."

"Gladly. The evenings grow longer, so I'll still be home before night falls. I'm sure Ingrid won't mind." Jason wheeled his bay gelding, and Samuel and Sofia fell in beside him.

Birds chirped their evening songs in the flourishing trees, and daffodils danced with bluebells on the roadside. The evening seemed full of spring's gentle spirit, full of hope. The *cheep-cheep-cheep* of a red-breasted robin warmed Samuel's heart as the meandering road snaked toward the manor; its spring song—powerful, confident, and upbeat—had made the crooner Father's favorite bird. Samuel dared to dream of his promise fulfilled.

". . . rumor that you're considering standing for a parliament seat. Hey, are you listening to me, Samuel?" Jason regarded him with raised eyebrows.

"I'm sorry, I was three thousand miles away. What did you say?"

As they rounded a bend outside Mickey Óg Spillane's tiny

cottage, two cavalrymen wearing blue tunics with the red cuffs and plastrons of the Royal Irish Dragoons restrained Samuel's laborer between them.

Jason stood in the stirrups. "What the devil's going on?"

"Why would the redbreasts harass Mickey?" Samuel heeled Belle into a canter.

"Now Samuel, don't do anything hasty." Sofia sped after him.

"What do you think you're doing? Unhand my man this second." His pulse beat faster. The civil authorities were becoming belligerent again, imagining Fenians and rebels behind every bush, and such aggression would only stir civil unrest.

One trooper came forward. "None of your business. And if I was you, I'd get the hell out of here before we arrest you with this Fenian bastard."

Samuel's heart pounded faster. Who had told the authorities this rubbish? "Are you kidding me?"

An overweight captain stalked from the cottage, where the splintered door hung ajar on its leather hinges. "What's the delay, Shelly? Get the manacles on him. I don't have all day."

Viscount Joseph Le Claire had gained weight since Samuel had last seen him on Lord Lucan's staff in Crimea. His yellow hair was as greasy as ever but thinner, unlike his jowly face and the belly that sagged over his belt buckle. He and Le Claire had been classmates at St. Matthew's College, surely Le Claire would sort this out.

Leather creaked as Sofia squirmed in the saddle as her usually honey-toned skin paled.

"Joseph, I'm glad to see you here. Please sort out this confusion for me. This is my cottier, who I've known all my life. I can assure you, he's no rebel." Samuel dismounted and approached Le Claire. "In fact, he's incapable of such deceit. He's a tad simple. He's harmless."

"You vouch for him, Kingston?" Despite his sheer bulk, Le Claire's voice was thin and reedy. "Of course you would. Your family always sides with the peasants. In fact, wasn't your father charged with treason several years ago? Why should—"

"You know damned well that's a lie. Was it Lucan who poisoned you against me?" Samuel grabbed Le Claire's elbow. They weren't taking Mickey to jail. No way. His simple soul would wither there.

"I don't have time to waste on you." Le Claire spun to face his men. "Bind the traitor, and let's be off."

How dare Le Claire dismiss him like this? Mickey wasn't going to jail. When they'd taken Father, he'd never come back.

Samuel snatched the revolver from Le Claire's holster. Cocking the hammer, he leveled it. "You're not taking Mickey anywhere. Get your men on your horses now, Joseph, and ride away."

"How dare you? Do you possibly think—"

"You know my reputation and I know yours, always the coward lurking behind the bullies. Do you believe for a second that I'll let you take my man? Mount your horse, and let this be the end of it. Mickey is harmless. He's innocent."

Biting his lip, Le Claire glanced back at the two troopers watching him with their mouths open, rooted in place, red-faced yokels who'd taken the Crown's shilling out of hunger, no doubt. One was blinking rapidly, and the other was rubbing his hand on his woolen trousers as he gaped at his officer. Samuel knew the cut of this regiment; these men were no threat.

"I'll send this revolver to your barracks later," Samuel finished.

Le Claire broke eye contact and swung sullenly onto his horse. "I'm the law around here, Kingston. You'll pay for—"

"I'd better not. Your foul father knows I have proof of his evil ways that would ruin his reputation. You don't want that published."

Le Claire spluttered. "What do you mean by—"

"Test me, and you'll find out. Or ask your pater." Samuel jabbed the revolver at Le Claire. "Now get off my estate."

Le Claire growled and spurred his horse up the lane. The troopers shoved Mickey aside, swung into their saddles without looking at Samuel, and followed their captain.

A bit jingled as Jason wheeled his horse to watch the departing cavalrymen with bulging eyes. "Damnation, Samuel, what have you done? That fat slug won't take this lying down."

Mickey stood with his lip quivering, as tall and as skinny as he'd been at fifteen.

Samuel placed a hand on Mickey's shoulder. "I'll fix this. But for the present, you must move Sheila and baby Rose somewhere safe. "How about taking them to Springbough, Jason?"

"The dragoons might search Mickey Senior's cottage, but I've an empty cottage they can hide in." Jason offered Mickey a reassuring smile. "I'll send your father over with a cart this evening to collect you."

When Samuel met Sofia's eyes, she pursed her lips and shook her head with disappointment. "I warned you not to do anything hasty. Now that wretch will come after you. What if those soldiers had fought back?"

"The Fifth Royal Irish are the worst regiment in the British Army," Samuel said. "They were disbanded in 1798 and erased from the army list records. They only reformed two years ago, and now they're scattered around Ireland. They don't even drill; I knew they'd back down. If Le Claire comes after me, I'll threaten him with the papers you took from Baltimore."

She wet her lips. "All the same, I wish you would think before you act."

"I wasn't going to let them take Mickey." He reined Belle around to face the road toward Las Peñitas. "Why're they after him, anyway?"

Jason fell in beside him. "I heard rumors that the Le Claire family and others are unhappy that you're buying up all the land around here."

Those people were unhappy with him, more likely, because he'd spoke up for the downtrodden. And they wouldn't leave him alone. He was a coward if he failed to take action. "As they should be. I'm using their money—well, the money of those financing Walker's war." If he could hold a consortium of that magnitude in check, he could handle that coward Joseph Le Claire and any others who moved against him. "That's why I've changed my mind about Rickard Deasy's offer. I will consider the solicitor general's invitation to run for the parliament seat. The inequality in Ireland must be addressed. Patriotic Anglo-Irishmen are rallying to the cause of equality and freedom in Ireland, and it's my duty to help them. To fight for what I believe in, what Father believed in, to make his dream come true."

Sofia clapped her hands together. "Finally. Finally, you've decided. I'm proud of you, Samuel."

Jason had a gleam in his eye as he edged his horse closer and punched Samuel's arm. My brother, the politician. Now we won't be able to believe a word that comes out of your mouth. All the same, you'll have my vote, and surely those of the middle class around here. This is so exciting. I can't wait to tell Ingrid."

Worries about Le Claire fell behind them as Samuel's thoughts drifted to bringing Father's remains home. The evening air smelled too sweet for such bitterness—the scent of wild-flowers and freshly cut grass, the first lambs frisking in the fields. He closed his eyes and drew a deep breath. It would feel so right to bring him home. "Isn't that smashing news about Father? I always hoped we'd find him."

"I recognize that tone," Sofia reached over and touched his arm. "You're contemplating a trip. You're going to bring him back."

She saw right through him. The corners of his mouth quirked. Well, not really. Not right away. Maybe."

"I understand how much this means to you. I do."

He forced himself to wait for whatever was coming next. Was she saying he should go?

"I was reminded the other day that it's been years since I saw

Filipe." Sofia plucked a plumb blackberry as Goldie ambled past a thorny branch reaching from the hedgerow. "Far too long. He was a boy then, and now he's a man running one of the largest haciendas in Nicaragua. I miss him."

He reined in. "You want to go back?"

"I've been meaning to ask you if we could visit him." She swallowed the berry and wiped a trickle of purple juice from her plump lips.

"But what about the children?"

"We'll only be gone about eight weeks. I'm certain Padraig's parents would move into the manor while we're gone. María would love to spend more time with them, and it wouldn't disrupt Jerry's responsibilities at Springbough. Jason wouldn't mind. Would you, Jason?"

Jason's ducked under a low-hanging branch of a willow tree blooming with yellow flowers. "It's a great idea. It will be wonderful to have Father in the crypt alongside Mother."

Samuel eyes raced, unfocused, over the grassy verge in the center of the road. "Eight weeks? More like twelve. It takes a month to travel there. And I don't even know if I can leave. Oscar Hayes is keen, but I'm not sure if he can manage the estate on his own yet. He's no Jerry Kerr."

"If Jerry is staying at Las Peñitas, he can keep an eye on Oscar," Jason said. "Springbough practically runs itself now—and besides, I'm there if there's a problem. You should go."

Belle snorted, baring teeth at Jason's mount.

"Easy, girl. This isn't a battlefield." Samuel tugged the reins gently. "Well, it's the right time of year for an Atlantic crossing, and Nicaragua should be safe now that Walker's on trial in New Orleans. I'll ask Padraig to come."

Sofia gave him that look of understanding that had kept his hopes alive during even his most desperate days in the jungle. "I'm sure he will. He's bored to death as a fisherman, and we might save his life if we take him away from his diving contraption. Come, let's go home and make plans."

CHAPTER FIVE

The Narrows protected the harbor at New York, not unlike Roche's Point did Queenstown, where the opposite headland shut out storms and pacified the water even when gales raged. The bay around Staten Island was almost as picturesque as the bay at home, with its islands and hilly shores shaped like a leaf. The transatlantic steamer slipped through the craggy harbor mouth, and the full expanse of New York opened before Samuel: the sweatshops and wharfs of Jersey, sweltering under a smudge of oily smoke; the buildings on Manhattan's cluttered skyline, peeping through a forest of masts and smokestacks; and eastward, the cranes and warehouses of the Brooklyn quays. Dumpy riverboats and tugs powered between square-riggers and schooners huffing smoke into the soiled sky.

All Samuel wished to do this week was to spoil Sofia until they sailed for Panama. He spread his hands on the guardrail next to his wife and friend as they drew in the stench of cooking fires and sewage, which knifed into their noses after the fresh ocean air. A strand of raven black hair billowed from Sofia's blue bonnet, and her light blue dress accentuated her lithe figure as it brushed the deck.

"This place is fascinating." Sofia tucked the wayward hair

under her hat. "It's so exciting to be back again. I want to buy Filipe a present. We must go shopping tomorrow."

He exchanged a knowing glance with Padraig. Shopping was a certain way to keep a woman happy, and this was, after all, his first worry-free trip to New York. Nobody was in danger. He'd silenced Lord Lucan and his cronies years ago, and William Walker was in New Orleans defending himself in court. He took her hand and chuckled. "I know what that means: It's going to be an expensive outing. Well, make the most of it. We've one week before the *Adriatic* sails for Panama."

"Thank you for letting me come." She rose on her tippy-toes and kissed his cheek. Her scent of apple blossom and perfumed soap overpowered the foul and acrid stench of the river. She pointed to the small boat steaming alongside theirs. "Is that the first-class ferry? I hope so. I can't wait to get ashore."

Padraig dropped his smoking cigarette butt over the side. "There's no hurry. They must offload our baggage first."

"Your baggage?" Samuel quipped. "That'll keep us here for days."

"Ha ha!" Sofia poked him with a sharp elbow. "But at least Padraig brought nice clothes. Why can't you dress as smartly?"

Samuel cast an eye over his friend. In his tweed frock coat from Whitakers', the best tailor in Cork, and one of those brightly colored waistcoats that were all the rage in London, Padraig did indeed look dapper.

Padraig's green eyes gleamed. "Sure, Samuel's an old married chap now. You'll be putting him out to graze any day."

"Old! I'm not even thirty, same as you. But unlike you, I'm not keen to draw attention to myself." He pulled the wide brim of his felt hat down to shade his eyes from the blazing sun. "I know you're a rich man now, but you shouldn't flaunt it. What if someone assaults you?"

Padraig patted his waist. "That's why I carry my trusty Colt. I'll tell you what. While Sofia is buying some beautiful dresses,

I'll take you to update your wardrobe. It's time you wore something more than plain dark suits."

"No, thanks. That's for you single men to draw the ladies. And, by golly, you need all the help you can get." He ducked Padraig's playful swat with a grin.

It took the better part of two hours before they boarded the first-class ferry, which spurted away from the transatlantic liner in a shower of sparks and smoke. Padraig hooted and pumped his fist in the air, causing the bearded man seated beside him to flinch.

Padraig blushed. "I'm sorry, sir, I didn't mean to alarm you. I'm excited to be back in New York. Sorry about that."

"Don't worry. I'm a bit jumpy, that's all." The stranger's eyes flickered to his long canvas case, now inches from Padraig's feet. He gave Padraig a broad smile. "Irish, are you?"

"I am. Padraig Kerr from Clonakilty. And you're American, I'd guess."

"Brilliant deduction, Mr. Kerr. Ben Henry from New Hampshire, now living in Connecticut."

"Pleasure to meet you, sir." Padraig shook Mr. Henry's hand. "May I present Samuel Kingston and his beautiful wife, Sofia? We're passing through on our way to visit Sofia's family in Nicaragua."

Henry raised his eyebrows as he shook Samuel's hand. "Nicaragua. Interesting. That place is in the news of late, what with William Walker's war and all."

Samuel plastered on a smile to cover his visceral reaction to Walker's name. "Old news. I read that Walker's on trial in New Orleans for breaching the Neutrality Act when he invaded Nicaragua and attacked Costa Rica. The government will lock him away."

"Not for certain. The *Times* says he's a lot of support in the South." Mr. Henry drew his long bag closer to his feet.

Samuel exchanged looks with Sofia as Padraig's mouth

dropped open. It was impossible that Walker could avoid a conviction. The evidence against him was irrefutable: thousands of dead in Nicaragua and Costa Rica, and a nation brought to its knees.

Henry was shaking Sofia's hand. "A pleasure to meet you, Mrs. Kingston."

"He might go free?" Samuel glared at Henry. "But how? That man is a tyrant."

Henry lifted his hands, palms out. "Oh, I agree with you. But Walker is popular in Louisiana."

Surely Walker wouldn't dare to return to Central America a third time? Samuel's gaze drifted over the ships moored at the Brooklyn wharfs. It was there he and Padraig had raided a factory where Walker's men were machining muskets into rifles four years earlier. Walker would never dare return to Nicaragua now. Surely it was safe to escort his wife there.

Sofia gathered his hand in hers and murmured in Spanish. "Don't worry, *cariño*, he won't return. He tried in fifty-eight and didn't make it up the river."

Padraig steadied his haversack as it tipped over. "I agree. Even Walker must've tired of war by now."

They were right. Walker would need a lot of money and powerful alliances to take back Nicaragua. "He's smart, but he's no Napoleon. He won't be back for another Waterloo."

"You all speak Spanish," Henry said, eyebrows raised. "Unusual for Irishmen."

"I apologize if switching languages offended you." Samuel dropped his hands to his lap. "It's a long story. Padraig's Spanish mother raised both of us."

A wave rocked the ferry, and Henry's long bag slid past Padraig and bumped against Samuel's ankle. Samuel knew that unyielding touch: rifles. He surveyed the man more closely: lean and fit, somewhere near forty, judging by the silver streaks running through his wavy black hair. "How did you enjoy Ireland, Mr. Henry?"

"My bad luck, but all I saw of Ireland was Queenstown when we made the stop. I was in London on business."

Padraig snorted. "Pah! London—dirtiest place on earth if you ask me."

"Then you've spent little time in New York." Henry flicked a fly from his close-cut beard.

The engine's roar slowed to a steady wheeze, and the ferry coasted into a berth two hundred yards from the sandstone walls of the Emigrant Landing Depot at Castle Clinton. The stench of fish and greasy smoke grew stronger, and the passengers fidgeted with their hand baggage as the crewmen lofted bow and stern lines to waiting dockhands. Some passengers stood and picked up their belongings, swaying precariously as the dockhands drew the boat alongside and others carried a narrow gangway toward the entry port. A more experienced sailor after his many jaunts with Padraig, Samuel appreciated the helmsman's skill in nudging the boat gently to the dock despite the strong current and two-foot waves lapping the pier.

Henry picked up his heavy bag and motioned Sofia ahead. "After you, Mrs. Kingston."

As Sofia brushed by him, a large wave, feathering from the prow of a passing tug, rocked the tender violently. Henry staggered under the weight of his bag, twisted in vain, and tumbled overboard.

Padraig grabbed for him but came up short, only managing to catch hold of his canvas bag's strap. He yanked the bag back to safety and slammed it onto the bench. Henry yelped and hit the water with a splash.

The boat swayed back and forth as the passengers stirred and cried out in alarm.

Padraig looked over the gunwale. "He's gone under. I can't see him."

Instinctively, Samuel whipped off his coat and handed it to Padraig. Sucking in deep breaths to fill his lungs, He kicked off his shoes and vaulted over the side into the water.

The cold, murky river sent a shock through him, and his muscles spasmed as the acrid water stung his eyes, but he'd swum here before. He squeezed his eyelids closed, kicked his legs, and pulled water with his hands. His only hope was to locate Henry by touch, since the dirty river was too cloudy to see anything. Chilly water invaded his ears as he sank deeper and his lungs burned, building pressure. He fought the profound urge to spew out his spent air, and his strokes became ragged.

When his fingers brushed something soft, he snatched at it, closed his fist, and drew Henry's body to his side. Samuel thrashed to orient himself, halted his descent, and swam for the dark surface. The primal urge to breathe grew unbearable. Air erupted from his lips, and water slammed into his gaping mouth and choked him. His throat froze, he couldn't breathe. He gagged and retched, sucking for air that wasn't coming, while the cloth slipped from his grip.

When his head broke the surface, he threw an arm around Henry's neck and pulled him to his chest, his heart pounding. He coughed painfully and gulped down another breath—stinking and foul, but it was air. A wave broke over him, and he slammed his mouth shut. Damnation, how could Henry be so heavy? His breath came in short painful bursts and heaves, but the vertigo subsided. He opened his stinging eyes.

The boat was a blur of faces above a white hull only yards away. He could make it. He tilted back his head, filled his complaining lungs, and paddled feebly, leg muscles burning with each pathetic stroke. The boat drew closer as he bobbed and spluttered. Water roared in his ears, together with the beat of the tender's engine. His head spun as acid bile burned its way up his throat. His lungs were on fire, and his throbbing legs had nothing more.

Two more yards, but he was sinking. He had to swim harder.

As he struck something solid and opened his stinging eyes, the hull loomed over him like a fuzzy falling wall ready to crush him. He pawed at it, and razor-sharp barnacles grazed his palms as he vainly sought a handhold. Nothing. He began sinking again.

Someone gripped his hair, and a rough hand grabbed under his armpit and lifted him. He cleared the surface to a pandemonium of shouts and scraped the boat's freeboard before they dragged him over the gunwale.

He thumped onto the deck. A second later, Henry's inert body flopped down beside him like a wet fish.

"Bloody hell, Samuel. Are you crazy?" Padraig dropped to his knees beside him.

Sofia knelt and cradled his head. "What were you thinking? You almost drowned. This is the second time in a month you've risked your life in the ocean. Damn it, Samuel, do you think you're Poseidon rescuing every drowning soul?" Her face was pallid. Lord, he was delighted to see her.

Shivering, he clutched her hand to his heaving breast. He couldn't speak. He let out a low moan and pointed to Henry on the deck.

"They'll look after him. Don't worry." Her voice trembled as tears streamed down her cheeks.

He tried to speak but only choked. Beside him, Henry coughed and vomited.

"He's awake. Give him some space," a man bawled. "Bring blankets, a coat, anything."

Samuel's stomach churned, but he didn't vomit, and his hungry lungs calmed. He sat up. "I'm fine. How is he?"

"Alive, thanks to one daft bugger." Padraig dropped his frock coat over Samuel's shoulders.

Sofia crushed her warm lips against his, and her tears were as salty as the sea. "You fine, foolish man. I could've lost you."

The gawkers shuffled back, and Henry sat up, reaching a quavering hand to Samuel. "My friend, how can I thank you? You saved my life."

Samuel's ears reddened as Padraig helped him to his feet. "Think nothing of it. Anybody would've done the same."

"No, I know what fortitude and effort it took. And look, you ruined your clothes." Henry squeezed Samuel's hand. "At least let me offer you and your companions a ride. My coach is waiting outside. Where's your hotel?"

The other passengers drifted toward the entry port now that the spectacle was over.

Samuel couldn't bother this stranger, not after the ordeal the poor man had endured. "We can't impose on you like that. We'll catch a cab."

Wincing, Henry removed his wet coat. "I insist. It's the least I can do. Now follow me. I'll help you through immigration."

It took no time to pass through the terminal and even less time for the two waiting coachmen to load their luggage on top of Henry's shiny black coach. The four horses pranced through the throng of drivers and hawkers clamoring for business outside the wooden terminal fence, hooves clattering on cobblestones.

The air was humid as the coach creaked to a halt outside the red-brick building of the Sovereign Hotel twenty minutes later, two blocks from New York's Washington Square.

"I'll see to the rooms." Padraig jumped out and clomped up the three marble steps leading to the lobby.

Samuel's damp trousers chapped his crotch as he stepped down and stretched his aching limbs. He'd worked his muscles hard during his unscheduled swim.

Henry clambered from the coach. "Thomas, Juan, let's have those trunks down, if you please, and take care with them."

A man watching them from the next corner caught Samuel's eye, a burly blond chap with an overlarge head, low forehead, and thick brows. The stranger's eyes flicked away to his smoking companion. That narrow fellow showed Samuel his back, dragged on his cigarette, and flicked it down the alleyway. Peculiar. What were they so interested in?

"Can you believe it?" Padraig stormed down the steps. "They don't allow Irish in this rubbish heap."

Samuel's head jerked back toward the marble entrance. Impossible. This was America. "What did you say to upset them?"

"Nothing. But as soon as I said we came from Ireland, the prick lifted his nose and claimed they were full."

"Let me talk to them." Samuel glanced at Henry, who observed them in silence. "I'm sure it's a blunder."

Inside, the hotel was well appointed with walnut paneling and gleaming bronze gas lamps standing on a white marble floor. The scent of polish, fresh flowers, and roasting beef filled the lobby. A man of about fifty, small-boned but with a well-fed paunch, stood rigid before the reception desk and raised his bushy eyebrows to greet Samuel.

"Good afternoon. I believe there's been some confusion." Samuel plastered on his best fake smile. "I reserved a suite with two bedrooms, please."

Crossing his arms, the hotelier spoke with a grating nasal whine. "You're with the Irishman, I presume? I'm the manager, Mr. Staple." His jaded blue eyes flicked to the door. "You're welcome, but not the blond fellow . . . We don't allow Irish in here. They're too much trouble."

What a creepy little churl. Samuel's gut tightened. "Explain why I'm welcome, but my dear friend is not."

Staple gave Samuel a knowing smile. "You're a British gentleman, not one of those diabolical peasants. It's their kind we don't want around here."

This was flat-out bigotry. Samuel's ears burned. "How can you stand there with a—"

"Mr. Kingston." Henry touched his elbow. "A word, if you please?" He drew Samuel aside. "I'm sorry, but we get a lot of religious friction here on the East Coast. This type of discrimination has been insidious ever since the famine refugees arrived in the late forties. You see it in black and white in job listings that state 'No Irish Need Apply' and businesses that post the same rubbish on their doors. It irks me to see prejudiced posters —even images of Celtic ape-men with cave dwellers' foreheads and atrocious appearances. But most here don't condone that, I assure you."

Samuel spun to face Staple. He would teach this woebegone wretch manners. "Now look here, you—"

"No." Henry tugged his arm. "I've a better idea. Stay in my town house. It's near here, it will delight me, and it's the least I can do. What say you?"

Nailed boots hammered on the steps and three policemen crowded through the front door, followed by Sofia.

Samuel huffed through his nose. "I'll be damned if I'll permit this bastard to abuse Padraig. I'm going to—"

"That's enough, Samuel." Sofia gave him a steady gaze. "Whatever the matter is, we don't need trouble now. We don't have time for it. We'll find another hotel."

"No need, Mrs. Kingston." Henry stepped over to her, drawing Samuel with him. "You would honor me by staying at my home tonight. After all, I'd be a dead man if it weren't for your husband. Besides, my wife is at my Connecticut estate, and I hate to dine alone. Company will delight me. I have plenty of room."

Sofia took Henry's hand in both of hers. "That's kind of you, sir, given that we are so out of sorts. If we're not imposing, perhaps you could put us up for one night, and we will search for a new hotel in the morning."

"Splendid." Henry rubbed his hands together. "I'll tell my men to load your trunks again."

It was fruitless to argue once Sofia made up her mind. Samuel stabbed his index finger at the manager. "Bad cess to you, you bastard. You've not heard the last of this." The stench of damp wool caught in his nose as he pushed past the policemen.

"Thank you, darling." Sofia's hand was warm on his shoulder

as she steered him down the steps. "We don't need them locking you up right now."

"Bloody wretch," Padraig hissed in Spanish. "I was going to smack him myself until I remembered how we upset those US marshals when we ran from the revenue men here when smuggling arms to Costa Rica. What were their names again? One was Tingle, was it?"

It had been quite some time since Samuel had thought of the day they'd sailed away after the district attorney for New York impounded their boat loaded with weapons. He licked his lips. But that was three years ago, and nobody had come to harm. They were not Americans. Could the authorities even convict them of breaching their precious Neutrality Act? "I don't remember their names. But you're right, we don't need to make a ruckus." He put on his smile again as Henry caught up. "I'm honored to be your guest, sir."

"And I'm embarrassed. That wretch must be a know-nothing. They've gained too much power here."

Samuel raised an eyebrow. What did Mr. Henry mean by "know-nothing?"

"Many Anglo Protestants whose ancestors fled here for refuge from their Catholic persecutors still vilify the Irish," Henry said. "They've rallied around the anti-Catholic, anti-immigrant American Party, whose members are called the know-nothings because if you question their politics, they claim to know nothing. Party members vowed to elect only native-born citizens —but only if they weren't Roman Catholics."

"I should have punched the bugger," Padraig growled.

"And you thought the Anglo-Irish were bad. We better scamper." Samuel opened the door of the coach. As she climbed inside, Sofia's flinty eyes made him smile. "After you, darling."

CHAPTER SIX

"I wish you would consider staying here for the duration of your trip." Ben Henry buttered his toasted bread. "I must return to the factory today, but my staff can take care of you."

Samuel lowered the coffee cup from his lips. "It's more than enough that your man found us rooms at the Shenandoah, Benjamin."

Early morning sunlight streamed through the windows, gilding the collection of rifles and handguns mounted on the walls. Samuel recognized an 1851 model of his own Colt. That beautifully engraved percussion revolver beside it had to be French-made. Oh, and that was an Enfield Pattern 1853 Cavalry carbine rifle, a British gun. Why the devil had the ordinance department not supplied those to the British cavalry in Crimea? They would have been much more practical than lances. "Great collection of guns, Benjamin. I like the Enfield, I don't know why they didn't arm the Light Brigade with those."

"That Enfield's nice and compact, but it's muzzle loaded—not much good for cavalry." Henry picked up the silver coffeepot. "More coffee, Mrs. Kingston?"

"Please." She slid her china cup closer to Henry.

"Few people can say they're acquainted with two heroes who

charged with the Light Brigade," he said as he poured. "'Theirs but to do and die. Into the valley of Death rode the six hundred.'"

Samuel grimaced. Six years after that fateful charge, he still had nightmares. "You're too kind. But it should never have happened. The British Army needs to modernize, promote leaders for their ability and not because they're aristocrats. And the role of the cavalry must change. No more lances or sabers. Cavalry should carry carbines, move into range swiftly to engage the enemy and retreat if necessary to minimize casualties."

"Bravo!" Henry clapped his hands. "I was saying the same thing to your war department in London last week. But they're enamored with the past, despite the fact that the Board of Ordinance was eliminated in fifty-five for that reason, and I couldn't convince them that a lancer would be better off with a repeating rifle than a lance. Perhaps you can." He rose and moved briskly to the door. "I have a gift for you because you saved my life and because I value your opinion. Now if you'll excuse me, I'll fetch it."

Samuel's ears heated. "I say, there's no need for a gift." All the same, he wondered what it could be. It sounded fascinating.

Henry waved a hand loftily and left the room with a chortle.

Padraig grinned. "Don't be too hasty saying no."

A slow smile spread across Sofia's face. She seemed as curious as the men.

As Henry bustled back in, the brass frame of a compact rifle in his hands gleamed in the morning light. Its barrel was thicker than Samuel's trusty Sharps. "What do you think about this beauty? I'd like to introduce you to the 1860 Henry repeating rifle."

Samuel and Padraig exchanged dubious glances.

"Mark my words, it'll change war forever. Holds sixteen rounds plus one before you need to reload. And it takes brass shells. No more fiddling with percussion caps." Metal jingled as

Henry rummaged in his pocket. He handed the rifle to Samuel and deposited a handful of copper cartridges on the table.

"Impossible." Padraig moved around the table beside Samuel, his eyes glued to the rifle. "How can you fit so many rounds? Where?"

The rifle felt heavier than Samuel's Sharps. He hefted it in both hands and spun it over. "Two barrels?"

"That's a tubular magazine below the barrel." Henry held out his hand. "May I? I'll show you how it works."

Samuel returned the rifle as Padraig pressed closer, rapt.

Henry rotated the gun and held it at an angle. "You twist a sleeve on the barrel and load the shells down the tube." He slid a silver tab down the magazine to the muzzle and twisted the sleeve. "There's a spring behind this follower that keeps forcing the shells down. Feed them in here." He slipped a shell into the tube. It slid down the spout, and he fed another in. "Simple as that. But don't hold the gun at too steep an angle. Otherwise, the shells might slide down fast and hard enough to detonate the next round inside."

Samuel drew back.

Henry worked the lever. "Unlikely, but why take a chance?"

"Insane." Padraig picked up a round from the table and examined it. "It loads that quickly? And seventeen rounds. That's a lot of kills."

Samuel shook his head. "Unbelievable. What's its range?"

"I hit targets consistently at one hundred yards, but it's good for two hundred." Henry pulled down the lever, and a long bolt slid back to cock the hammer as a round ejected from the shiny brass elevator. "Now it has a fresh round. Quick, isn't it?"

"Revolutionary. What a beauty." Samuel shook his head slowly.

"It's yours." Henry thrust the rifle into his hands. "I've filed the patent already, but it won't be legal until the fall. That's when we begin production. Until then, you'll be the only man out there with a repeating rifle."

Samuel stroked the smooth brass frame absentmindedly. He'd love to have this gun. "I can't accept this. It's too much."

"You'll be doing me a favor if you used it and wrote a brief report on it." Henry grinned. "I've an ulterior motive."

"Oh?"

"Testimony from a man with your record might convince those pencil pushers at the War Department to buy my guns. You'd be doing me a favor."

"I'd like to, really I would, but—"

"It's yours. Fires .44 caliber rounds. I suggest you take five hundred rounds for the present. Once the rifles are on the market, it'll be easy to buy more ammunition, but until then, you'll want to save your shells and reload them."

Samuel squeezed the gun in his hands. Why not? "Thank you, Benjamin, I love it. I can't wait to try it out."

"Great. I've a cartridge belt here somewhere. Let me dig it out while you pack for the road. Now let's finish breakfast. I reckon your wife is chafing at the bit to visit the shops."

An hour later, the cab swept them away from the townhouse as Henry was preparing to depart for his Connecticut home. The morning was muggy and hot as the cab carried them south, and Samuel's shirt was already dampening with sweat.

"Remarkable man. He's going to revolutionize warfare." Samuel unbuttoned his frock coat. Padraig was squinting at the canvas bag behind Samuel's heels. "You lucky bugger. I can't believe he gave you that weapon. You lucky, lucky bugger."

Samuel laughed. "You can have it whenever you like. It would've been useful in Crimea or even Nicaragua, but not now. Not when we're men of peace. I'll stop by the post office and mail it home before we leave for Panama."

"No, you won't." Sofia elbowed him. "We're going to try it out in Chinandega. We'll go hunting."

Samuel gave her a playful nudge. "Look at you. You're as envious as Padraig." He kissed the top of her head. "Next time, you take the swim."

The squalid area they were threading through looked more like the dreaded Five Points slum than Madison Square. Broken windows and open doors sagged from the tenements, where washing flapped on lines stretching across the road from sill to sill. Ragged children raced beside the cab, begging for coins. Perhaps this was a shortcut. Samuel fiddled with the window latch. "Where's he taking us?"

The coach lurched to a halt, and the door on Padraig's side flew open to reveal the blond man Samuel had observed lurking outside the Sovereign Hotel the evening before, with a pistol. Samuel's hand flew to his Colt as the opposite door came ajar, and a narrow fellow jammed a pistol in his ribs.

"What the devil!" Samuel pushed Sofia behind him.

"Don't do anything stupid, Kingston. We only want to trade with you." The black dot of the muzzle flickered in the blond man's hand. "Squeeze up. My friends and I will be joining you."

The hair prickled on the nape of Samuel's neck. They'd used his name. This was no random attack. The skinny middle-aged fellow had been outside the hotel too.

The driver appeared beside the blond man. "Don't dawdle, Biggs. We need to tuck them away before we're spotted."

So the blond fellow was Biggs. The name didn't ring a bell.

The skinny man prodded Samuel with the pistol. "You heard him. Shove over."

"Get in, Brown." Bigg's head swiveled, checking up and down the road. "We don't have all day."

Brown growled and spat over his shoulder. "Back off, I'm going as fast as I can."

Samuel took the chance, knowing Padraig would act too. He shoved Brown's gun skyward with one hand as he drew his Colt with the other, cocking the hammer as Brown's pistol barked and a slug tore through the coach's roof. Smoke stung his eyes, but he held steady and fired. The shot hit Brown in the breast. Were there others outside? He lunged past Brown's falling body, jumped down from the cab, and scanned around him as he cocked the Colt. Nobody. Padraig and the blond man had disappeared.

"They're over here, on the ground." Sofia was pale but composed.

Bits clinked, prancing hooves drummed the cobblestones, and the cab jolted forward a yard.

"Out this side, quickly. The horses might run."

Samuel sprinted around the cab. Padraig was on his knees beside the unconscious blond man, Biggs. The driver was writhing on the ground behind them, blood pumping between the fingers clutching his shoulder.

"I knocked the pistol out of this one's hand, but I had to shoot the driver." Padraig punched the unconscious Biggs and grinned at Samuel. "To be sure, to be sure."

"Are you all right?" Sofia appeared from around the cab, her face white.

Samuel slumped against the coach's warm panel. "They knew me. This isn't random."

Shouts sounded up and down the street, and several tough-looking loafers shuffled closer, chattering and gesturing.

Samuel's shoulders tightened. They had to get away before the constables arrived. He tapped Biggs with the toe of his boot. "I'll throw this wretch into the cab and secure him. Padraig, you drive. We'll question him when he wakes up."

"But where to?"

"I've no clue. Anywhere but here. Sofia, get in."

The horses threw up their heads and pranced as Padraig vaulted into the driver's seat and gathered up the reins.

After heaving Biggs on the coach's floor beside Sofia, Samuel clambered in and rapped on the roof of the cab. "Ready!"

"Go. Yeah, go!" The cab surged ahead, throwing Samuel against the leather upholstery as gawkers leaped out of the way. Something outside smashed against the door, and another blow shattered the window as the coach careened around the corner, almost rising on two wheels.

Samuel slapped Bigg's face.

Sofia wiped the sweat from her forehead with her sleeve and picked up Samuel's revolver. "That's right. Wake him. We must make him talk. I can't believe this is happening again."

They'd been cruising through the streets for ten minutes, and the blond thug was still unconscious.

"Drat. How hard did Padraig hit him? They called him Biggs." Samuel slapped the blond man's face again, stinging the pads of his fingers.

"I don't know." Sofia frowned.

"Biggs. That's right." Samuel hit Biggs again. "Biggs, wake up, you wretch."

Biggs groaned.

Sofia clutched the Colt to her bosom. "He's waking."

Samuel clenched his teeth. They couldn't ride around in circles all day. They had to discover who they were up against. He grabbed Biggs's shirt front and shook him. "Wake up!"

Biggs's eyes opened, and he cringed. "What . . . Who—?"

"Why did you attack us?" Blood pulsed in Samuel's ears. The gall of these fellows, attacking them in daylight.

"Kingston." Biggs flopped his head back onto the floor.

Boom! The Colt kicked in Sofia's hand, and Biggs arched his back with a scream. Samuel recoiled, gaping at Sofia with bulging eyes.

She cocked the smoking Colt. "Next bullet goes through your heart. We don't have time for games."

Biggs mewled and clutched his bleeding foot.

The cab slowed.

"What happened?" Padraig's voice was shrill.

Samuel hammered on the roof of the cab. "It's fine. Keep going." She was incredible, his wife. He forced his attention back to the wounded man on the floor of the carriage.

Biggs's eyes bulged as blood seeped through his fingers. "Damn you, you're going to pay for this. It was Walker. Walker sent us."

"Why?" Samuel barked. Damnation—like the last time they clashed, Walker was a move ahead of them. How did he know they were in New York, and what else did he know of their plans?

"He wanted you held prisoner until you gave back his money. He ordered us not to harm you, though, I was—argh!"

Sofia's kick cut Biggs off. "Walker has gone after my family once too often. You've one minute to answer all our questions." She poked the Colt at Biggs's gut.

"Easy, Sofia. He's talking." Samuel swiped spit balls from the corners of his mouth with his cuff. Biggs couldn't inform them if she killed him, and he was their only lead.

"What do want to know?" Biggs nursed his bleeding foot on the floor of the swaying coach. Terraced houses and storefronts swept past the windows in a blur, and the sound of hoofbeats and hawkers swelled and faded.

"Who told you we were coming?" Sofia was a lioness defending her pride. Samuel's mouth fell open. He'd understood she was tough, but here she was merciless. "Why kidnap us?"

"Walker's returning to Nicaragua as soon as the court frees him, but he needs money to fund his campaign."

"And what has that to do with us?" Samuel demanded.

"He said you had his money, so he lured you here with news of your father's body."

Father! It was nothing but a ruse. Samuel grabbed a clump of his sweaty hair. "My God, it was all a lie. His remains could be anywhe—"

"Samuel, stop." Sofia's voice was granite. "Filipe wouldn't lie about that part. He has your father, I'm sure of it."

Samuel clutched the front of Biggs's shirt. "Is it true? How did Walker discover Filipe had Father's remains?"

Biggs sniffed back the snot running from his nose. "A one-armed filibuster named French was there when he died. General Walker had his allies spread the word about where they buried him, I guess, so your relative would get word. I dunno, I had nothing to do with it. The general promised each of us one hundred and fifty acres in Nicaragua when—"

"I thought we killed him in San Juan del Sur." Samuel lowered his forehead to Sofia's shoulder. French. That snake was back.

"One got away, remember?" She touched his hair. "It must've been French."

Biggs groaned. "Mate, I need a doctor. Please. I told you everything."

Samuel's head whipped up. "I don't think so. Let's talk facts. How many of you are in New York? What—"

"Whoa there, my beauties." Outside in the driver's seat, Padraig's command was urgent, and the coach skidded to a halt. "Good morning, constables."

The occupants of the cab exchanged pale glances.

"Where are you going in such a hurry, boy?" The voice was gruff and irritated. "You can't race through the streets like that."

"Going a bit fast, was I? I'm sorry, but we—the lady has a medical emergency. She's expecting, and, oh my God, she started bleeding." Padraig played the part of a nervous man quite well.

"Damned paddy." The voice was an angry growl. "You could kill someone driving like that."

Taking the Colt from Sofia, Samuel threw the seat rug over the filibuster. "Don't move, Biggs. Don't even squeak."

Sofia ran a hand through the sticky blood pooled under Biggs and rubbed it down the front of her blue silk dress. "I can't bear this pain," she called in a quavering voice. "We must save my baby."

"I want to see this woman for myself." Heavy footsteps clomped to the window and a jowly face scowled through, the sun glistening on the double row of brass buttons on his blue tunic. "That true, missus, are you—oh, my Lord, you're bleeding."

Samuel froze his bouncing knee. He couldn't shoot his way out of this. They never should've left the scene of the fight. Now they appeared as guilty as Biggs.

Sofia's face contorted in agony and she scrubbed a bloody hand down her cheek, leaving a crimson smear. "I can't stand it. I think I'm dying."

The policeman flushed and hopped back a step. "Let them go, Joseph, I'll not have a woman die on my watch. I'm so sorry, missus. Go on with you, and the best of luck to you."

"Thank you, sir." Samuel pressed the Colt to his knee beneath the blanket to stop his hand from trembling.

"Good day to you, gentlemen, and God bless you for this," Padraig called. A whip cracked, and the coach lurched forward.

Samuel slumped back in the leather seat. "Thank goodness. You were incredible, darling."

Sofia tugged his shirt collar. "How many of you are in New York? Is French here?"

Samuel sank back in the leather seat. Sofia was relentless. Needing a boost to steady his nerves, he pulled out his silver cigarette case and took out a cigarette he'd rolled earlier.

"Four of us here today. French is in Nicaragua already."

"Are there more of you in the city?" Samuel lit the cigarette and took a long drag.

"Only Colonel Anderson. Frank Anderson. He's looking for investors. They need boats to do something or other. To transport volunteers, yeah, down to Nicaragua."

Samuel stared at Biggs, sucking in a lungful of smoke. How could this be happening again? The evil that was William Walker was returning anew to plague Nicaragua. "Where's Anderson now?"

Biggs dragged a wrist across his eyes. "For God's sake, man, I'm dying. Help me or—"

Samuel clipped Biggs's head with the Colt and exhaled a stream of smoke. "Where's Anderson now?"

Biggs's voice grew muffled as his hands curled over his face.

"The Royal Canadian Hotel off Union Square. I've told you all I—"

"We need to lock this guy away until we leave." Samuel rubbed the back of his neck and puffed on the cigarette. "This changes everything. We can't go—"

Two loud thumps, and the roof of the cab flexed under Padraig's fist. "What in damnation's going on? I've slowed down to avoid drawing more cops onto us, but I can't drive aimlessly all bloody day."

Samuel flicked the cigarette out the shattered window, still a lavish butt. "Pull into any ally."

The cab creaked to a halt minutes later, and Samuel updated Padraig as soon as he appeared at the window.

Padraig craned his head both ways, checking the street. "So what now?"

Samuel pointed a thumb at Biggs. "We lock this one up and make a plan. We need to find Brogan. He'll have an idea where to hide the wretch."

Padraig peered down at the prisoner. "He needs a doctor."

"Well, he can't have one," Sofia spat. "We protect each other first. He can have a doctor when we sail for Panama."

"Fair enough. I've seen men survive worse wounds." Padraig grinned at Sofia. "Jazus, woman, you're a tiger."

She crossed her arms. "Whatever it takes to protect my family."

"Head to the river to Brogan's tug," Samuel drew his shoes back from the creeping puddle of blood on the floor. "Remember where it is?"

"Vaguely, on the Hudson side." Padraig climbed lightly back into the coachman's seat. "But I'm a New York City driver. I'll be sure to know the wharf when I see it."

~

"There's the tug, pier forty-two." Padraig sounded his unflappable self as the coach halted alongside the bustling quay packed three and four deep with sailing ships and steamboats. The toad-like black hull of the *Macaw* snubbed her mooring lines at the nearby jetty.

Samuel patted Sofia's knee in relief. "He's here. It's going to be fine."

"I hope so." She held out her hand. "Give me the revolver. I'll watch Biggs while you talk with Frank."

"Are you sure you can manage?"

"For goodness' sake, he's a wreck. Give me the gun, darling."

"All right, but be careful." He handed it over and descended from the carriage. "Come on, Padraig. Sofia's watching Biggs."

"Ahoy on board," Padraig called out to the *Macaw*.

The squat tug hardly stirred as Samuel stepped on board. "Frank, you there?"

Brogan popped his face out of the companionway, and his mouth fell open. "Well, I'll be. Padraig, Samuel. You're the last people on earth I expected." He wiped his grease-stained hands on a rag and climbed on deck.

"It's great to see you, Frank." Samuel hugged the lean Irishman. "How's your boy?"

"Growing like a weed—and can you believe it, he speaks like a Yankee."

Padraig embraced Brogan. "Earragh, what do you expect, and you raising him here?"

"Yeah, but this is a hard place to raise an Irish child. Too much discrimination. He's not too fond of the place. I'm thinking about returning to Nicaragua."

Samuel and Padraig exchanged a dark look.

"He'd like it there. With the war over, it'll be safe." Brogan pulled up short as he took in their expressions. "What brings you over here? Wait, hold that thought. I'll pour us a whiskey."

"No time. I'm afraid we're in a spot of bother. We need your help." Samuel leaned against the bulkhead.

A seagull landed on the bowsprit with a croak and fixed its beady black eyes on them as he filled Brogan in.

"I can lock the wretch up in my workshop. Nobody would find him there. But what are you planning to do?" Brogan rolled down the sleeves of his shirt.

"I don't know. I think—"

A gun barked on the quay.

Samuel's heart hammered. "Sofia!"

All three men raced ashore, where the horses pranced in their traces and tossed their heads, tugging at the reins secured to a steel bollard. Samuel yanked the coach door. Sofia sat wide-eyed with the smoking Colt in her hand. The cab reeked of brimstone, sweat, and blood.

"He attacked me," she said simply. "I had to. I had to shoot him."

Samuel stooped inside and embraced her sweaty body. "It's all right. He was scum. He'd have killed you in a flash. We must get rid of the corpse. Now. Frank?"

Brogan appeared at the window. "We'll take him aboard *Macaw*, and I'll dump him in the bay tonight."

Five minutes later, Brogan and Padraig wrapped the body in a tarp and lugged it to the tugboat while Samuel did what he could to mop up the blood with rags Brogan provided. His mind raced as fast as his pulse. Walker was after them, and they had a dead body on their hands.

Sofia drew a deep breath and let it out slowly. "He'll never leave us alone. He'll keep attacking until he gets his gold back or destroys us. We must stop him."

Samuel grimaced. He'd dragged his family into this mess again. "It's too dangerous. Father would understand why we must leave his remains with Filipe. Perhaps later—"

"Not if Walker takes over Nicaragua. And he won't stop there, you know he won't. He came after us once in Ireland, and he'll do it again. He'll harm Filipe to vex us. We have to fight him."

"Damnation, Sofia, I can't let—" He sat back and scratched his sweating neck. "Well, I can't say I disagree. But how?"

Sofia smoothed her stained dress. "What a mess."

They'd be lucky to get away with dumping the body. And Walker was after them again. Samuel's stomach dropped, but he tried to lighten the moment as he finished mopping up the blood. It reeked like copper. "Yes, isn't it, literally. There. That's the worst of it. Brogan knows a quiet place to burn the coach tonight. It's best we get rid of it."

Sofia looked out the window. "Here come the lads now. I don't know what we can do about Walker. Yet. But. I'm sick of him. Five years of watching over our shoulders. There must be some way to stop him."

Samuel tapped his fingers on the side of the coach as warehouses and wharfs blurred past the window. The salt air was rich with the aroma of coffee and spices, somewhat softening the stench of death inside the coach. What they needed was a way to trap Walker. But what bait? What did Walker want? What did he need?

He reviewed what Biggs told them, and his breath hitched. Investors and ships—that's what Walker needed, and that's precisely what Samuel would supply.

He drew Sofia close and nuzzled her neck. "Don't worry, my darling. I have an idea."

CHAPTER SEVEN

Early the following morning, Samuel helped Sofia down from a coach outside a familiar two-story office building on West Fourth Street. Frank Brogan followed, and they waited while Padraig paid the driver. The street hadn't changed since he'd last visited Cornelius Vanderbilt three years before. It still bustled with workers in dusty coveralls, wealthy men in tailored suits, and women in hooped dresses and feathered bonnets. The sooty air vibrated with the creak of cartwheels, snatches of conversations, the cries of street hawkers, and drivers' curses. The place was alive with confusion as cabs and horse-drawn omnibuses zipped between lumbering wagons and pedestrians dodged through the traffic.

"Are you certain this is the place?" Sofia shaded her eyes to peer at the array of hats filling the windows on the second floor.

Samuel caught her elbow and drew her to the steps leading to an unmarked door. "We've been here before." Like Samuel, Vanderbilt would have assumed his enemy, Walker, was doomed. He wouldn't be happy that Walker was free again, and that might work to Samuel's advantage. If anybody knew where Samuel could charter an ocean-going vessel Vanderbilt would.

"You'd think the richest man in the world could afford a sign," she grumbled.

He opened the brass-trimmed door inward and stepped aside to let Sofia proceed them into an anteroom, where paintings of steamships lined the bland walls. The same wizened clerk they'd met before guarded the double doors to the inner sanctum, and his bushy eyebrows popped up his skull when he saw them. A half dozen men in business suits perched on wooden chairs along the wall perked up and ogled Sofia as she crossed the room, her Lancashire print dress sweeping the floor. Lecherous bastards, he'd half a mind to rattle them.

The clerk frowned up at him. "Captain Kingston. We weren't expecting you."

"I'm sorry." Samuel held his hands up, palms out. "We arrived in the city yesterday, and I've an urgent proposition for the Commodore. I'm certain he'll be interested."

"I'm sorry, sir, but that's impossible. I book the Commodore's schedule weeks ahead of time." The clerk's eyes flicked to the men tilting their heads or blinking at the honey-complexioned beauty standing at Samuel's elbow.

The room was uncomfortably warm and smelled of wood polish and cigars. Samuel held his smile. "It's an emergency. We don't have time to wait. I'm certain Mr. Vanderbilt will want to hear what I have to say."

"I'm afraid you must make an appointment."

Samuel took one step toward a chair. "I'm sorry, but that's not acceptable. I'll wait."

The clerk groaned theatrically. "Please don't make this difficult, Captain. I'm afraid I must ask you to leave if you don't wish to make an appointment."

Yes, it was poor form, but getting in to see Vanderbilt was important, perhaps a matter of life and death. Samuel thrust out his jaw. "It will be too late by then."

The clerk rounded the desk and pointed at the door. "Get out."

He didn't have time for this. Samuel stalked across the room and rapped on one of the double doors.

"How dare you." The clerk yanked Samuel's arm. "Get out this instant or I'll have you arrested."

The double doors flew open. "Rabb, what's the meaning of —" Vanderbilt's flushed face appeared. "Kingston, what on earth are you doing here?"

"I'm sorry to interrupt, Mr. Vanderbilt, but this is an urgent matter." Samuel lowered his voice. "It's William Walker. He intends to attack Nicaragua again."

Vanderbilt plucked at the voluminous white whiskers brushed back from his angular face as his eyes narrowed. "Blast it. This is most irregular. I don't—"

"I'm sorry, sir. He barged past me. Mister, you must leave now." The clerk jostled Samuel's arm.

Samuel twisted away and stepped in front of the smaller man. "I'll leave when I've said my piece. The commodore knows me. Knows I'm not here to trifle."

Vanderbilt's thin lips hardened into a smile. "Very well. Five minutes—after I finish my meeting." He clicked the door closed.

The other supplicants frowned their disapproval as Rabb sauntered to his desk and made a show of examining his appointment diary.

Samuel lifted his hands and let them fall. "I'm sorry, gentlemen, but this is truly an emergency."

A middle-aged man with short black hair stood up. "I'm certain it is. Mr. Vanderbilt doesn't normally let folks barge in on him." He gave a brittle laugh and faced Sofia. "Madam, please take my seat."

"Thank you, sir." Sofia flashed her winsome smile. "I appreciate that kindness, but I'll stand. I've been sitting far too much these days."

Ten minutes later, Vanderbilt reopened the inner door. ". . . expect you to keep a sharp eye on them. Don't let those tight-fisted bastards skimp on the paneling. Only quality stuff."

The rotund man departing knuckled his weathered forehead. "You can depend on me, Commodore. No shipyard has ever diddled Captain Jasper Summers."

"Good man, Jasper. I knew I could rely on you."

The captain headed for the exit with the rolling gait of a sailor.

Vanderbilt beamed at Sofia. "You must be the intrepid Mrs. Kingston. Caused quite a stir before, didn't you? Well, I'm glad everything worked out and we got you safely home."

Samuel plastered the fake smile back on his face. *He got her safely home.* Humph. All Vanderbilt had done was make things more difficult and carve off his own pound of flesh. "Yes, Mr. Vanderbilt, this is Sofia. Sofia, Cornelius Vanderbilt."

Vanderbilt's keen eyes measured her as he shook her hand. "I can see why your husband rocked a nation to get you back, Mrs. Kingston."

Lecherous old goat couldn't wait to tear off her britches, but Sofia could well handle such compliments. "Why thank you, Mr. Vanderbilt."

Samuel exchanged a glance with Padraig. Vanderbilt's habits were infamous. "And you remember Lieutenant Kerr?"

"Yes, I guess so." Vanderbilt glanced over his shoulder at the mantel clock. "Come in. I have little time."

Four scale models of steamships sat beside the clock and more paintings of steamships lined the walls of his otherwise Spartan office. Samuel remembered the stuffed striped cat sitting on a rolltop desk in the corner as he guided Sofia to the two seats in front of Vanderbilt's long uncluttered desk.

"Sit down, please, Mrs. Kingston." Vanderbilt took a cigar from the desk drawer. "Now what's this about Walker? That man has more lives than a cat. He got clean away with his piracy in Nicaragua. Shows the American obsession with manifest destiny. What's so urgent, Captain?"

"Walker's returning to Nicaragua, sir."

"What?" Vanderbilt's voice rose. "He wouldn't dare."

Samuel related what had happened since they arrived, except of course the part about dumping Biggs's body in the harbor under the cover of darkness last night. "It's a fact, and I hope you'll help me stop him. After all, the last time he was there, he stole your concession to operate the Nicaraguan transit route."

Vanderbilt shook his head disparagingly. "Damned the bastard, he did, and I punished him for it. But even if he conquers Nicaragua, he can't harm me now. I've killed the Nicaraguan route; it's more profitable to operate through Panama now."

"I understand, sir, but Nicaragua—"

"I've made a deal with Aspinwall to share the Panama route. It's quite profitable with our East Coast and West Coast shipping concerns merged. Several of my ships joined Aspinwall's Pacific fleet, and I'm a major shareholder of his Pacific Steamship Company. We've cornered the California traffic as well, so it makes sense to continue to use Panama."

Samuel exchanged glances with Sofia. He hadn't expected the magnate to be so forgiving.

Vanderbilt stiffened. "I despise William Walker, but I won't waste another dime on that tin soldier."

Greedy old bastard. The Panama route might have been more profitable for him, but it was longer and more dangerous for his passengers. But Samuel hadn't expected Vanderbilt to reject the prospect of revenge. The shipping magnate had once sworn to destroy Walker, but now he was backing down—profits before vengeance.

"Walker will sell the Nicaraguan transit route concession to one of your competitors." Samuel gestured to the map of the Americas on the wall. "It's a much shorter route."

"Let him. Whoever sets up in Nicaragua, I'll beat them on price. I have the US Mail contract. I can afford to run lean." Vanderbilt fixed his eyes on Samuel. "I'm curious. You intend to stop him?"

Sofia reached for Samuel and squeezed his hand.

"I have plans. Walker may have stopped meddling in your business, but he's still attacking my family. I was hoping you might know where I can charter an ocean-going vessel, sir?"

Vanderbilt's head flinched back slightly. "An ocean-going vessel?"

"I want to use it to set a trap." He wouldn't tell Vanderbilt any more than he had to. "Don't worry, I'll return the ship unha—"

"No." Vanderbilt lifted a wrinkled hand. "The less I know the better. Hmm . . . It can't be one of mine, they're far too conspicuous."

Samuel scooched forward in his chair. "Of course. Perhaps you know someone with a sailing vessel like the old *Spartacus*? She's ideal, but I've no idea how to find Captain Keller."

"God only knows where that old pirate is." Vanderbilt scratched his receding hairline then picked a pen from the inkwell on his desk and scribbled on a notepad." Try this fellow. He's shifty enough for a job like this. Remember, you never got his name from me. Tell me no more, so I need not deny it later."

Samuel rose alongside his wife with a smile, took the note, and extended his hand to the magnate. "Thank you, sir."

Vanderbilt shook his hand and bowed slightly to Sofia. "The best of luck to you."

Padraig squirmed as he pushed back his chair, surely not pleased that Vanderbilt had ignored him.

It seemed Samuel had a lead on a ship, but the rest of his desperate plan was going to be far more complicated. He bit his lip and offered Sofia his arm.

The day after their meeting with Vanderbilt, every muscle in Samuel's body ached by the time he picked up a room key at the Willard Hotel on Pennsylvania Avenue in Washington, DC. Hours of riding on stuffy trains, barraged by the grate and squeal of iron wheels on bumpy tracks, had exhausted him, and he was grimy from the ash and cinders spewed by the wood-burning locomotives.

His headlong rush to the nation's capital was part of a madcap plan, but he'd no other option. Sofia and Padraig had remained in New York to arrange financing for Brogan, who was searching for the broker Vanderbilt had suggested—no mean feat on short notice. It was Samuel's job to convince the British ambassador, Lord Richard Lyons, to mobilize the Royal Navy.

The British embassy staff denied him entry not an hour ago. Why would the ambassador meet with a nobody? But Samuel's luck changed outside the gates, where he bumped into a colonel in the distinctive red pantaloons of the Eleventh Hussars. Samuel struck up a conversation and mentioned he was a veteran of the Seventeenth Lancers. Delighted to find another soldier who'd charged with the Light Brigade, Colonel Donald Pennington suggested Samuel waylay Ambassador Lyons at his favorite haunt, the Willard Hotel, the center of political gossip in Washington.

The odor of disinfectant in his immaculate bedroom was a welcome change from the locomotive's wood smoke, and if he crouched, he could glimpse a corner of the White House between the buildings on the other side of the busy street. He brushed the dust and ash from his frock coat, scrubbed the grime and sweat from his body, and put on a clean shirt.

As he stood at the mirror and tried to tame his wavy black hair, he considered what Colonel Pennington had told him about the ambassador. Though Lyons had already served as Britain's ambassador to Athens, Saxony, and Tuscany, his appointment here to Washington had displeased the American president because he was so young, still in his early thirties. But Lyons's tact, staunchness, and stoicism in negotiating a peaceful resolution to the Pig War had earned President Buchanan's respect. Samuel had never heard of the Pig War; he'd have to ask Colonel Pennington about that, if he got the chance. From what

Pennington had said, Lord Lyons wasn't the typical arrogant aristocrat, not prejudiced against other races and religions, and he strongly opposed slavery, a fact that might work in Samuel's favor.

He shoved the Colt under the pillow, stubbed his smoking cigarette in the ashtray, and headed for the door.

The Red Robin Bar downstairs was luxuriously appointed, with pictures of American statesmen and military figures lining the oak-paneled walls. Guests already occupied most of the leather-upholstered chairs at the marble-topped tables. The air was heavy with the scent of perfume, hot bodies, and cigarette smoke.

Colonel Pennington beckoned him to the circular bar. He was a short man, fit and lively for his fifty years, with white hair that stood out stiffly like a horse brush. He'd changed his Cherry Picker uniform for a plain dark suit, flowery waistcoat, and black cravat. "Red Robin's signature drink is a mint julep: Kentucky bourbon, lots of sugar, and mint leaves. Fancy one?"

Samuel would need a clear head to deal with the ambassador. "Water, please. It's been a long day."

Pennington jerked his head back playfully. "You sure you're a lancer? Right then, water it is." When the barman moved away, Pennington pointed discreetly to a colorful group in one corner. "The Japanese ambassador is staying here. Look at their swords. Imagine if we pranced around here with our sabers?"

Samuel was too focused to spare more than a glance for the men in long patterned dresses carrying swords not unlike the shashkas the Cossacks had carried in Crimea. "Are you certain he'll be here?"

"Yes, yes, old chap." Pennington glanced around conspiratorially, and a surge of nervous energy flittered across Samuel's fidgeting shoulders. "You know, your name rang a bell when we met, and I believe I remember where I heard it. That old firebrand Colin Campbell of the Highlanders mentioned you. It must be you, eh? Surely there weren't two Kingstons in the

Seventeenth. Was it you who helped the Thin Red Line hold back the Russian attack?"

Even a few years ago, the mere mention of the Battle of Balaklava would have triggered horrible images—charging Russian cavalry, bearded faces snarling above flaring muzzles that huffed mist into the air, brittle sunlight dancing on whetted blades, round shot gouging the earth between flying hooves—but he was in a better place now, thanks to Sofia and his family. "General Bingham ordered me to help him."

Pennington slapped the table with an open palm. "You're a bloody hero, man. Colin said you and your company also charged with the Heavy Brigade, said he put you in for the Victoria Cross. Did you get it?"

Samuel didn't want to revisit that. "I was never on good terms with General Bingham." He hadn't been on good terms with any of the bumbling aristocrats who ran the Crimean campaign, damned their eyes.

Pennington scoffed. "That can only stand you in good stead. Lucan's an old blowhard." He twitched his silver goblet toward the door. "Here comes Lord Lyons now."

His passion for opulent dinner parties had made Ambassador Richard Lyons chunky despite his youth. His dark hair was oiled and plastered to the side, and sunken eyes in a round face lent him a contemplative look. He passed his top hat to one of the two men in business suits following him and headed to one of the few empty tables.

"Come, I'll introduce you before he's mobbed. Lyons is popular." Pennington picked up his goblet and strode toward the ambassador.

The two men standing behind the diplomat tensed at their approach but relaxed when they recognized the colonel. They took a step back and continued to eye the room.

"Lord Lyons." Pennington bowed slightly. "How do you do, Your Excellency? May I intrude for a moment, please?"

"Colonel Pennington, what a pleasure." Lyons rose and

extended his hand. "I've always time for the men who protect the empire. Please, take a seat. My guests aren't due for another thirty minutes. I thought I'd sneak an early julep to fortify myself before their attack." He grinned boyishly. "Allow me to buy you a drink."

"Thank you, Your Excellency, we already have sustenance. May I introduce Lieutenant Samuel Kingston, formerly of the Seventeenth Lancers and a genuine hero of the empire? He's the only officer who fought in all three engagements during the Battle of Balaklava. He helped General Campbell's Ninety-Third Highlanders turn the Russian cavalry from their Thin Red Line. Then he and his company hit the Russian flank as they attacked the Heavy Brigade, and he still had enough steam left to charge with the Light Brigade later the same day."

Lyons moved his silver-handled cane from the seat beside him. "I'm truly honored, Lieutenant. Sit, please."

His hand was fleshy but the grip was firm and reassuring. Samuel squeezed back. "How do you do, Your Excellency? My junior, Lieutenant Davis, rode in all three skirmishes that day too. Unfortunately, he didn't survive the last charge. Too few did."

The ambassador squeezed his dark eyes shut briefly. "Many good men fell in that folly. What a waste. What a stupid war. The London mob howled for blood, and—" He threw up his hands and sank back into the overstuffed leather chair. "I won't get started. So where's home for you now, Lieutenant?"

"A small town called Clonakilty in the Southwest of Ireland, Your Excellency."

"Ireland. What a beautiful country. It's given us many heroes —and Wellington, of course." Lyons crossed his arms. "What brings you to the United States, Lieutenant?"

Samuel wet his parched mouth with water from his glass. He shouldn't have come—and it wasn't too late to rein in his galloping plan. He glanced at the intelligent eyes watching him intently. Too much depended on this, not only his family's safety but the fate of nations.

"I was passing through New York on my way to collect my father's remains in Nicaragua, but now that I'm here, I find that my past has caught up with me." He related how his family's enemies had forced him to fight in Nicaragua for Walker, and how he'd returned a year later to help the Costa Ricans capture the San Juan River and cut Walker's supply route. He explained how that move had led to Walker's eventual defeat.

By the time Samuel paused, Lyons was wringing the napkin at his place setting. "I can't understand how the Americans cheer for Walker."

"Well, I can imagine the slave states support him," Pennington added.

"This slavery issue threatens to tear America apart, and where will that leave Britain?" Lyons glanced around and lowered his voice. "I used to consider it impossible that the South would be mad enough to dissolve the Union, but now I fear it's inevitable. And which side should Britain take?"

What was the right response? Samuel waited out the pause.

Ice clinked as Lyons swirled his julep with a silver stirring stick. "But enough of that. If Walker begins another war down there, it will additionally pressure our interests in Central America. I despise slavery. I won't have that. But we can't touch him unless he invades a country, and by then it'll be too late."

"What if I could guide the Royal Navy fleet in the Caribbean to Walker and a boatload of armed men, sir?" Samuel stopped his foot tapping frantically beneath the table and moved to the edge of his seat.

"And why would Walker take a boatload of—how would you . . . Go on."

"Can you assure me that you would convict him as the American courts seem unable to do? That's the only way to curb his ambition." Samuel was dying for a smoke but settled for pulling out his snuffbox.

Lyons twirled a silver fork on the table and raised an eyebrow at Pennington.

Pennington placed his goblet on the table. "We've fifteen frigates in the Caribbean right now. If we had a rough idea of when Walker planned to sail, they could wait out there and—"

"Uuuup the Fenians!"

Samuel's head jerked back at the ragged shout. A bearded man was charging across the bar, a revolver aimed at Samuel's table. Samuel snatched up Lyons's silver-handled cane as the gun went off. One bodyguard fell with a scream. Patrons stampeded from the room to the sound of screams and breaking glass.

Swinging the cane, Samuel lunged from his seat and struck the attacker's arm. The gun flew from his hand. The second guard threw himself over Lyons like a human shield as Samuel pounded the attacker in the face.

The guard rolled away from the fracas and pulled Lyons to his feet. "We must go, Excellency."

As the attacker lolled on the floor, Samuel snatched the revolver, cocked it, and scanned the room. "He's the only one. Must've been acting alone."

Lyons was pale and trembling. "The Fenian Brotherhood. My God, I thought they were all bluster."

Pennington stooped and lifted a gun from the fallen body-guard's belt. "I'll check there's no more of them." He scurried across the barroom.

A Fenian. Samuel rose and pointed the gun at the prone attacker. Word of that organization was spreading in Ireland. Its Irish American supporters believed Ireland had a natural right to independence and were proposing an armed revolution. The assassination of Britain's ambassador would have been quite a coup. "He seems to have acted alone, but there might be others outside. We should wait here until the police arrive." He pointed to the unconscious guard. "Check your comrade. I'll cover the door."

The guard's forehead wrinkled, and he glanced at Lyons.

"Do as he said, man." The color was returning to Lyons's face as he assertively took command.

Blood blackened the fallen bodyguard's shirt. His colleague placed a trembling hand on his companion's neck and shook his head. "Gone, Excellency. Peter's dead."

Lyons stared at the body and spoke in a monotone voice. "I never thought a man would die because of me. I'll see these Fenians hanged, all of them. A free Ireland." He huffed. "Never! Ireland is part of the British Empire. We'll never let them go."

Samuel pinched his lips together. He disagreed with violence and would never support it, but Ireland should be free, just as America was. But this wasn't the time to broach that subject.

Outside the bar, the hotel appeared to be alive with mischief, with people shouting and racing back and forth before the Round Robin's doors. Samuel nudged the assassin with his foot. Still out cold. Never taking his eyes off the man, he sank to the edge of his seat to take the weight off his buckling legs. "Are you all right, Excellency?"

"Thanks to you, Lieutenant." Lyons dapped the sweat beading his forehead with his napkin. "Pennington was right about you. You're a man of action, and I owe my life to you."

Four uniformed policemen appeared at the door, pistols drawn.

Samuel had to ask, or he'd never get another chance. "Excellency, about the Walker affair?"

Lyons's features softened. "My word, but you're a persistent bugger. You should be a politician. But yes, let me think on it. Come to the embassy in the morning."

"Thank you, Your Excellency." Samuel slumped back in his seat as the policeman rushed toward them.

There was hope for his Walker plan yet. And who knew? Perhaps he would become a politician; it seemed the only hope of bringing equality to Ireland.

But that was another day's challenge.

CHAPTER EIGHT

Four days after landing in New York, Samuel adjusted his slouch hat and stepped from the coach into the heat and humidity. "Frank? Are you certain you want to do this? I can find someone else."

Thank God the American filibusters had billeted separately from Samuel and his Nicaraguan troops back during the Nicaraguan civil war. He'd never met Frank Anderson, so he wouldn't be recognized, and Brogan would need help navigating this negotiation. Anderson, now Walker's trusted deputy, had a reputation as a tough soldier, passionate about excellent horses and fine brandy but hard as nails. But if Brogan backed out, it would be next to impossible to find an experienced sailor committed enough to do what was needed.

"I told you New York was no place for the Irish. They treat us like dirt here. I was serious about returning to Nicaragua with my lad, and since I don't want to live in the Nicaragua Walker intends, we must stop him."

"Good man." Under his coat, Samuel settled the Colt in his belt. "Remember, I'm Samuel Morris from Devon, England. And let me do most of the talking."

"Lead the way."

The Laughing Man was typical of the bars near the Five Points slum—dark, the air heavy with tobacco smoke, reeking of body odor and stale booze. Anderson probably found it a good place to tempt poor and desperate men with Walker's promises of gold and land in Nicaragua. The chatter of a dozen conversations washed over Samuel: several voices too loud, drunk patrons catcalling the few women who dared to frequent the dump.

The bronzed, clean-shaven man of indeterminate age rigidly perched at the last table against the wood-paneled wall had to be Anderson. Samuel knew the filibuster had served in the Mexican War. Unlike the four men in shirt sleeves sitting at the table littered with tankards, Anderson wore an expensive suit, was well groomed, and sat upright, every inch a soldier. His eyes flew to Samuel as soon as they entered. This was a cautious man.

One of the toughs at Anderson's table coughed, a slow hacking sound between sharp intakes of breath. Samuel sauntered over and offered his best smile. "Good afternoon, gentlemen. I'm Samuel Morris, and my friend here is Captain Brogan. We're looking for Frank Anderson."

"Afternoon." Anderson's glass scraped as he rotated it on the table. "And what's your business with this Frank Anderson?"

Samuel lowered his voice. "We heard you were looking for investors, Colonel Anderson, and we might be interested."

"You're an Englishman?"

"Yes."

"And him?" Anderson gestured with his thumb.

Brogan tilted his head back. "Irish, and the best damned sea captain on both sides of the Atlantic."

Anderson fidgeted with a coin on the beer-splashed table. A second later, he motioned to his companions, who stood and drifted back from the table. He pointed to the empty stools. "Sit. I'll buy you a drink, and you can tell me what you think I'm looking for."

"Thank you, Mr. Anderson." Samuel sat.

"General. You can call me General. I got a promotion."

"Very well, General, and I won't mince words. We heard William Walker is preparing an expedition to reclaim his presidency of Nicaragua. We can help if he makes it worthwhile. We're in the shipping business, and we'd like to reopen the Transit Road route through Nicaragua. It's much faster than a passage through Panama. That's why Cornelius Vanderbilt fought so hard when Walker took his concession to operate the Nicaraguan Transit Route. But Vanderbilt and his partner have cornered the market and the mail contract with his Panama route now, and he'll never work with Walker. Too much bad blood." Samuel sat back. He didn't want to sound too eager for a deal. "Those drinks? I'm partial to a good Scotch, and Frank likes his Irish whiskey."

Anderson motioned to one of the standing men. "Two whiskeys, a Scotch and an Irish, Tom."

Samuel inclined his head. "Thanks."

Anderson appraised Samuel with intelligent blue eyes. "Opening that route again will take deep pockets."

"Not a problem. What I want is a deal. I can have two brigs in New Orleans by the beginning of June."

Anderson shot Brogan a dubious look.

"They can easily carry four hundred men and all the weapons you need," Brogan said, "with room for artillery and . . ."

An hour later, Anderson sat back and ran a hand through his hair. "I like the plan, and the terms are reasonable. Are you certain the brigs can be in New Orleans in time?"

"Yes." Brogan nodded once.

"And they're large enough to carry all the supplies, the artillery, and two hundred men?"

Brogan intertwined his fingers and extended his arms into a stretch. "Yes. More if you wish."

"I like it, but I need to run it by General Walker." Anderson tugged the cuffs of his jacket. "Where can I contact you?"

It dawned on Samuel that he knew the confident walk of the tall, lean man entering the bar: Captain Charles Hornsby. They'd fought together in Walker's army; Hornsby would recognize him in a heartbeat.

Samuel pulled the brim of his hat low on his forehead and made a show of checking his silver pocket watch. "My word, is that the time?" He clicked the cover shut and rose from the table. "I'm terribly sorry, General, but I've an urgent appointment across town."

Brogan's eyebrows sprang up.

"You're rushing off now?" Anderson lowered his glass with a frown.

It took great effort not to look at Hornsby by the bar again. Samuel offered his hand to Anderson. "I'm afraid I must if I'm to make my appointment to sign for the funds from my bank in England—the money needed for this enterprise. Frank will arrange the logistics with you."

In the corner of his eye, Hornsby collected a glass from the bar and faced their table.

"Good day to you, gentlemen. Frank, I'll see you at the hotel." For goodness' sake, if Brogan didn't pick up his dropped jaw and take the cue, they were in trouble.

"Oh right. The bank." Brogan forced a smile. "It's fortunate, you remembered it. Now then, General Anderson, when do you think . . ."

Looking down, Samuel scurried to the door. Hornsby's lanky frame slowed as he passed. Samuel yanked open the door and fled into the clammy evening.

It had been a close escape, but the hunt was on.

Having returned to New York, Samuel found the heat unbearable. Even with windows thrown wide open, sweat trickled down his back as he waited with Sofia and Padraig in the hotel's restaurant, surrounded by the smells of tobacco smoke, baking pastry, and fresh coffee. China rattled as a waiter passed with a tray of steaming food, and laughter punctuated the drone of murmuring patrons.

Where was Brogan? He needed confirmation all was arranged with Anderson before they boarded the *Adriatic*. The steamship would sail for Panama the next morning. Samuel opened the top button of his shirt. "Padraig, stop jiggling your knee. You're rocking the table."

Sofia gave Padraig an understanding smile. "Brogan will be here any time now. With luck, he'll bring good news."

Turning his head aside, Samuel exhaled a stream of cigarette smoke. "I hope so. There's not another boat to Panama for two weeks."

"Ugh, I don't want to stay in New York another two weeks," Sofia said. "I'm ready to see Filipe again, to see the old place."

"I'm not keen on that delay, either. That would extend our trip quite a bit, make it longer before we see the children. But we must be certain Walker embarks with his volunteers on the brigs. Colonel Pennington is waiting aboard a Royal Navy steam frigate in the harbor for confirmation that Walker took the bait. Once he's certain of it, the frigate will sail for the British base in Bluefields. They've five warships based in Nicaragua and ten more scattered across the Caribbean—plenty to bag Walker. Look there, Frank's coming."

A sheen of perspiration covered Brogan's youthful face as he pulled out a chair to join them. The tug captain hung his bowler hat on the ear of the chair and beamed around the table. "It's on. Walker accepted our deal and will embark with his troops in New Orleans. In return, we get the rights to operate the Transit Road route when Walker retakes the country." Brogan chuckled and smoothed the breasts of his dark tweed jacket. "Fat chance of him even reaching Nicaragua."

"No chance, you mean." Padraig backhanded Samuel's

shoulder and relaxed back in his seat. "Walker will be president of a British jail cell."

"I hope it's Newgate Prison." The memory of his time in that notorious jail's damp cells flashed through Samuel, reminding him of its reek of rot, feces, and human despair. Imprisoning Walker in Newgate would make a fine twist.

"It's agreed, then." Brogan dragged on his cigarette and picked a flake of tobacco off his lip as he puffed smoke out. "I'd like you all to come to my place for dinner this evening. Now, the house is tiny, nothing like you're used to, but Brice, my son, is eager to meet you. I told him about you years ago—not the bloody stuff, of course, but how you fed our family at the height of the Great Famine. Kathy, my sister, wants to thank you herself. She says this time, it's her turn to feed you."

Brogan's grin was infectious, and Samuel had to smile. "We'd love to, thank you." What kind of present should they buy for an eight-year-old boy? His little John would want a saber. He toyed with the edge of the tablecloth, missing the children terribly. Remembering the time little John had copied Padraig's scar with charcoal on his nose and swatted wildly with his play sword stretched his smile even farther.

"I can't think of a better way to spend our last evening in New York," Sofia swirled the coffee in her china cup and took a sip. "And I hope you don't mind if I stuff Brice with sweets."

Brogan laughed.

"Great, that's settled then." Samuel stubbed his cigarette in the ashtray and glanced around for a waiter. "I think we deserve a proper drink. I've had enough coffee."

"I must get on home and warn Kathy." Brogan twisted around to pick his bowler hat off the chair's ear. "She's fussy. She'll want all the time we can give her to prepare. Shall we say six o'clock?"

Six it is, Frank. I'm looking forward to meeting them." Samuel shook the tug captain's hand.

Sofia pushed away her cup and rose. "I won't stay for a drink,

I need to pack. It's going to be hard to fit everything since you filled most of one trunk with ammunition for your new toy."

"I'll have a quick whiskey with Padraig, then." He pecked Sofia on the cheek, and the scent of her fresh sweat and her new jasmine perfume stirred him. He'd make it a very quick drink.

When their Irish whiskeys arrived, Padraig took a long whiff. "Smells like burnt toast at breakfast time." He raised his drink. "To finally locking Walker away."

The tumblers clinked together.

Movement beyond the stained-glass doors caught Samuel's eye, and something about it made him look again. It could be waiters or a patron fumbling to enter, but the movement seemed stealthy.

He plonked his glass on the table. "Something's wrong."

"What the—" Padraig's eyes flicked to the entrance.

"Quickly, out the back door."

Padraig sprang to his feet, knocking over his chair. "Police. Scatter."

"Through the bar." Samuel kicked open the half door under the counter and ducked behind the bar.

The overweight barman dropped his tea towel and grabbed for Samuel. "You can't come in here. This is—"

"Sorry, friend." He shouldered past the barman and slipped into the back room. Most bars had a back door for bringing in bottles and casks.

And there it was.

Shouting erupted behind them in the dining room. "US marshals! Stop those fugitives."

Footsteps close behind him reassured Samuel that Padraig was on his heels. The narrow passage stank of stale alcohol and mold as they dashed past stacks of bottles and wooden casks. Glass shattered, and Padraig cursed. Samuel craned around. Padraig was toppling crates of bottles as he ran. Behind him came a man with a grizzled face and a familiar walrus mustache.

They burst into a narrow alley between sooty red-brick walls, and the stench of urine and rotting rubbish was overpowering.

"Hurry, they've drawn pistols," Padraig panted.

Fifty yards ahead, pedestrians thronged the street in the sunlight, and cabs and carts trundled in both directions.

Samuel dashed for the crowds. Perhaps they could hide among them.

Padraig drew up next to him as they ran. "That was the deputy marshal."

Raine, US Marshal Raine—that's who Walrus Face was. Samuel stumbled, flailed back into balance, and dizzily plunged on. Raine, the US marshal he'd outwitted several years earlier, was pursuing him again.

Samuel dodged right at the street and bowled into a well-dressed couple, knocking the woman to the ground. Padraig yelped and leaped over her. The man cursed and swung his cane as Samuel hurled an apology over his shoulder. The cane landed a stinging blow on his neck.

A dozen heads swiveled to stare, jaws dropping, eyes glaring, followed by a chorus of squeals and gasps. The broad sidewalk was packed with people and hemmed in by towering buildings while cabs, carts, and horsemen zipped in both directions in the street beyond. Two policemen and a fellow with his bowler hat in hand dodged between the horse-drawn traffic a hundred yards ahead, angling to cut them off.

"Watch out, they're ahead of us." Padraig slowed, his breath heaving in exhausted spurts.

Samuel glanced back. Pedestrians were parting like the Red Sea, and US Marshal Raine and two strangers weaved between them. One of the men carried a baton, and the second wore a long coat despite the heat, a hand tucked inside as if concealing a weapon. Samuel sped on, his leg muscles burning and his lungs rasping.

"This way." He dodged into another wide street.

Iron railings barred access to the park ahead. A dead end.

Samuel slowed to a fast walk and risked a glance behind. Padraig was right there, sweat streaming down his flushed face. Raine appeared around the corner, followed by the man in the long coat. Samuel whirled around. They couldn't advance—the park was closed off—nor could they retreat.

He caught Padraig's arm and dragged him behind a marble column in the archway of some fancy office building.

Momentarily oblivious that they'd gone to ground, Raine continued forward. Samuel had to take the chance and thin the odds, even with the others so close behind. He drew his Colt. Padraig flattened against the wall and balled his fists.

As Raine swayed into sight, Padraig darted out and tripped him. Before he hit the ground, Samuel cracked him on the head.

They dashed toward the park.

"I hope . . . you . . . didn't kill him," Padraig panted. Both horsemen, neither were used to hoofing it.

A shrill whistle cut the air. "Stop those fugitives!"

"Criminals escaping!"

The crunch of boots behind them lifted the hair on the nape of Samuel's neck, and he pumped his legs harder, his breath burning the back of his throat. The park was only thirty yards away, but the double gates were closed and chained in the wrought-iron fence. He swerved into a side street, but two more policemen were there, dashing toward them.

Samuel skidded to a halt. "Not this way."

Padraig bumped into him. "Buggers are everywhere."

They hastily backtracked. Samuel winced at the spikes atop the park fence, but the trimmed lawns of the park beyond were enticingly empty. "Over the railings. I'll give you a leg up." He threw his back against the iron bars and cupped his hands.

"You first."

There wasn't time for Padraig's undying loyalty. Samuel, the taller of the pair, had the best chance of climbing the fence unassisted. "Get up, you fool, or we'll both be taken."

"Bloody hell." Padraig caught Samuel's neck with a sweaty

hand, and his hard boot ground into Samuel's palms as he stepped up and pulled, assisted by a well-timed heave. He planted a foot between the spikes with the agility of a boy who'd grown up pinching apples from orchards, balanced on top for a heartbeat, and dropped into the park. He landed like a cat on his palms and the balls of his feet.

"Hurry."

Samuel grasped the bars below their sharp spikes and heaved himself up, his feet scrabbling for traction on the slick metal. Upward, upward . . . His eyes came level with the spikes, sharp as the blade of a lance—they'd gut him for any faux pas. Shoulders screaming with the effort, he dragged his torso level with the spikes. Six more inches and he'd be over.

A hand clamped his ankle. "Got you."

He kicked with his free foot, but his muscles gave out and he toppled backward. His coat caught on a spike and ripped with a rending tear before he hit the ground. His teeth cracked together, and the fall drove the wind from him with a loud *huff*.

Running feet came closer, and the policeman who'd felled him locked a sweaty arm about his neck.

"Go," Samuel yelled. "Tell the others."

As they hauled him to his feet, he glimpsed Padraig sprinting across the park. He closed his eyes and shook his reeling head. At least one of them had escaped.

Rough hands spun him around into the swarthy sweating face of Deputy US Marshal Stone—the lawman he made a fool of during his last visit to New York.

Stone slapped him across the face. "I've waited years for this, Kingston. You made a laughingstock of me, and now you'll pay for it. You're under arrest for breaching the Neutrality Act in eighty-six when you smuggled arms to Costa Rica, and more— resisting arrest, assaulting a federal officer, and several other charges. You're looking at ten years' hard labor on Blackwell Island." He rubbed his hands together and sneered. "Take this criminal to the station. The rest of you, stop gawking and catch the other one."

Samuel's head reeled as they marched him down the road. Just when he almost had Walker in his grasp, things had spiraled out of control. He'd blown it. He only hoped that the others would follow the plan, leading Walker into the trap.

The policeman on his right gave him a shove. "Move it, you blackguard."

CHAPTER NINE

It was the poke in the ribs that woke Samuel, the elbow of a ragged drunk with abysmal breath who rolled against him in the crowded cell. He jolted upright and scooted back against the sopping stone wall. The hot cell stank of human waste and sweat of the thirty men crammed in there, farting, cursing, and snoring in conditions that made Newgate Prison seem like a hotel. He gagged and plucked a louse from his armpit.

The dove-gray light seeping through the narrow-barred window high in the wall promised dawn. It felt as if he'd been there a week. Anyone seeking a long life should go to prison; time dragged there. He rolled his shoulders to ease aching muscles, flopped his head forward, and ran a hand through his lank and sweaty hair. The *Adriatic* would sail on the ebb tide that afternoon, and it would depart without them. Sofia and Padraig would never leave without him.

Even when he stood on the tips of his toes, he couldn't reach the tiny window high in the wall. "Damnation!"

Steel gates clanged, and prisoners stirred in a chorus of curses peeling out from the cells along the corridor. Three guards appeared with a jangle of keys, vague in the gloomy light. One rattled his baton along the bars. "Kingston, which one of you is Kingston? Hop it now, quickly, I can't abide the stink of you lot."

A key rattled in the lock as Samuel picked his way through the tangle of limbs, bleeding sores, and upturned eyes filled with fear or malice.

"The cop basher," growled the guard with the baton. "I hope I get a crack at you."

They seized his arms and marched him down the corridor past cells teeming with misery and a single window overlooking a worn noose, swinging listlessly on the gallows. A rusty metal door at the end of the corridor creaked open as if of its own accord, and an angelic face appeared behind a guard. Samuel pressed his grimy palms to his eyes. He had to be imagining this.

Sofia sprang forward with a squeal.

"No!" The guard with the baton held her back. "Stay clear of the prisoner."

"How dare you touch the lady? 'The prisoner'? Can't you read, moron?" Clipped disdain poured from a bald man in an expensively cut suit. "Mr. Kingston's record is clear—more so than yours, I dare say. Get out of my sight before I lock you up in your own cell." The gentleman stepped forward and held out a manicured hand. "A letter of pardon signed by President Buchanan himself. I'm Thaddeus Young, federal judge for the Southern District of New York. You're a free man, Mr. Kingston. I hope your stay here wasn't too unpleasant."

Thanking him, Samuel rushed forward and embraced Sofia. Her sweet scent was an oasis in that stinking hell; she wore her favorite apple perfume. Her fleshy lips crushed his, and she was soft as cream to his touch after the hard bodies crushing against him. He was out of this mess, reunited with Sofia, free to collect Father's remains and go home. He hugged her even closer.

He drew his head back only inches. "Darling, how did you manage this?"

Her lilting laugh was full of joy. "You made powerful allies in Washington. I didn't realize you were such a charming man."

Samuel disengaged as Colonel Pennington, holding a bowler hat and walking cane, stepped closer. "I was awaiting confirmation that Walker took the bait," Pennington said, reaching for a handshake, "but when Mrs. Kingston brought news of your imprisonment, I wired Ambassador Lyons. Only two hours later, I received his telegram with word that President Buchanan had ordered your release."

The corners of Sofia's mouth quirked. "A compassionate man, the American president."

Pennington popped the bowler on his head and adjusted it to a jaunty angle. "Apparently, he doesn't speak against Walker publicly for fear of further alienating the slave states, but privately, he despises Walker's ambitions and feels his incarceration would bring a happy change. Old boy, you're not alone in your endeavors." He clapped Samuel on the shoulder and wrinkled his nose. "Phew, you're in desperate need of a bath. I've arranged a hotel where you can clean up, but we must make haste. You've a boat to catch."

"Colonel, I'm grateful to you and the ambassador. Please convey that to him." He needed to hold Sofia again and feel her lithe arms wrapped around him.

Young and Pennington bustled for the exit, but Samuel drew his wife close and kissed her. To hell with the leering guards across the room. "Thank you, darling."

"But of course. I didn't want to travel to Nicaragua alone."

He drew back slightly. "Padraig?"

"Outside with the coach and baggage. After escaping through the park, he sneaked into the hotel and alerted me. I'm sorry it took us so long to get you out." She gave him an impish smile. "I guess it takes time to rouse the president of the United States in the wee small hours."

The chuckle warmed him all the way through. "Believe me, I'm not disappointed. You've worked miracles." He was vibrating with excitement. Fate had snatched him from the brink of disaster, and soon Britain would capture William Walker. All that remained now was to bring Father home. He couldn't wait to see the children again. "Come along. A hot bath awaits."

Sofia held her nose. "Thank goodness. But perhaps you should ride up front with the driver." She stuck out her tongue before leading him to the exit.

~

The fore-and-aft tilt of SS *Adriatic*'s two masts and her red funnels gave her a rakish form that promised a speedy passage, and the forty-foot paddle wheels to port and starboard were the business ends that would deliver it. The steamy air smelled of salt and the fish guts thrown overboard by passing boats. Seagulls soared and wheeled in the smoke-smudged sky, gluttons screaming and diving for the bloody scraps.

It was almost noon, and the *Adriatic* would sail at two to take advantage of the ebb tide. His stay in prison had almost made them miss the boat, but now they were back on track. The Royal Navy would capture Walker, and the British courts would lock him away for years. All that remained was to visit Filipe, collect Father's body, and hurry home to the children. Samuel paused thirty yards from the gangplank. "What a beauty. Those paddle wheels are huge. It must take an enormous engine to power them."

"It is." Padraig's haversack exhaled as he laid it down to survey the 350-foot black hull and white superstructure. "Two oscillating cylinders, one hundred inches in diameter, each capable of producing thirty-six hundred horsepower with a steam pressure of twenty pounds to the square inch."

Of course, Mr. Know-It-All had researched both ships on their route. Samuel caught Sofia's smirk and rolled his eyes. "You know, it would delight your mother if you attended mass with the same reverence."

Padraig snorted. "Bloody landlubber."

"Perhaps the captain will let you steer her."

"Can we board, please?" Sofia said. "This sooty air is going to ruin my dress."

"It's the coal." Smoke spiraled from Padraig's mouth as he spoke around his cigarette. "This behemoth burns ninety tons of coal a day."

As Padraig stooped to pick up his haversack, a young woman cutting between them bumped against him. She fell with a squeal, and her valise flew from her hand to burst open as it struck the ground. The wind scattered filmy garments across the stone pier like leaves.

"Oh, I'm terribly sorry." Padraig dropped his cigarette and stooped to help her.

The young woman flushed and shook her arm free as Samuel and Sofia chased down her garments. "You should be. Why don't you watch where you're going, clod? You could've killed me."

It wasn't her belligerence as much as her cramped Dublin vowels that stopped Samuel from chasing stitches of clothing to inspect her. She was a pretty sight to behold. Young—early to mid-twenties—with skin the color of alabaster except for the tips of her ears, which had flushed from anger. A forest-green ribbon tied down her green bonnet, and strands of hair had broken free to dangle past the soft curves of her pale shoulders like golden-red ropes. Her diamond-shaped nose was perfect, although her colorless lips were narrow, and her eyes, blue as a sun-kissed lagoon, blazed as she berated Padraig for an accident that had been entirely her fault. Samuel dropped his chin to hide a smirk. It would be interesting to see how the ladies' man handled this assault.

But the veteran who'd charged the Don Cossack artillery cringed from her ire.

". . . attention." Sofia thrust her face into his. "Are you helping or not?"

"I am, I am." He scooped up a coal dust-blackened petticoat and dropped the clothes in the suitcase with a chuckle. Sofia was jealous.

Closing the valise, Sofia handed it to the young woman. "Here you are, my dear. But you shouldn't be so hard on Padraig. You bumped into him."

The girl snatched the luggage and stepped back. "I bumped into him? I'll have you know . . ." Her golden-red eyebrows pinched together, and she let out a hard sigh. "You're right. I'm so clumsy. It's, it's all too much. I'm sorry." A tear dribbled from the corner of one eye, and her dress brushed the stone pavers as she spun on her heel and walked away.

"Wait." Sofia hurried after her. "Are you all right? You had quite a fall. Let us help you. Samuel will carry your bag. I'm certain the steward in first class can launder your clothes."

Halting, the woman pushed a strand of hair from her face. "I can't go with you. My ticket is for steerage."

Sofia's face softened. "Never mind that. If someone objects to our helping a woman up the gangplank, I'll sort them out quickly. We ladies must stick together. Come along, my dear."

When Padraig hesitated, Samuel shouldered the long bag with his new Henry rifle and their Sharps rifles and took the case from the girl. "I'm Samuel from Clonakilty, and this is my wife, Sofia." He couldn't resist the urge to tease. "And the handsome man you fell for is Padraig."

Samuel craned around to catch Padraig blushing.

"Where are your manners?" Sofia punched his arm playfully.

The girl's fingers flew to her parted lips. "My gosh. You're Irish? You sounded English to me, at least until you started speaking Latin."

Samuel had heard that all his life. "I went to school in England. You're from Dublin. I'd recognize that accent anywhere."

She bobbed her head. "Sara Brennan from Drumcondra. I'm on my way to Nicaragua."

Sofia's head came up in horror. "You're traveling to Nicaragua alone? Why on earth would you? It's not like Ireland. It's much wilder."

"Oh, not where I'm going. Colonel Ivan Garcia contracted me as his children's governess. He has a sugar plantation close to a place called Shinnandeego."

"Chinandega." A tentative smile formed on Sofia's cherry-red lips. "Isn't that a coincidence? We're going to Chinandega too."

It *was* a surprise. Most if not all the Panama-bound passengers would continue on to San Francisco. Samuel chuckled to himself. How many English speakers would Colonel Garcia's children surprise once they picked up that Dublin accent?

A purser ushered them aboard like royalty. Sofia insisted on keeping Sara's suitcase and having her clothes laundered before returning it to her. Padraig had a faraway look when they parted from Sara and headed to the first-class cabins.

The Spartan conditions on the lower deck reminded Samuel that while the steam engine had abolished the constraints of time and space, and could potentially even strengthen the touchy ties between Britain and America through regular steamship service, the passenger ships it powered followed the same stratification by class as Britain and the British Army. There was still that vast divide he'd grown to detest. Father had stood up to that precedent and demanded more rights for the working man. Samuel's brow furrowed. He should do more for that cause, pick up Father's torch. But first, he'd bring him home.

The passenger berths were arranged around the first-class dining salon and a luminous grand saloon. Glittering columns of patterned glass stretched to a skylight in the spar deck above, while sunlight poured through stained-glass windows to shower a rainbow of colors across the rich carpets, and artfully spaced mirrors projected the illusion of spaciousness. Knots of passengers seated on brightly upholstered Louis XIV furniture conversed around the tables topped with Italian marble.

Their steward opened the door numbered 112 with a flourish and stepped aside to allow them to enter a spacious cabin with a big brass bed.

As soon as the steward departed with Padraig, Sofia sat and bounced on the mattress. "Oh my, what a comfortable bed. I can't wait to see if it squeaks."

Samuel flopped down beside her. "Really? And what happened to my jealous wife?"

"Me? Never. I wanted you to rescue that poor woman's clothing, that's all, instead of standing there like an oaf, relishing Padraig's discomfort. Didn't you say he needed a wife?"

"No, Mrs. Meddlesome, that was you."

Mrs. Meddlesome's slim finger began meddling with his lower lip.

He kissed the soft pads of her finger. "That redhead's pretty, but she might be too fiery for Padraig."

"Do you mean that literally, or are you referring to the color of her hair?" He couldn't stop looking at her parted lips, a sensuous bow.

"Never mind, husband. I'll show you what I mean by fiery." She swung lithely to her feet, a flame of beauty in the sunlight streaming through the brass porthole, petticoats rustling with a flash of silk stockings and honey-brown thighs. As her blue shawl glided away from her unblemished flesh, she crooked a finger and slid her dress off one shapely shoulder with the other hand. "What's the matter, darling? Are you too hot?"

Desire flowered in Samuel with shocking speed and force, stirring his need, fanning his love. He dropped his frock coat on the floor, kicked off his shoes, and lay down, drawing her to him as blood rushed through his body. "Let me stoke those flames before I quench them."

Her lips were like plump cherries, and her moist mouth tasted as sweet as strawberries.

"Only six days?" she whispered against his lips. "What a pity. Next time, my love, we should sail to China instead."

~

On the third day of the voyage, the *Adriatic* shouldered the emerald sea, her towering paddles churning steadily and her sails billowing in the fresh north-by-northwest breeze. The sun was a flaming ball sinking in the sky strewn with high clouds glowing white and pink. Samuel rode the deck's rolling motion with his arm around Sofia and watched the spray break over the bow to shower the deck with rosy diamonds as the wind strummed the taut forestays. The air was fresh and salty, free from the taint of smoke, paint, and other humans.

Sofia craned around to peer at the spar deck and raised her eyebrows. "They're at it again. I can't believe she kisses him like that in public. I wonder about her. What do you think?"

Samuel drew back and slipped his hands into his pockets. It didn't matter what he thought when these two women weren't getting along. He didn't want to have to warn Padraig to take it easy—Padraig was a grown man—but Sofia kept insisting, and there would be no peace until he broached the matter. His friend was smitten with Sara, but no one liked to be told to take it easy when he was galloping a beautiful girl across the Caribbean Sea. "I don't have the foggiest, but Padraig thinks he loves her."

"He bought her a first-class ticket and moved her into his cabin. What will María think of a skilamalink like that?"

"Look at you with your fancy words." Perhaps he could lighten the moment. "You've expanded your vocabulary since leaving Nicaragua. That ticket is chicken feed to a wealthy man like him."

She tucked her arm in his. "I love him like Filipe, but I'm concerned she's hiding something. I told you I saw her arguing with a man on the lower deck the day after we departed, before Padraig moved her into his cabin. He was an angry-looking fellow with hair down to his shoulders. What would she want with a man like that?"

"But I thought you asked her about it."

"She said I was mistaken."

"You probably were."

"Mistaken!" She released his forearm and stepped back, hands on her hips.

"Why can't you two women get along?"

"It's not about two women getting along, Samuel Kingston, and I'm not blind. That woman lied to me."

"Padraig's a big boy. He can take care of himself." He sneaked a glance at the spar deck. Padraig had chosen a fine way to take care of himself, indeed. Sara might have been a skilamalink, but she was a curvy one.

"Even if there's nothing too it, she's making a fool of Padraig." Sofia threw up her hands. "She's not right for him. This won't end well. Padraig acts the joker but he's sensitive, and she's going to break his heart. At the least caution him to take it slow. María will thank you for it. Any mother would."

He felt the heat where her arm had rested on him and squeezed his eyes shut. He wouldn't let this silly argument spoil an idyllic trip. "All right, darling, I'll talk to him. But please don't tell María, no matter what happens. Soldiers never bring back tales like this."

"They don't? So I'll never discover what you got up to in your army days?" She rewarded him with the quick smile and ready laugh that had won his heart years before. "Well, I'm not a soldier. Those stupid rules don't apply to me." Her windblown hair glistened like liquid onyx in the fading light.

He drew her into his arms. "Tell the filibusters you shot that you're not a soldier."

Every time the sails billowed, the stays shivered and twanged as tight as lyre strings. From time to time, he glanced at the couple on the spar deck. He'd better get it over with soon, but he could think of no way to tactfully broach the subject. The first stars pierced the darkening sky and a quarter moon bloomed in the west as the sun dipped beneath the bronze sea. Sara kissed Padraig and sashayed toward their accommodations.

It was time.

Samuel nuzzled Sofia's neck, released her, and tugged the

collar of his shirt. "Sara's gone inside. I'll stroll down and talk to him."

She eyed the deck below. "You're doing the right thing. I'll wait by their cabin and stall her if she tries to return."

He lit a cigarette and dragged on it hard. Was this the right approach, or was he doing it to appease Sofia? "I'll see you in a while, darling. If he doesn't toss me overboard."

She gave his hand a squeeze as he peeled away toward the companionway.

Padraig was tapping an easy beat with his foot and reading a book.

"Another book?" Samuel gently shook the back of the chair. "What's this one about, engines or military strategy?"

Padraig beamed up at him and threw his arms back into a luxurious stretch. "I saw you kissing Sofia on the bow, you dirty dog. Nothing like being in love, eh?"

He wasn't going to make this easy, was he?

"Sara's gone back to freshen up before dinner," Padraig continued. Beats me why women take so long at that, but it's worth it. When they show up, they're perfectly lovely. Sit down, I'll order us a drink. Whiskey?"

"Please, a double." He perched on the edge of Sara's chair.

Padraig beckoned a steward. "Yes, you." He raised his glass and held up two fingers. "Two whiskeys." His voice became light and airy as he placed his hands behind his head and considered the night sky, now filling with sparkling stars. "Isn't it wonderful that everything's working out? We've boxed Walker in at last. He'll be locked away in a British jail by the time we're back in Ireland. And I've met the girl of my dreams."

"Come on, Fred, there's going to be a tug-of-war. Bet my dad's side wins. "Two little boys wearing peaked caps and long woolen shorts rushed past and joined a small crowd gathering on the deck farther forward.

"Tug-of-war sounds like hard work." Samuel scraped with his

nail at the varnish peeling from the arm of the chair. "I'm glad we didn't sign up for that."

"Bloody right." Padraig dragged his chair around for a better view of the men dividing into two groups with a hemp rope laid along the deck between them. "Look at the men dressed in suits and overcoats; imagine how they're going to sweat. Nah, I'd rather tug on a whiskey."

One of the stewards dropped his hand and the onlookers cheered as the men hauled on the rope, grunting with their leather shoes slipping and scratching on the wooden deck. The two teams of six men each inched fore and aft.

"They seem evenly matched," Samuel squinted at Padraig from the corner of his eye. Was there any easy way to approach this thorny subject? "Fancy a wager, my money is on the team on the aft side, the one with the tall fellow wearing the John Bull hat."

"To hell with that," Padraig stretched like a lazy cat sunning itself. "Look, here come our drinks."

"Thank you." Samuel picked up one of the glasses.

"Imagine meeting an Irish girl all the way out here, a perfect girl, even if she's from Dublin." Padraig sat upright and fixed his gleaming eyes on Samuel. "She is perfect, isn't she? Mam's going to love her."

This would be harder than he thought. Samuel gulped down a slug of whiskey, and it stung the back of his throat. He coughed to one side.

"Getting old? You married men can't hold your booze. Shoot me if that happens to me when I marry."

Samuel coughed again and forced a laugh. "Are you going—do you think . . . Is this not a bit rushed, your . . . ." Darn it, he couldn't call this a relationship. He stubbed out his cigarette and tipped back another mouthful of whiskey. "You only met this Sara a couple of days ago. Don't—"

"'This Sara'?" Padraig lowered his brow. "My Sara, you mean. There isn't any other."

"Yes, of course, your Sara." Samuel rubbed the back of his neck. "No, what I mean is you should wait until you're better acquainted before making long-term plans. Anyway, didn't she say she'll be with her employer's family for two years?"

Padraig tugged down a sleeve. "Not anymore. She's returning to Ireland with us."

Samuel spluttered on his whiskey. When he recovered, he had to force himself to speak. "But you don't have the faintest idea who she is."

"I love her. What else matters?"

"I mean, does she come from a decent family, does—"

"A good family! I'm not a Proddy like you, and I'm not some arrogant Anglo trading up my social position for a dowry. I don't need money, I'm one of the two richest men in Munster. You're the other." The air that had been comfortable between them grew taut as Padraig sullenly regarded the billowing sails.

It was like talking to a horse—no, a horse would pay attention. Samuel tapped his finger on the arm of the chair. "I want you to be happy, that's all that matters to me. To Sofia. But something's out of sorts. Look, Sofia saw her arguing with a man down in steerage the day we sailed. She may not be alone. It's—"

"So that's why Sofia's suspicious? Holy Mother, that's the reason" Padraig grabbed a clump of his dusty blond hair and tilted his face skyward. "She told me about him, some American who was pestering her to have a drink with him down there, and she warned him to leave her alone. I'd go down there and punch him if I didn't think it would get me confined to my cabin or worse."

Sofia's imagination was running wild. Sara had done nothing wrong. Samuel's ears reddened.

"She said she denied it because it was none of Sofia's business. Look, I don't want to fight about this, not with my best friend. "Why can't you be happy for me?"

Samuel plonked his glass on the deck. "I'm only looking out for you. Listen, you—"

"You don't want me settled, don't want me married. You want me at your beck and call to rescue you on stupid missions like this."

This was growing tedious. "That's ridiculous. You're acting like—"

"In fact, if you'll remember, I met Sofia first and you took her from me. Remember—"

Samuel jumped up. "Out of order. You were a playboy back then. You still are. You met Sofia twenty minutes before I did, and she never—"

Padraig rose as well. "I don't need this rubbish from you. From now on, fight your fights without me. I'm taking this ship back to New York, going home, and Sara's sailing with me." He stormed across the deck.

Slumping back in his seat, Samuel groped for his cigarettes. He and Padraig had been together since María had wet-nursed them, yet they'd never had a proper fight. His head pounded as Padraig disappeared through the companionway with nary a glance. What had he done? And what was that woman Sara up to? His hands were awkward as he opened the silver cigarette case. Somehow he had to fix this and fix it quickly before the *Adriatic* took Padraig back to New York. But he'd no idea how.

CHAPTER TEN

Mangrove and twisting vines strangled the swamp surrounding the ramshackle port of Colón, where crocodiles and reptiles abounded in the slimy mud bordering the bay. Pestilential swarms of mosquitoes and black clouds of sandflies roiled Samuel's stomach as he listlessly stirred the roast pork and rice around his plate. The so-called dining room of the Colón Hotel seemed more like a stable, with no walls and a roof of molding banana leaves propped up by crudely trimmed tree trunks. The smell of fried pork and plantains mingling with the reek of rotting vegetation was no sauce to spur his appetite.

Sofia plucked at her damp blouse and fanned her face with her napkin. "You must eat something, my love. You didn't touch your supper last night."

"I'm not hungry." All he wanted to do was get on the train and leave this miserable place.

"At least drink your champagne. I doused it with quinine to ward off malaria." Her eyebrows drew together. "You mustn't worry about Padraig. You two have been through so much together. He'll get over this. He'll take Sara home, and María and Jerry will hate her—and so will he once he gets to know her. I'm certain something's the matter with that woman."

Women. Why did they have to be so petty, always competing? Sofia needed to let this go. She was driving a wedge between them and Padraig. He shoved the plate away and gave his wife a sharp look.

"She's hiding something."

"I should never have mentioned her to him. He'll never forgive me." Lord he needed a smoke. He reached for one of the cigarettes he'd rolled earlier and stored in his silver case, reminding him that his throat felt dry and scratchy from too many, and took a sip of champagne instead.

She covered her sweaty face with her hands. "I'm so sorry I asked you to talk to him. I only wanted to protect him. Look, we don't need his help to bring your father—"

"I understand that. But he's always been there for me, and I feel I'm letting him down." He clasped her hands in his own. "We're not certain Sara's up to anything. She's Irish, for heaven's sake, and we shouldn't doubt her. I'm more worried about Padraig. I've knocked on his door twice this morning, but he didn't answer, didn't say a word to me. He's perfectly furious with—"

"Samuel, Sofia!" Padraig rushed into the humble dining area. "Have you seen Sara? She was gone when I woke this morning." He scraped a hand through his tousled hair and scanned the muddy plaza. "She's all alone out there, a woman, and she hasn't a word of Spanish."

Sofia bit her lip and glanced at Samuel.

A foreign woman abroad in this wild town didn't stand a chance. Samuel swabbed his forehead with his napkin and dropped it onto the slice of tree trunk that served as a table. "I'll help you find her. Let me get my coat and gun. Have you your Colt?"

"Yes, yes, of course." Padraig wrung his hands together and peered outside. "Where on earth could she have gone?"

"I'll come too." Sofia struggled to push back her heavy chair.

Samuel rested a hand on her shoulder. "It's going to rain again. You'll get soaked."

"Rubbish. I was born in Central America. I grew up in tropical rain." Sofia pushed her chair back—no mean feat, carved as it was from thick hardwood.

He'd already put her in too much danger. Samuel pressed her down in the seat. "Please wait in the hotel, darling. It's too dangerous."

Sofia brushed off his hand.

"The hotel manager warned us not to venture out. Besides, the cart will be here to take our baggage to the train station any time now. Someone must be here to meet them."

She folded her arms. "The weather's not that bad. And I want to help."

He picked up the yellow steamship ticket on the table. "Did you read this? 'The danger of the seas, lakes, rivers, and harbors, restraint of governments, collision, detention, discomforts, and ailments arising therefrom . . .' blah, blah . . . And it goes on."

She appeared unmoved.

"Think of the children."

"All right. I'll wait in the hotel. Take care out there. The children need both of us." Her features softened. "And you too, Padraig. You are so dear to us both."

Samuel kissed her cheek and stepped into the misty street with Padraig. They hired a Carib porter named Pedro to guide them through the ankle-deep mud and rotting rubbish, past teetering wooden shops and hawkers living off the travelers' trade. Colón was a different world to two young men from West Cork, a maze of narrow run-down lanes between bamboo and rough-hewn walls intersecting tight winding alleys both dark and sweltering. Samuel's eyes widened at the pimps standing blatantly outside their shacks, boasting the claims of their lovelies, and he recoiled when one propelled a drunk in through the swinging doors of a stall. He averted his eyes, only to catch a glimpse of another pimp dragging two fair-skinned girls away down an alleyway.

He froze and groped for the guide's arm. "Were those girls American?"

"Maybe, sir, or European." Pedro beckoned Samuel along without breaking stride. "Their kind are popular down here. But they don't last long before the fever takes them. Buttocks and twangs, we call the girls and their pimps. They sleep all day and work all night."

"Blessed Virgin," Padraig murmured. "We must find Sara quickly. What if one of those pimps kidnapped her?"

Samuel followed mutely. He'd seen three-penny-uprights plying their trade outside fleshpots wherever the business of war had taken him, but he never got used to the sight of such suffering. His stride slowed to a trudge. So many wrongs to right in the world. Where could one begin?

A fearsome stench smote Samuel's nose near the river. Two bodies floated facedown, naked, crabs and beasties crawling over them even amidst the water.

Samuel groped for the reassuring butt of the Colt inside his coat. "Murder?"

Pedro didn't even break his stride. "Happens every morning, sir. Lured down an ally by a buttock, and her twang slit their gullets."

Padraig's Adam's apple jounced. "Dear God, this place is a cess pit."

"If the lady's not this side of the river, she must be in Barrio España." Pedro pointed across the bridge to the crush of rotting wooden hovels packing a slum more dilapidated than any London rookery. A hodgepodge of tilting wooden tenements with slime leaking beneath the decaying wooden walls.

Samuel pinched his lips shut and followed Pedro across the wobbling deck boards. They followed the meandering trench in front of the hovels that was covered with rainbow-colored scum and banked with heaps of indescribable filth. The pestilent air stank like a graveyard.

"There she is." Padraig's cry spurred Samuel on. "Sara! Look, Samuel—no, in the doorway over there, that shack to the left."

Bedraggled, her red-golden locks plastered across her tear-streaked face, Sara shivered against the rough-hewn trunk propping up the roof of a bar. The long green dress clinging to her hourglass form was soggy and spattered with mud. The wail she let out tore into Samuel's heart.

She collapsed into Padraig's arms. "Thank God you found me. I thought I'd die in this dreadful place."

"You're safe now." Padraig rocked her tenderly. "Where did you go? I searched everywhere for you."

"I'm sorry, so sorry. I woke with a powerful pain, a woman's pain, and went in search of a doctor. I should have roused you, but I was . . . It was personal, you know? With your argument yesterday and all, I didn't want to cause more trouble." She burst into tears.

Samuel sidled away to give them privacy. He'd been such a churl, judging this poor woman who was traveling all alone, far from home. What if she'd ended up like those doxies down the road, all because of his suspicions. Sofia's suspicions?

Padraig draped his coat over her shoulders. "I'm the one who should apologize. Can you ever forgive me?"

"Padraig?" Samuel laid a tentative hand on his friend's shoulder. "I'm sorry I interfered."

Padraig kept his eyes on the coat, which he wrapped more snugly around Sara. "I'm sorry too. I've felt like shite since we fought."

Samuel was the shit, shifting from foot to foot in the mud while their bright-eyed guide devoured the whole scene. "And today? Will you still return to Ireland, or will you carry on with us?"

Padraig straightened, the usual fire gleaming in his eyes. "Of course we'll go with you. Sara can give Colonel Garcia her notice in person. Come along, Sara. We've a train to catch."

Sara slunk closer to Padraig, and her blue eyes flashed. That look: had it been one of satisfaction? Samuel glanced at Padraig, but his friend was busy tucking his coat around Sara's shoulders.

Panama City's coast was an endless strip of white strand along turquoise waters, stretching as far as the eye could see. Sailing ships of all sizes bobbed at anchor on the whitecaps. A bath and a full night's sleep in a feather bed had refreshed Samuel. How sly of Sofia to remain at the room they'd taken in the Corona del Mar Hotel right there on the beach while they searched for the boat headed to Nicaragua. He led Padraig and Sara into the shed that served as the harbormaster's headquarters.

"Ah, here we are, another den of corruption." Padraig opened the door with a flourish. He believed that every government official was crooked, and he was often right.

The harbormaster's rheumy eyes lifted from his ledger as he scratched his well-nurtured paunch. "Good morning. And where did you come from? I didn't see any craft sail in this morning."

Samuel placed his hands on the dusty counter. "We arrived yesterday on the train from Colón. I'd appreciate it if you'd please point out the brig that calls into San Juan del Sur. We want to travel there."

"Oh, I'm afraid *La Tranquilidad* no longer sails the San Juan del Sur route." The harbormaster folded his arms. "Trade in Nicaragua went to hell during the war and never recovered."

"But there must be some boat going north. Anything?"

"The steamship for San Francisco, but she left on the morning tide and she never stops in Nicaragua." The harbormaster bit the inside of his cheek. "Maybe a coastal trader? But who knows when that'll happen."

Padraig craned his neck to look at the harbormaster's register.

The harbormaster closed the heavy leather cover with a soft crack and motioned toward the water. "A coffee baron chartered that lugger out there. She's headed for Nicaragua, but the captain's a prickly wretch. He won't take you. I could ask around. These are such hard times for all of us. I might find more if I had some silver."

Of course the harbormaster was a greedy woebegone. Padraig raised his eyebrows in that "told you so" way of his.

Samuel palmed a silver coin onto the counter. "I'll help you out if you can locate a boat. You'll find us in the Corona del Mar Hotel."

"Right you are, *caballero*."

The blistering sun stung Samuel's eyes when they stepped outside and he paused, blinking. The beach had a different heat to the isthmus swamps, marginally drier but still humid enough to coat a fully clothed European with sweat.

"What a bloody disaster." Padraig kicked a piece of bleached driftwood off the path into the powdery sand. "Stuck here in this oven of a country. I thought Nicaragua was hot, but it's the Arctic compared to this place. What I wouldn't give to have one of my steamboats here." He removed his wide-brimmed hat and held it up to block the sun and appraise the lugger pitching on the gentle combers. "She'd do all right, though. Trim lines and looks well-preserved for a boat in these parts."

"You heard what the harbormaster said. They're not the kind to help us. The hacienda barons are as greedy as the aristocrats back home. Come along, we'll pick up Sofia and ask around the waterfront bars. Someone might know of a boat going north."

"I hate this place." Sara shuffled along the sandy path beside Padraig. "I wish I never agreed to come here. It's so hot and dirty, and the food's terrible. Rice and beans, rice and bananas—"

"—rice and beans." Samuel and Padraig finished, grinning

despite their predicament. It was their old joke: Every meal served in Central America was the same.

"Don't worry, Sara. In Nicaragua they sometimes cook iguana, too." Padraig slipped a hand around her waist and drew her closer.

She pulled a face. "What's that? It sounds disgusting."

"It tastes like chicken." Padraig waggled his eyebrows at Samuel.

It was good to see Padraig back in good humor. Samuel still had reservations about Sara. How had she ended up in that slum? It was obviously not the place one would find a doctor, but on the other hand she might have been disorientated and got lost. But that quick flash in her eye back in the Colón slum, it was triumph. Nah, he was overthinking it. Sofia's suspicions might have fired his imagination; no woman would visit such a place intentionally. He'd been right not to have mentioned his misgivings to Padraig, it would only have caused another falling-out.

Padraig slipped an arm around Sara shoulder. "I'll give that money-grabbing bastard Vanderbilt a piece of my mind the next time I see him. He never should've shut down the Nicaraguan transit route. It's harsh we have to sail all the way down to Panama to get to Chinandega. It'd be easier to get to the moon."

"It's better than sailing to the bottom of South America to round Cape Horn." Samuel pursed his lips. Padraig had the right of it: It would be a long time before they came to Nicaragua again, and that would be hard on Sofia, not seeing her brother for God knew how many years.

It was cooler inside the colonial-style Corona del Mar Hotel, where the doors and windows were wide open to the salty sea breeze and fresh-cut flowers arranged in colorful bouquets against the white-washed walls perfumed the air.

"Samuel, over here. In the restaurant." Sofia beckoned from the shaded terrace overlooking the ocean.

He pecked her on the cheek and dropped into the seat

beside her. "More bad news, I'm afraid, darling. The ship no longer sails to Nicaragua. We're marooned."

Sofia pinched his cheek and grinned at Padraig. "Isn't my husband amusing? He likes nothing more than to bait me."

"No, no, he's serious, he is." Padraig pulled out a chair for Sara. "Apparently *La Tranquilidad's* owner couldn't find enough trade in Nicaragua and dropped the route."

Sofia stopped her wine glass before her lips and raised mournful eyes. "What are we going to do now? We've don't have time for delays."

"Sofia . . ." Samuel spread his fingers wide, palms on the smooth wooden table.

"We must finish our visit and bring your father home." Sofia tapped the table with her fingers.

Samuel covered her hand on the table with his. "I know that we—"

She drew back her hand and gazed over the sparkling blue sea. "I miss the children terribly already."

He rushed to reassure her. "Darling, I—"

"Can't you charter a boat or something? It's not as if you're—"

"Good morning. Please pardon my intrusion."

Samuel turned to see a fair-skinned man in an expensively cut suit.

The stranger bowed slightly to Sofia and to Sara. "Franklin Harcourt from San Francisco. I manage the US affairs of Colonel Ivan Garcia." He paused as if Garcia's name would ring a bell.

Sara perked up in her seat. "Colonel Garcia of Chinandee . . . Sinan . . ."

"Chinandega, yes, the very man." Women would've called Harcourt handsome for his neat haircut, sculpted face, and broad shoulders that strained the seams of his fantastically colored shirt. "I'm looking for a Miss Sara Brennan."

Sofia touched fingers to her parted lips as Samuel shot her a sidelong glance. Now, this was a strange turn.

Sara clapped her hands to her cheeks. "That's me! I'm Sara Brennan."

"The very lady I'm looking for." Harcourt bowed with a flourish. "I had business in Costa Rica, and when Colonel Garcia heard there was no longer a Panamanian ship calling into San Juan del Sur, he asked me to sail south and collect you. I can take you directly to Chinandega."

Samuel smoothed his shirt. That would please Sofia.

"Good thing, too." Sara snorted loudly. "We're stuck in this awful place, and it's so hot, so tiresome, so full of . . . of natives. But how—"

"I've a chartered lugger here, miss, and if the wind holds, *La Esparanza* can deliver you to Chinandega in a couple days."

Sara clapped her hands together. "Thank God. But wait. My friends, they helped me out, and they're going to Shinan—to that place too. Can we bring them?"

"Not exactly Chinandega, but El Realejo, a small harbor about five miles from Chinandega. The town itself is inland, but of course we can take your friends." He grinned at Sofia and winked at Samuel. "Plenty of room."

A way out of Panama after all. Samuel surreptitiously surveyed Sofia again, but she didn't stir. What was the matter now? A moment ago, she couldn't wait to leave Panama. "Thank you, Mr. Harcourt, that's a generous offer. We are—"

"Samuel?" Sofia squeezed his arm. "May I have a word in private, please?"

"Of course, my dear." Heat crept across his cheeks. "Please excuse us one moment."

Padraig scowled as Sofia led Samuel to the edge of the terrace.

"I don't want to be beholden to this Colonel Garcia," she whispered, "to Sara, or to anyone else. We must find another way."

She'd been in such a hurry to get to Chinandega, but now, when the opportunity to do so had landed in their laps, she was making a fuss. Samuel ran a hand over his jaw. "Is this part of the age-old Democrat versus Legitimist feud? Mm, that's it. That must be it. Garcia must be a Legitimist. You reacted to his name when Sara mentioned—"

She seized his forearm and pulled him closer. "Don't be daft. I recognize the name, all right, but Garcia's a Democrat, as Papa was. But you know how the ruling class are. They always expect favor rewarded."

"Well then, what gives?"

"It's Sara. Something's not right there. I don't . . . I'm certain she's hiding something. I mean, what on earth was she doing back there in Colón?"

Samuel took a deep breath and released it. "Don't start that again, please. Do you want to set Padraig off? We agreed to avoid the topic. To monitor her. To keep watch."

"I don't want Padraig hurt."

"Padraig's a big boy and can look after himself." He pointed to the blue ocean. "Look out there. There aren't many other choices, if any. No big ships will divert to San Juan de Sur or El Realejo, and it'll take a while to find a smaller craft to carry us. We could be stuck here for weeks."

She glanced over his shoulder at the others then down at the tiles. "There must be something available. What if you offered to pay double?"

"To whom exactly would I make that offer?" Her stubborn Spanish pride was giving him a headache. Perhaps she was simply jealous of Sara. Well, there was no reason for that. María Kerr had said it often: A man could never understand the workings of a female mind, but the brain of a Spanish woman was a Gordian knot. Sofia had imagined Sara was plotting with some fellow in the steamer when there had been a simple explanation. She had to stop with this nonsense. "If we don't accept Mr. Harcourt's offer, we could be stuck here for a fortnight. I thought you missed the children."

"Oh, I do, terribly. I wish we'd brought them with us. I miss them so much." She tapped her fingers on the low wall separating them from the white sand. He could see she was coming around to the idea of Harcourt's boat.

"Panama's too dangerous: wild animals, bandits, diseases. They'd catch malaria or worse. Perhaps we can bring them here when Vanderbilt reopens the Trans-Nicaraguan Route. The San Juan River is a safer bet."

"Fine." She threw up her hands. "What choice do we have?"

He folded his arms and gave her his best mock scowl. "And you'll be nice? I don't want you pouting for the entire two days of the voyage."

"Yes, yes, I will. Don't lecture me." She stalked back to the table, where the others were doing their utmost to appear not to be watching them intently.

He lit a cigarette and eyed the hazy horizon. This trip was careening out of control. Perhaps he should call it off and take the next boat home. It would be the last chance to retreat, while they were still close to the train and the next boat back to New York. But there were Father's remains to be brought home, and they were so close to accomplishing that.

He pushed up his sleeves and strode back to the others. They would continue on.

CHAPTER ELEVEN

Chez Moi in New Orleans's French Quarter wasn't the kind of restaurant you could simply walk into and get a table for lunch. One had to make a reservation weeks in advance—unless you were William Walker. Walker dragged his irritable gaze away from the view out the bay window over Bourbon Street back to the cloying flowers on the mahogany table. Piano music tinkled in the background, and the air was as sultry as the morning, laden with the odor of fried fish, spices, and cigar smoke.

Jethro MacIntosh stuffed his jowly face with another forkful of ham and pawed away the grease trickling down his chin. The wealthy plantation owner's physique reminded Walker of a hog, compact, squat, and coarse. At least the Anglo-Irish lords, his incompetent previous allies, had been gentlemen. MacIntosh and beak-nosed Bernard Fullerton, seated beside him, were ignorant slobs compared to those Brits. Robert de Burg had possessed a mean streak but he'd been a gentleman. It hadn't surprised Walker to discover the man was none other than Louis Greenfell, the Earl of Baltimore.

But that wretched Samuel Kingston—he was no gentleman. The oaf was a mere pretender who'd managed to muddle so many of Walker's affairs, slaying Greenfell, stealing a fortune in gold, and blackmailing the aristocrats into abandoning their alliance with him. Oh yes, Kingston would pay for leaving him no option but to ally with the ridiculous Masonic pro-slavery group here at the table tonight. The Knights of the Golden Circle were unsavory at best, but he needed their money to enforce his vision on Central America, unifying the petty little nations into a vast rubber-, cotton-, and fruit-producing empire.

Fullerton swirled the red wine in his glass and sniffed it. "There'll be civil war before long, and I fear the slavery states will lose. It'll be impossible to operate plantations profitably without slaves."

"That's why we must act now." MacIntosh spat gristle onto his plate. "We need this new empire if we've any hope of keeping our slaves."

"And when you reintroduce slavery down there, William," Fullerton interjected, "make English the official language. I don't want to hear any of that greaser prattle."

These fools were insufferable. Walker drummed his fingers on the table. It was an unfair world that granted money and power to these ignorant masons, but he was stuck with them. The judge had doubled the bribe, leaving him no choice but to return to the masons, cap in hand, for more money.

"I'm still confused why you're beginning your campaign in Roatán." Fullerton frowned as MacIntosh's knife skid over his ham and splashed his sleeve with gravy. "Why not attack the mainland?"

These people were a waste of time. If only he wasn't dependent on their funds. Walker folded his arms. "Roatán and the other four Bay Islands have enjoyed being a full-fledged British colony since 1852, but now Britain is bowing to pressure from America and handing the islands back to Honduras. According to the Wykes-Cruz Treaty, this will happen next month despite the Bay Islanders' petitioning Queen Victoria to keep the territory in the empire. When the Queen ignored them, they asked me to help them set up an independent Bay Islands republic with myself as president."

"President Walker, eh?" MacIntosh grinned around a cheek full of meat.

"A president who'll take care of his friends." Walker tugged at his cravat. "Everything, all our future plans depend on getting an acquittal, and to assure that, I gave the judge a gift." They didn't need to know he'd also bribed two jurors and threatened several more.

"Prudent of you." MacIntosh picked grizzle from his yellow teeth.

"And that left me short for future expenses. I was wondering if you gentlemen could advance me another five thousand until I take control down there."

"But I still don't see why this island matters." Fullerton frowned at McIntosh and pushed away his plate. It seemed McIntosh's foul table-manners disgusted him too.

"Roatán is only forty miles from the mainland, a perfect place to launch an attack on Honduras or Nicaragua. My American and German volunteers are already infiltrating the island, dozens of them sneaking in on the fruit boats. Of course, the islanders are unaware of my—our—greater plan for all Central America." He pulled his watch from his pocket. Was that the time already? He needed to wrap this up. "Can you loan the five thousand?"

MacIntosh choked and spluttered chewed food onto his plate.

"Five thousand dollars." Fullerton toyed with his greasy plate. "I don't have that sum lying around. It was hard enough to hide the funds I paid to you already from the family.

"Me neither." MacIntosh mumbled through his soiled napkin.

Clowns. Now it was imperative to capture Kingston and wring the money out of him.

"I understand. Forgive me, but I'm due in court. We must continue this later." More's the pity.

But if Frank Anderson arrived with those two brigs today, he could embark his army tonight, and that would be the last he'd see of these obnoxious men for months. Of course, everything hinged on whether the court would find him guilty of breaching the Neutrality Act. He bit his lip. The newspapers were on his side, that should sway the jury, and he had paid off the judge even though the bribe had dented his meager war chest. He smoothed the lapels of his frock coat. Dear God, it had to work out.

"Tonight, then," MacIntosh said with his mouth full. "Good luck."

Walker rose stiffly. "Luck has nothing to do with it. The Lord is on our side." But would Jesus win his trial for him? That was all that mattered.

The United States District Court of Louisiana, Judge Brian Parker on the bench, assembled at two o'clock, and onlookers packed the wooden seats inside the courtroom, sweating profusely in a haze of humidity, tobacco, and boozy breath. A rousing cheer greeted Walker's entrance, and he stretched to his full height as his spirits soared. They loved him down here in the South. Why wouldn't they? He was a hero.

The jurors were already in their box: a short fellow with drooping eyelids, always sleepy; a second, who Walker marked by his big head with white hair standing out stiffly around it; a third with ears like jug handles and bushy brows that burrowed together studiously; and the rest of them . . . Well, it didn't matter. He already had them eating out of his hand. What a bunch of oafs, all chewing their lips, blinking stupidly, and following him with bulging eyes. To them—to most men in the South—he was already a legend. They would never convict him.

He drew back his shoulders and strode to the dock, planting his hands wide on the pulpit. The touch of hard wood reassured him as he saluted the jurors and waited for the cheers to subside. His training as a physician meant he understood more than most men about how the mind worked, how to manipulate it, and as an experienced lawyer, he knew how to manipulate a courtroom. He knew he cut a dashing figure with his clean-shaven face, prominent brow, and black suit. He was the darling of the press who'd fought duels for honor, an expert swordsman who'd carved a throne in another country, and they'd proclaimed him the gray-eyed man of destiny ordained to expand the United States of America. If only he'd been taller, more imposing than his modest five feet two—why, he'd have ruled the world. As it was, he'd settle for Central America. Soon.

Judge Parker adjusted his bulging waistcoat and squinted at him through rheumy eyes that were enormous behind the thick lenses of his horn-rimmed glasses. "Mister Walker, your lawyer, Mr. Maloney commenced the defense's closing arguments before we broke for lunch, and I believe you wish to finish them. Is that correct?"

"Yes, and may it please Your Honor and Gentlemen of the jury—since the adjournment of the Court this morning, I have considered this frivolous case as I reasonably could and will wrap this up within the shortest possible time."

The throng in the courtroom stirred, feet shuffling, some onlookers whispering, and others leaning forward with eager eyes fixed on him.

Walker took a deep calming breath and reminded himself again: He was William Walker, doctor, lawyer, and soldier, and it would be a very long time before the world forgot him. The court of public opinion had already ruled in his favor, and he'd had enough of this circus.

He feigned addressing the judge with a glance and a tilt of his head, but his words appealed directly to the jurors. "Good morning, and thank you for coming here today to defend liberty and the American way. I won't keep you long." His hands glided apart on the smooth wooden railing, an invitation into his world. "You've heard all the indisputable facts, how foreign powers and devious abolitionists are seeking to deprive loyal Americans of the right to expand our great country and attacking our long-standing Southern institutions. It's for that reason that I'm willing to rest my case, trusting that this fine Southern jury will declare my intentions to be honorable and my patriotic actions to be innocent. Dark forces seek to rip the fabric of our great nation apart and deprive Southerners of our basic rights. Your vindication of me will send a clear message north that they cannot trifle with the South."

The ensuing clamor—men shouting, pounding fists, and stamping feet—electrified the jury. Every one of them bolted upright in their benches. Even the sleepy idiot jolted wide awake.

Judge Parker pounded the sound block with his gavel. "Silence. Silence in the court."

Gavel thuds echoed through the courtroom for a minute rising in intensity until the uproar died down, and all the while the jurors pressed their heads together, faces animated and lips nibbling the law, while Walker rewarded acquaintances in the gallery with winks, nods, and salutes.

Judge Parker greeted the hush with a final slam of his gavel. "This is outrageous. Another outburst like that, and I'll instruct the marshals to clear the courtroom. Gentlemen of the jury, please withdraw and consider your verdict."

Eyes downcast, the jury shuffled from their benches and left the court as voices rose in the gallery, many called their good wishes and encouragement to Walker as he joined Maloney at the defense table.

Maloney shuffled his chair closer. "Great job, Mr. Walker. I think you swayed them our way."

"President Walker, you mean. I'm the elected President of

Nicaragua. And they'd be fools not to see I acted for America and the greater good. They will exonerate me."

The door to the jury room door opened twenty minutes later.

My Lord, they're back already. That must be bad news, a guilty verdict. He let out a hard sigh and closed his eyes. No, it couldn't be a guilty verdict. Maloney had bribed two jurors, and Czarnowski had threatened three more. He sat straight and peered at the jurors filing into their seats.

At that moment, more people crowded into the courtroom and filled all the space, pressing around Walker, hot and sticky, stinking of cigarette smoke, bad breath, and sweat. He dismissed the blur of expectant faces and necks stretching to witness the closing act and scanned the jury. The short fellow with drooping eyelids flashed him a knowing smile, the mouse-faced man in a threadbare coat rubbed his chest almost imperceptibly, and the jug-eared juror's bushy brows drew together as he beheld Walker with soft eyes.

They would not convict him. He spread his feet wide and rested his fists on his hips, collected and indomitable.

"Silence in the courtroom. "Judge Parker rapped the block with his gavel. "Clerk of the Court, please recapitulate the offence set forth in the indictment."

The thin-boned clerk smoothed his black robe and faced the jurors. "William Walker stands accused of breaching the Neutrality Act of 1794, which prohibits private individuals from accepting a foreign military commission, outfitting military vessels for a foreign state, or enlisting or hiring persons for the service of a foreign state."

The populace stood perfectly still and silent, Maloney squirmed beside him, and a blue jay whistled outside the closest window. This was it. All his future plans for a new Central America depended on these jurors.

"Gentlemen of the jury," the clerk continued, "what say you? Is the accused at the bar, William Walker, guilty or not guilty?"

Walker held his breath in the hush.

The jury foreman cleared his throat. "Not guilty."

Walker drew a deep satisfying breath and faced the erupting crowd.

Bowler hats, top hats, and felt hats sailed into the air on a wave of cheers, and red-faced celebrants surged toward Walker. Rough hands plucked him up, and his head spun as they hoisted him on their shoulders and carried him from the building. Swaying on those mismatched shoulders was unsettling, but he shook every hand that met his as he searched for Anderson's face. The ships better arrive soon. He was free to embark now on his next campaign, and there wasn't a moment to lose. He bared his teeth. Would these clowns ever set him down?

"All right, boys, that's enough." Joe Czarnowski halted the men carrying Walker. "We don't want to drop President Walker, do we?"

His guards cleared a space, and Czarnowski helped him down from the sweating shoulders.

He grasped Czarnowski's elbow. "Have you seen Colonel Anderson?"

A red-faced man with enormous whiskers and a belly busting the seams of his stained waistcoat stepped in front of him. "God bless you, General Walker. You showed them Yankees, didn't you? It's our God-given right to expand the United States—first Texas, then California, and now Nicaragua." His breath stank of cheap whiskey. He slapped Walker's back and sent him staggering forward. "Take me with you."

Czarnowski shoved the man away. "Get the hell back."

"Easy there, Joe." Walker faced his enthusiastic supporter. "Thank you, friend. So you believe in manifest destiny?"

"Huh?"

What a fool. But they needed every man he could muster to the red star on his blue-striped Nicaraguan flag. "Do you think it's America's destiny to expand our territories? To civilize the world? Do you deserve a piece of that?"

"Hell yes, I deserve it."

"Good man." He shook the fat fellow's hand and beckoned to one of his senior commanders, Anthony Rudler. "Colonel, we may have a recruit here. Speak with him and see if he's free to join our expedition."

Rudler's face tightened as he eyed the prospect. "Um, General, he's not the recruit we're seeking. Look at him, three sheets to the wind."

Walker's head pulsed. Must every officer debate his orders? "We need all the recruits we can muster. Talk to him."

"Yes sir, I'll take care of him." Rudler threw him a smart salute. "Any update on when we leave?"

"Soon. I hope Colonel Anderson has news for us." He beckoned Czarnowski. "Take me to the hotel."

"Stick close, Mr. President, it might get a bit rough." Czarnowski pointed to a crowd of whiskered men in gloomy suits, some wearing religious collars, accompanied by pinched-faced women in beaky-white bonnets, all singing a slavery hymn beside a tall wooden cross.

Walker flexed his fingers. "Those confounded Bible-thumpers don't scare me. Push through."

At the iron gate of the courthouse grounds, the abolitionists closed ranks around them with snarling faces, animals ready to tear him apart. Before Walker could brace himself, a larger mob swarmed the abolitionists in turn.

"Go home, thieving Yankees!" bellowed a man inches behind Walker. "Leave the South to the Southerners."

A hook-nosed man with a broken front tooth jostled Czarnowski aside to block the northerners from approaching Walker. "Our livelihood, our slaves."

Dozens of supporters spilled down the courthouse steps and swarmed the modest circle of abolitionists, fists flying, clubs rising and falling. The rough fabric of an abolitionist's coat brushed Walker's hand as the silver-haired man was bludgeoned, and drops of warm blood splattered onto his lips, tasting like copper and salt. Served the fanatical bastards right.

Walker scrubbed his lip with a hand and shoved Czarnowski forward. "Let's get out of here. I don't want the authorities blaming me for this." But it was the anti-slavers' fault, not his. Every state in the South allowed a man to own slaves. Why should America deny him the same rights in Nicaragua? It was the only way that country could thrive.

He tucked in behind Czarnowski and his men, shouldering at right angles through the crowd as his supporters carried him forward in the crush. Though there was no fighting in this direction, the tension in the crowd was palpable. The acrid stink of body odor, whiskey breath, and cheap perfume stung his nose as the mob swept him along. With any luck, they would lose them in the approaching alley. The South was a tinderbox, and he didn't want to be the match that lit a blaze. He had his own war to fight.

The crowd thinned abruptly, the road cleared ahead, and the shouts, screeches, and curses behind them dwindled.

"Czarnowski." He slowed down. "It's imperative we find Colonel Anderson."

Czarnowski dropped back beside him. "Perhaps he's at the training camp."

"Then we'll go there. This court case has drawn too much attention. The last thing we need is federal marshals showing up to impound our weapons and supplies. I've had it with these sanctimonious buffoons."

The filibuster training camp was an hour's ride out of town, far enough to avoid scrutiny but close enough to visit during his trial. Walker banged open the door to the ranch house that served as headquarters, wiping the sweat from his forehead, and checked his watch again. Four thirty!

He scowled at Colonel Rudler, who stood pinned against the door in an idiotically stiff salute. "Anderson should've been here by now." He threw his handkerchief on the desk. "At ease."

Rudler relaxed and sank into a chair. "We're not behind schedule, are—"

"This morning's riot at the courthouse could draw the federal marshals on us. We must sail as soon as possible."

"They don't come more reliable than Frank Anderson, sir. I'm certain he'll be here." Rudler cocked his long leg over the arm of the chair. "Unless this Brogan character double-crossed us."

It was muggy, and the odor of the crawfish the farmer's ancient wife was boiling in the kitchen filled the room. Walker tugged at the cuff of his coat. "Why would he do that? I've promised him the Transit Road and San Juan River concession, and if anyone comprehends its value, he does. He captained a boat on that river. Are the men ready? What do you think of them?"

"For the most part, they're good men and have learned their drills. They've trained hard. There's the usual handful of drunks and idlers, but we can't turn them away. We're short of volunteers." Rudler ran a hand through his close-cropped hair. "One hundred and thirty men. Is that enough?"

Born in France and raised in Georgia, Rudler had served as a captain with the Second Louisiana Infantry during the Mexican War, and he was one of Walker's most experienced officers. Walker took a deep breath and exhaled. It was time to share the rest of his plan. "I'd hoped for more men, to be honest, but after what happened last time when Anderson abandoned his expedition, we need a win before the public believes in us again. Then volunteers will be clamoring to sign up."

He lifted his elbows from the table as the wizened farmer's wife approached. She plonked a steaming plate of red crawfish in front of him. "There you are, Mr. President, finest food in the South. Spicy, to put the fight in you."

"That wasn't Frank's fault," Rudler said. "The stupid captain ran the schooner up on the rocks off Belize. Frank and his men were lucky to get home. I'm more worried about this expedition. We don't—"

There was a rap on the door, and Colonel Frank Anderson's face appeared. "Bad time, Mr. President?"

Walker paused peeling the skin from a hot, spiky crawfish. "Hell no, General. Come in and take a seat. You're a welcome sight. I hope you bring good news." He wiped his hand clean on a napkin and extended it to Anderson.

Anderson shook hands with both men and sat at the table. "The brigs are here, fine sailing vessels with plenty of room for the troops. When do you plan to leave, sir? We can't keep the boats secret for long. Too many people use those wharfs."

"As soon as we've loaded the ships. Tonight." He'd waited two years for this moment, and he wasn't about to let loose lips on the dock stop him. He sucked the meat from the shell. Spicy. Delicious.

Rudler swung his leg to the floor and headed to the sideboard. "Whiskey?"

"A small one." Anderson followed Rudler's every move as he poured the golden liquid and cleared his throat. "Sir, only one hundred and thirty men are—"

"Enough," Walker snapped. "There's more to this plan, much more. General José Trinidad Cabañas, the old fox, wants to be president of Honduras again."

Anderson's eyebrows flew up. "Wasn't he deposed—"

"—around the same time the US Navy unlawfully removed me from office in Nicaragua," Walker finished. "Cabañas will help me to retake Nicaragua in return for my support. He'll join us with three hundred rebel troops in Honduras."

"I thought we were going to Greytown in Nicaragua," Rudler said.

"Everything in Central America is complicated and connected, especially politics." Walker drew a map from the rosewood box on the table. "The leaders on Roatán realize that Britain will soon give up its interests in Honduras, and they want independence from Honduras when that happens. Cabañas promised them autonomy if they help him to power."

Anderson's head began to bob. "And so . . ."

"And so he's arranged to hide the volunteers I'm sending there." Walker slid his red-stained plate aside, spread out the map, and jabbed a finger at it. "We'll land here in Coxen Hole, capture the island, and leave a garrison before meeting Cabañas on the mainland. He'll guide us across the country to El Triunfo in the west."

Rudler moved forward alongside Anderson, pinching his lips together.

Walker traced the route with his finger. "From there, it's only a hop across the border to Chinandega into Nicaragua. We'll avoid any interference from the Royal Navy in Greytown."

Anderson raised his eyebrows quizzically.

"Even if word of this expedition leaks, everyone believes we're sailing to Greytown." Walker tilted back his chair and placed his hands behind his head. "The Royal Navy will wait in the wrong place."

Rudler tapped the map with a finger and sat back. "Might work. It concerned me that the ships' owners might shoot their mouths off, but even if they do, they'll be passing false information."

Anderson shook his head. "I don't trust the Hondurans. You should postpone until we gather more volunteers. We need Americans to—"

What impudence. Walker sat up. "Who commands here, General? I do. And I won't waste another day here. I will—"

"This is more madness." Anderson slammed the table. "You sent me down there half-cocked before, and I almost drowned when the fool captain ran the ship into a rock. This is your fourth throw of the dice, and I'll not face a Honduran firing squad because of you."

Walker slammed a fist on the table. "Are you refusing to obey my orders?"

"Darn right, I am," Anderson snarled. "I stood by your side in the last war down there and faced odds of ten to one for you, but I won't do it again. I won't sail with fewer than four hundred men."

Walker surged to his feet and pointed to the door. "Then you won't sail at all. Get out." But while Anderson held his ground by the table, Rudler flinched and looked away.

"Get out of my sight. We're better off without a coward like you." Walker's words crashed down like stones between them.

Anderson hurled his glass against the wall, where it shattered into vicious shards. "To hell with you. I ought to call—"

"Call me out? A duel, is it?" Walker had fought duels before. They didn't concern him. He'd make an example of this coward, and the others would fall in line.

Anderson snatched up his hat and stormed to the door. "To hell with you."

Rudler approached the table after the other commander left, eyebrows raised.

"Pah, let him go." Walker dismissed Anderson from his mind; he didn't need naysayers in his army. He reverted his attention to the map. "We're better off without him. You're my deputy commander now."

Rudler lifted his glass in a toast. "The San Juan River route never worked out for us. This time we'll be attacking from a totally different direction."

Walker nodded briskly. "We need the San Juan River route as well. How else can volunteers join us from the East Coast? I'll have a loyal Nicaraguan commander capture it for me."

"What about Samuel Kingston? He eluded capture in New York." Rudler eased down onto a chair.

"I already sent Parker French ahead to Chinandega with twenty men. By now, he'll have captured the Valle hacienda. He'll seize Kingston when he arrives."

"Plans within plans." Rudler sipped his whiskey.

That was how empires were carved out. Walker signaled the old lady to clear his plate. "We'll force the wretch to return the money he stole, more than enough to mobilize thousands of men. Within months, we'll control all of Central America."

"All of it?" Rudler's head jerked back. "What about General Cabañas? I thought you agreed to help him take Honduras."

Walker scoffed. Rudler had no imagination. "That old fool is only a stepping-stone. I'll help him take Honduras, all right. For me." He clapped his hands together. "Now shall we begin, Colonel? I want the army and supplies loaded tonight. We sail on the morning tide."

CHAPTER TWELVE

Samuel was unsure whether he'd heard the dull thump in a dream or whether he was drifting on the fringe of sleep while still awake and had heard it. *La Esparanza* rolled and groaned, snubbing the anchor rope, but the wind no longer thrummed the rigging and the rain had ceased. By now, the moon would be bright on the sea outside. Bad luck that they'd almost lost the mainmast when a shroud had parted at sea; Harcourt had been forced to anchor the brig in a secluded cove south of San Juan de Sur for repairs. His crew would fix the rigging in the first light of dawn and they would once again be underway.

All he heard (besides the tinnitus from his injury in the Crimean War, of course) was the rhythmic rattle of halyards slapping the mast and waves lapping the hull. Sofia snored ever so softly, a drowsy tangle of sweaty limbs beside him. The cabin smelled of pitch, hemp, and sweat oozing from the timbers. Nothing seemed amiss, but he learned long ago not to ignore this tingle in his nerves.

As he rolled from the bunk and picked up his rifle, a soft cooing arose from the crew accommodation up forward, what Padraig called the fo'c'sle. Samuel halted midstride. Pigeons? Onboard? Imposs—

The pad of feet on deck made his heart skip a beat. He darted from the cabin and bounded silently up the steps to the hatch. Four crouching figures were frozen in the shadows between silvery streamers of moonlight.

They were being robbed or attacked. His heart raced. "Boarders!"

Pistols blazed, burning yellow vignettes inside his eyeballs, and he threw himself down as lead thumped the mainmast close by. A jolt of pain shot up his leg as his knee hit the deck. He fired a shot and drew back, disoriented. The gun's feel, the way it kicked in his hand, was unfamiliar. Of course—this wasn't his Sharps. It was the new Henry with sixteen rounds.

"Samuel, stay there." Padraig's Colt barked behind him. "Come on, ye bastards, bring it on." He fired again and again.

Samuel worked the lever, and the spent shell ejected from the elevator, arcing brass sparkling like gold in the moonlight. He pulled up the lever, and another shell clicked into the breech. He fired at the roiling shadows, shooting as fast as he could work the lever. Brass shells bounced and tinkled onto the deck.

Boots scuffed the timbers ahead, and someone grunted.

"Christ, must be an army of them," one of the boarders clamored. "Retreat. Into the boat before we're slaughtered."

An American. Why were Americans raiding the lugger? Well, the Henry would see them off. Benjamin was right about that; it was as deadly as a squad of riflemen. He kept firing, counting his shots, as the barrel grew warmer and warmer in his hand. By the twelfth round, it was too hot to hold, and he drew up to peer into the shadows. Something thumped the hull on the port side, and urgent voices whispered beyond the gunwales. The boarders were retreating. He held his breath and crawled to the gunwale. Figures scrambled in a boat below—five or six people, at least.

Sara reared up from among them and screamed.

Guns blazed from below on the little cutter, spitting flames from the darkness, and he ducked as bullets peppered the hull. Samuel peeped over the side but dared not fire for fear of striking Sara. Pearls of moonlight dripped from the oars as the smaller craft slid away.

Samuel pounded the rail with his fist.

"You all right?" Padraig slammed into the gunwale beside him, wearing nothing but his drawers. "Who were they? What are they after?"

"Sara. They took Sara."

"What?"

"They sounded like Americans."

Padraig rubbed his brow and glowered over the transom at the silvered sea. "Are you certain?"

"She was with you. You should know."

"I—she said I was too hot, sweating too much, and she went to sleep on deck." Padraig rubbed the back of his neck. "I should've—"

"Argh!" The groan came from the other side of the deck.

Exchanging glances, Samuel and Padraig padded over with guns leveled.

Harcourt lay in the bow, blood seeping through the fingers he held to the back of his head. "Did you get them? Who was it?"

"What happened to you?" Samuel laid the carbine against the gunwale and hunkered beside Harcourt.

"Something woke me, and I came on deck to check all was well." Harcourt sat up, and his head jerked around. "Where's the watchman? He had the anchor watch. He should have raised the alarm."

They found a small and compact man, lying on the starboard side, a pool of blood spreading like a black claw beneath him.

"Stabbed through the heart." Time slowed as Samuel tried to pierce the gloom shrouding the ocean. Sara was in real danger. "There were Americans with them, maybe Europeans. Surely they won't harm her. But who could they be?"

Sofia climbed on deck wearing riding breeches, still buttoning her blouse. "Are you all right? What happened?"

Samuel beckoned her over. "It's safe now." It was best to let her see. She'd seen dead men before, even killed a few herself; she wouldn't thank him for trying to hide what had happened.

Harcourt fished out a handkerchief and dabbed his bleeding head. "Could be deserters from Walker's old army. Some of his soldiers dodged the navy when Walker surrendered, and they stayed in country. They . . ." His voice faded as he sagged against the coach roof.

Padraig darted toward the main hatch. "We must go after them and bring her back."

"Her? Who?" Sofia's hand flew to her lips. "My God. Sara?"

"The bandits took her." The cool breeze tickled the sweat streaming down Samuel's naked torso.

Sofia squinted at the dark ocean and drew Samuel to one side by his sleeve. "She's gone again. This is the second time she's—"

"What?" She can't be seriously thinking this is Sara's fault. Samuel wagged an index finger. "Pirates, bandits have taken the poor woman. She's in mortal danger, and you continue to be suspicious of her. Look at the trouble you caused about that man she spoke to in the steamer, and all for nothing. She had a perfectly good explanation."

"But why did she deny—"

"Because she was sick of you hounding her, I dare say. She told Padraig about him."

"Only after I confronted her."

"Enough, Sofia, please. I'm getting dressed and going after her with Padraig. Harcourt and the crew can stand watch in case the bandits return while we're gone." That was very unlikely, only a fool would attempt another assault now the crew was alert. "Lock yourself in the cabin until we return."

"If you return. I can't believe you'd risk your lives for that . . . that woman." Sofia tugged his wrist. "But if you're going, I'm coming with you. I don't want to stay here alone. Bring the Henry rifle for me."

She was so jealous of Sara; she was being impossible. He

wouldn't risk her ashore, especially when she was not thinking clearly "It's not safe."

"And it is here?" Sofia released his wrist and balled her fists. What if they return? I must come with you."

Harcourt approached still nursing his wound. "We have to rescue that young woman."

There were a half dozen bandits in that boat, and they might return. Samuel glanced at the shadowed shoreline. "No, you should stay here and guard the boat with the crew. Have they guns on board?"

"Most boats have weapons to fend off pirates; I'll find out. And I have a rifle." Harcourt seemed a steady fellow for a toff.

"Samuel, come on!" Padraig yelled up from the main hatch.

"You and your men must keep watch here." Samuel started toward the companionway. "If they come back while we're gone, we're buggered. Padraig and I will go after the bandits. We've done this kind of thing before—you too, darling." She would probably be safer beside him, and she was better with a rifle than most men.

Every mile nearer to Chinandega seemed to take them farther away and into greater danger, he reflected as he dressed hastily below. He should've quit when they had a chance. Pulling on his boot, he hesitated. Perhaps he shouldn't go or drag Sofia further into danger. He might never see the children again; if things went wrong, they'd be orphans. But they couldn't leave Sara in the hands of those criminals, and if he didn't go, Padraig would go alone. He had to stand beside his friend. He shoved his foot in the boot and picked up his belt. *Dear God, I know I'm courting danger again, but please watch over us tonight.*

The longboat glided over the silver waves, and well-greased thole pins were silent as the oars dipped into the water. Careful not to miss a stroke, Samuel stretched out his leg and touched Sofia's foot, where she gripped the tiller in the stern. Her face was icy in the moonlight, stubborn and tight, her eyes fixed on the sand and the forest beyond. He was placing her at risk again. If she died, his soul would fall beside her.

She met his eyes, and her lips quirked into a thin smile before mouthing *Te amo*. He squeezed the oars until his knuckles were white. Curse the bad luck that had landed them here.

The whisper of waves rustling the sand grew now, and he craned over his shoulder. Four paces to the shoreline. "Three hard strokes. Drive her up on the strand."

He hauled on the oars with all his might, lifted, dipped, and pulled again. The boat surged forward. When he shipped the oars, he was rocked backward as the bottom scraped over the shallows. He and Padraig leaped out and dragged the boat up onto the beach, boots sinking in the soft sand amidst frothy wavelets fizzling around them. There was a loud clunk—Sofia levering a round under the hammer of the Henry as he hurried back to help her out of the boat.

"I'm fine." She shooed him away. "Watch out for an ambush."

The yielding sand hardened underfoot as they dashed into the tree line, and Samuel halted beside a palm tree to listen, tilting his head. The only sounds were the whispering waves and the breeze stirring the moonlight-dappled palm trees. The earthy smell of withered leaves and rotting wood colored the sea air.

He edged closer to the others. "Keep to the foliage bordering the beach. South first. Search for their boat or tracks in the sand where they dragged it up to the tree line. Stay ten yards behind me. Don't make a sound."

Sofia's face was chiseled marble in the moonlight as she padded beside him. Padraig rubbed the scar on his nose several times as they walked for half a mile and found no tracks. A night animal snuffled and shuffled through the forest behind them.

Samuel halted and scanned the beach strewn with driftwood. "They wouldn't have landed this far south of the boat. Let's backtrack, go north of where we landed." He used the lugger's position offshore to estimate where the bandits had come ashore. "They'd never have gone farther than this. Their boat must be in the other direction."

Padraig booted a waterlogged coconut across the sand. "Who knows what the bastards are doing to her."

Sofia met Samuel's gaze; this was off form for Padraig.

Samuel checked his pocket watch by the moonlight. "Four twenty. Daylight in an hour." He jogged back the way they came, his thighs burning as the sand sucked at his feet, sweat streaming down his face and soaking his shirt.

Padraig slogged up alongside him.

"I counted about six men in the boat. I think at least three were Americans or Europeans. I wonder how many more there are?" Samuel wiped the sweat from his eyes as he panted for breath.

"They kidnapped a woman. What kind of men are they?" Sofia glanced at Samuel wild-eyed. Now she had to believe Sara was the victim.

They slowed to a walk, and Samuel checked his bearings based on the lugger's position. If these men were veterans of the Filibuster War, overcoming them would be a challenge.

A nightingale sang out in the trees, adding to the chorus of whirring insects.

Padraig tugged a leaf off a tree. "They're bastards, and I'm going to kill anyone who touched so much as a hair on her head."

Samuel stretched out an arm to stop the others. "There's our tender. Fall back ten yards behind me and follow, same as before. Not a sound."

He picked his way over the tangle of withering palm fronds, pausing intermittently to listen. Were they watching from the forest and laughing as he hurried into their trap? Was he too late? He pushed away images of Sara pinned down like the Tartar girl he'd rescued in Crimea years ago. A mosquito buzzed his ear, and he swatted at it in vain.

Catching a whiff of cigarette smoke, he threw up one hand and dropped into a crouch. A guard? An ambush? He glanced back to see Sofia's and Padraig's shadows melting into the trees. He tiptoed to a leaning palm tree and placed his hand on the prickly bark to peep around the trunk. Nothing. He slowed his breath and scanned the shadows where the forest met the beach. There it was again, the pungent smell of tobacco smoke. An orange ember glowed twenty yards away.

A guard.

He crossed his forearms, signaling the others stay put, and drew his knife. Taking a deep breath, he crept forward with his pulse beating in his ears. If the guard glanced his way, the jig was up.

Thud!

He froze. Dead leaves rustled, and the glow of the cigarette floated down. That noise hadn't come from the guard. Something, probably a coconut, had fallen nearby. Sweat trickled down Samuel's face as he hovered like a flesh statue.

The guard coughed in a phlegmy hack and spat before he sauntered to the edge of the sand and made water into the sea.

Samuel raced toward the guard, the knife handle sticky in his clammy hands, his feet whispering across the powdered sand. He grabbed a fistful of greasy hair and put his blade to the guard's neck. "Not a word or you die."

The guard flinched. "Wha—? No. Who's—"

"Shut up." Samuel pressed the knife—easy, just a fraction.

The guard slumped. "Don't kill me."

"Don't give me reason." The guard had no sidearm. "Weapons?"

The man shook his head.

Only a fool would stand watch without a weapon. Samuel yanked the guard's head back, and the man yelped. "Lie again and I'll slit your jugular. Where are your weapons?"

"Back in the trees. A rifle. You're from the boat? I didn't—"

"Silence. Put your prick away."

Padraig appeared soundlessly and jabbed his Colt into the man's spine. "Where's the girl? If you harmed a hair—"

"I didn't, I swear, I—"

"Quiet. Both of you." It would soon be dawn. Samuel didn't have time for this. "Turn around."

The guard was older, his stout body giving way to folds of fat.

"I'll ask one time." Samuel ran his finger over the blade's edge. "The wrong answer, and . . . Where's the woman?"

"I'd nothing to do with taking her. She's at the cottage. Mile from here. I can guide you there."

Padraig grabbed the man's shirt. "Is she hurt?"

"No. She was on the deck, and we—they, they took her to silence her while they set up the attack. Look, I had nothing to—"

"It's almost daylight; we need to get going." Padraig clubbed the guard with his Colt.

Samuel exhaled in disgust. "What have you done? How the hell are we going to find them now?"

"We saw their trail as we waited for you," Sofia said. "The boat too, up there, covered with palm fronds."

He never even heard Sofia approach; she was stealthy. He nudged the guard with his toe. "Padraig, there must be rope in their boat. Fetch it and tie this bugger up." He grabbed Padraig's arm. "And cool down. We're going to get her back, but if you behave like a hothead, you'll get us killed."

"It's—" Padraig kicked the toe of his boot into the sand. "Sorry. She's important to me."

If only they knew what they were up against. Samuel threw up his hands. "Get the rope, quickly."

Twenty minutes later, a faint glow flickered through the undergrowth ahead, and Samuel put out a hand to stop Sofia behind him. "Quietly now."

Testing the ground before every step, they crept toward the light of the dying campfire. An animal roared in the trees overhead, and Samuel jumped. It reminded him of the inhuman clamoring he'd heard on his last trip to Central America, a howler monkey marking its territory with a shriek too big for its little body. He brushed Sofia's arm to reassure her and started forward again.

Bottles and rubbish littered the trampled clearing outside a wooden shack. They crouched in the undergrowth and observed for an interminable minute.

Samuel drew his Colt. "They're asleep. Cover me while I see what we're up against. If there are only five or six, Padraig and I will go in."

Sofia flinched. "That's madness."

He pointed to the scattered bottles glinting in the moonlight. "They've been drinking. With luck they're drunk."

Padraig surged ahead.

"Blinking hothead," Samuel whispered. Padraig was never like this. This Sara, this relationship with her . . . He cupped Sofia's sweaty head to his neck. "Promise me if something goes wrong, you'll get the hell out of here. Don't do anything stupid." He kissed her and sped after Padraig, giving her no time to answer.

The cottage was little more than a shed of rotting planks, its rickety shutters thrown wide open. Padraig was rising to peer inside when Samuel caught his arm.

Padraig grimaced. "Nobody. The place—"

"What have we here?" The Southern drawl made Samuel whirl around.

Three men with unkempt hair and clothes mended long past decent stood on the edge of the clearing, rifles pointed at Samuel and Padraig. Samuel's core chilled.

A man with a matted beard and a single bushy eyebrow bridging his forehead gestured with his rifle. "Handguns on the ground. Don't try anything funny."

A thin-boned bandit nudged the man with one eyebrow. "Look at that, Reggie. Are them there those fancy revolvers with six shots apiece?"

Samuel clenched his Colt so hard his knuckles were white. What a bloody fool. He should've taken more care before barging in. If only Padraig hadn't raced ahead—but Samuel had been the idiot who followed him.

"Shut up, Curtis, and watch them. These are dangerous fellers." Reggie jerked his rifle. "Now I ain't telling you twice, boy. You too, blondie."

"I told you I seen 'em." The third man was short and round with a pockmarked face. "On the beach."

This was hopeless. Samuel's shoulders sagged, and he dropped his Colt. Padraig stiffened beside him. "Padraig, that's suicide. Drop your gun."

Padraig's nostrils flared as he hurled down his revolver. "A cess on them. You should've fought."

Reggie barked a laugh. "Well, boys, I reckon this prize will please the boss."

Of all the stupid mistakes he'd ever made . . . Samuel resisted the urge to check for Sofia in the woods. At least she was safe. She better do as he told her and return to the ship; one woman stood no chance against these men. Perhaps he could tempt them with money, but if they wanted the boat . . . Oh, dear Lord. They should've gone home to Ireland long ago.

A gun barked, and Reggie pitched back as a flock of pigeons flapped from the trees behind Samuel.

Click-clunk. The gun discharged again, and the two surviving bandits ducked. Another shot, and Curtis spun around, dropping his rifle to clutch his shoulder. A second shot, and the fat man collapsed with a scream.

Only the Henry rifle could shoot that fast.

Sofia!

Samuel dived for his Colt, but by the time he rolled to his knees, cocking the weapon, it was all over.

Curtis clawed his bleeding shoulder. "Don't shoot! I surrender."

Click-clunk. The undergrowth rustled. "Don't stir a muscle. I've thirteen more rounds here, an unlucky number . . . for you." Sofia stepped from the trees with the smoking rifle. Strands of hair had slipped free of her wide-brimmed hat, and her sweat-soaked blouse clung to her like skin.

Samuel's legs wobbled as he climbed to his feet and laughed shakily. "I thought I told you to go back to the boat."

"When have I ever listened to you?"

"Christ, Sofia, I wouldn't doubt you, girl." Padraig picked up his Colt and stalked over to Curtis. "Where's Sara?"

Curtis was deathly pale. His lips moved, but no words came out.

Padraig grabbed a fistful of the bandit's hair and jammed the Colt into his cheek. "Where's the—"

"It's not like you think," Curtis squeaked. "We were told—"

"Where . . . is . . . she?"

"The cabin, dear God, the cabin. She's unharmed."

"Watch him, Samuel." Padraig shoved Curtis backward and sprinted for the cabin. Samuel had never seen him so angry or scared. He was incandescent.

"It could be a trap," he called after his friend. "Be careful."

Sofia stepped into the clearing near the bandit with the heavy brow, whose ribs rose and fell in ragged breaths like the last wheeze of a torn bellows. He'd be dead any moment, like the fat man sprawled in a pool of blood close by.

Padraig swung the door of the shack wide, cursed, and fired his Colt into the darkness. Another gun barked within.

Samuel's heart skipped a beat as he barreled Sofia off her feet. She hit the ground, and the Henry flew from her hands. He sat up clumsily and swung his Colt to cover Curtis. "Don't move." He glanced at the cabin. "Padraig! You all right?"

Breathless, she pushed to her feet and recovered the Henry. "Help Padraig. I'll watch these two."

Samuel sprinted to the shack, threw himself against the wall, and peered around the doorway. Someone lay on the floor, blood soaking the earthen floor around him. Padraig stood farther back, his arms wrapped around Sara as she whimpered in the gloom.

"You harmed?" Samuel scanned the single roomed shack. "What happened?"

"This one was waiting to ambush us, but I was too fast for him." Padraig poked the dead man with his boot. "Hush now, Sara, you're safe. I'll let no one harm you."

Sara twisted her hand in Padraig's shirt. "He—they came out of nowhere and . . ."

Padraig drew back his head and peered into her teary eyes. "Easy, you're safe now. Take a deep breath and tell us from the beginning."

"I don't . . . I couldn't sleep. It was so hot, and you were snoring, so I climbed on deck for some air. They came from nowhere and dragged me to one side before I could make a sound." She buried her face in Padraig's shoulder. "When someone fired—at one of you, I guess—they dragged me over the side into their boat. Then everybody began shooting." She drew back her head to peer at Padraig. "I thought I'd die, trapped with those horrible men, and them shouting and swearing. I must have fainted because I woke up when their boat thumped onto the beach."

Padraig's nostrils flared. "Did they harm you? In any way?"

Her mouth opened, but no words came forth as she panted shallow breaths, tears streaming down her cheeks. "They, he, the skinny one tried to—"

"Bastard!"

Before Samuel could check him, Padraig whirled out the door, barreling toward their only prisoner. He'd never seen Padraig so angry. God alone knew what he would do. "Sara, I'll be right back."

Outside, Sofia was tugging Padraig's gun away from Curtis's

head. "Don't, Padraig, don't. You must listen to what he's saying. It was a setup, a—"

Setup? Samuel's mind raced. "What do you mean by—"

"I don't care, the bastards attacked her." Padraig twisted his gun free.

What had the prisoner told Sofia? What else had he told Sofia? Samuel raised his voice emphatically. "Padraig, we need him alive."

Click. The sound of the Colt's hammer cocking was loud in the clearing.

He grabbed Padraig's wrist. "No."

Spittle flecked the corner of Padraig's mouth, and his empty hand clenched and unclenched.

The hair rose on the back of Samuel's neck. Padraig was out of control, and he'd kill the bandit before they could interrogate him. What had he told Sofia?

Sofia placed her hand gently on Padraig's shoulder. "Padraig, stop it now. Listen to what he has to say."

Padraig cursed and punched Curtis in the gut, knocking him to the ground. On with you, then, ask your bloody questions. Then I'll kill him."

"Stop it now." Sofia pulled Padraig's shirt. "These are Walker's men. Living here since the last war. Ask him."

Walker's men here, how? Samuel's eyes darted around the clearing. If there were more, they were in immediate danger. He stooped and yanked Curtis into a sitting position. "That true? How many more of you are there?"

Curtis spat at him. "Go to hell."

Jerking back, Samuel wiped the spit from his cheek with his forearm.

"Hell, is it? Talk now or I'll send you there." Padraig lashed Curtis with the barrel of his Colt.

Curtis cried out, and his hand flew to his face. "All right. We've been here since fifty-seven when Walker surrendered. We hid when the U.S. Navy rounded up the other volunteers to ship them home. We scattered along the coast and tried to survive until he kept his oath to return."

They'd waited three years for Walker. "You believed he'd come back?"

Curtis wiped blood from his split lip with a grimy hand. "He assured us he would before he surrendered. He's coming. Mark brought orders for the volunteers to assemble in Chinandega. We were going to trek there, but your boat was a quicker and easier way to travel north."

Sofia palm flew to her mouth. "Chinandega. Filipe's in danger."

It took effort, but Samuel kept his voice calm. "We don't know that, yet." Filipe was stubborn enough to fight the filibusters, and Cortez and the other Euronicas would support him. He shook Curtis and steeled his voice as Curtis's shirt ripped. "How many filibusters stayed behind when Walker surrendered?"

"Don't rightly know. Maybe three, four dozen." Curtis spat out blood.

As many as forty men. That was a powerful force. "And why Chinandega?"

"How the hell would I know? We—"

A gun roared behind Samuel, and he spun around. Smoke swirled from the barrel of the pistol in Sara's trembling hands.

"Bastard attacked me."

Curtis lay in the dirt with a hole in his forehead, blood and brains colored the trampled grass behind him.

"My God." Sofia's palm flew to her mouth.

Sara dropped the pistol and fell to her knees sobbing.

Padraig kneeled beside her and wrapped an arm around her shoulders. "It's all right, Sara. He deserved it. I'm here. I'll always be here."

Samuel was speechless. She must've picked up the bandit's pistol inside the cabin. He should've stayed with her, but Padraig would've—well, the filibuster was dead now anyway.

Sofia fixed Sara with a narrowing glare. "Now we'll get no more information. Convenient."

"They attacked me," Sara cried. "They—I don't know what—I had to kill the bastard. I had to."

"Hush now. Of course you did." Padraig rained kisses on her tearstained face. "It's over now. I'm here."

Sofia skewered Sara with an unflinching scowl. "You shot him to silence him, didn't you?"

"Damn it, Sofia," Padraig's eyes blazed. "Samuel . . ."

Things were spinning out of control. They couldn't turn on each other. Samuel took a firm grip of Sofia and drew her to the edge of the clearing. "That's enough, Sofia. They assaulted her; she's terrified out of her mind. Doesn't know what she's doing."

Sofia face was limestone as she unclamped her tight lips. "Listen to yourself. I know what the hussy is doing. She's betraying us."

"That's a wild assumption. How—"

"Wild! Wild is you men fawning over the pretty lost woman there. Tripping over her barefaced lies. We must get to Chinandega. Take me back to the boat. Which way is it?" Each syllable rapped out as hard and sharp as the blade of a saber, then she stalked toward the trees bordering the clearing.

Samuel sprinted after her. "We don't know if they'll attack Filipe's hacienda. We don't even know if filibusters assaulted Chinandega. That bastard could have lied. We'll leave right away. It's not far now. And even if filibusters are there, without Walker, this rising has no chance."

She slowed down, trembling. He draped an arm around her and pulled her close.

She shook her head. "I don't know. What if the Royal Navy doesn't capture him in the Caribbean?"

"The best navy in the world? They'll catch him." Samuel chewed his cheek. He had to sound more confident than he felt. He didn't want to concern Sofia further.

"Walker's sent word he's returning, and the filibusters here are helping him. What if more are still up north and they go after Filipe?"

"After him? Why?" But the filibusters knew that Samuel had married Colonel Valle's daughter. If Walker had them pursued in New York, he might also have sent men after Filipe. Samuel took a deep breath. "That won't happen. If the Royal Navy hasn't caught Walker already, he's sailing into their gun sights as we speak. Nevertheless, let's return to the boat and push Harcourt to finish his repairs." He twisted around. Padraig was trailing them with his arm around Sara, scowling and keeping his distance.

Thirty minutes later, the gray tails of dawn streaked the sky as Samuel dipped his oars and heaved back to power the tender clear of the gentle surf. Thoughts of the cabin in the woods niggled him. "Those men were living rough back there. You'd think they'd have mixed in with the locals by now. They've been here three years."

Padraig was stiff as he rowed, and he said nothing. Samuel's chest caved. How could he ever heal this rift between Sofia and his friend? This was the last thing they needed now.

On the tiller, Sofia shaded her eyes with her hand. "Look at that. A bird flew off the boat."

Samuel craned around to see.

"Looks like a pigeon," Sofia said. "Poor thing must've been lost. I hope he finds his way back to land."

Samuel saw it then, a flapping shadow flying north northeast toward the shore. "Must be a seagull. It can't be a pigeon."

"Too dark to be a seagull." She continued to track the bird.

"I've seen seagulls with brown feathers." Padraig grunted as he pulled on his oars.

"Well, I think it's a pigeon, but it doesn't matter. I hope the poor thing makes it home, that's all."

And the rest of them, too. Samuel's limbs tingled. Danger was closing in, but there was no turning back now, not when

Walker's men might be after Filipe as well. But they would achieve little with this animosity dividing them.

Padraig rowed silently, his eyes fixed on Sara as she held her blanket over her face and sniffed loudly.

Samuel bit his cheek. He had to decide who was right about Sara, and he'd lose either Sofia or Padraig when he did.

CHAPTER THIRTEEN

"How could those fools have let the Royal Navy capture the *Clifton*?" Walker glared across the turquoise waters at the white sands of Cozumel from the deck of the brig, *John C. Taylor*. "We lost arms, ammunition, and men we badly need to capture Roatán."

Rudler scratched his stubble. "Unfortunate luck, Mr. President. The Caribbean is crawling with Royal Navy frigates. It could've been us as handily."

"Well, they didn't catch us. And I'm tired of hiding off this Mexican island. It's been four weeks already. If we don't go back soon, Roatán will be fortified and impregnable. I promised Cabañas I'd capture the island before we head to the mainland to link with him in El Triunfo. From there, it's a quick march over the border into Chinandega. Coronel Garcia's men would've captured Kingston by now." He couldn't wait to see the look on Kingston's face through iron bars.

Rudler cleared his throat. "About the men, sir. They're unhappy. Some are frightened."

"What do you mean? Where did you find these cowards?"

"They . . . they feel we're too few to continue. There's talk of turning back, returning to New Orleans."

Walker pounded the guardrail. "Cowards. If he only had General Henningsen and the heroes who'd defended Granada. Pressure surged through his veins. "Retreat? Never. Assemble those quitters. Gather them this instant."

Rudler recoiled, saluted, and stalked off.

The men gathered in the brig's waist, brown from weeks in the Caribbean, except the few whose sunburned skin peeled continuously, their eyes fixed on Walker. One stout black-whiskered villain, with his belt straining the last hole, took a surreptitious sip from a flask which he sneaked back into his pocket. Rudler should've confiscated all liquor long ago. Walker ground his teeth and scanned the tight faces. Save for a dozen American and German mercenaries, this rabble couldn't compare to the fine warriors who defended Granada in fifty-six, but they were all he had. He could brook no insubordination from this bunch.

A gust of wind ruffled the wavelets lapping the ship and rattled the rigging. Three gulls launched from the mainsail yardarm to wheel between the masts, crying mournfully.

Walker scanned the malevolent faces and placed his hands behind his back, grasping one wrist with the other hand. "Men, the opposition to our landing in Roatán was only a setback. Rest assured, I haven't been idle during this leisure thrust on us against our wills. I've been reviewing our options and know they are strong. By now, Major French will be entrenched in Northern Nicaragua, in Chinandega, and Nicaraguans loyal to our cause will march south to seize control of the San Juan River, opening the route for thousands of volunteers to join our noble enterprise."

Several men exchanged sidelong glances or pulled at their clothing. Only a handful met his gaze.

"Don't let our present position and the timidity of a few weaken your resolve. We do God's work here. This struggle between the old and the new elements in Central American society is not passing or accidental but natural and inevitable.

And the pure white American race cannot save the mixed race in Central America from its self-destructive indolence without the employment of force. By the cross thou shalt—"

"Horseshit." A broad-faced man with a bushy grey beard took a step forward. "We lost too many men when they captured the *Clifton*. Too much ammunition—"

"What's your name?" Walker boiled under his collar. How dare this wretch speak to his commanding officer like that?

"Francis Cole. From Tennessee."

He'd stop this mutiny dead on this deck. "Lieutenant Blocker, Sergeant McCabe, seize Rifleman Cole. Corporal King, raise a grating to the mast. I'll teach this blackguard to challenge me."

The men fell back with bulging eyes, speechless, as Blocker and McCabe grabbed Cole.

Walker stalked to an inch-thick mooring line coiled on the deck and cut two feet of rope from the bitter end. "Rip off his shirt."

"You can't do this," Cole screeched as they bound his hands to the grating. The bare flesh of his back was blindingly pale against his suntanned neck.

"Twenty lashes, Corporal." He handed the rope to King, the burliest man here. Cole needed to feel the pain, and the men needed to see blood. King's jaw dropped. "Don't spare him or you'll be next."

As Rudler drew his revolver, Walker stepped to one side and folded his arms. These weak wretches wouldn't dare object. The tension was palpable as the men stiffened, mouths open, hands fluttering, eyes narrowed or dull. King twisted the rope in his meaty hands as he regarded the scarred deck. Did any of them have the courage to do what was needed?

"Get on with it, Corporal."

King struck. The rope landed with a crack like a pistol shot, and Cole arched back with a scream. King glanced sidelong at Walker.

"Another." The men would remember this lesson. They'd never challenge him again.

By the last lash, red welts crisscrossed Cole's back, and blood dribbled where the rope end had broken skin. Cole was a sobbing wreck.

"That's twenty, sir." Corporal King was as shaken as the tight-faced volunteers.

"Walker surveyed the bloody back. That would teach them discipline. "Take him below. I want him shipshape by the time we reach Roatán, Doctor Albright."

The men stirred, eyes blinking, tight lipped.

"That's right, we're returning to Roatán." His harsh voice cracked across the deck, loud as King's bloodied whip. "We're going to make history."

He showed them his back and headed for his cabin. He shouldn't have had to waste his time disciplining the men. Perhaps Rudler wasn't up to the task after all. No matter, he would write a page of American history impossible to forget or erase, and nobody, least of all his men, would stop him.

CHAPTER FOURTEEN

The pyramid of sails boomed above Samuel and Sofia each time the lugger surfed down a wave, and the forestay thrummed. The salt air was fresh after the reek of death in the forest. The one-hundred-and-twenty-mile journey from the bay to El Realejo should've taken twenty-four hours, but this northerly wind would stretch the voyage to three days, a torturous trip where Sofia and Padraig had ignored each other, leaving Samuel chilled between them.

Samuel glanced aft at Padraig and Sara, wrapped together at the guardrail amidships. They were kissing again.

"Don't tell me I'm overreacting." Sofia twisted her fingers in the hem of her shirt. "She killed that bandit to silence him."

"Rubbish. She shot him because he'd violated her. Poor woman's at her wits' end." Samuel rubbed the back of his neck. Sofia was like a horse pointed toward home, fighting the bit and pulling toward the stable, toward a conclusion. But what if she was right? Sara's explanation of her disappearance back in Panama was lame, and now a kidnapping? In the light of day, catching up with Walker's men on the beach seemed quite the coincidence. Padraig was the one who usually unraveled these puzzles, but Sara was blinding him. She was leading him around by the nose—no, by his . . .

"You must believe me, Samuel. That woman's trouble. Talk to Padraig. He's ignoring me. If the filibusters harm Filipe because you two refused to—"

"All right, I'll talk to him." Oh, God, how did it come to this? He would have to choose between his wife and his best friend. His head pounded. Something didn't add up.

"And that Harcourt." Sofia glanced aft at the canted deck, where two of the crew were preparing for the next tack, coiling down the braces and belaying them at their marks, set to be released. "Something about him smells off as well. Despite his clean-cut looks, he's slimy. Have you seen the way he stares at Sara? His yearning ogle."

Samuel blinked. Sofia might be right. It was possible Harcourt could have damaged the rigging as an excuse to anchor back there, that he was in league with the filibusters. They could have knocked him on the head to cover his tracks.

She grabbed the forestay, rose on her tiptoes, and peered back at Padraig and Sara. "Still clinging together brazenly. That girl's a hussy. María will be in tears if he brings that one back to her. I can't stand it. I'm going below." She pushed off and swayed across the rolling deck, sure-footed as a cat, taking the leeward side as far from Sara as possible.

Samuel found a sheltered spot and took out his tobacco. Harcourt was deep in conversation with the captain at the helm. Captain Molina was weathered and old but stood straight as a lance. He and his eight crewmen kept to themselves, as if they resented the landlubbers who'd invaded their ship. No matter; Molina only had to endure them until he delivered them to El Realejo, and that couldn't come a moment too soon. Samuel bit his lip as he spread tobacco in the cigarette paper. The country was like a sleeping volcano, holding its breath in the shadow of Walker's return. They'd waited a long time to finish Walker off, but once the Royal Navy swept him up, the country would settle down. Or would it? Walker seemed to have pawns shifting on all sides: men in New York, loyalists along Nicaragua's coast, and an army at sea in the Caribbean. And somehow this was all converging once again on Chinandega. They needed to reach Filipe and confirm he was safe.

It took three matches to light his cigarette, and he greedily sucked the smoke deep in the hope it would settle his roiling nerves. The nimble lugger forged ahead, shouldering through the moon-silvered sea as Samuel divided his uneasy attention between the kissing couple amidships and the dark horizon.

He was puffing on the stub of his second cigarette, the hot ash heating his fingers, when Sara separated from Padraig and swayed across the pitching deck toward the companionway. He took out his watch and angled it to catch the moonlight. Eight thirty. He stuffed his watch in his pocket and dug out his cigarette paper. The topic of Sara was going to infuriate Padraig. Perhaps after another cigarette . . . Now he was stalling. He thrust out his jaw and strode aft before he could change his mind.

Padraig was leaning on the weather guardrail aft of the mainmast, his upturned face pale in the moonlight. His eyes sparkled when he faced Samuel. "What a wonderful night: fresh air, a million stars, and the wind whistling in the rigging—a sailor's dream. I wish it could last forever."

Now he was being nice. What had become of all his anger? Padraig was losing his mind. "It's a fine night, all right, but it would be better if we didn't have to tack back and forth all the way to El Realejo."

Padraig's smile broadened into a stupid grin—not his usual cheeky grin, but the infuriatingly silly smile of a man possessed. "I don't mind how long it takes. I'm having a great time." He took a large, deep breath and seemed to savor it. "What fresh air. What a wonderful balmy night. It's perfect."

Samuel forced himself to continue. "Hardly. Not with the filibusters marching on Chinandega. Filipe, Chavez, Cortez, all of the Euronicas are in danger. The country is about to explode into war. Pull yourself together. We need to talk. What if they attack the Valle hacienda to prepare for Walker's arrival? What will happen to Filipe, to all our friends?"

Padraig tilted his head back and blew out a stream of smoke. "You're worrying about nothing. By now the Royal Navy will have snagged Walker in our trap, and to be sure, they won't let him out of the snare, not like the Americans did. You worry too much. Enjoy the cruise."

"Have you been paying attention at all?" Samuel swallowed hard. He should walk away before he said something he regretted. "This boat pulled in at a so-called random spot on the coast for repairs and just there were Walker's men. Too much of a coincidence. But we'll never learn the truth because Sara shot the prisoner before we could finish questioning him. All we have—"

"Whoa there, hold your horses." Padraig's nostrils flared. "So this is what it's really about, then? I'm surprised at you, and even more surprised at Sofia. I never figured her for a snob, and I thought you shed your airs and graces years ago."

"You're overlooking the—"

"But no, you both disliked her from the beginning because she's a common girl from Dublin. Don't think I failed to notice your condescending looks. They cut me."

"Listen to me. Get your head in the game. I need your help. We're facing—"

"I'm not facing anything." Padraig pushed off the railing and stepped back. "When we reach El Realejo, Sara and I are continuing on to San Francisco. This is the last insult, and I've had enough. We'll part as soon as we dock."

This was exactly what Samuel had been afraid of. Drat, he should've left well enough alone. "Please, calm down and think th—"

"*Psst!*" The hiss shot toward them from across the deck. "We need to talk. It's urgent." Sofia darted up beside Samuel, flushed and out of breath.

Padraig pounded the gunwale with his fist. "What's it now, Sofia? What new fantasy have you conjured to make my life miserable?"

Heat flushed through Samuel's body. The churl. How dare he speak to Sofia like that? "Don't address my wife that way." He stabbed a finger into his friend's chest several times for emphasis.

Padraig batted his hand aside. "What's this? If you—"

"Shut up, both of you, you fools." Sofia's voice, low and commanding, made both men pause. "That *was* a pigeon I saw flying from the boat yesterday, a messenger pigeon, and they've three more down below in the forward cubbyhole room or whatever you call it. Sara's sending messages. I found these blank pieces of paper in her case, along with Noah Webster's American dictionary, all marked—"

"You searched her belongings?" Padraig spluttered. "How could you—"

"Be quiet, Padraig Kerr, and listen." She grabbed Padraig's shoulder and shook him. "Someone's marked up the dictionary. It's a code: a number for the page, a letter showing the column, and a number for the entry of the column. It's a *code*."

Padraig's mouth fell open, and he shook his head.

Samuel's stared across deck, seeing nothing. "But how—"

"Hush. Not here. Our cabin." She clamped a hand onto Padraig's arm and drew him to the companionway.

Samuel's mind was dull as he glanced from her receding figure to Padraig's gaping face as he trailed her. "Come on, we must know the truth." His feet dragged as he followed them.

They seemed to be hurtling toward a carefully planned disaster hatched a long time ago, long before they had even left Ireland.

~

Sofia drew Padraig into the hot cabin ahead of Samuel. By the time he closed the door, his wife and his best friend were already squared off in the cramped space. The stale air smelled of mildew, wood, and the body odor baked into the old timber bulkheads.

"It's Scovell's method." Sofia swayed with a roll of the ship and flopped onto the narrow bunk.

"Rubbish." Padraig grabbed a deck beam to steady himself.

Samuel struck a match and lit the lantern rocking on gimbals screwed to the timbers. "How do you know about codes?"

She crossed her arms. "I read it in a mathematics book. You're not the only one who reads books from the Kingston library, Padraig Kerr."

Padraig flopped down on the opposite bunk, facing Sofia. "Argh!" He pulled Samuel's sheath knife out from under him and dropped it to one side. "Damn, don't leave your knife lying around. I almost impaled myself."

"Look before you sit." Samuel stooped to move the knife. Too hell with that, it was his bunk; he'd leave it there. "You should worry about Sara and what other surprises she's planned."

The timbers creaked in rhythm with the boat's rocking movement, and the rush of water past the hull was a constant muted whoosh.

Sofia lifted a hand. "There's more. I searched Harcourt's cabin as well. I smelled a woman's perfume—lemon oil, the same as Sara uses. She's been in there with him."

The light from the swinging lantern bloated and shrunk their shadows on the dew-splattered bulkheads as all three fell silent. Samuel's stomach clenched. If Sara was sleeping with Harcourt, then she was stringing Padraig along. Who else was in on this? The captain? The crew? "My God, that's—"

"She can't be with him, she can't." Padraig bowed his head and grabbed a fistful of damp hair with a groan. "But that night the filibusters took her, she wasn't . . . she wasn't in my . . ."

"She was on deck with Harcourt." Sofia cupped her hand on

Padraig's shoulder. "It's been eating at me all this time, how she inveigled her way into our party." She ticked points off on her fingers. "Her disappearance in Panama. You found her in a slum, for God's sake. And now that I dwell on it, that could've been Harcourt I spotted with her in steerage in the steamship. He's following us. Maybe she met him in Colón, not a doctor."

Samuel shook his head. "That didn't look like—"

"Perhaps he was wearing a wig and dressed like a settler. He's working with her."

"Oh God, it can't be." Padraig's hands slid loosely into his lap. "I love—"

The cabin door swung open and smashed against the bulkhead. Harcourt stood outside with a revolver.

"I told you the sly cow was snooping," Sara spat from behind him.

Sofia drew herself up from Padraig's side. "You filthy harlot. I'm going t—"

"Sofia . . ." Samuel grabbed her elbow and pulled her close.

As he did, Padraig's arm flashed forward. Light blinked on the twirling blade, and Harcourt rocked back clutching his throat.

"Got him." Padraig sprang to the door and pounced on Harcourt where he lay outside.

Sofia broke free from Samuel's grasp and punched Sara in the jaw with a balled fist. Sara's head cracked against the bulkhead, and Sofia leaped on her. "You heartless tart. He's a fine man, and you used him. What—"

It was all happening too fast, the madness. Samuel's skin crawled. What was the sense of it? Why? He caught Sofia's sinewy arms and dragged her off the stunned Sara. "Enough, Sofia, you'll kill her."

Padraig rose, his shirt soaked with blood. "I had to do it. Serves the bastard right for—"

"Padraig." Samuel grabbed his friend's arm. "We need to stay focused. The crew."

Padraig undid a button on his blood-stained shirt. "Are they part of it?"

"I doubt it." Samuel shook his head. "It's a chartered boat, but let's keep Harcourt's death quiet until we know, until we have a plan. Keep Sara in here, Sofia, while we hide Harcourt's body in his cabin."

Samuel hurried to the companionway, climbed the stairs, and checked that no one was close by. The captain was standing aft beside the helmsman. "It's clear, move him quickly."

Padraig removed his shirt and helped Samuel drag the corpse down the short passageway to Harcourt's cabin. His mind racing, Samuel helped Padraig roll the stiff body beneath Harcourt's bunk. Sara had to be working with Walker. Walker had been ahead of them at every turn; the attack in New York and planting a pretty Irish girl in their party both smacked of his genius touch. What else did the man know? If he knew the brigs were a trap, all of them were in danger.

He rummaged through Harcourt's clothes, found two shirts, and pushed one into Padraig's hand as they left the cabin. "We've more to worry about than this crew. It's Filipe. He's in danger, I sense it."

"I was thinking the same." Padraig scrubbed a hand across his face. "Aw, Sam, I'm a gal sneaker. She played me for a fool."

Samuel pushed him down the corridor. "You're a man, that's all. Thank God, we caught her in time." He stopped outside his cabin and used the other shirt to mop up the bloodstain.

"I love her. I thought she was the one." Padraig slumped against the bulkhead.

"I've heard you say that before, and you got over it." Samuel knelt back. The planks were black and ancient; the stain would hardly be noticeable. "Not too bad, is it? A man on a galloping horse would never see it. Pull yourself together. Let's see what Sara knows."

They crowded into the cabin to more sniveling from Sara. ". . . governess to Harcourt's children."

Sofia's hand was a blur as she slapped Sara yet again. "Stop that nonsense. We've no time for this. You'll tell me everything or you'll go overboard with your lover."

Padraig flinched but said nothing.

Sara buried her head in her hands. "I d-didn't mean any b-badness. I couldn't find work in New York because many businesses won't hire the Irish. So I ended up as a . . . as a ringer."

Sofia raised her eyebrows. Of course she wouldn't know that word.

"A prostitute." Discrimination had set Sara on this cruel path. Samuel's lip curled. No. She brought this fate on herself when she choose to lie and betray them, to betray Padraig, who cared for her.

"Franklin was a perfect gentleman—at first. I fell in love with him. When he offered to take me away from that life, I grabbed the chance. He was going to marry me." Sara sobbed. "He was going to marry me. And now he's dead." She shuddered.

Sofia's lip curled up. "He played you for a fool."

"No. He loved me."

"And that's why he sent you to Padraig. Get some sense, woman." Sofia shook her.

Tears streamed down Sara's freckled face. "He said it was the only way to discover your plans. He said you were thieves who'd stolen vital papers from Walker. He promised a life together on his Nicaraguan estate. But I had to find some papers you have that really belonged to someone else named Baltimore."

The Baltimore papers. Walker had expected Samuel to carry them.

"Baltimore's papers." Sofia's hand flew to her mouth. "Why would Walker, Harcourt—whoever— think you had them with you?"

"Because Walker's men stole them from Clonakilty last time. They figured I'd bring them with me to keep them safe." But those papers were secure in a hidden safe in the Kerr's house, and no one would ever think of looking there. "And if Walker has the papers, there's nothing to stop Lord Lucan and the aristocrat consortium for financing Walker's plot."

Sara eyes flicked from one listener to another. "I'd be a lady, with servants, pretty—"

"Foolish woman." Sofia shot Samuel a venomous scowl. He wouldn't stop her pressing for answers, not now. "And the message? What did the message say? The pigeon?"

"I didn't . . . It wasn't my—"

Slap!

Sara cried out and cringed from Sofia.

"What did it say?" Sofia was a lioness protecting her pride.

A red handprint blossomed on Sara's cheek. "All right, stop smacking me. I'll talk." She pushed her hair back from her face. "That was Franklin warning Colonel Garcia that our men failed to catch you back there. He advised Colone Garcia to ambush you when we land in El Realejo."

The tic started under Samuel's left eye. Walker's forces were operating all over the country; nowhere was safe. They were sailing into a trap, but they couldn't turn back, not with Filipe and all the Euronicas in danger. If Walker had a prominent official like Garcia on his side, Filipe and all his old company were in peril. "What about this ship's crew and the captain, are they working with Harcourt?"

Padraig wiped Samuel's knife clean and stuffed his bloody shirt under the bunk. "They can't be. Didn't the filibusters murder one of them when they boarded the boat?"

Sara sobbed and whimpered.

"Are they?" Sofia grabbed her shoulder and shook her. "Are the crew part of this?"

"No. Franklin warned me to beware of them when I searched your cabin."

Samuel stepped closer to her. "And why were you in that slum in Colón?"

"Franklin wanted to meet . . . He missed me. But he became furious when I reported I failed to find those stupid papers."

Padraig blanched. "You met that bastard."

"He slipped me a message to see him."

Sofia kneeled in front of Sara. "So I did see you with him on the ship. He *was* following us. You went with him, and he left you in that disgusting slum. How can you think that brute loved you?"

"He does . . . did." Sara sniveled. "But he got angry sometimes. I met him outside the hotel, and he took me to a shack he'd rented to . . ."

To lay with her. Samuel drew away from Sara speechless.

"Blessed Virgin save us." Padraig threw a hand up and backed into the bulkhead.

"He got angry when I had little news. He beat me, and I ran away. I got lost, and that's when you found me." She pawed the tears from her eyes. "I know he didn't mean to hurt me. He got so angry sometimes, but wasn't that my fault. I know he loved me. Why can't you see that?"

Padraig covered his face with his palms. "Shut up, you stupid hoor. I can't believe . . . I can't deal with this." He yanked open the door and stomped out.

Sofia jerked her head toward the door. "Get him back, Samuel. Don't let him go on deck."

Outside, Padraig leaned against a bulkhead. "I'm such a fool. I should have listened to—"

Samuel placed a hand on Padraig's shoulder. "No. She deceived me also. I would never have believed a pretty girl could be so devious."

Sofia stepped from the cabin and closed the door. "That hussy's going nowhere."

Padraig's shoulders sagged. "What now? We can't sail into El Realejo'"

"And we can't abandon Filipe." Samuel leaned against the bulkhead opposite Padraig. "I don't know."

Sofia squinted her eyes. "Walker's not the only one with allies in Nicaragua. He won't do this to us again. Here's what we'll do."

Her eyes had steel in them that he'd never seen before, and Samuel's lungs expanded as she outlined her plan. He knew his wife. The love of his life was a fighter; he'd seen her in action before, full of power and confidence. But this time the odds were stacked against them: three people, alone on a coast where filibusters ran berserk and old allies savaged each other for the promise of power and land. A country where few could be trusted.

Samuel's lungs deflated in a long sigh.

Major Hernan Valle's hacienda was a sprawling colonial home with white walls and columns nestled between fields of cane and corn. The damp air smelled of freshly cut sugarcane, vegetation, and rain. Samuel willed the cart to go faster as the last half mile dawdled on forever. The driver who transported them from the coast had heard nothing of a disturbance at Major Hernan's estate, but Samuel needed to know about Filipe. Was Sofia's brother safe? And what about the Euronicas? They would find the answer here.

"Wow. How long did I sleep?" Sofia sat up, rubbed her eyes, and stretched her hands toward the brooding sky. She was beautiful, even with a dirty face and straw poking from her disheveled hair.

"Ever since we left the beach." He checked his watch. "Over two hours. It took longer than we expected. Padraig, you all right?"

Padraig had said little since the sailors rowed them ashore. He touched the scar on his nose. "Fine, fine. Well, I'm still . . . I mean, to let Sara use me like that."

Samuel exchanged sympathetic glances with Sofia.

"But now I'm wondering if it was smart to send her back to Panama on the lugger," Padraig winced and adjusted his position in the cart. "I know I suggested it. I couldn't stand it if we kept her around, even as a prisoner. I never want to see her face again." Samuel had paid Captain Molina to take Sara back to Panama, happy to be rid of her.

"You did the right thing." Sofia ran fingers through her tangled hair. "She'd have slowed us down. And where would we have locked her up? Here? *Tio* Hernan doesn't need that headache."

Samuel shifted the holster to stop the Colt digging into his side. "The lugger's charter ended when Harcourt died, and the captain was heading back to Panama anyway. Paying him to take Sara along was the best plan. Now she's no longer a threat."

Sofia cried out and pointed to the house with a moss-speckled Spanish-tiled roof. "Look at this place, it hasn't changed a bit. I hope Tio's home. I'm desperate for news of Filipe."

Perching on a trunk in the cart for two hours had aggravated Samuel's leg wound from the Crimea War, so he massaged it. *Twenty-seven going on seventy. All this action has aged me, and now I must act again to stop William Walker.* "I hope Major Hernan can really help us."

"Of course he can!" Sofia waved at a woman and child dressed in ragged clothes standing on the wild grass of the verge to let the cart pass.

"He was an officer in the *Democrático* army, but that no longer exists."

"It's hard to know who has power these days, with the government so fractured," Padraig scratched at an angry red bite on his forehead.

Axels squeaking and wooden sides creaking, the cart jounced up a rutted road between fields of golden corn, and shirtless men and women in long faded smocks raised their heads to enjoy the distraction—anything to interrupt the monotony of their back-breaking labor. Two skinny boys dropped their rakes and ran beside the cart. A woman in a frayed red dress with a toddler beside her called them back to work.

"Tio will do what he can for us and he'll have news of Filipe." Sofia took off her sweat-soaked hat and wiped her brow. "We're only ten miles from Filipe's hacienda. If Walker's men are stirring up trouble, he'll know." She tapped the driver's shoulder and pointed to the courtyard in front the house. "*Por aqui, a la derecha. Gracias.*"

"And this Garcia fellow who's out to capture us." Samuel handed Sofia his handkerchief. It wasn't exactly clean but it was better than her grubby hand. "We need to know what he's playing at. He must be closely connected to Walker, if he's willing to stick his neck out like this."

She tugged off her oilskin coat. "Look at the state of me. *Tia* Angela will think we're peasants." She shook pearls of rain from the coat and folded it neatly.

As the cart halted on the cobblestone driveway before the imposing double doors made of polished hardwood fastened with gleaming brass studs, one door sung ajar, and a small woman appeared.

"Sofia, *querida*, is that you?" Tia Angela bounded down the stone steps with energy that belied her middle years. "Where did you come from, rolling up in a cart of all things?"

Sofia vaulted over the sideboard and ran to meet her. "Tia, you appear well, *hermosa*." She threw her arms around her aunt and kissed her cheek. "Have you heard from Filipe? We're worried about him."

Angela's eyebrows wormed together as she stepped back. "No. We've not heard from him in several weeks. Hernan was going to ride over there, but bandits raided several of the tenants' homes, and Hernan rode out to hunt for them."

"Where, Tia?"

"Quebrada Amarilla. He left yesterday." Angela's brow wrinkled. "He should have been back by now."

"He went alone?" Samuel glanced sidelong at Padraig. Had Hernan run afoul of filibusters, of Colonel Garcia?

"No, he took ten of the men." Angela shook her head. "Tsk!

I'm sure he's fine. You all look done in. Shame on me for keeping you out here in the sun. Come inside and drink something."

Samuel twisted the brim of his hat in his hand. No word from Filipe, and raiders roaming the plain. The unrest had to be linked to Walker. It was vital to check on Filipe as soon as possible.

An hour later, freshly bathed and dressed in clean clothes, the travelers sat on the shaded veranda eating pork, green vegetables, and sweet potatoes while Angela fussed and directed the two young maids serving them. Samuel fidgeted with the salt cellar as Angela twisted a strand of gray hair. She was worried but trying to hide it. Angela wasn't the only one concerned; Samuel was eager to ride to Filipe's place as soon as they had eaten.

When Sofia finished her story, Angela topped up Padraig's glass of whiskey and swept back the gray curl she'd twisted over and over. "Walker returning . . . That explains all this instability, it's frightening news. We still haven't recovered from his last war —thousands dead, Granada a pile of ashes, neighbors eyeing neighbors with suspicion."

"Well he's not here, Tia." Sofia patted her aunt's wrist. "By now, he's on his way to a British prison."

"It must be his filibusters stirring trouble then." Angela dabbed her shiny forehead with a silk handkerchief. "The robberies, people disappearing. Hernan was right, there's mischief afoot."

"Sofia!" The cry came from the hallway. "You're really here."

The tall girl striding to join them resembled Sofia, but with a lighter complexion and green eyes like Angela's. Her hair swirled like long strands of black silk as she tossed her head, breathless. "Prima Sofia, when Soyla said you were here, we thought she'd been drinking her cooking sherry."

Sofia clapped her hands together and embraced her cousin. "Prima Nelly, look at you! Last time I saw you was when we camped in Las Peñitas. You were only a girl, remember? And now you're a stunning woman. Let me see you." She broke their embrace and stepped back to appraise Nelly.

"You brought your handsome soldier with you . . . and his friend." Nelly's long black eyelashes fluttered like moth wings as she boldly offered Padraig her hand.

"Señorita Nelly, *es un placer volver a verse*. When we met last, you were riding pillion behind some young man." Padraig's cheeks glowed as he released Nelly's hand.

"Oh for goodness sake, Lieutenant, I was only a child then, and Papa insisted I be kind to Major Suñe's brats. I thought boys were perfectly horrible back then, all sweaty and grubby. Now I ride astride like Sofia, even if Mama hates to see me in breeches. I look dashing in them—admit it, Mama, better than this dowdy dress." Nelly spun, whirling her yellow hooped dress in a way that emphasized her slim waist.

Padraig flashed that silly grin he produced for Sara only couple of weeks ago. "Well, we must go riding then. All of us, of course." He flushed under his sunburn and touched the scar on his bridle hand—a wound from the same stroke of the Cossack shashka that had slashed his nose.

Sofia's tender smile at Padraig somehow conveyed both indulgence and impatience. God, Samuel loved that woman. "We won't have time for that. We must discover what—"

Ten pairs of horsemen trotted up the long driveway. The first two peeled off around the house to the stables, while the rest disappeared behind a hedge of purple bougainvillea.

"There's Hernan now." Angela slumped back with a slow smile. "He's going to be surprised."

Moments later, boots clacked on the tiles inside the house, and Hernan Valle strode onto the veranda accompanied by a dark-haired young man. "Sofia! I can't believe it. How? Where did—"

Sofia surged into the major's embrace. "Tio, it's so good to see you."

Major Hernan was heavier than his brother had been, but his dark eyes—sharp as the point of a bayonet—reflected his strong character. The serious young man who settled beside his father, watching and listening intently, had to be his son Lorenzo; Samuel had never met him.

After exchanging greetings, Hernan became all business and ordered them to explain their unexpected arrival. The stream of cigar smoke he blew into the air reminded Samuel of Sofia's father. "Even if the Royal Navy captures Walker, we still have his filibusters to worry about. And his local allies. What will Colonel Garcia do when you don't show up in El Realejo? What exactly did this Harcourt tell him in the message that pigeon carried?"

Samuel pushed away his plate with a sigh. "Sofia related all we know. The message said filibusters failed to capture us down there and he should apprehend us when we landed. What do you know about Garcia, señor?"

Major Hernan blew on the tip of his cigar, and it glowed red. "We fought the *Legitimistas* together, but I never trusted him. He's a landowner, but always covets more. He's now director of Chinandega Department, but it doesn't surprise me he's thrown in with Walker for the promise of more land on top of a political position."

Samuel wet his dry mouth with a sip of whiskey. It tasted bitter and rough. "Director. He'll command a couple of companies, then?"

"Aye, maybe eighty soldiers." Major Hernan spat to the side. "Conscripts and bandits."

Angela frowned at the gob of spittle on the tiles.

"This country's been lawless since the war. Tomás Martínez may be president, but he can't control the warlords grabbing land all over the country. The Central American countries put Martínez in power because he's weak. That way, Nicaragua will never threaten them. Wretches." Major Hernan almost spat again but stopped when his wife knitted her brow. "I keep ten of my old soldiers on the payroll, so men like Garcia don't drive me out. But if Walker's—"

"I'm worried about Filipe, Tio," Sofia burst out. "Tia says you've not seen him for a long time."

"A couple of weeks." Major Hernan tipped his cigar in the ashtray and smiled at Angela. "But that's not unusual. You know how young people are. I'm sure he's fine."

Lorenzo scooted to the edge if his seat. "Come to think of it, Papa, Filipe promised to loan me a stallion to cover Paloma. He should've brought it last week."

The skin prickled on Samuel's arms. "I'd must ride over and see Filipe immediately."

He wouldn't say it, but his sinking stomach told him that they were already too late.

Sofia brushed her fingers down his arm. "You think they have him. Dear God."

Hernan's face tightened. "And what of Garcia and his men at El Realejo?"

Samuel covered her hand on his arm. "If they have Filipe's hacienda, we'll be exposed between two forces." He eyed Padraig, who was apparently dividing his time between smiling at nothing and stealing looks at Nelly who was still batting her eyelids at him. "What do you think, Padraig?"

"About what?"

Samuel sighed and faced Hernan. "We must check on Filipe right away, then we'll worry about Garcia."

"Lorenzo can ride to the coast and watch Garcia." Major Hernan crushed his cigar in the ashtray and looked at his son. "But don't take any chances, lad. Let's get you some horses, and we'll visit Filipe."

CHAPTER FIFTEEN

Sweat trickled down Samuel's back as he skirted the cane field bordering Filipe's house. Major Hernan and his men were waiting a mile down the road while Sofia, Samuel, and Padraig reconnoitered the hacienda. But in the three hours they laid on the edge of the field beneath the scorching sun, they only saw Americans on the property; there was no sign of Filipe or his workers, the Euronica veterans. After leaving Sofia and Padraig to watch the main house, Samuel circled to check the outhouses. Filipe and the others had to be imprisoned somewhere.

He dropped flat in the prickly grass and aimed his spyglass at the granary. A man sat in the shade to the right of the door. His heart skipped a beat. A guard; his friends must be locked inside. He scanned the building. Just one guard—good. If they could free the Euronicas, it would improve the odds, and combined with Hernan's men they might be enough to overcome the fili-busters. They had to be. A mosquito buzzed in his ear, making his skin crawl, and he slapped at it.

Cane plants rustled behind them, and Padraig appeared between the stringy green leaves. "Hernan's looking for an update. It'll be dusk soon, and we need to act." He stiffened and peered at the granary. "There's a—"

Samuel touched his lips with a grubby finger and motioned Padraig to withdraw. A hawk screeched overhead, flapping its wings rapidly, gliding gracefully up into the azure-blue sky.

"Yes, a guard. They must be holding them there. Where's—"

"I saw French on the west veranda, I'd know that one-armed bastard anywhere, it looks like the hoor's in command." Padraig's words were like stones falling on the sunbaked earth. "It's a wonder Walker still trusts him after he lost the gold to us."

French, the man who' double-crossed them their first time in country, was there and in command. Not for long. Samuel drew Padraig along with him. "Filipe and the others are in the granary. We'll free them after dark. So French *was* the rider who escaped that night we took the gold."

"And he was one of the last men to see your father alive. He must've known where they buried him. I think he's the one who spread the information around . . . set the trap."

"Makes sense. It was no coincidence that Filipe found Father's remains. Come, let's tell Sofia and Hernan the plan."

Padraig pushed through the rustling cane after Samuel. "He did it to lure you back to Nicaragua."

Samuel let out a weighted sigh. "Walker wants to force me to return the gold. Or perhaps he just wants revenge."

"Sure, he wants his gold back. Ughh!" Padraig brushed a spider from his sleeve. "Nasty little bugger. We know Walker's short of money. That's why he has men scouring America for backers. There's Major Hernan and his men with Sofia."

Standing behind the major in a trampled clearing at the edge of the cane field, his veterans were a head shorter than Samuel, with dark faces leathered from the equatorial sun beneath their straw hats. Major Hernan swore they were reliable, but Samuel questioned how effective their older rifles would be against the heavily armed Americans.

The sight of Nelly in riding breeches stopped Samuel midstride. "Hernan let her come. Isn't that danger—"

Padraig's low whistle interrupted him. "Sofia's cousin is beautiful. I'll keep her safe. I'm glad she's here."

Sofia lit up and slipped an arm around Samuel's waist. "I saw Filipe when he appeared on his bedroom balcony. He looks well. The others?"

Filipe was in the house, not in the granary. Samuel cursed under his breath. His plan to free them all at once wouldn't work.

Major Hernan ground his cigar stub into the mud. "How many of the bastards are there?"

Samuel fished out his grubby handkerchief and dabbed his neck. "We've counted twenty or so. The Euronicas are locked in the granary, but with Filipe separated from them, it's going to be complicated. Somehow, we must rescue him and the others at the same time. We can't leave hostages they can use against us."

"That will be a challenge. They outnumber us." Major Hernan gazed absently across the cane field in the direction of the house.

"Have you heard from Lorenzo?" Samuel drew his Colt and checked its charges.

"No. He should have been here by now." Major Hernan removed his wide-brimmed hat and ran a hand jerkily through his gray hair. "I hope he's not in trouble."

"He's a sharp lad. He must have found Garcia and settled down to watch him. I'm sure if anything changes in El Realejo, he'll let us know. But we lack the men to assault the house and the granary at the same time." Samuel twisted Father's signet ring on his finger. Padraig wasn't paying attention; only Nelly seemed to interest him. First Sara, now Nelly. If Padraig didn't focus, he'd get someone killed. He kept his voice low and resisted the urge to shake his friend. "Padraig."

The silly grin disappeared from Padraig's face. "Yes?"

"What do you think?"

"Sorry. About what?" The tips of Padraig's ears reddened.

"How can we rescue Filipe and the others at the same time?"

Padraig bit the inside of his lip and squinted down.

He was no help. Samuel drew a deep breath and released it before speaking. "If we free the men, the numbers will be in our favor to attack the house, but that may alert the filibusters, and they might use Filipe as a hostage."

Major Hernan offered a water canteen to Samuel. "Whatever we do, we need to act tonight before Garcia tires of waiting for your boat."

Sofia tugged Samuel's sleeve, causing him to spill water on his shirt. "But what about Filipe? They'll kill him."

Samuel would never allow Filipe to die. He took a long drink to ease his parched throat as his mind raced, then returned the major's canteen. "I've an idea.' He drew his knife, dropped to his haunches, and began to sketch the Valle compound in the dirt. He'd once sworn to never fight again, but he'd fight now to protect those he loved.

He'd fight now to secure his family's future.

The main house and its two wings gleamed pearly white in the moonlight dribbling through the clouds. Lights still burned in several ground-floor windows, but the drunken singing and loud chatter had died an hour ago, before eleven. No doubt the filibusters had helped themselves to the alcohol in Filipe's cellar, and with any luck, they were all deep in a drunken slumber.

Samuel wiped the sweat dripping from his nose and slipped out of the sugarcane field into the shadows on the manicured lawn. It had been five years since his only visit to the Valle estate, and his feelings for Sofia had distracted him then, but tonight she described the house in detail and showed him where he could climb to the balcony outside Filipe's bedroom before the bullets flew.

Stress twitched his left cheek as he rolled his shoulders and loosened the Colt in its holster. Crickets whined a crescendo, and a night bird twittered in the trees. He scanned the hedgerows bordering the driveway. Good, not a sign of Sofia and Nelly where they lay aiming their rifles at the main door. At his suggestion, Hernan's Nicaraguans shed their white shirts and blackened their faces. The disguise worked; he couldn't see them hiding in the fields bordering the lawns.

He rolled his tongue in his parched mouth. It was time.

The tang of limes tickled his nostrils as he dashed between palms and citrus trees to the nearest of the arcades extending across the lawn like the spokes of a wheel. Designed so the family could walk the gardens on rainy days, the arcades provided cover as he raced to the rear of the house. He stopped to catch his breath below a trestle matted with sweet-scented climbing plants at the edge of the veranda beneath Filipe's bedroom. As his panting subsided, he listened. Nothing but the ever-present whine of crickets and the insistent call of a nightjar seeking a mate. Not a sound from inside the house.

He blew on his fingers, flexed them, and stretched high up the trestle for a crosspiece. It creaked when he tested it, but it held his weight. He shoved the tip of his boot through the curtain of green creepers and climbed with the scent of fresh blooms filling his nostrils.

A crosspiece broke with a loud crack, and only a firm grip saved him from falling. He pawed for another crosspiece, his heartbeat pulsing in his ears. Clinging to the rough wood, he hung there, fingers aching. If someone heard that trestle snap, they'd come running.

Not a sound came from the house.

He swung a leg over the balcony rail and landed on the tiled floor. He slipped through the open door into the dark room. It smelled of wood polish and damp clothes.

An arm circled his neck as a blade brushed his windpipe. "*No te meuvas* or I'll kill you."

"Filipe, it's Samuel," he whispered.

"Samuel? *Como—*"

Gunfire popped in the yard. The filibusters had discovered Padraig's rescue of the Euronicas. "We've got to go. To the balcony, *rapido*."

"Hold on." Filipe released him, and the bed creaked as he sat on the mattress to pull on a boot. He had grown and added a lot of muscle. This wasn't the youngster they left behind in San Carlos three years ago; now Filipe was a man.

Shouts came from somewhere inside the house. "Wake up! It's an attack."

"Valle, Valle, Valle—get him, quickly."

"Leave the boots," Samuel hissed, drawing his Colt and cocking the hammer. "We've must leave."

"Ready." Filipe sprang off the bed and darted to the balcony.

Hard soles clattered on the stairs, and a shadow appeared in the landing, outlined against the white tiles. Samuel fired, and a tongue of flame licked out in the darkness. The figure on the landing toppled back with a screech.

Samuel whirled for the balcony, and the trestle creaked as Filipe's head disappeared below the balustrade. He holstered the Colt and swung a leg onto the trestle. Guns barked all around the grounds and inside the house, where men roared and cursed.

Halfway down, the trestle squeaked and swayed away from the balcony with a crack. He flinched. Time moved like treacle as the frame, plant and all, parted from the balcony and pivoted free. He glimpsed Filipe's strained face, pale as marble in the moonlight, before he released his grip and fell with arms flailing. Pain stabbed through his back as the impact punched the air from his lungs. His head struck the ground with a thump, and pins of light flashed before his eyes.

"Here's one," someone drawled.

Click.

He wrenched his eyes open. A disheveled American was lowering a pistol toward his face.

Filipe lunged around a marble column and slashed the man's throat. Crimson blood sprayed the air, glittering rubies in the moonlight. Filipe hurled the body aside as Samuel sat up and held his head. Footsteps clattered in the house behind them.

"Come on." Filipe pulled him to his feet and dragged him across the lawn.

A gun roared, and a bullet drilled the earth a yard to Samuel's right. Shouts in the open air behind them—pursuers. He fumbled out the Colt and fired without aiming. A yelp, and the quiet thunk of someone hitting the turf.

Samuel's toe caught the uneven ground, which sent him sprawling. He rolled with the fall but was so rattled he couldn't gather his feet under him. A second figure skidded to a halt by the fallen filibuster, and the empty left sleeve of his jacket flapped.

Parker French! The smooth-talking swindler who did Walker's dirty work.

Samuel swung the Colt to cover him. "Drop the pistol, French."

"Samuel!" Filipe yelled from the darkness ahead.

French stepped back with a squeak. "Kingston?"

Samuel scrambled to his feet, the Colt unwavering.

French raised his own revolver in reply.

Time for some answers. Samuel fired a shot over French's head. "Next won't miss."

French's handsome face tightened, and he lowered his weapon.

"Get his gun, Filipe."

Filipe wrenched the weapon from French's hand and jammed it into his back.

"This way. Into the cane field." Samuel shook his head to clear it as Filipe shoved French across the moonlit lawn.

"You'll never get away with this," French hissed. "Walker's coming back, and he's going to kill you."

More shouts came from the house, and four filibusters raced onto the veranda. Samuel propelled French onward with a push toward the cane field twenty yards away. Guns barked behind them, and a bullet tugged his sleeve.

Filipe fired over his shoulder three times. "*Bastardos, esta es mi casa.*"

French slowed and halted. He was lean but strong, digging in his heels. Samuel fired the Colt close to French's left ear.

"Curse you, Kingston!" French threw his only hand across his face to touch his ear and staggered forward as musketry crackled all around the grounds, and rifles barked from inside the house.

Samuel sensed filibusters closing in. "They're coming. Hurry, they'll catch us."

Rifle muzzles flared from the field in front of them, the booms echoing across the flatland, and cries of pain split the air behind them.

"This way," Padraig called from the cane.

French staggered and cursed, but Samuel steadied him while forcing him between the closely packed plants. Leaves slapped and scratched at his flesh as they plunged into the thick of it.

"French!" Padraig yelped somewhere ahead in the cane. "Sweet Virgin Mary. Nice catch, Samuel. Hello there, Filipe."

Men yelled and cursed in the distance, and guns roared from the gardens, but the lawn was empty. Nobody was chasing them. Samuel pushed through the tall leaves toward Padraig's voice, halted French, and poked the Colt's barrel at his chest. "Call off your men—now. If they don't throw down their weapons and surrender, the Nicaraguans will slaughter them. But you'll die first."

"All right." French's voice was shrill. "I'll talk to them." As cowardly as ever when it came down to it.

Thank God it was over.

Padraig embraced Filipe. "You've grown. I hardly recognize the scrawny sprat I knew."

Samuel touched Padraig's arm, as much for comfort as to catch his attention. "What went wrong over there? The shots?"

Padraig pawed the sweat beading his upper lip. "I never saw

the second guard, but he was inside. He shot Calvo. He killed Calvo before I could stop him."

Roberto Calvo had been with the Euronicas from the beginning. They used to joke that the light-complexioned Calvo, with his green eyes, looked like a chubby Irishman. Samuel winced, remembering how Calvo had risked infection to care for the soldiers stricken with cholera on the voyage from El Realejo to San Juan del Sur several years ago.

"He's dead, Calvo's dead." Padraig's voice broke as he lowered his gaze.

Samuel's breath hitched. Their world was spinning out of control. Poor, harmless Calvo. He'd always fought with heart, but the little man had been too gentle to be a soldier. That was why he'd been the only Euronica not to join Samuel's attack on the San Juan River forts in fifty-seven. How many more would die to feed Walker's ambition?

Filipe punched Parker in the stomach. "You people don't belong here. I'm—"

"Not now." Samuel stepped between them and shoved Parker back toward the house. "Come on, we're going to call off your dogs."

Padraig and Filipe fell in beside him.

Samuel lowered his voice. "The others? Chavez, Cortez?"

"The rest are safe. Twenty of them." Padraig sounded exhausted. "Bloody filibusters, we should hang them all. What next? What else has Walker planned?"

Samuel stared down at his hands. Calvo dead. This madness had to stop.

They had to stop Walker.

∽

The odor of unwashed bodies, tobacco smoke, and damp clothing was overpowering in the drawing room where the Euronicas, Major Hernan, and Samuel's party had gathered.

Emanuel Chavez, the short, muscular Indian who'd once been a priest, was the Euronicas' unofficial chief. Even wiry Sergeant Zamora followed his lead. Defrocked for his unconsummated love for a nun named Teresa, Chavez had enlisted in the Democrat army to avoid prison back in eighty-four at the height of Nicaragua's civil war. Chavez and Teresa had become Samuel's trusted friends, and eventually moved to the Valle hacienda as Filipe's advisors.

The filibusters inside the hacienda had apparently believed themselves surrounded by a hundred troops, and surrendered immediately. Now they were locked up the granary where they'd imprisoned the Euronicas.

Besides Chavez, Pedro Cortez was the only Euronica who spoke English; the young African Carib had grown up near the British naval base at Bluefields, north of Greytown on the Caribbean coast. He hadn't stopped flashing his gap-toothed grin since his release from the granary.

Shifting from foot to foot, Samuel scanned the familiar faces. They were the best soldiers he'd ever trained, but he'd not seen them in over three years, and people changed, circumstances changed. Would they follow him now? He lifted his hands. "*Silencio.*" When the excited chatter petered out, he gestured to the pile of dry wood stacked outside the window. "The threat of burning the filibusters alive, as General Guardiola did to their comrades a few years ago, untangled French's tongue. His news isn't good, I'm afraid."

A murmur of Spanish swelled.

Samuel steeled himself to lay bare his failings to the men who'd once trusted him with their lives. "My plan to have the Royal Navy capture Walker and his volunteers offshore of Greytown. It's finished. It won't work. Walker outsmarted me. He never intended to sail to Greytown as I'd believed. French revealed he's taking his army to Roatán, an island in the Caribbean. Once he captures it, he'll join forces with the Honduran rebel leader, General Cabañas, and they'll march west across Honduras to El Triunfo and cross the frontier into Nicaragua."

"Sweet Blessed Virgin, save us." Chavez touched the wooden cross at his neck. "That will put them only twenty-five miles from here."

Samuel sat on the arm of Sofia's overstuffed chair. Chavez was right to be alarmed. "Walker's coming to Chinandega. He promised this estate to French."

Men gasped and swore, several of the Euronicas' jaws slackened, and Sofia slumped back in the chair as conversations broke out around the room.

Filipe clapped his chest. "I'll die before that *bastardo* sets foot in our home."

"And yet his filibusters captured the estate." Samuel tapped the rolled-up map in his hand with a finger. He provided the ships for Walker's invasion, forgetting that a man of Walker's exceptional intellect would always be three moves ahead of his enemies. But he refused to berate himself for playing into Walker's hands. "Well, Filipe, he'll be here soon if we do nothing to stop him. There's another wrinkle according to French. Colonel Garcia has orders to commandeer a riverboat at La Virgen after he captures us. He'll use it to seize the forts at San Carlos and El Castillo."

They'll control the San Juan River then." Cortez's dark eyes flicked back and forth between Samuel and Padraig.

"Exactly, allowing more volunteers from America to cross the isthmus and swell Walker's new army." But not if Samuel could help it.

"We have some time if Garcia is at the dock waiting for us to arrive." At the back of the room, Padraig winked at Nelly.

"I fear not. Remember that northerly wind delayed *La Esperanza* for days. We're overdue, and Garcia must suspect something's awry. For all we know, Garcia may have decided to move on and attack the forts." If only Lorenzo would report in. What was keeping him?

Sofia touched Samuel's hand. "But Sara's pigeon would have warned Garcia we're coming."

Samuel forgot the messenger pigeon in all the fuss. "Then he'll still be waiting for us in El Realejo. That's good, but it doesn't change the plan. Padraig and I will ride to Greytown to warn the Royal Navy. There's still time to divert the warships to Roatán, but we must hurry."

What does the Royal Navy have to do with it?" Cortez tugged his collar and undid the button at his throat.

"They're already under orders to capture Walker. Roatán and the other Bay Islands are British territories, and Britain doesn't want Walker meddling there." Samuel sucked his cheeks in. The navy had better catch the filibuster.

Padraig's broad forehead creased. "How do you know French isn't lying again?"

Samuel stood and spread his feet wide. "He didn't. He even told me the name of the inn where the rebels meet in Tela, on the mainland, El Oveja Negra."

"The Black Sheep." Padraig rolled his eyes. "How appropriate. But how does he know that?"

Why didn't Padraig just trust Samuel's instincts? French hadn't lied. Samuel released a slow breath. "French was to send a messenger there for Walker once he and Colonel Garcia had captured me." Walker wasn't going to get that message anytime soon.

Padraig raised an eyebrow. "We'll give Walker a very different message when the navy surprises him in Roatán."

"Quiet." Major Hernan raised a hand to quell the chatter of several conversations in the heating room. "One person speak at a time. Walker could be in Roatán already. How can you catch him? It's a two day ride from here to La Virgen and another full day and night on a riverboat to reach Greytown."

Chavez rubbed the back of his thick neck. "How long will it take the Royal Navy to mobilize?"

Samuel rushed to answer him. There was no time to waste on

a debate. "They should be waiting off Greytown for him already." But Walker wasn't going there, he had never intended to. "If he's in Roatán already, the navy will have to follow him there."

Throwing up his hands, Padraig moved to the center of the room beside Samuel. "Good luck with that. If Walker reaches mainland Honduras, I can't see a bunch of marines catching him in the jungle. He and his volunteers will run rings around those lobsters.

"That's why we're going to help the British." Samuel pushed up his sleeves and glanced at Sofia. She did not meet his eyes. He'd failed to dissuade her from coming, but at least she agreed to stay in Greytown. If they had to pursue Walker, the jungle was no place for a genteel woman, no matter how brave and handy she was with a gun. He scanned the frowning faces in the room. "I've no right to ask this of you, but it's your country, your freedom we're fighting for, and you are the most experienced pathfinders in Central America. Together we can track Walker down before he links with Cabañas's main rebel force, and together we can stop him once and for all. I ask you to ride with Padraig and me."

The room erupted as men closed around Samuel, shouting their agreement and volunteering noisily. He raised a hand for quiet, but before he could continue, Filipe pushed through the others. Filipe had to be eighteen, nineteen now, but he commanded the men's attention. Samuel glanced at Sofia. Their father would've been proud of him.

Filipe gestured to the men. "Of course we'll join you. You taught Chavez and Jimenez to ride like lancers years ago, and I insisted they train the others. Nicaragua has been lawless since the civil war, and we learned to defend ourselves. We are ready, and we can ride. We dropped our guard once, and those pirates caught us by surprise. It won't happen again."

Seated at the head of the table, Major Hernan steepled his fingers. "I'll remain here with my men in case Garcia sweeps by here on his way to La Virgen."

"He outnumbers you eight to one." Samuel didn't want another Valle murdered.

"I know." Major Hernan jut out his jaw. "But my men are veterans, experienced and all mounted. We'll harass them from a distance and force them to fight for every yard they advance."

Their body heat flushed Samuel as the men fidgeted and closed in. He glanced at the windows that had been thrown wide open. There wasn't a puff of breeze to cool him. "Garcia will make for La Virgen, señor, but you should wait here in case I'm wrong. Now . . . We'll need horses if we're to have any hope getting there before him. We'll commandeer a steamer at La Virgen. Padraig can helm it across Lake Nicaragua and down the San Juan River to Greytown."

Major Hernan frowned. "What about the rapids at El Castillo?"

Samuel perched on the arm of Sofia's chair again. "With any luck there'll be another riverboat moored downstream from the rocks. If not, we must risk powering over them. We managed it back in fifty-five."

"And almost ripped the bottom out of the boat." Sofia laughed nervously.

Far more lives were at stake this time. Samuel pitched his voice low and evenly, ignoring the knot in his stomach. "The second time is always a charm."

Filipe lifted his chin. "Between Tio Hernan and myself, we can muster at least twenty-five horses. That enough?"

The others whispered animatedly as Samuel calculated the numbers. "Should be. We'll also—"

Lorenzo trotted into the room, his shirt soaked with sweat, and everyone talked at once as he spoke in the major's ear. Samuel held his breath.

Hernan patted his son's shoulder and clapped his hands. "Silencio." When the men fell silent, he dipped his head in approval. "Garcia has loaded his men on a ship call *La Esparanza* and sailed south."

La Esparanza! Why had the lugger continued north after dropping them off? Samuel grimaced. Sara must have convinced Captain Molina to carry on to El Realejo, perhaps with the promise of a reward. So she wasn't the innocent victim she'd claimed to be but rather a cold and calculating trickster. "*La Esparanza* is the boat that delivered us here."

"That wretched woman." Sofia pounded a hand on the table.

"And warned Colonel Garcia we'd avoided his trap." Samuel unrolled the map. But why would Garcia embark his men on *La Esparanza*?

The scar on Padraig's nose purpled as a flush crept across his cheeks. "He's sailing to San Juan del Sur."

Lorenzo darted a glance at his father. "That's what delayed me. I crept close enough to overhear his men. They were happy the boat showed up as it saved them a long march south to La Virgen."

Sofia squeezed Samuel's hand. "He's going to seize the forts on the river."

"French told the truth." The enemy was a step ahead again. Samuel scanned the wide-eyed faces around the room. "And traveling by sea, he'll get there quickly."

Spontaneous conversations filled the room.

Samuel raised his arm for quiet. "Silencio. For God's sake, be quiet."

The room settled.

"If we stop Walker, Garcia will fold. What's he got left to fight for?" Samuel's throat was parched. He picked up his glass of whiskey and took a drink, the bitter liquid stung his throat.

Sofia nodded her agreement.

"Then we'd best ride hard." Samuel rolled his shoulders and adjusted the Colt at his waist. "If Garcia beats us to the river, he'll control the riverboats. Hernan, this makes your mission easier. Now you only need to worry about French and the other filibuster prisoners. Watch out for more factions like the ones who boarded our ship. Fortunately, they are few and scattered, but you'll have to round them up when this is over."

Hernan tossed back the rest of his rum. "We'll keep French and his cronies locked up, and if more Filibusters appear, we'll deal with them. You concentrate on Walker. Nicaragua's fate lies in your hands. Catch Walker in Roatán, and his ally, Cabañas, won't dare invade us."

Samuel stood poised with a lightness he didn't feel. They faced a hard ride south during the rainy season in a race against time and nature, and if Garcia beat them to Lake Nicaragua, they'd battle a force four times larger than their own. Padraig shoved his hands in his pockets and peered away out the window. It was obvious he felt the same. If only Sofia weren't adamant about going. But he knew better than to waste time arguing with her; he'd lost that argument five years ago.

Bedlam erupted in the room: people shouting and arguing, chest-bumping and bravado. Samuel pounded his fist on the table. "Enough. Gather weapons and horses. Filipe, have your servants pack tortillas and dried meat, some of the lads will help. We leave in one hour, and may God ride with us. If Walker triumphs, he'll abolish the slavery ban and make slaves of you and your families. Nicaragua's freedom—your freedom— depends on you now."

CHAPTER SIXTEEN

The chestnut mare was breathing hard as she approached the top of the last rise before La Virgen Bay, her flanks lathered with sweat and flecked with mud. The brooding sky promised rain. Lots of it. Samuel rubbed his gritty eyes and peered north at the hill where Legitimist scouts had killed Arias and Sabora five years ago, at the beginning of the Battle of La Virgen, the first Euronicas sacrificed at the altar of Walker's unbridled ambition. He coughed to clear his scratchy throat. How many more had to die before he brought Walker to justice? None, if he could help it. In Greytown he'd drop Ambassador Lyons's name shamelessly to convince the Royal Navy to divert to Roatán.

Padraig coaxed his horse alongside Samuel. "Last time we came this way, we carried a fortune in gold. We were rushing to catch a boat that time, too."

"I'd return it all to see Walker ruined." Samuel reined in the mare.

Lake Nicaragua stretched to the misty horizon, vast as an ocean and glittering like beaten bronze in the light of the setting sun. Six miles offshore smoke floated from the hollow top of Concepción volcano on Ometepe Island, crowning the jagged cone like a cotton garland. At the lakeshore below them lay their destination: La Virgen. The Accessory Transit Company terminal, established by Cornelius Vanderbilt, hadn't changed a bit since he'd helped Walker win his first victory. The substantial offices of the ATC dwarfed the small hotel and businesses lining both sides of the one-street village.

The sight of two riverboats at the narrow jetty made Samuel grope for his spyglass.

Padraig's mare threw up her head, and her bridle clinked as she chomped at the wild grass. He teased back the reins. "Steady, girl . . . Two boats."

Samuel scanned the side-wheelers floating either side of the dock with bows pointing at the endless lake, each with a black funnel in stark contrast to their white hulls pinked in the setting sun. "We can take our pick."

Padraig pulled his spyglass from his pocket and rose in the stirrups. "The bigger one looks like the *Wheeler*. I remember it. The other could be the *Machuca*, the boat we used to capture the forts last time we were here. We should take her; she's bound to bring us luck."

"Forget your superstition. We'll take the fastest one." Samuel moved his lens to the street. Nothing stirred.

"How the hell do I know which one's fastest?" Padraig swept both boats with his own spyglass. "Smoke's coming from the *Machuca's* funnel . . . her boiler's fired. That's the one we must take."

"If she hasn't sailed by the time we bring the men up." They left Sofia and the others at the farm of a Valle family acquaintance close to town. The owner would keep the horses until they returned.

Samuel swiveled his lens to the smaller boat. A chain of four men were passing logs from a pile at the end of the jetty onto the lower deck, but he saw nobody else on board. Likely there were firemen and an engineer down in the engine room. It was hard to see inside the lower deck in the failing light, although Samuel scrutinized it yard by yard. A flash of white drew his attention. A man in the shabby white shirt and trousers worn by most soldiers in Central America appeared and threw a cigarette into the water.

Samuel's stomach sank. "Garcia beat us to it. Look at the entry port."

Padraig jerked his spyglass around. "Two guards."

"Where are the rest of his men?" Samuel surveyed the main street again. "He must be holding them out of town until they're ready to sail so they don't get drunk. Go tell the others to hurry. I'll scout the town for Garcia's men. We need to sail on the *Machuca* before they do."

"True. If not, it'll take hours to raise steam on the *Wheeler*." Padraig shut his spyglass. "If they reach the fort at the river mouth first—"

"—they can turn the fort's guns on us," Samuel finished.

"Well for goodness' sake, don't take any stupid risks when you go down there. Where shall we meet?"

Where indeed? Samuel scanned the village. "The stable where we bivouacked the last time, on the edge of town. All the lads will remember it. I'll mark where Garcia's troops are holed up so you can steer clear." He adjusted the cartridge belt on his shoulder, dismounted, and handed his reins to Padraig.

"Fair enough. Be careful." Padraig wheeled his horse and trotted off leading Samuel's chestnut. Samuel needed stealth and would continue through the village on foot.

Thirty minutes later, the sky darkened, and the rain began, drops as big as grapes pounding the muddy road. Samuel pulled on his oilskin coat. He could no longer see the town he was scouting, but that was a good thing—he'd be less visible. Tucking the Henry rifle under his coat, he started down the hill, scanning both sides of the road. Visibility was down to four yards. His back and legs ached, the two-day ride had chafed his thighs, and his clothing stank, sticking stiffly to him. He prowled past the deep puddles and rain-filled ruts toward the lake. Nobody had added more gravel to the mettaled road since the Accessory

Transit Company stopped sailing to Nicaragua. Not surprising. The Filibuster War had impoverished the country. Heaven help the people if Walker ignited another conflict.

Samuel passed the blurry shadows of wooden shacks typical of this region, frequently cocking his head to listen with his good ear. The sound of a cough rewarded him, and he froze. A sentry? He sidestepped onto the grassy verge and followed it until a cluster of rickety buildings loomed from the mist. A farm. A door creaked open, and the miserly light from within revealed a soldier stepping inside. There was no guard—typical of a sloppy conscript army.

Crouching, he rushed to the farmhouse and flattened his back against the rough boards of the wall. Faint beams of light trickled from the gaps in the vertical siding planks. The muted conversation inside was barely audible above the drumming rain. He pulled off his drenched hat and pressed his face against the rough boards, and warm smoky air stung his eye as he peeped through a gap. Soldiers packed the house, all in tattered white shirts, trousers rolled up to their knees, and their bare feet covered in mud.

Garcia's men.

A burst of laughter erupted from the outhouse behind the farmhouse. More soldiers. Samuel retreated to the road, where he knotted his handkerchief to the branch of a tree. Padraig would understand the warning and bypass the farm. He slunk toward the terrace of adobe houses where he'd attacked a flank of charging Legitimist troops in eighty-five, pushing away the memory of the bloodied bodies littering the road and wounded men crying out for help.

A shirtless figure plodded past him, head down against the rain. Loud voices issued from the open shutters of a terraced building on the north side of the street, the commercial part of town. Samuel crossed to the shadows on the south side and paused. Inside the open window three officers in black uniforms were walking through the smoky restaurant toward the door.

Coming outside.

He darted east toward the lake and ducked behind a low fence. Light spilled onto the muddy street, and the three officers stepped outside. Pale-complexioned and tall, likely they were typical of the wealthy officers who'd served on both sides in the civil war. Legitimist or Democrat, it hadn't mattered; they'd fought to seize property from the other side, and their victims were the peasants they whipped into battle to do their dirty work.

One, with a rakish tilt to his peaked cap, lit the long cheroot slanted between his fingers and exhaled a stream of smoke. "I don't care if it's raining. The riverboat has steam up, and we must leave. It'll take all night to cross the lake, and I want to land at San Carlos before dawn. Get that scum aboard her."

Icy fingers slid down Samuel's spine. Padraig and the others would be on their way by now, but he couldn't go back to warn them. These officers would spot him. He could only trust that Padraig would see his handkerchief and take to the adjoining fields. Samuel would have to carry on and somehow delay the boat.

The rain ceased with tropical swiftness as he crouched beside the palisade surrounding the Accessory Transit Company depot. Nobody moved on either of the riverboats at the jetty, but sparks squirted from the smaller boat's funnel, and it was, indeed, the *Machuca*. The guards *had* to be there.

He sucked in his cheek and fingered the rifle lever under his coat. Nothing was going to plan. Garcia shouldn't have arrived first, and now he and his men would march up that road any minute and take to the lake, denying Samuel the boat. There had to be some way to stall him, but nothing came to mind. His only hope was the narrowness of the jetty stretching across the shallows into the lake, a bottleneck—that and the Henry rifle with the firepower of ten men.

If Garcia had eighty soldiers, those were overwhelming odds against Samuel's twenty-three rifles. But Garcia's men were conscripts, ill-trained and ill-disciplined compared to the Euronicas, who could fire volleys as fast as the vaunted Black Watch Highlanders. If he had to, he would hold the jetty and hope his men would come running when the gunfire started.

He pressed his lips together, drew his Colt, and sprinted to the inky lake. In the sudden silence, he realized the rain had stopped and moonlight silvered the parting clouds.

His boots sank in the damp sand before clunking on the timber jetty. Speed was his only hope. He headed for the *Machuca*, the boat he'd used to capture the river three years ago. Would she be lucky as Padraig had said? He raced up the gangplank, past two sleeping guards who never stirred as he tossed their muskets into the lake and slipped between them. Steam hissed up from the companionway; the firemen and engineer must be down in the engine room. They wouldn't hear him above the racket down there.

Cocking the Colt, he nudged one guard with his boot. "*Levántate*. On your feet."

The man stirred, opened his dark eyes, and yelped. He bolted upright as his companion woke and cringed.

"Don't shoot me." The second guard threw up his arm like a shield.

"*Cállate*." Samuel pointed to the narrow companionway. "Get below to the engine room."

The ashen-faced pair shambled across the deck with a cowed demeanor that assured him they'd be no trouble. He scowled and jabbed the air with the Colt. "Get below and tell the engineer if I don't have full steam when I call for it, I'll slaughter all of you."

He slammed the door behind them and tied off the handle with a piece of rope cut from a fender. Now for the captain. More rope in hand, he skipped up the stairs to the top deck, crossed to the wheelhouse steps, and continued climbing to the wheelhouse. The captain was dozing behind his spoked wheel, a small, unshaven man with receding hair and a weather-whittled face.

"*Levántate.* Quickly." Samuel poked him.

The captain jumped to his feet with a curse. "*Qué?* What the —who are you?"

"*Cállate.* I'm taking your boat. Come out here and face the gunwale." He bound the man's hands and tied him to the guardrail. "Move an inch and I'll kill you. Understand?"

"*Sí, sí.*" The captain bobbed his head like a bird.

Now came the hardest part: waiting. Samuel moved to the forward rail on the port side of the wheelhouse, where he could cover the jetty, and removed his coat. Time for a smoke. He was puffing his second cigarette when white-clad figures appeared at the corner of the ATC building. He took one last drag, quenched the stub on the guardrail, and removed his cartridge belt for easy access.

When he made out a black uniform among the white ones, he brought the rifle to his shoulder. The smooth stock was cool against his cheek, reassuring. Sighting the officer, he held his breath and squeezed the trigger. The muzzle flash blinded him fleetingly as he sidestepped along the rail, firing as quickly as he could work the lever. Halting at the wheelhouse, he worked his way toward the jetty side again, firing all the while. He would convince the enemy there were many defenders on the boat.

By the time the Henry was empty, Garcia's men were crouching on the beach and shouting into the chaos. Let the confused buggers puzzle over how many they faced. He tipped the hot barrel to forty-five degrees, slid up the tab, twisted the sleeve, and fed shells down the tube. As he worked, a handful of muskets blazed along the sand, wild shots that came nowhere near him.

He finished loading and peered through the darkness at the beach. An officer swinging his sword was driving a dozen men forward. Samuel fired at them and dodged left with lead balls pecking the boat's hull beneath him. Thank God those muskets were inaccurate at that range.

A wave of white-clad soldiers advanced down the beach, and Samuel fired over and over, until the air stank of gun smoke and hot metal. The rifle's fore end grew so hot he could no longer hold it, so he rested the barrel on the guardrail. His shoulders curled. When the Henry ran out of rounds, he would not dare to reload the hot gun; he couldn't even hold the barrel. He fired again, and a white figure danced grotesquely before collapsing on the beach. Six bodies lay scattered about, but dozens of soldiers advanced across the silver sand. They paused to fire their muskets and took a knee to reload. Thank God they were undrilled and slow.

Click! The Henry was empty again.

Moonlight glimmered on bayonets as screaming officers drove the hesitant attackers closer. The first line was ten yards from the jetty now, their curses and bellows flooding the tropical night air. The Henry's barrel was steaming and the stock slippery with sweat when he laid it on the deck and drew his Colt. His lip trembled. Where were his comrades? Time suspended, every-thing happening slowly, drawn out like an infinite thread. *Come on, Padraig, come on.* Heartbeat thrumming in his temple, he kept firing, counting off the shots. He tensed, brittle and grim-faced, and pulled the trigger again.

The first man to charge the jetty clutched his ribs and toppled into the shallow water. Samuel shot at an officer who was shoving men closer. He missed.

"Damn you."

He fired again, acrid gun smoke stinging his eyes, and the officer spun back clutching his shoulder. The men by the jetty hesitated as the officer hit the ground. Samuel fired his last shot, holstered the Colt—it would take too long to load— and braced himself to pick up the steaming rifle.

"*Adelante*, you cowards," someone roared from the beach.

The Henry's fore end scorched Samuel's fingers as he fed

bullets into the tube. A soldier bellowed, jumped up, and charged down the jetty. Five shells must serve. He twisted the sleeve back, released the follower, and worked the lever as the sound of bare feet pounded closer.

When he hefted the rifle, the soldier was ten yards away, his dark face twisted with aggression. Samuel fired from the hip, and the Henry kicked in his hands. A black rose blossomed on the soldier's white shirt as the slug hurled him back onto the jetty's planks.

Samuel aimed at the men hesitating behind their fallen comrade and pulled the trigger. Nothing happened.

His rifle was jammed.

He dropped the Henry and fumbled for his cartridge box and the Colt. He'd never reload in time. Oh Lord, he was out of time.

Shouts erupted from the main street, where dark figures double-timed onto the beach into two lines.

"Firing by rank," called a voice from the far end. "Front row, ready. Aim."

Rifles stocks swung to a dozen shoulders. Several bullets slipped from Samuel's fumbling fingers and clattered onto the planks.

"Fuego!"

The rifles blazed yellow tongues in the moonlight with an eruption like thunder. Samuel squeezed his eyes shut.

Screams and thuds sounded from the jetty. Samuel opened his eyes. A handful of Garcia's men toppled, and the men who had been advancing up the jetty were falling back.

"Front row, load. Rear row, aim." That was Sergeant Zamora's voice, as calm as Sergeant Major Wagner's from Samuel's days with the Seventeenth Lancers. "Fuego!"

Twelve rifles barked as one in the swirling smoke, and minié balls cut down four more white-clad soldiers. Several others spun on their bare heels and raced north up the beach. Twenty seconds later the Euronicas fired another volley, and more of Garcia's men fell. The rest of his troops stuttered to a halt and retreated.

"Fix bayonets."

Rasp.

The metallic snicks made Samuel's heart soar as he rammed a ball into the Colt's chamber. The lads were faster than ever. Filipe must have kept them drilling for months.

"Charge." Padraig's bark launched the Euronicas toward Garcia's wavering band, leaving Sofia alone.

Garcia's men broke and ran, many dropping their muskets as they fled.

Sofia sprinted down the beach and up the jetty. "Samuel." Her voice was barely audible above the cheers and Padraig's sharp recall whistle to the men.

Samuel holstered the Colt and hurried to the lower deck. "Here. I'm fine."

By the time he hugged Sofia, the Euronicas were streaming to the jetty, chattering loudly and clapping one another's backs.

Sofia's shirt was damp with sweat, but she smelled like apple blossoms when he kissed her lips. "In the nick of time, darling. We must away, leave before they regroup."

Padraig approached with his cheeky grin. "This is getting old. How many times must I save your ass?"

He shook Padraig's clammy hand, plans already filling his mind. "The captain's up top, but you helm the boat. Let's get going. Where are Florez and Rivera? They worked the engine room for Spencer last time. They can guard the firemen."

Sofia had discovered two casks on the starboard side. "This is gunpowder and lead shot. They must've loaded it already."

"We've enough with us, and the lead shot won't work. The lads' rifles fire minié balls. Sergeant Zamora, guard the jetty."

They completed preparations for departure in less than

twenty minutes, and there was still no sign of the enemy by the time Padraig conned the steamer onto the lake. Samuel untied the captain—the man's name was Cardoso—since the old fellow was no threat.

"Sorry, *Capitán*, but I assure you we mean no harm." Samuel drew his Colt and rummaged in his cartridge box for his powder horn. "You'll get your boat back when we reach Greytown if the rapids don't rip the keel off her. But *Tempest* crossed them once, we can do it again."

Cardoso gaped at Samuel. "You're the ones, eh? The Europeans who captured the river forts in the war. I never believed the stories, but it's true."

"Hmm?" Samuel cast him a bemused smile.

"You speak perfect Spanish, and you fight like demons. It must be you." A broad smile cracked the captain's face. "God bless you for ridding us of Walker. You're welcome to the boat. It's not mine anyway. But why now? Why are you back?"

"Walker's begun another invasion, and we need to reach Greytown to have any chance of stopping him. Those men back on the jetty serve Walker."

"Colonel Garcia?"

"Si. I'm afraid so."

"So he's a traitor." Cardoso spat over the gunwale. "May he rot in hell."

"If he's rotting, he'll have to do it back there." Padraig emerged from the wheelhouse. "Would you like the helm back, Capitán? I need to roll a smoke."

"Aye . . ." Cardoso hesitated.

Something was wrong. Samuel tilted his head and fixed eyes on Cardoso. "What's the matter?"

"Did you see how many of them there were back there? There must've been a hundred of them." Padraig paused spreading tobacco on his paper and winked at Cardoso. "Sixty left now. If they're lucky. Don't worry about them, Skipper."

Samuel frowned. Sometimes Padraig's jokes went too far. The

men back there hadn't deserved to die. They hadn't even known why they were fighting. But Garcia and his officers, they were a different story.

"But even you can't defeat sixty men." Cardoso squinted down at his compass and teased his helm to port.

"We don't have to." Padraig slapped the bulkhead with a chuckle. "We're on the lake, and they're stuck back there."

A vein pulsed in the wrinkled skin of Cardoso's neck. "Garcia will chase you in the *Wheeler*, and she's a much faster boat."

"By the time he gets up steam, we'll be over the horizon." Padraig ducked his head into the wheelhouse and lit his cigarette.

Cardoso eyed the smoking cigarette and licked his lips. "It's a long way—seventy miles across the lake and one hundred and twenty miles down the San Juan River to Greytown."

"I know." Padraig pulled out his tobacco. "Want a smoke?"

Cardoso nodded rapidly. "Si. But there's no riverboat scheduled to dock on the other side of the rapids at El Castillo. This boat's older now; I don't think she'll survive a run over the rapids. You'll be stuck at El Castillo if Garcia doesn't catch you first."

Samuel numbed inside, and he cast his eyes to the dark horizon to hide his despair. Surprise had overcome the odds for now, but once Garcia caught them on the river, trapping them between his sixty muskets, the jagged rocks, and whirlpools of the rapids, they would be in trouble.

"This afflicted country." Padraig pounded the guardrail. "We never get a break."

The engine panted rhythmically, and the paddles churned the water, propelling *Machuca* across the lake stretched like a silver mirror to the horizon beneath a billion twinkling stars, a tranquil, watery paradise. But on the river, at the storming rapids, they'd have to fight for their lives. Samuel's eyes found Sofia standing with Cortez and Chavez on the lower deck, and his hand trembled. Had he doomed his beloved?

~

Six hours of sleep revived Samuel and lifted his spirits. His desperate plan even seemed possible as he stood beside Padraig on the small platform outside the wheelhouse, squinting against the morning sun at the shadowed walls of Fort San Carlos high above the turquoise waters of the lake. The eight cannons crouching like toads at the crenulations on the ancient Spanish fort's walls were no threat. The small garrison would've grown soft in peacetime. They'd no idea another war was coming.

Samuel accepted a neatly rolled cigarette from Padraig. "Are the logs ready?"

Padraig displayed a half dozen fresh cuts on his hands. "Jimenez and I scraped them out last night—sliced our hands to shit, we did. Dry wood's the worst to work on. But they're stuffed and glued, so nobody can tell we meddled with them."

"Good. When we take on fuel, make sure you leave them on top of the pile at the depot. It's imperative the *Wheeler* takes them aboard."

"I know. Look, Sofia's calling you down to breakfast. She and Nelly share a resemblance, no? I think I'll visit Nelly in Chinandega when this is all over."

Samuel tugged at his stinking shirt. If they survived. "Brothers-in-arms become brothers-in-law?"

Padraig grinned.

Samuel stuck his head into the wheelhouse and lit his cigarette. Was Padraig rushing into another relationship again? This time the family dynamics were complicated; Nelly was Sofia's cousin. He watched the end of his cigarette glow for a few seconds. "Nelly's sweet and seems capable, but don't rush things this time. Remember what your father says: 'marry in haste—"

"—and repent at leisure.'" Padraig rubbed the back of his neck. "I know, I know. It's just that I . . . This time it's different. Nelly's different. But I'll take it slowly . . . I promise."

Samuel nudged him, shoulder to shoulder. "Then, I'll

support you. I'm sure we'll get along fine, much better than the Earls of Lucan and Cardigan." He didn't have to force a smile at the memory of the squabbling cavalry commanders in Crimea.

"Buggers nearly got us all killed. I hope you wouldn't do the same." Padraig slid an arm over his shoulder. "I'm the skipper here. Who knows when we'll eat next? Go eat your rice and beans, rice and beans—"

"—rice and beans, rice and beans," Samuel joined in.

They laughed.

But even some time later, after noon, Samuel's stomach still grumbled—thanks to the beans—as he sat on the upper deck with Sofia teaching Cortez, Chavez, and Jimenez to play his favorite card game, Patience.

Tapping his fingers on the table, Cortez peered at the cards, his sweating face shining like polished mahogany. He was a handsome young man despite the acne scars that marred his face.

"Stop wasting time, Cortez. You're stuck," Jimenez gloated. "It's my turn."

Cortez ran a hand through his tight black curls. "You can't even count."

Jimenez gave a disgusted snort. "The numbers only go to nine, and there are pictures anyway. I got all the cards out last time, didn't I?"

Chavez exchanged looks with Cortez and wiggled his eyebrows. "Because you cheated. There's no such thing as an honest thief."

"Oh, go back to your saints, Chavez." Jimenez poked a finger at the tattered bible in Chavez's hand. "Come on, Cortez, give up. You're stuck."

Cortez huffed and scattered his cards on the scarred tabletop. "Pah, what a stupid game. It's pointless, wasting all this time only to get stuck. Why can't you teach us that game the *yanquis* play?"

"Poker?" Jimenez caught a windswept card in midair. "That's

a gambling game, isn't it? You think you can take our money then, Cortez?"

"Like you could," Cortez scoffed.

Typical soldiers, all they did was argue and complain. At least the card game was keeping their mind off the dangers ahead. Samuel's stomach rumbled again. Bloody beans.

Sofia nudged him. "Stomach problems? Don't forget to lift the toilet seat before you go."

He laughed despite his quivering stomach. She was a little devil to prod him about the accident that had caused them to meet five years ago. "That only happens going upriver. We should reach El Castillo soon, then we'll see what the *Machuca*'s made of."

"I hope there's a boat there."

"If not—"

"If not, we should wait." Sofia rubbed her hands down her breeches. "It's madness to drive the boat over the rapids."

That looming threat had Samuel's already delicate stomach in knots, but what choice did they have?

A burst of excited chatter aft caused him to twist around.

"Capitán." Roy Perez raced forward and pointed behind his shoulder. "Another steamboat at the river bend."

"They've caught us." Samuel jumped to his feet and snatched up his rifle. Sofia was already standing. "Darling, please—"

"Not again, Samuel. I'm fighting." Sofia clutched his Sharps rifle to her breast like a shield. "This is my country."

He checked the loads in his Colt. "You're a woman. You should stay clear of—"

"So you'll fight, risking your life, and leave me skulking back here."

He gave her a long, level look. "It's for your safety."

"But shouldn't I fight for my country too?"

Samuel stepped close and laid his hands on her warm shoulders. "That's different! You can't deny that."

"How churlish. My commitment to liberty and Nicaragua is as important to me as your desire to—to end this."

How had an argument developed—and now, of all times? He should've known better. She had always insisted on sharing the danger. Samuel cupped her oval face in his hands. "Just be careful."

Padraig pounded up the deck. "All that chipping wood, carving, and bleeding hands for bloody nothing. I'm sorry."

"It was an unlikely plan. It's not surprising. Not my brightest idea."

"What now?"

"We'll pick as many off as we can with the rifles before they catch us. After that . . ." Samuel holstered the Colt and picked up the Henry rifle. "Sofia, stay close to me so I can mind you."

She bridled. "I don't need minding."

"Everyone needs someone to guard their back. Padraig, watch Filipe."

"Don't worry about Señorito Filipe, Capitán." Chavez pointed his thumb at Filipe, who was animatedly talking with Sergeant Zamora on the lower deck. "He fights better than any of us."

"And he's as stubborn as his sister." Samuel grinned at Sofia.

"My Teresa's the same, Nicaraguan women." Chavez kissed the wooden cross on his neck. "Let's go teach this traitor Garcia a lesson."

The Euronicas on the afterdeck parted to let Samuel and the others through. Behind them, the *Wheeler* was powering out of the forested bend a quarter of a mile back, twin bow waves frothing from her prow like the wings of a tern. Dozens of white-clad soldiers clustered at her forward rails on both decks, but it was the black muzzle on the bow that made Samuel's heart skip a beat.

"*Bendita Virgen.*" Chavez took a step back. "They've mounted a cannon."

"Bastards." Samuel raised his spyglass. "Walker did that in the old days."

Three times as many men plus a cannon. Samuel's cheek ticked beneath his left eye. They might've held off the musket-wielding conscripts, but the cannon would smash the *Machuca*'s hull to kindling.

"Who cares about the pig's cannon? *Teniente* can hit the gunners with his Sharps." Jimenez curled all the fingers of his right fist save for the middle one and wagged it at the *Wheeler*.

Padraig gave a high-pitched laugh and slapped Jimenez on the back. "Clever lad. You can't speak English but you can sign it."

The blurred image of the cannon centered in Samuel's lens, and he scrutinized the gun. There was an iron plate around the barrel to shield the gunners. Even Padraig would find it difficult to strike the men behind it. He swiveled his spyglass to the wheelhouse on the upper deck, where another plate protected the helmsman. Colonel Garcia stood on the platform outside the wheelhouse, leaning over the rail and gesticulating to the gun crew below.

"Damn them," Samuel growled. "They've shielded the gun and the helmsman. It'd be easier to coax a pot of gold from a leprechaun than to hit them."

Padraig was still raising the ladder sight on his Sharps rifle when the cannon vomited yellow flame. The *Wheeler*'s bow bucked as a round shot arced over the river and slammed into the trees thirty yards astern of the *Machuca*. The bark of Padraig's Sharps was a feeble reply, and his bullet pinged off the cannon's shield. Nevertheless, the mass of men on the lower deck ducked below the guardrail.

"It bounced right off." Padraig cranked down the lever and jammed another cartridge into the breech.

It was hopeless. If the next round shot didn't cripple the *Machuca*, the following one would. Samuel glanced at Sofia, wishing he'd got her to safety. The woman was so stubborn. He lifted the Henry, searching, but Garcia was out of sight. Padraig should've shot at him instead of the gunners. Samuel fired at the wheelhouse, hoping for a lucky strike.

The cannon's black muzzle was inching to the left, an adjustment that would send the next round into the *Machuca*'s stern or blow a paddlewheel asunder. They'd be helpless to stop Garcia from slaughtering them at his leisure. Samuel fired at the gunners as fast as he could work the Henry's lever. The bullets bounced off the steel plate.

An enormous explosion rent the air as flames spurted up from the *Wheeler*, and her hull expanded like a balloon. The blast punched Samuel even though it was a quarter mile away. The *Wheeler*'s upper deck and wheelhouse blew apart in smithereens. Soldiers and shattered planks tumbled through the smoke-filled air. Flames licked across the hull as men and blackened timbers showered the river.

"Lord almighty." Chavez covered his mouth with his hand.

Sofia paled, frozen in the act of lifting Samuel's Sharps to her shoulder.

"It worked, Teniente, it worked." Jimenez danced a jig among the cheering Euronicas.

Soldiers darted around the *Wheeler*'s blazing deck in between jets of steam spraying up from the shattered boiler.

"Not a moment too soon." Padraig mopped his sweating brow. "Leaving logs filled with gunpowder at the last AC Transit wood depot—a brilliant idea, Samuel."

Samuel flushed, averting his eyes from the men thrashing in the river, the bodies floating around the crippled riverboat. He'd meant to take out the boiler, not kill the soldiers—the treacherous colonel, yes, but not the men who'd been forced to follow him. "The grenades you made last time we were here gave me the idea, but this . . ." He swallowed. "I meant to damage the burner and boiler. That's all."

Padraig hugged Jimenez, who was pounding him on the back.

"Perhaps we got carried away, eh, Jimenez? Serves Garcia right for leaving that gunpowder—"

"Capitán, quickly! The rapids." Cardoso's shout from the wheelhouse was shrill.

Samuel and Padraig dashed up the steps to the wheelhouse. Three hundred yards ahead, the angry river frothed with white-caps over jagged rocks. On the left bank, the village of El Castillo huddled in a jumble of shacks clustered around an aban-doned hotel, while the ancient Spanish fortress brooded on the hill above. Upstream from the rapids the jetty was empty, nor was a steamer moored at the jetty downstream of the whirling waters.

Samuel pressed his hands to his temples. Before he'd passed out from exhaustion during their voyage across Lake Nicaragua, with his mind reeling from the challenges ahead, he'd decided they had no choice but to run the rapids if there was no boat on the other side.

"We must take the *Machuca* through," he told the captain.

Cardoso's weathered face paled. "That's madness. I can't do it. We'll all drown."

"Fine, Capitán, Padraig will helm. Step aside, please." He smelled cold sweat as he drew Cardoso away.

Padraig squeezed past Cardoso, rubbing his hands together. "I've always wanted to do this. Brogan said the trick is to pick the least rocky path."

But there were rocks everywhere, stabbing up from the churning river, and Samuel couldn't see any route at all, rocky or smooth. It was a death trap.

"Don't worry. Vanderbilt built her for this." Padraig pushed the engine order telegraph all the way to the right. "I hope they're awake in the engine room. I need full steam to jump her over the rocks."

Samuel's knuckles whitened on the handrail. The bugger was actually enjoying himself. "Remember, you're not riding a horse."

The *Machuca* hit the first rock, slewed sideways, and surged ahead as Padraig spun the wheel. "Yes, you beast. Go, girl!"

The steamboat bashed against another rock but continued scraping and lurching forward, her paddles churning the boiling water and stone while painfully treading over the rapids, using those paddle wheels like feet. Samuel forced himself to keep his eyes on the jetty ahead.

The moment *Machuca* surged into the smoother waters downstream, Samuel released a huge breath to a volley of cheers from aft.

"There you are, you beauty." Padraig slapped the wheel and grinned at Samuel.

Samuel returned the grin. The remaining rapids were nothing compared to that, but still their mission was fraught with danger. He eyeballed the river scouring the banks as it raced relentlessly to the sea and twisted Father's signet ring on his finger. Their way to Greytown was relatively assured at this point.

But when they found Walker and his army, he still had to defeat the tyrant.

CHAPTER SEVENTEEN

Commander Salmon of HMS *Icarus* steadied his spyglass on the twinkling lights of the town on the mainland of Honduras. "There's Tela."

The sleek frigate steamed directly into the wind with the sails furled on her three masts and a plume of smoke trailing from her black funnel. Forward of the wheel where Samuel stood beside the young commander, the Euronicas were scattered along the guardrails watching sailors lower one of the four longboats dangling from davits on either side of the flush deck.

Two days after the *Wheeler* exploded, they docked the *Machuca* at the Royal Navy base in Bluefield only to find all the frigates were at sea. Sofia's old acquaintance, Captain Simpson convinced the base commander that Samuel was trustworthy and was indeed working with Ambassador Lyons. Samuel learned British forces foiled Walker's landing at Coxen Hole, Roatán's main harbor, on July twenty-ninth, and the filibuster had disappeared. A Royal Navy lugger delivering dispatches to the fleet hunting Walker in the Caribbean carried Samuel's cadre to the *Icarus*. Frustrated by HMS *Gladiator's* failure to apprehend the filibusters at Coxen Hole, Commander Salmon was searching every bay on the Honduran mainland for Walker's remaining brig. But that was a month ago, and the navy had found no trace of the filibusters since.

"I don't think you'll hear word of Walker here. We seized his second brig, the *Clifton*, all the way over in Georgetown. Walker's ship, the *John C. Taylor*, could be anywhere in the Caribbean." Salmon waved to catch his first lieutenant's attention. "The *Clifton* was loaded to the gunwales with weapons and ammunition—yes, Mr. Buckingham, hold her up a point, I want to shelter the longboat in our lee, that's it—but Walker still has a hundred men on the other brig."

"My lead is all you have, Commander. I might hear word of him at El Oveja Negra inn. It's a rebel meeting place."

"A long shot, and you're on your own from here. I dare not go closer. If anyone spots a Royal Navy frigate anchoring along the coast, it could create an international incident. America is already upset that we delayed signing the treaty with Honduras. They want Britain out of the Bay Islands."

"A long shot, but our only shot. Our best chance to track Walker down.'" Samuel drew his Colt to check the charges.

"I doubt you'll find news about him here." Despite the humidity and heat, Salmon wore his full uniform: cream waistcoat, white facings gleaming on his embroidered blue coat, white breeches and stockings, and burnished steel buckles on his black shoes. "If he has any sense, he sailed back to America when he didn't land at Roatán."

"They should've apprehended him when they had the chance," Sofia said. "This would be over now. I'm going to collect my gear."

Samuel winced and bit back another plea that she remain on the frigate. She hadn't even waited in Greytown as she earlier agreed. She wouldn't stay, despite anything he said, despite the danger.

"By the time *Gladiator* had gathered her crew from shore leave on the island, Walker had disappeared again. But I agree, she should have caught him." Salmon met his first lieutenant's questioning eyes. "Yes, now, Mr. Buckingham. Heave to, if you please. It's time. I don't know how Walker slipped past our frigates in the first place. You warned us of his plans weeks ago."

Samuel couldn't have agreed more. Delay after delay, it was already the beginning of August, and it had been over three months since he'd seen the children. He shifted uncomfortably "Walker's out there somewhere; I sense it. And if he still has a hundred volunteers, that's more men than he started with when he conquered Nicaragua the first time. It's not in his nature to retreat."

"It's up to you then. You all speak fluent Spanish and can snoop around without a fuss."

Ever vigilant, Salmon scrutinized the *Icarus's* position relative to the wind and sea. "Rumors of Walker's presence on this coast have jeopardized completion of the treaty. We must apprehend him. It's time to go."

"I'll do my best, Commander." Samuel holstered his Colt and followed the commander to the entry port where the others were climbing down to the longboat.

As the longboat skimmed toward the beach east of Tela, the prospect of discovering news of Walker or the rebel general suddenly seemed slim. Samuel glumly contemplated the shadowed outline of palms and canopied trees on the flat coastline. If he couldn't uncover a lead to Walker soon, Commander Salmon wouldn't be able to justify diverting from his orders any longer.

Constantly making small adjustments to the tiller, Padraig rested an arm on the gunwale and squinted at the foresail in the dim moonlight. "Trim that jib, Quintero, it's flapping like Jimenez's mouth."

"His mouth's not flapping, Teniente, it's trembling," Cortez said. "How does that British capitán expect us to confront the rebel general with no muskets, no bayonets?"

The plan made sense: Weapons would attract too much attention. Cortez was overly fond of his bayonet. "You have a pistol, that's enough. We need to keep a low profile, move around unnoticed, and ask questions."

Jimenez stared across the tranquil water at the twinkling lights. "The capitán's not native Spanish. And no way you are, Teniente, not with your yellow hair and green eyes."

"The officers speak Spanish like natives, you thick donkey." Cortez never missed an opportunity to have a crack at Jimenez, who was happy to give as good as he received. "They can say they're from Spain, with their snobby Castilian accents, and you can be their servant if you like."

"I'm no servant!"

"Ah sí, forget that. Only thing you're good for is thieving. When we find Walker, you can rob him."

Jimenez flashed his knife with a grin. "If you don't shut your crooked mouth, Cortez, I'll steal your tongue. You know I don't steal no more."

Despite the challenge of landing in a strange land and infiltrating a rebel town, the men were in good spirits. Samuel had picked the best of the Euronicas for the mission. Chavez was a fighter who could read and write. As a Carib, Cortez would blend in well with the local population. Jimenez was tall for a Central American, but his skills as a burglar had assisted Samuel before. Quintero had grown up as a fisherman and would help Padraig sail the boat. And Sofia and Filipe, they insisted on coming too.

A wave broke over the gunwale, and Samuel turned his face away as warm salty water splashed over. If only Sofia hadn't joined them; it was too dangerous.

Sofia touched his arm. "What if we can't find the Oveja Negra inn?"

He covered her hand with his and rubbed his thumb in small circles to reassure her. "We must. How difficult can it be? It's a small town. The lads can mingle and discreetly ask about General Cabañas."

She grew still. "That's dangerous, isn't it?"

"Not for them, they look like locals."

"Do they speak English here, like in Roatán?" She brushed a strand of hair under her broad-brimmed hat. Dressed in a short jacket, breeches, and soft leather boots, she intended to pass for a man. A very pretty man, Samuel thought as he hid his smile.

"On the mainland, even this close to the Bay Islands, they speak Spanish. They only speak English in Belize." Samuel picked up the wooden pail rolling back and forth on the floorboards, scooped some of the water splashing about in the shallow bilges, and tossed the water over the side.

Padraig passed the mainsheet to his tiller hand and hauled it in with the other hand. "Ease the jib a bit, Quintero. Good lad. I wish I had one of my steamboats here, we'd be ashore already."

"I'd love to crew on a steam-powered fishing boat, *Teniente*. Will you take me back to Ireland to work for you?" Quintero bit his bottom lip.

Samuel glanced at him in double take. Quintero seldom spoke.

"Really?" Watching the mainsail as he let the mainsheet slip out through his fingers, Padraig closed his fist on the rope when the front of the sail flickered. He drew the sheet back a few inches. "There, that's as good as we'll set her. So you want to come to Ireland, then? I hope you like the cold, Quintero, because you'll freeze your bollocks off."

Jimenez sat up from lighting a hand-rolled cigarette out of the wind below the gunwale. "Cold weather would be a nice change. I'd like to go as well, there's nothing for us here in Nicaragua."

Filipe stopped sharpening his knife and glared at Jimenez. "What do—"

"You're a terrible *capatas*, then, Filipe, a cruel taskmaster?" Samuel nudged Filipe to cover his surprise.

"I ahh . . . I don't . . . I give you a home and I pay you well. What do you mean?" Filipe's shoulders slumped.

"It's not that, Don Filipe. You take good care of us all."

Jimenez blushed and shifted in his seat. "I'd like to see the world."

Padraig moved the dark lantern to better focus the narrow beam on the compass. "Well, I'm always looking for experienced fishermen, Quintero, and though Jimenez is a bit of a donkey, but we can teach him the ropes."

"I've no interest in fishing. Perhaps the capitán can give me a job." Jimenez cupped his cigarette and dragged on it.

Cortez had taken over bailing the boat. He pursed his lips and exhaled. "A job burgling all those castles, you mean, robbing lords and ladies of their crowns and jewels. Anyway, what good would you be over there without a word of English?"

Jimenez flicked him with the bitter end of a rope. "Lords and ladies don't have crowns, idiota, only the king of Ireland has one."

Sofia rocked against Samuel with a peel of laughter. "Oh, Carlos, you won't be popular at mass if you tell the Irish they have a king. Britain has a queen, Victoria, but they're not pleased she rules them."

"I rest my case, Jimenez. You're too thick to travel anywhere." Cortez sat back against the gunwale like a pugilist who'd won his bout with a hook to the jaw.

Samuel clutched Sofia and laughed. "I don't think the queen will trouble you in Clonakilty, Carlos, and if you want to return with us, you're welcome. You're a smart man, you'll learn English soon enough."

Learning English, "Are ye, now? Sure why would you do that? 'Tis Irish you'll be needing in Ireland." Padraig never took his eyes off the sails, but his lips twitched into a smile.

"I want to come also. I speak English perfectly. Stop with the rope, Jimenez." Cortez dodged another flick from Jimenez's rope end and splashed his comrade with water from the bailing bucket.

Samuel looked at Sofia and quirked his eyebrows. Jimenez

and Cortez would be useful men around the estate. "Why not? I'll find work for both of you."

"Honest work, Jimenez, mind you. Honest work." Padraig glanced over at Quintero where he trimmed the jib. "I could use you to skipper my dive boat. I've not tried my diving suit offshore yet. Someone dragged me over here before I had the chance."

The ocean was mercury beneath the waning moon as the long-boat glided toward the narrow strip of sand thirty minutes later. Anticipation had hushed the crew; the only sounds were the lap of water against the hull and the whisper of tiny waves frothing up the sand.

"Spill the wind." Padraig released the mainsheet, Quintero slacked the jib sheet, and the sails flapped in the gentle breeze.

The tender's bow slid from the water, scraped over the sand, and halted abruptly. Filipe and Chavez jumped out with bare feet and hauled the bow out of the water. Samuel's boots sank in the wet sand as he took Sofia's hand. Cortez ran up the beach to the screen of tall trees—palms, most of them—fanning up into the haziness that trees wrap around themselves at night. His whistle confirmed that nobody was about, and they dragged the boat to the hightide mark and left it in Quintero's care.

Samuel's damp shirt clung to his back like a second skin, aggravating the bites he acquired by the time they located the Oveja Negra inn, four blocks back from the beach. It was a jaded, two-story building in the center of Tela, with bleached wooden walls splitting from years beneath the blistering sun. The adjoining bar was nothing more than a thatched roof on stripped logs, half full of Caribs and other lighter-skinned patrons. It was a lively place, where drunken voices competed with three drummers and a guitarist pounding a fast, almost sexual beat in one corner. A haze of smoke floated on the humid air as it only did in the tropics, atop the acrid smell of sweat and *guaro*, the cheap alcohol made from sugarcane. The tables were slices from the trunks of enormous trees, covered with slops and strewn with wooden mugs and *jicaras*.

Samuel wrinkled his nose as he led Sofia to a table. "Not exactly the Army and Navy Club, is it?"

Padraig gyrated to the rhythm of the drums. "No, thank God. I'll take this nanty narking over those braggarts any day."

Ignoring Cortez, who had entered earlier and was already playing dominos with five bronze-skinned locals in the corner. Samuel pulled up a heavy chair hewn from hardwood. Remembering that Sofia was posing as a man, he hastily took it himself while Sofia pulled down the brim of her hat and sat beside him. The rhythm of the drums was hypnotic; no wonder the patrons couldn't stand still. Jimenez ordered rum all around and paid with silver. Samuel checked his watch. Seven thirty; the night was still an infant.

Forty minutes later, they were stretching out their second rum when three barefooted men in dark shirts strode into the bar. Samuel resisted reacting as one of them, a young man with a scraggly black beard, appraised him bluntly. The second man nudged the first and murmured something lost beneath his heavy mustache, and all three headed toward Cortez's table.

The man with the mustache yanked Cortez from his seat with the help of his bearded companion.

"What're you doing?" Cortez struggled between them.

A lean man with a scar on his cheek, punched Cortez in the kidney. Cortez arched his back with a grunt. The musicians halted in an abrupt attenuation of forsaken notes as the other patrons scrambled away.

Scarface stepped between the men holding Cortez and grabbed a fistful of shirt. "Who sent you? What do you want with General Cabañas?"

Samuel bit his lip as Padraig stiffened.

Cortez cocked his head, and his back went rigid. "And who are you? It's none of your damned business wh—"

His brave words were chopped off with a grunt when Scarface punched him again. "Aren't you a stubborn Carrib? Outside." He jabbed a thumb toward the entrance. "I'll loosen his tongue."

Samuel sprang to his feet, and the others followed his lead. "Why are you attacking that man? He's minding his—"

A pistol blasted. Sofia grunted, clutched her side, and collapsed with a moan. Samuel's heart dropped as he took a knee beside her.

Outside, four men aimed pistols over the wooden railing, smoke swirling from one muzzle.

"Sofia." Trembling, Samuel touched her chest. "My God, you're hit."

"Don't, strangers." Scarface brandished a pistol at the others. "My men will shoot anyone who moves."

Padraig stood frozen with his hand inside his coat. Chavez, Filipe, and Jimenez slowly withdrew hands from their weapons.

Sofia's face was pallid, and her breath came in shallow rattles as blood leaked between her fingers pressed to her side.

"Get up." Scarface kicked Samuel in the back and sent him sprawling over Sofia.

She screamed in pain, and Samuel shivered as he pushed himself off her, her warm blood sticky on his abdomen. This wasn't happening. Dear Lord, not Sofia.

Feet padded and women shrieked as patrons ducked under the railings and fled into the night.

"Pick her up and carry her outside." Scarface punched Samuel between his shoulders.

"I'm going to kill you, you bastard," Padraig growled.

Samuel glowered a warning at Padraig. The men outside still menaced them with pistols; this wasn't the time for heroics. He had to convince Scarface to let him get Sofia to a doctor. He moved her bloody hand and placed his handkerchief over the wound. "Press this to it. It doesn't look too bad. You're going to be fine."

The sight of her spilling blood made him dizzy. *Oh Lord, why Sofia? Please don't take her from me.* Her skin was gray, drawn tight across her contorted face, and her sunken eyes pleaded to him. Sweat soaked her shirt even as her blood blackened it. Her body felt too light as he and Padraig picked her up and his men crowded around.

Filipe stared at Sofia vacantly. "Don't let her die, Samuel. She's all I have left." Tears welled in his eyes. Abruptly, his hand flew to his belt.

"No!" Jimenez caught his wrist. "You've no chance."

Scarface brandished a pistol in Filipe's face. "Outside. Now. I won't ask again."

As they left the bar, two dozen soldiers in dark shirts and floppy-brimmed hats emerged from the darkness, pounding down the street toward them.

Scarface whipped his head around. "Army. Leave the yanquis. Save yourselves."

Red blotches colored his face as he pushed past Samuel and scurried to the side of the bar counter. Bare feet slapped the earth as his men scrambled to follow him.

Filipe spun along with them and stabbed Scarface. The rebel threw up his hands and pitched forward with a grunt. Candle-light flickered on the blade as Filipe drew it back to strike again.

"Drop it." A swarthy sergeant muscled in and rammed the butt of his musket between Filipe's shoulder blades, sending him sprawling on top of his victim.

Soldiers piled up in front of the bar, breathless, aiming muskets at Samuel and the others as two officers in rumpled black uniforms emerged from their midst.

"He's dead." The sergeant hauled Filipe to his feet, plucked the revolver from Filipe's belt, and manhandled him toward Jimenez and Cortez. "Any more trouble from you, and I'll shoot you. Save the hangman some work."

"Go to hell, you fat bastard. He shot my sister." Filipe's face was bright red as he broke free of the sergeant's grip.

The hothead was going to get hurt. Still holding Sofia, Samuel lashed out with his boot, grazing Filipe's knee. "Stop, you fool. The man's dead, and you'll die too."

Another officer with gray hair pushed through the soldiers and pointed across the empty bar. "After them, you fools."

"Sí, *Mayor* Varela." The lieutenants rushed through the bar, followed by half the soldiers. The remaining men surrounded Samuel and his companions.

Suspended between Samuel and Padraig, Sofia moaned feebly, and Samuel's breath hitched. Lord, he was losing her.

The officer pulled off Padraig's slouch hat, and his eyes sparked at the sight of blond hair. "Filibusters! So our information was true. Where's Walker, *yanqui*?"

"My wife needs a doctor," Samuel pleaded. "She's . . . she's dying."

"*Cállate*, filibuster. Let the *pera* die. Where's Walker?"

"We're not filibusters, *bastardo*." Muscles corded on Padraig's neck.

Samuel would've lunged at the officer if he hadn't been supporting Sofia.

"*Españoles!*" The short officer's eyebrows shot up his skull. "What are you—never mind. General Guardiola will want to interrogate you himself." He pivoted on his heel. "Bring them to the barracks. Cano, apologize to His Excellency for the intrusion and ask him to meet us there. He's going to want to see these people. Tell him Españoles have joined the insurgency."

Samuel and Padraig exchanged stunned glances. General "The Butcher" Guardiola had burned his American prisoners alive when he commanded the Legitimist army that won the First Battle of Rivas. What atrocities would he inflict if he discovered that he captured the men who'd orchestrated the defeat that disgraced him in Nicaragua? He would never provide a doctor for Sofia then. She would die—they'd all die horrible deaths. Samuel's lips pinched together as he held her tighter to his chest. *Oh, my darling, what have I done? Dear God, save her at least.*

In the musty-smelling cell at the barracks, Samuel guessed it must be after nine at night. His watch had been taken along with their weapons and belongings before they were all crammed into a single cell.

Sofia's twisted face, shallow breathing, and the blood seeping from the wound in her side gutted him. The cursed lead was still inside, poisoning her. Samuel's limbs tingled. He had to convince their captors to send a doctor to remove the bullet.

The cell door flew open, and four guards marched in.

One jabbed a finger toward Samuel and Padraig. "You two, the general will see you now."

Samuel hated leaving Sofia. "Don't make trouble, Padraig. It's our only hope of talking our way out of this."

One guard grabbed Padraig's arm.

"Get your stinking paws off me. "Padraig shrugged off the offending hand.

"No, Padraig." The chains on his manacled wrists clinked as Samuel twisted the tail of his stinking shirt and shuffled ahead of the guards.

Padraig followed without further fuss. "She'll be all right. We've been in worse trouble than this and you found a way out." But his dragging shoulders belied the optimism in his forced smile.

Somehow Samuel had to convince Guardiola they were on the same side this time, that Samuel and his men could eliminate the threat Walker presented to Honduras as well as to Nicaragua.

It was the only way Sofia would get the medical help she needed.

As Varela led the way into a dusty room, the tic began under

Samuel's eye when he recognized the man leafing through their personal papers at the desk. General José Santos Guardiola had piled on the weight since Samuel had last seen him through a spyglass five years before, when Guardiola led his men against Walker's army in La Virgen. He combed his sparse graying hair across his pate like a greasy flap, and gold epaulets and gold braid festooned his black uniform.

Two guards positioned themselves on either side of Samuel and Padraig and stopped them a yard from the chipped wooden desk.

Guardiola laid down Samuel's identity papers and flexed his fat fingers. "I've prayed for this moment, Kingston. I've lost count of the nights I lay awake reliving that battle in La Virgen, the humiliation when all Central America scorned me for losing to that dwarf—that coward, Walker—and not a soul believed me when I told them it was the trickery of two British officers that caused my downfall. And no matter how I've racked my brains, I can't discern what devilry gave you victory. I had ten times the men, yet you routed my army. I prayed to the almighty for revenge, and he's delivered you to me." He picked up the papers again and crumpled them whole. "What are you doing in my country?"

Tyrants like Guardiola expected deference, and Samuel wasn't about to antagonize him. He stared down, avoiding the general's eyes. "General Guardiola, we're working with the British navy to capture William Walker. The British don't want him disrupting the new treaty with your country."

Silence. Samuel went on to relate how he was helping the Royal Navy to hunt Walker.

More silence. Finally, Guardiola flapped a hand dismissively. "We don't need the help of a mercenary like you. Cabañas has fled the area already, and the British will capture Walker. It's time you paid for your crimes against the legitimate government of Nicaragua. As president of the republic, I hereby sentence you both, and Sofia Valle, to die by firing squad tomorrow at noon."

Samuel's vision grayed. He expected Guardiola to be difficult but summary execution? "You can't do this. We came here in good faith to help your country. We haven't been tried for any crime." Oh Lord, not Sofia too. He'd die willingly, twice over, to save her. "I beg you, sir, my wife had nothing to do with that business all those years ago. Please spare her. We deserve to have our side heard. I demand you send for Commander Salmon."

For once Padraig was quiet, gaping at Guardiola.

The president's fat neck flushed. "Ah, the dashing young British commander. I'll ask his forgiveness afterward. I don't need him interfering. As for your trial, this is a military tribunal. I've reviewed your case, and I find you and your coconspirators guilty of insurrection against the republics of Nicaragua and Honduras. Both . . ."

He was going to murder them.

". . . taken to the barracks square and shot at noon tomorrow. Thereafter, your bodies will be interred in unmarked graves so as not to encourage—"

"That's madness." Chains jangled as Samuel cracked his knuckles. "You'll never get away with it."

Stepping so close Samuel could smell the tobacco in his breath, Guardiola chuckled unpleasantly. "Of course I will. I'm the president." He poked Samuel's chest with a fat finger. "And furthermore, I condemn your men to four years' hard labor in the copper mines."

"You bastard." Padraig thrust out his manacled hands and lunged at Guardiola.

The guards pulled him back, but Padraig was broader and taller than both, and he dragged them forward. Varela drew his pistol. As Padraig stretched for Guardiola, Samuel exploded and thrust off his guards, sending them staggering back with eyes bulging.

With surprising speed for a man his age, Varela slammed

Padraig in the head with his pistol. Padraig collapsed, and all four guards piled on Samuel, driving him to the hard floor.

His face purple, Guardiola jumped to his feet. "Get these wretches out of my sight. Noon, Kingston! You die at noon."

They hauled Samuel to his feet as more guards rushed into the room.

He jerked his head around to look at Guardiola. "General, please, not Sofia. She's a mother." He inhaled a breath into his heaving lungs. "She's innocent. Spare—"

"Innocent?" Guardiola bellowed. "You don't think I recognize her name? Her father opposed me, and now she opposes me. She's an insurgent!"

Samuel's head spun. "A doctor, at least a doctor to treat her wound. I beg you, señor."

"She dies today, she dies tomorrow—what difference does it make?" Spittle flew from Guardiola's lips. "Remove this scum from my sight."

The chair creaked as Guardiola slumped back into it, panting for breath. One guard grabbed Samuel's hair, and three of them marched him from the room while more dragged Padraig after him.

That was it. They were going to die, and John and baby Maria—none of the family—would have any idea what had happened to them, not until Filipe emerged from the hell of hard labor in the mines—if he emerged at all. Four years' hard labor? Samuel had been imprisoned in a Central American mine once. Nobody there had survived four months.

CHAPTER EIGHTEEN

"Hurry, Jimenez." Motes swirled around Cortez like gold dust in the sunlight where he stood on his toes and peered through the tiny window. "The sun's been up for hours. We're out of time."

"Cállate. You try picking a lock with a piece of wood." Jimenez fumbled the sliver he pried from the door frame. He cursed and stretched his hands wide before relaxing them.

It stank of sweat, feces, and blood in the crowded cell where the Euronicas had been held for two days, packed elbow to elbow, straining away from Sofia and Samuel to give them a few inches of privacy. Dried blood flaked from his fingers like rust as Samuel rubbed his gritty eyes and touched Sofia's forehead. Burning up—a fever, for sure.

He kissed her dank cheek. "Hang in there, my love. Fight it. Fight for the children. Fight for me." He didn't recognize his raspy voice.

A gate banged open down the corridor, and boots clacked on the stone floor. A moment later the door opened, and Major Varela appeared with several guards behind him.

Samuel's head spun. Not now. It was too early to die.

Varela squinted into the gloom. "Kingston, Kerr, outside. The president demands to see you."

The breath caught in Samuel's chest as he looked down at Sofia. He couldn't leave her, not like this. "My wife's dying. She needs a doctor."

"You've bigger problems than that, boy. Now, you can walk out of here or we can carry you."

"You're not taking him anywhere." Filipe thrust himself between Samuel and Varela.

An older soldier wearing a straw hat struck Filipe in the back with the butt of his musket.

"Bastardo!" Padraig spun and hit the older man with a straight right. The blow landed perfectly, next to the man's left eye.

But the soldier was a solid fellow and not easily discouraged. He swung around and lashed out at Padraig with his musket. Padraig dodged the blow and hit him twice more.

At the same moment, the other three soldiers lowered their weapons to the ominous click of cocking hammers as the Euronicas surged to their feet while simultaneously Varela whipped out his pistol with surprising speed and jammed the barrel to Filipe's head where he struggled to rise to his knees. "Stop! Anyone moves a muscle and the boy dies."

As Samuel shielded Sofia from the brawl, Padraig's fist connected with the older soldier's cheek, breaking the skin, but his left hook, his knockout punch, froze in midair. "All right. Don't harm Filipe." He dropped his arms in surrender as the battered soldier backed away.

"On your knees, all of you, and up against the wall." Varela jammed his pistol in Samuel's gut. "No more trouble or you die."

It was hopeless. The soldiers couldn't shoot them all, not with a single shot apiece. But nobody else should die. Samuel's hands went limp. "Do as he says. You win, Varela. We'll come. But my wife, she—"

"That's up to the president." Varela's teeth ground together as he pushed Samuel, the pistol's muzzle never wavering from his gut.

"So help me, you pig, if—"

"Enough, Filipe. Now's not the time." The pulse beat in Samuel's throat as he ripped his eyes from Sofia's sweating face. *Lord, save her, please. I can't live without her.*

The Euronicas murmured and cursed as he and Padraig were shoved to the door.

"You'll pay for this, Varela." Padraig was breathing heavy and his faced was flushed as he was bundled into the corridor ahead of Samuel.

The trip to the dusty office was a blur, but when Samuel saw Commander Salmon sitting at ease before Guardiola's desk, his jaw dropped. The commander was the last person he expected to see. Salmon had always made it clear the Royal Navy would not encroach on Honduras' mainland.

Guardiola greeted them with a scowl and glared out the window.

Salmon rose with haste. "Captain Kingston, you look dreadful. And your wife? Is—"

"Dying." Samuel jabbed a finger toward Guardiola. "This butcher refused to send a doctor."

Guardiola sat on the edge of the chair. "How dare you use that—"

"Mr. President." Salmon spread his hands. "Captain Kingston's clearly overwrought. Forgive him, please. We must work together if we're to capture Walker. Kingston and his men are experienced pathfinders; they're our only chance of apprehending Walker if he leads his men into the jungle."

Walker in the jungle? What?

Guardiola's nostrils flared. "Your people reported Walker was missing."

Salmon retook his seat, pulling it back to include the two prisoners. "He was, but he anchored off a remote part of Roatán two days ago. Our marines discovered one of his mercenaries left behind on the island; he was drunk in a bar when rebels ferried the rest of them out to Walker's brig. We interrogated him, and he revealed the filibusters' contingency plan: to land on the Honduran mainland and link with Cabañas' rebels." He glanced at Guardiola, who glowered at Samuel. "I've five Royal Navy boats searching up and down the coast for him, but I fear he'll have landed by now. If you agree to help us catch him, the president will set you free."

Samuel's knees wobbled. A chance . . . But Sofia . . . A naval surgeon would know how to treat a gunshot wound. "My wife is on her deathbed. She needs a surgeon. You must take her to your ship."

"The Valle woman stays here." Guardiola wagged a finger at Salmon. "If they don't bring Walker to me, I'll carry out her sentence."

Samuel dug his nails into the palms of his hands. Everything depended on remaining calm. "We'll capture Walker, no matter what it takes. But we're not leaving until the *Icarus'* surgeon removes the bullet from my wife."

"None of us." Padraig scowled.

Salmon stood. "I'll send for the surgeon and his assistant to operate right away. Furthermore, I'll leave the assistant to care for Mistress Sofia until we return."

Nodding to Salmon, Samuel palmed his chest.

Salmon pointed to the chains. "Mr. President, please be so kind as to remove the manacles from these gentlemen. And I trust you'll relocate Mrs. Kingston to more suitable place for the operation."

Guardiola scowled. "But if Kingston fails to deliver Walker here within a month, on the third of September, to the hour, dead or alive, I'll execute the woman. That should pin the hunters' noses to the trail."

Drawing himself erect, the young commander placed his hat on Guardiola's desk. "I would not advise that, Mr. President." His voice scraped like a the *Manchuca's* hull across the rapid's jagged rocks, "These British citizens came here to help, and such a barbaric action would turn the world against you."

"Where was the world when Walker invaded us?" Guardiola slammed a pudgy fist on the desk. "I'll do as I please, and there's nothing you can do about it, sir. And one more thing. I received word my political rival, Mariano Alvarez, has marched from Tegucigalpa with seven hundred troops to search for Walker, and I'll be damned if this corrupt general will make political hay by capturing him. If that happens, our deal is off, and the woman dies. So every minute counts. Were I you, I'd get underway."

Outside the office, as the soldiers removed his chains, Samuel tipped his head back. He had until September third—one month to land on a strange coast, track Walker through the jungle, and defeat one hundred men—it was an impossible task. But life without Sofia, that was equally inconceivable, and the children . . . He'd grown up without a mother. They would not.

Later that morning, Samuel wiped the sweat from his lip and checked his watch again. Eleven o'clock. He shot another glance at the closed door, slumped onto the bench beside Padraig, and jammed his hands into his armpits. "How long will it take? The surgeon's been operating for over an hour already. I can't stand this. I should never have brought her back to Nicaragua."

Padraig moved closer and offered him a freshly rolled cigarette. "You can't blame yourself for that. She's stubborn. You've known that all along. You couldn't have stopped her."

Accepting the cigarette, Samuel eyed his friend bleakly. That was easy for Padraig to say, but it was Samuel who'd given in and let Sofia come to Honduras. Tears blistered the corners of his eyes.

"She'll pull through. Commander Salmon said Mr. Tomkins, the surgeon, has a lot of experience with gunshot wounds. Jazus, by the look of his wrinkles, I'd wager he patched up Nelson." Padraig scratched a match and touched the flame to Samuel's cigarette.

Harsh, the smoke scratched his throat; Samuel's mouth tasted like an ashtray. Glancing at the tall marine lieutenant with sunburned skin pacing outside the door, he moaned. "I won't get on the *Icarus* until I know she's all right. I can't. I couldn't bear not knowing she's out of danger." If she even made it. The surgeon said the bullet was deep.

He drooped forward and draped his hands limply over his knees. This wasn't helping. He should pray. If he'd prayed more often in his life, more fervently, these awful things wouldn't keep happening.

"Of course we're not leaving until she's safe, and she's going to pull through." Padraig dropped a cigarette butt on the stone floor and crushed it with his boot.

At the same instant, the door creaked open, and the wizened surgeon emerged, drying his hands on a bloodstained towel. His eyes were dull under a storm of gray brows, and his chin dropped when Samuel leaped to his feet.

"How is she?" Samuel's eyes flicked from the doctor to the door ajar behind him, but he couldn't see Sofia.

The surgeon smelled of carbolic soap and pipe tobacco. "I did everything possible, but she was hemorrhaging. That bullet was deep, close to the—"

"Will she live?" Samuel grabbed a fistful of the surgeon's blood-stained apron.

The surgeon recoiled. "I had to dig around. Too much. But I promise you I did everything possible. I think I removed all the foreign bodies, but there may be nerve damage. It's in the Lord's hands now."

"The Lord's hands? What does that mean?" She couldn't die. He'd be lost without her. Panic peaked in his gut, and he swallowed down the bitter taste. "What are her chances?"

"I'm no gambler, but if I were, I'd say fifty-fifty. But we did our best. Roy, my loblolly boy, is very experienced; admiralty will assign him as a ship's surgeon when we return to England. He'll do all he can for her."

A fifty percent chance she might die. Samuel's vision blurred. "I must see her." He lunged for the door.

The surgeon caught his arm, his grip surprisingly strong for an old man. "She looks bad, but she's been through much. She has a chance. Don't lose hope."

Without a word, Samuel rushed into a noxious haze of chloroform, cerate, and blood. Sofia was unconscious on the makeshift operating table, breathing shallowly through cracked gray lips, her skin sallow and tight across her wasted face.

Samuel sagged to his knees and clasped her cold, stiff hand. "She's barely breathing. Sofia, my darling." His head flopped forward. "Is she dying?"

How could you do this to me, Lord?

A warm hand touched his shoulder. He hadn't noticed anyone else when he'd rushed into the room with Padraig.

"She's alive, trust me, but she needs rest. Lots of it. I promise you, we're taking care of her." The surgeon's mate's voice was deep and confident.

"Please, you must. And I'll stay right here with you until I know she's—"

The door sprung open, and Major Varela stomped in with two soldiers. "*El doctor ha terminado.* You must board the frigate immediately. The president is already furious at these delays."

Samuel heaved to his feet with balled fists. "Go to hell, I will not. I won't leave until I know she's all right. What if she—" He couldn't say it.

Varela's dark eyes flicked toward his guards, he nodded curtly, and they pointed their muskets. "If you don't, I've orders to shoot both of you immediately."

Time slowed. Padraig shifted like a cornered fox beside Samuel, and the surgeon's mate blanched, retreating to the window.

They couldn't win. If they resisted now, the Honduran guards would shoot them. Sofia would be alone. Might die alone. He'd no choice. He had to pursue Walker and leave Sofia in God's hands.

He stepped back, knees trembling, and spoke to Padraig in English, his voice thick with emotion. "We'll go. We can't help her if we're dead. The sooner we find Walker, the sooner this nightmare ends."

Padraig's eyes blazed at Varela. "If she dies, I'm coming for you. You'll look over your shoulder never knowing when that bullet will strike, your throat will be cut, or you'll roast in the burning shell of your home."

Sweat beaded Sofia's hot brow when Samuel kissed it. "Live, darling, for the children. Live for me." He ripped his eyes from her and shuffled to the door.

"I'll do everything I can for her, Captain," the surgeon's mate called after him. "She's strong. She'll fight."

In the hallway, Samuel ignored the marine lieutenant who tugged the tails of his red coat and fell in behind them. William Walker's twisted ambition had caused Father's lonely death, and now Sofia was . . . He pressed his lips together as his stride increased unbidden. He'd capture Walker, but not alive. Not this time.

This time, he was going to kill the bastard.

CHAPTER NINETEEN

Even with the sails furled on her three masts, the Icarus moved like the wind thanks to the powerful steam engine throbbing beneath Samuel's pacing feet. He was grateful when engine trouble delayed their departure from Tela for three days, allowing the surgeon to visit Sofia again. Alarmingly, Dr. Tomkins reported no improvement. *I've wasted enough time on things I can't control. Now I must focus on finding Walker's brig, for Sofia's sake.*

Samuel glanced at Commander Salmon in an animated discussion with Lieutenant Buckingham on his quarterdeck and rolled his tongue in his dry mouth. After five days scouring Honduras' Caribbean Coast, searching bay after bay, Salmon was growing impatient. Nobody had sighted the *John C. Taylor*, and the commander was convinced that Walker had fled back to New Orleans. Samuel refused to accept that; if it were true, Sofia was lost.

Slowly shaking his head, Salmon beckoned him.

Something was amiss. Samuel's heart shrank as he plodded aft.

"We've been searching for almost a week, now, HMS *Gladiator* also, and found nothing. I'm convinced Walker's sailed to

America. This is a waste of time." Salmon fussed with his cravat. "I can't divert *Icarus* and *Gladiator* any longer. I'm sorry, when we rendezvous with *Gladiator*, I must call off the search."

That would be the end of everything. Samuel numbed inside. Lost for words, he shifted from foot to foot as he stared at Salmon.

"I've orders from—"

"Commander, I beg you. I know Walker, he's here, close by, marshaling his pawns to strike. We'll find him, we must. You can't stop. You heard Guardiola, he'll kill Sofia."

"Orders, captain. I've already stayed out here too long. I'm sorry, but when we meet with *Gladiator*, I must take both frigates back to Barbados and report to the admiral. Walker is gone, long gone." Salmon swallowed and angled away. "I'm truly sorry."

This wasn't happening. If they abandoned the quest now. . . Sofia was . . . Samuel swayed on his feet. "But, Commander, you can't—"

"Deck there, I see sails." The shout came from the crow's nest on the main mast.

Salmon glanced up at the lookout, cupping hands over his mouth. "Where away?"

"To windward, sir. Starboard side and making straight for us. Square rigged."

"Very well. Keep a sharp eye on her, and let me know when you discern her colors." Salmon nodded to his first lieutenant. "Mr. Buckingham, set a course to intercept."

Square sails. Could be a brig. Samuel rushed to the starboard gunwale. *Please, please, let it be Walker.* But only whitecaps rolled on the empty blue sea stretching to the horizon.

Padraig padded up. "You think it's them?"

"I dearly hope so, but I can't see her yet. If not, we're finished. Salmon called off the search."

Padraig jerked around to stare at the commander beside his helmsman. "He can't. What the hell is he thinking. What about—"

"He's doing it." Samuel drew a breath and released it before speaking. "Well, if this isn't Walker, Salmon must put us ashore, and we'll hunt for Walker on foot." It was a hopeless plan, but he wouldn't give up—never.

Padraig lifted his spyglass. "She's hull down, too far away to see her yet."

He followed Padraig's example and glassed the horizon, but the pitching, blurred skyline looked empty.

Five minutes later, Padraig halted his swiveling spyglass. "There, I see her royals in the northwest."

Samuel peeked around his eyepiece at the direction Padraig was looking and pointed his spyglass at the same place. The ocean pitched wildly, in and out of focus, but the speck of a sail flashed like a tiny white crown gilded pink in the sun. Trying to pin the sail in his lens as her topgallants topped the horizon made him dizzy.

It took forever to close on the ship. He lowered the spyglass to rest his eye and wrung it in his hands as the minutes ticked away.

"It's a brig." Padraig pocketed his spyglass before scrambling ten feet up the ratlines and fishing it out again.

Samuel followed him to the waist and paused. There was no reason for Walker to sail south when his plan was to disembark his army on the mainland. It made little sense. He didn't climb up after Padraig. His legs were too shaky. He watched the brig's lines firm up as she crawled closer.

"It's a Honduran flag, and she's small. It's not the *Taylor*." Padraig shoved the spyglass in his pocket and scrambled down.

Samuel he slumped against the gunwales. It wasn't Walker. *Icarus's* bow arced slowly to port, away from the brig. Salmon had realized this wasn't their prey. But what if the brig had seen the *John C. Taylor*? He hurried to the quarterdeck.

"It's not Walker. She's a Honduran vessel, coaster probably." Salmon didn't meet his eye.

He felt bad about giving up the hunt. And so the bugger

should. "We must at least ask her if she's seen the *Taylor*." Samuel's voice quavered. They had to try everything possible to find Walker—to save Sofia.

Salmon swallowed and peered at the brig. "Waste of time. We'll be late for our rendezvous with *Gladiator*. Carry on, Mr. Buckingham."

To hell with *Gladiator*, they needed to know. Samuel needed to know for sure that there was no chance. "I implore you, Commander. It's a matter of my wife's life."

Glancing from the brig to his first mate, Salmon fidgeted with a brass button on his frock coat.

"Please, Commander."

"All right. Head for the brig, Mr. Buckingham." Salmon fished a bullhorn from the cubbyhole beside the wheel and passed it to Samuel. "You speak with them, my Spanish is mediocre at best."

"Have you seen a brig in these parts," Samuel bellowed across the water thirty minutes later when *Icarus* took station on the leeward side of the sailing vessel. *Please let them have news, please.* "A vessel called the *John C. Taylor*?"

A frail, clean-shaven man clinging to a shroud amidships on the brig lifted his bullhorn. "A brig, you say, is it? I only seen one, anchored in Trujillo Bay. We passed too far away to note her name though."

Nearby, Padraig and Filipe whooped and clapped each other's backs as the Euronicas lining the gunwale cheered.

That had to be the *Taylor*. Samuel's belly fluttered. "We have him, by God. "Gracias, señor." He clutched the bullhorn to his chest and faced Commander Salmon. "They saw a brig in Trujillo Bay."

"Don't get your hopes up yet, Captain. But it's certainly worth a look."

"It's him, I know it is. Thank you, Commander."

Salmon smiled tightly. "Come, let's see how far it is on the charts. I reckon some fifty miles or so.

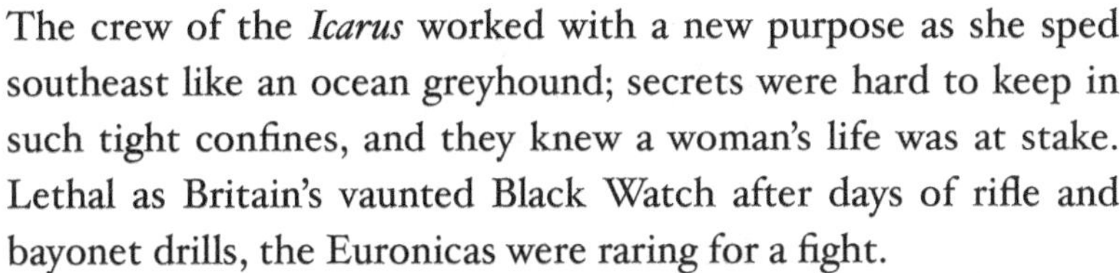

The crew of the *Icarus* worked with a new purpose as she sped southeast like an ocean greyhound; secrets were hard to keep in such tight confines, and they knew a woman's life was at stake. Lethal as Britain's vaunted Black Watch after days of rifle and bayonet drills, the Euronicas were raring for a fight.

Another weapons' practice ended; Samuel paced the deck again. It had to be Walker in Trujillo, it was the last throw of the dice. Time was stampeding like a half-trained cavalry horse. It was the twelfth of August already, and if he didn't deliver Walker back to Tela by the third of September, Sofia would die.

Choices and uncertainties spun in his mind, making his head ache. Enough! He strode to Padraig and Filipe at the bow. "It's taking forever to get to Trujillo Beach."

Fumbling with his spyglass, Padraig dropped his cigarette stub. He scooped it up and glanced around furtively. "Bloody hell, if the boson saw me messing up his holystoned deck . . . Samuel, your impatience is exhausting me. You should've rested."

"Can't. Not now."

"Well, we're hours away from Trujillo, and no matter how far you pace, we won't arrive any faster. Really, you should rest. You won't get another chance. If Walker's on that beach, there'll be wigs on the green."

"Did you say wigs?" Filipe paused from cleaning his revolver for the second time. "Hair? That makes no sense."

"It's from the old days back home, when men wore wigs. When they fought, their wigs often rolled off onto the green."

"Imagine wearing a wig out here." Filipe raised his eyebrows at Samuel. "You'd be roasted."

Samuel couldn't indulge in idle chatter, not with the image of Sofia, pale as death and barely breathing through colorless lips, burned into his mind. If Walker escaped across Honduras and Guardiola murdered her, he'd never forgive himself. The filibuster was evil, and only execution would halt his ambitions.

Walker had to die. If he'd killed him years ago, Sofia would be safe at home with the children. He shook his head to clear his thoughts. "Do you think it's him—Walker in Trujillo?"

"It can't be anybody else." Padraig dropped the cigarette butt over the side and pointed his spyglass at the coastline. "Makes sense. You saw the chart, and Trujillo Beach is as good an anchorage as any on this stretch of coastline."

"One hundred filibusters." Samuel's heart shrank. "The *Icarus* only has twenty marines on board; even with the twenty-four in our cadre, Walker outnumbers us two to one."

"Ah, but we're the Euronicas. We're used to facing great odds."

Filipe dropped his loaded Colt in his holster with practiced ease. "Don't worry," "We'll get him."

The *Icarus* forged ahead through truculent seas beneath a sky stacked with black cumulus clouds. Jimenez, Delgado, and Soto were throwing dice and smoking in the shade of the steam-driven longboat suspended from davits on deck. Samuel hadn't had time to catch up with Delgado and Soto since his return. A chat might rest his troubled mind and make the time go faster.

Soto was taller and broader than the rest of the Nicaraguans, but that didn't stop the men from teasing him for being a townie from León. He'd been a baker's assistant before the Democrático army conscripted him at sixteen; now he worked in the kitchen at Filipe's hacienda. Delgado was a short, wiry country boy, like most the Euronicas, who fancied himself a gambler.

The three dice rolled up a total of sixteen, and Soto clapped his hands. "That's two cups you owe me now, Delgado."

"Hell, no." Delgado's dark face flushed. "I gave you my ration three days ago. Those dice must be loaded."

"They're not." Soto snatched up the dice. "Here's the capitán, he can judge them." Soto was a good soldier, but he was slick, fully capable of pulling the wool over Delgado's eyes. He stuck out his hand. "Señor, Delgado thinks I'm cheating. Do you see anything wrong with these?"

Samuel took the warm dice and hefted them one by one. He seldom played dice—he preferred cards—but he didn't feel anything unusual. He rolled them onto the deck: a three, a one, and a five. "They feel fine to me."

"See! I'm not cheating. You better pay up when we get our ration tomorrow."

Jimenez wet his fingers and quenched the stub of his cigarette. "If you can't pay your debts, Delgado, you shouldn't gamble. What you need is a good woman to keep you in line."

"Pah, all the girls my age on the hacienda have nothing but wool between their ears. I won't settle down with a girl like that. I don't know if they'll ever grow up and get some sense." Delgado pulled the stopper from his *jicara*, drank, and wiped his mouth with his forearm.

Samuel hid a smile. They all knew Delgado preferred to pay for his company, to walk away with no ties.

"Then find a mature woman." Jimenez grinned. "What do you think of a wife in her thirties?"

Delgado exaggerated his mouth dropping open. "Not a chance. I'm only twenty-one."

Soto scooped up the coins in the pot. "I think two wives of eighteen would be better, papi. If you fellows aren't playing, I'll try my luck with Quintero."

If he was asking these men to hunt Walker again, they needed to know he was one of them. Samuel pulled a few coins from his pocket. "I'll play, Soto."

Jimenez sat up straighter. "If you're playing, señor, I'll play too. Soto won't cheat if you're here."

"I don't cheat." Soto scowled. "I'll give back Delgado's drink, if he wants."

Samuel sat on the warm deck and dropped silver. "I'll fund you, boys. How about three coins each, and we'll see who lasts longest?"

Delgado clutched his fists to his breast and pretended to faint. "Nice one, Capitán."

Nearby, Guido Lopez blew a reedy note on his bamboo flute. The young Indian from Chinandega always carried his instrument. He raised the flute to his mouth and played the opening notes of a haunting traditional song.

"I'm in." Jimenez scooted closer to Samuel, glaring daggers at Lopez. "But why does he have to start up with that din? Sounds like a strangled cat."

Delgado reached for the scattered coins. "Can I take my share and not play?"

"No!" All barked at him together, including Samuel; the object of the exercise, after all, was to build camaraderie.

The clouds thinned above them over the next hour, but the dense cumulus layer still brooded over the mainland.

"Look, a ship," Delgado called from the gunwale, where he'd joined Gutierrez after losing his coins in three rolls of the dice.

A pillar of smoke smudged the sky to the south. Samuel fished out his spyglass and hurried to join Padraig near the stern. Forging toward them through the waves came a black frigate with a blunt bow and bare masts swayed back at the same rakish angle as her long, fat funnel.

A great marksman, Padraig had the vision of an eagle. "HMS *Gladiator*. Look at her fly. Steamships are the only way to travel."

"She's running up signal flags." Samuel grabbed a shroud to keep his balance on the rolling deck. "Let's go to the quarterdeck and find out what she's saying."

Commander Salmon stood behind the helmsman with his spyglass trained on the flags shooting up the *Gladiator*'s mast, but he must've had eyes in the back of his head, for he beckoned Samuel and Padraig without lowering his lens. Beside him, Buckingham, his dour first lieutenant, didn't acknowledge their arrival.

"Twenty more marines on the *Gladiator*," Padraig whispered

from the corner of his mouth as Samuel started up the steps. "I'd say the odds are improving."

Salmon spoke without changing his position. "Mr. Buckingham, acknowledge, if you please, and ask them to take station astern of us. We'll need all the help we can get." He straightened and fronted his visitors. "Gentlemen, I'm afraid they reported nothing of significance. No matter, I'm peckish. Do you fancy a late lunch? Mr. Buckingham, you have the conn."

The British Army could jest about the Royal Navy, but naval officers dined well, and Samuel dug into the meal of baked bread, fish, exotic vegetables, and fresh fruits from Tela. He realized he hadn't eaten in twenty-four hours, and even the smell of paint, tar, and wood polish failed to spoil his appetite.

Commander Salmon had also served in the Crimean War, and he had warmed to Samuel and Padraig on the voyage up from Greytown when he learned they were not only survivors of the Charge of the Light Brigade but also the men who helped topple William Walker three years before. He proved a charming host, entertaining them with tales of growing up as the son of a preacher in Hampshire and of his adventures serving on *HMS Shannon* in Lucknow during the mutiny. The discovery that all three of them had served in India strengthened their bond.

Samuel appreciated the perspective he gained during their meal. Salmon was a new breed of officer, promoted despite being a commoner and based on his own merits. He was a capable commander who would go far in the modern navy switching from sailing ships to steamships. He swelled with satisfaction to see command awarded not to lordships but to bright, hard-working men.

As the meal went from course to course, his anxieties rose again, and he caught himself biting his lip. It couldn't be long now. With any luck, Walker would be right where they expected. In a matter of hours, Samuel would face the man who'd destroyed so many lives in Central America and now threatened his wife. But what if that wasn't enough? What if Guardiola let the Royal Navy have him and Walker talked his way out of the next indictment too? Even if they condemned him to life in prison, it wouldn't be enough. For all he'd ruined, the churl deserved worse than to rot in a cell for the rest of his life—he deserved to die.

Salmon laid down his napkin. "I'm sorry, Captain, I see you looking at your watch for the tenth time. You must be beside yourself with worry. Shall we return to the deck? We should soon be close enough to see the old Spanish fortress on the hill above Trujillo."

Now they would know. It was all Samuel could do not to leap from his chair. Somewhere along the Honduran mainland nearby, William Walker was now within his reach, but it was already the twelfth of August. The deadline for Sofia's execution, the third of September, loomed closer. Samuel's chest twinged as he headed for the door. They had to catch Walker quickly.

Three miles west, the coast lay dark beneath the gloomy clouds, and a mile astern, the *Gladiator* followed with her black funnel spewing smoke into the air. The Euronicas hooted and jeered in the frigate's waist behind the steam-driven tender suspended from davits on the port side. Padraig's eyebrows flashed up, and he and Samuel sprinted down the rolling deck toward the cluster of shouting men.

Samuel pushed through the Euronicas even as Jimenez loosed a savage snarl and lunged at Filipe's breast, with the bayonet fixed to his rifle. Filipe skipped back with a yelp. Steel rang as he swept the bayonet aside with his saber, stepped in, and slapped Jimenez's thigh with the flat of his blade.

The men roared and pushed each other, and Jimenez threw down his rifle with a curse.

"Move over, Chavez." Sergeant Zamora shoved Chavez aside to make space for Samuel and Padraig. "Jimenez is the finest of us at bayonet drill, but Señorito Filipe has bested him three out of three."

Chavez clapped Samuel on the back. "Boy's a credit to you, Capitán. A great swordsman, a proper gentleman, and a generous employer. The men love him."

"Didn't my snarl scare you, Don Filipe?" Jimenez shook Filipe's hand with a grin.

Muscles rippled beneath Filipe's mud-stained shirt as he pumped Jimenez's hand and pulled the wiry ex-thief into an embrace. "I wasn't watching your mouth flapping, Jimenez. When your eyes fixed on my torso, you signaled your intentions before you attacked."

Padraig nudged Samuel. "I told you I'd make a silk purse out of this sow's ear one day. I couldn't have fought better myself."

"See, Chavez? Padraig should get the credit for training him." Samuel's chest expanded, not only because Filipe had so easily bested the likes of Jimenez but more from Chavez's compliment that Filipe had become a leader and a gentleman. Sofia would be equally proud.

Sofia. The thought of her fighting for her life prickled goose bumps on his arms.

As the men dispersed to the shade of the longboats, a hand touched Samuel's shoulder.

"My compliments on your men, sir." The tall marine lieutenant with a sunburned face extended his hand. "Lieutenant Sherman, Royal Marines. We haven't had time for introductions before. I observed your native troops drilling this last hour despite this infernal heat, and I've never seen the like. They can load and fire a round in fifteen seconds, and they're lethal with bayonets. I'd wager that they're better than the Highlanders."

"Thank you, Lieutenant, that's quite a compliment." Samuel had fought beside the Ninety-Third Highlanders in the Battle of Balaklava; they were warriors indeed. He shook Buckingham's sweaty hand. "These men were my soldiers years ago. Now I'm proud to say they're my friends—they're no longer in the army. They're here as patriots to stop Walker's return."

"Commander Salmon said they—you—are all pathfinders? Experts in jungle warfare? We've had no such experience, and we're not dressed or equipped for it." Sherman touched the breast of his scarlet jacket. "We won't exactly blend in, but the Royal Navy is a stickler about dress code. I wanted to say I'm glad to have you along."

"Thank you, Lieutenant. I look forward to working with you." A heartening moment indeed.

Samuel strode to the gunwale and pulled out his spyglass. The land sloped gently from the strip of golden sand to densely forested hills and on to cone-shaped mountains. He moved the lens northward, searching for Trujillo.

Padraig joined him. "There's the fort. Not there, farther north on that hill."

As Samuel lowered the spyglass to find his bearings, a beam of sunlight burst through the clouds—almost mystical, like an image on a stained-glass window—gilding the sea silver and illuminating the stone fort.

"Must be Fortaleza de Santa Bárbara." Padraig rubbed his beefy hands together. "Now let's see if we have the bastard."

Samuel scanned down toward the beach to a three-masted brig floating on the cyan waters below the fort.

Walker.

Samuel's heartbeat raced. Now, if he could only capture Walker in time. He studied every inch of the deck. "Only a handful of sailors. Is it—"

"That's the *John C. Taylor*, all right." Padraig moved to the ratlines and climbed five feet up the mesh of hemp ropes. "But I can't see any—wait. There. There are a couple of lads, you're right. But no soldiers."

Bare feet padded on the deck behind them as sailors streamed by to man the guns below. Sherman strode from the quarterdeck, calling his marines, who were gathering amidships.

Samuel aimed his spyglass back on the fort. Where were Walker's men?

"It's Walker's boat, Captain Kingston." Sherman spoke from behind Samuel's shoulder. "Commander's compliments, he asks that your men stand to at the entry port to reinforce my boarding party. Walker would be a fool to resist two frigates."

The wind shifted, and Samuel could see the flag rippling above the fort—a red star on white between two horizontal blue bars. Cold dread washed over him. "My God, he's captured the fort."

Padraig swung down to the deck. "This changes everything. We'll never winkle him out of there, not with the handful of men we have."

Samuel focused his spyglass on the fort, swaying with the frigate's roll. Men clustered around four of the ten cannons along the steep stone embankment. "The wretch is there, all right, and he's got several cannons working."

"No . . ." Padraig threw up a hand to shade his eyes and peered at the fort. "How?"

Samuel touched Padraig's arm. "Come. Let's go talk to the commander. I don't want him damaging the brig if Walker's in the fort. Remember, I paid to charter it."

Salmon was already abreast of the situation when they arrived at the quarterdeck. "The scoundrel seized the fort, and there are men standing by several of the cannons."

A wave surged under the hull, and Samuel grabbed the combing to steady himself. "He must've repaired those carriages and mounted the guns."

Salmon frowned and pushed back his cocked hat. "Our round shot will bounce off that stone embankment. See how canted it is? It's going to be difficult to force Walker out of there, gentlemen."

"We must." Samuel jutted out his chin. He refused to quit. Sofia's salvation was within his grasp.

"One hundred men behind the stone walls of a fort." Salmon

locked eyes with Samuel. "Between my *Icarus* and the *Gladiator*, we can muster forty marines. And how many Nicaraguans have you? Twenty odd? Not enough. Not enough at all."

This wouldn't serve. Samuel flashed Salmon an encouraging smile and shrugged. "My men and I have faced greater odds than that, Commander, as did you at the siege of Lucknow."

"All very well, Captain Kingston, but I hardly think we are in a position to—"

"The British government regards Walker as a menace, sir. It's your duty to capture him."

Salmon raised his eyebrows.

Samuel threw back his shoulders. "As for us, if you won't help us, then put me and my men ashore. We'll take him ourselves."

"Hold on there, Captain." Salmon lifted his hands, palms outward. "I want him as badly as—"

"No sir, you do not. If we fail to deliver Walker to the Hondurans, that butcher Guardiola will murder my wife. He'll do it. I've seen his evil work before."

Salmon stroked his chin. "Sherman reports good things about your men. All right then, shall we crack on? I'll take control of the brig first, so he can't turn back. Perhaps the sight of two men-of-war will be enough to make him surrender. I'll anchor beyond the range of the cannon, run up a white flag, and open negotiations."

Samuel shook his head. Whatever his faults, Walker was clever and devious. He wouldn't sit still and negotiate. "Negotiate if you must, Commander, but I know this man. He'll stall you while he plans his escape. I urge you to put your marines ashore with us, and we'll surround the fort. The—"

"This is my ship, Captain, and I give the orders."

Samuel drew a deep breath. "My wife is in mortal danger, sir. And those men over there?"—he pointed to the Euronicas gathered in the waist—"Walker will enslave their country, their families. We're going ashore."

The commander tipped his head up and eyed Samuel silently.

Samuel bit his lip. He was getting too emotional. Salmon was doing the best he could. "I'm sorry, Commander. I'm concerned for my wife."

The helmsman and first lieutenant were watching them now, listening. Samuel took Salmon's elbow and drew him to the starboard gunwale. "You're a sailor, Commander, and I'm a soldier. I know this enemy, and I know how to campaign on land. Together, we can do this. Please trust me when I tell you, Walker's already looking at his back door. We must close it."

Salmon's eyebrows wormed closer together. "We can't capture that fort. Even if your men and my marines surround it, Walker can hold out for months. Our best chance is a negotiated surrender."

Sofia didn't have months. She had days. "Surrounding Walker, denying him the option of retreat, will strengthen your position, Commander."

"True." Salmon thumbed his ear and said nothing for an endless moment. Samuel resisted the urge to tap his foot. "Very well, Captain, I'll put your men and my marines ashore while I open negotiations."

"Thank you, Commander. You're making the right decision."

"I hope I am. Our cook will provide you with victuals for your time ashore. Now if you'll excuse me, I must update Lieutenant Buckingham."

Samuel strode back to the men, who watched him with dark irises expanding.

"Set him right, did you? Good for you." Padraig rubbed the scar on his nose, a sure sign he was preparing for a fight. "Salmon's no coward. He'll back us."

"We're going ashore with the marines." Samuel jabbed a finger towards Sergeant Zamora. "Take Chavez to the galley and ask the cook for five days' food for every man."

Zamora snaped off a smart salute. "Si señor. And we will catch him I promise you."

"Jimenez." Samuel closed with Jimenez and looked around,

checking none of *Icarus'* crew was within earshot. "Snoop around and see if you can liberate a map from the Sailing Master."

Jimenez's face, usually stoic, broke into a grin, and he bobbed his head before backing away through the throng of men.

The Euronicas cheered and thumped one another's backs as if they'd already captured Walker. It was a beginning, and Samuel was heartened. But onshore, William Walker was entrenched and prepared. Even with the marines from both frigates, the filibuster outnumbered them two to one, and he would never surrender his final roll of the dice. Samuel forced a smile for his keen men.

CHAPTER TWENTY

Gnawing pain in Samuel's gut woke him again. The men were still sleeping, and the only sounds were snores, the chirp of crickets, and the *swish* of waves whispering over the sand. His muscles creaked painfully from sleeping on the beach for ten days in a row. He checked his watch with unsteady hands. Five a.m.! Only thirteen more days to Guardiola's deadline, to Sofia's execution. So little time. His shoulders stiffened and drooped. They had to attack this minute. It was time—beyond time. Curse Commander Salmon for holding them back so long.

It was a standoff at the vast bay curving in a graceful arc of rolling green hills and silver sand from the hook of Puerto Castillo on his right that sheltered Trujillo all the way west to Tela where poor Sofia languished over a hundred miles away. *Icarus* and *Gladiator* were shadows in the bluing light of dawn, anchored fore and aft to train their heavy guns, 24- and 32-pounders, on the fort, and the filibusters' cannons pointed back at them from the lofty embankment like accusing fingers.

Eager to avoid bloodshed, Commander Salmon had exchanged letters with Walker for ten blasted days that Sofia didn't have to spare. It was already the twenty-second of August, yet Salmon and Walker were arguing over money and government paper left in the customhouse, of all things, a sum of $2,025. Desperate for a peaceful resolution, Salmon couldn't see that Walker was stringing him along. Every day he had assured Samuel that Walker was surrendering, and every day the sun had set on the barred gates of the fortress.

He was an idiot. He shouldn't have listened to the commander, shouldn't have gone along with this timorous strategy. Even if he managed the impossible and they took the fort, it would be a scramble to deliver Walker to Guardiola in time to save Sofia.

He had to do it. He had to risk an attack.

Samuel pushed his left foot into his boot, the invasive sand gritty between his toes, and eyed the bluff above him. The steep grass slope and stone embankment capping it presented a daunting climb. The nine- and twelve-pounder cannons bristling along the wall presented another challenge; with their height, they could strike the Royal Navy frigates in the inky bay. The frigates had sharp teeth too, which is why both sides were so reluctant to spark a full-scale artillery duel. So it fell to Samuel to break this stalemate.

As he dragged on his other boot, he couldn't make out the morning watch on the *Icarus* below. Good. That meant they couldn't see his preparations either. But if he could read his pocket watch by the light of the half moon, Walker's sentries could spot any attack across the open ground in front of the fort.

He shook Padraig awake. "It's time. Even that waning moon's too bright to approach the west wall. We must climb the embankment from the beach."

"Right, I'm ready." Padraig sat up and scrubbed the sleep from his eyes. "But are you sure about this? Salmon believes Walker will surrender. They exchanged correspondence again yesterday."

"Arguing back and forth about the customhouse regulations." Samuel daubed his face with boot polish. "Walker's stalling him, and we're out of time. Why did I wait so long?"

Padraig rolled his eyes. "Salmon should've unloaded a nine-pound cannon and blown the gate off its hinges."

"Walker would've sunk any longboat carrying a cannon ashore. Lieutenant Sherman has run out of patience too, and I convinced him to storm the gate if he arose one morning to find an attack in progress."

Padraig let out a low whistle. "Commander Salmon won't be happy about that."

Samuel belted on his saber. "Sherman will say he'd no choice but to attack when he heard us fighting inside."

"Salmon's feelings are the least of our worries." Padraig squinted up at the stone embankment. "The odds are against us. Walker has a hundred men up there, and we have twenty-three."

"We'll be fine. You're worth ten men." Samuel tried to sound more confident than he was as he poked Filipe with his toe. "Filipe, it's time."

"I'm ready. I've been awake for hours." Filipe sat up spryly and shoved the revolver lying beside him into his belt.

"I'm worth only ten men? You undervalue me." Padraig closed the flap on his holster. "Pray we can reach that gate."

"Exactly." Samuel's stomach twinged again, and he rubbed it absently as he passed the tin of boot polish to his friend. "Let's check the men are ready."

"Your stomach hurts. No wonder. You've eaten little since we left Tela."

"Can't. I'm too worried about . . . Come along."

Save for Padraig, whose skin never held a tan but only burned, the men were almost invisible with their dark complexions and forest-green shirts. Equipment clinking, they crowded around Samuel and Padraig, whispering as Zamora and Chavez jostled them into position.

"Secure that rattling gear." Samuel slung his Henry rifle over his shoulder. "Cortez and Jimenez will cross the wall first and take out the sentries."

He led the way across the sand to the foot of the bluff and

waited for the men to spread out. The shadows hid them here, but moonlight showered over the top, and they'd be in plain sight when they crested the embankment. He smelled wet clay and salt as he picked his climbing route.

Jimenez ascended through the whispering tall grass as easily as if there were stairs. He paused and tilted his head to one side, listening. All Samuel heard were waves breaking on the sand below and the whine of crickets. When Jimenez beckoned, he began the steep climb with Padraig right behind him. He rolled his tongue around his dry mouth. Sofia's life depended on his success. If he fell, they were both dead, and the children would grow up as orphans. He clenched his jaw and focused on grabbing his next handhold in the soft clay. It was too late to dwell on anything else.

Jimenez offered a hand at the top. Scree rattled underfoot as he pulled himself onto the crumbling ledge, his nose grazing the damp stone.

"Nothing stirring, Capitán. Cortez is ready. Go?"

Samuel patted him on the shoulder, and Jimenez skittered up the canted wall like a spider, sprinkling Samuel with sandy clay and pebbles.

Samuel heaved Padraig up beside him. "Never say I don't take you sightseeing."

Padraig sniggered and adjusted his slouch hat. "Let's do it."

Samuel rubbed his hands together, stretched for a gap in the jigsaw of uneven stones, and pulled himself up as he probed with the tip of his boot for an opening. The rough rock brushed his cheeks as he clambered from handhold to toehold.

A moonlit shadow appeared at the top, and Jimenez helped him over the low wall. "No sentries, Capitán. Strange. I'll check the barracks." He adjusted the machete hanging from his waist and looped away toward the only building where light flickered within.

The fort appeared far less formidable from the inside, a single-story stone barrack room against the walls and a two-level guardroom to the left of the wooden gates on the town side. Far below, the two frigates rode at anchor like toy boats on a silver pond. The susurration of crickets drowned the sounds of the Euronicas clearing the wall. They reeked of cold sweat when they joined him, their war faces gray as limestone in the pale moonlight as they fitted bayonets with metallic *snicks*. Samuel's spirits buoyed despite the gravity of their situation. These men would fight to the death for him.

He unslung his rifle and chopped his hand forward curtly. Padraig led the first band to the right, and Sergeant Zamora took seven men toward the single-story buildings. Samuel darted across the trampled grass of the square.

Jimenez appeared from the corner of the barracks holding his rifle across his chest. "A dozen wounded men, nobody else. He's gone, Capitán."

Not again. Samuel's toes curled up in his boots. The bastard had slipped away in the night. It was several seconds before he could bring himself to turn back to Jimenez and proceed. "Are they armed?"

"Guns, but no fight left in them."

"Samuel!" Padraig called. "Nobody's here."

Zamora trotted up. "Same on this side. What happened, señor?"

"I don't know, I don't know. Walker's gone." Samuel yanked off his hat and dragged a hand through his matted hair. "Padraig, come with me. We'll talk to the wounded. The rest of you, stay alert. This could still be a trap."

The barracks was an empty stone cavern, where the animal stench of waste and blood was overpowering. The light of a dwindling fire flickered across the men lying on the floor or propped against the wall. Despite their terrible wounds, all seemed stoic, resigned to whatever tragedy fate had planned.

Samuel kicked up dust that tickled his nose as he and Padraig approached a captain in a vintage US Army jacket. "Where's Walker?"

The captain glanced at them disinterestedly. "Gone."

"What happened here?" Samuel slung his rifle over his shoulder.

"Those you see here, their wounds prevented them from breaking out with him." The captain groaned and would've fallen forward if Samuel hadn't caught him.

"Easy, soldier. Where are you hit?"

The captain held up a bloody stump, and Samuel winced. "A musket ball at point blank as I fired over the wall. They took my hand."

"Did they get your pistol too?" Padraig sniped. He stepped close to examine the bandaged arm. "Look here, Captain Filibuster, Walker's a ruthless man with dangerous ambitions that've already killed thousands. We must end this. Where's he headed?"

"That's all I'll tell you."

Padraig removed his coat. "Tell us where he's headed and his plans so we can stop him."

"Screw you, Irish prick."

"Want to play tough, then? Fine by me." Padraig rolled up a sleeve. "Jimenez, pass me your machete."

The prisoners behind Samuel squirmed and whispered, but when Jimenez drew his machete with a rasp, the room fell silent. He could've heard a pin drop.

Padraig took the machete and seized the captain's good hand. "If you don't tell me where Walker's gone, you'll be picking your nose with a big toe."

Samuel swiveled his face away to hide the flicker of a smile. Broad-shouldered and marred by the livid scar across his nose, Padraig cut a frightening figure, but he would never follow through with such a cruel act. Still, he played his part well.

The filibuster crumpled against the wall. "Inland."

"Eh? Where inland?"

"To rendezvous with General Cabañas."

"And?" Padraig raised the machete.

"And what? I don't know what you want! I'll tell you anything, but I don't know what you want."

"What are Walker and Cabañas planning to do?"

"They're going to cross Honduras to a place called El Trunfo or something." Sweat rolled off the captain's forehead. "Close to the Pacific coast."

Jimenez sucked in a breath. "El Triunfo. Close to the Nicaraguan frontier, north of Chinandega."

Filipe inhaled sharply. "It's true then. They're going to attack our home."

The machete inched higher. "And then what are they going to do?"

"The boy's right. They'll march on Nicaragua. Please don't do it, sir. I've children." The captain sagged into a faint.

"I knew it." Jimenez punched the palm of his hand. "El Triunfo."

Samuel stooped beside the injured captain. "Bring water. This man is burning up."

Padraig took out his tobacco and waved it in front of the prisoners. "Anyone for a smoke?"

Another prisoner cried out, and Samuel rose to see what happened. A man near the door was cringing away from Sergeant Zamora, Carmona, and Soto as they entered.

"Don't let the natives slaughter us." The prisoner's voice was a shriek.

Central American soldiers seldom took prisoners, and filibusters could expect a painful death. Samuel lifted his hands, palms forward. "We won't harm you. We'll hand you to the Royal Navy, and their sawbones will treat your wounds." He scrubbed a grimy hand across his face in exasperation; "sawbones" was a poor choice of words in front of a man who'd lost his hand and might also lose the arm. He beckoned to Zamora. "There's a dozen wounded here. Take their weapons outside, and let the boys pick what they want."

"Sí, señor. Gracias."

"I'm going to open the main gate for the marines and update Lieutenant Sherman." Samuel picked a torch from the pail by the door and lit it from the failing fire. The greasy smoke stung his eyes as he hurried from the chamber.

Urgency flogged his pace across the square. He couldn't believe Walker had escaped again. Commander Salmon would be furious about this morning's attack, and it was doubtful he'd allow Samuel to pursue Walker inland. He took the worn steps to the guardroom three at a time. He'd leave right away, before Salmon even knew Walker had fled.

The guardroom stank of chalk and urine, and insects scuttled into the shadows as he made his way to the small window. A falling ember burned his hand as he thrust the torch through the opening and tossed his signal outside. Now the marines wouldn't fire on them when he opened the gate.

Sweat glistened on Cortez's forehead where he stood by the gate with Quintero. "Easy one, Captain, eh? I think that pirate Walker's afraid of us. Ready to let the redcoats in?"

An owl hooted twice somewhere in the ancient eaves of the fort as the gate creaked open. The white breeches and cross belts of the two dozen marines waiting outside gleamed in the moonlight. In their cylindrical shakos and tight tailcoats, they reminded Samuel of red crickets.

"What happened?" Lieutenant Sherman called as his men passed through the gate. "Surely you didn't capture the fort without a shot."

Samuel surveyed the marines quickly. They clutched their rifles with white knuckles and exchanged wide-eyed glances, but they looked determined If only they could join him on the hunt. "Walker's gone, left the wounded and disappeared. Didn't your lads see anything?"

"Gone? I assure you, he didn't come this way. I doubled the guard last night."

Chavez pushed through the marines at the gate, already rattling off a report in Spanish. "Capitán, they went over the south wall. I saw tracks leading into the jungle."

"English, Chavez, English." Samuel didn't have time to translate for Sherman.

Chavez pointed south. "I found a rope where they went over the wall."

Muscles tautened in Sherman's neck and he glared bleakly a Samuel. "Bloody hell, I thought that side was unscalable. I should've posted men there. Commander Salmon will be furious."

There was no time to waste. If Walker made it to General Cabañas, he'd use Cabañas's rebel troops to invade Nicaragua. "We must pursue him immediately."

Sherman removed his shako and scrubbed a hand across his sweaty forehead. "Not without orders. I must report to the commander."

"No time for that." Samuel glanced at Chavez. "Take Cortez and Quintero. Question the townsfolk. Find a suitable guide if you can, perhaps a local hunter. Lieutenant, follow us as soon as you can. I'll slow Walker down."

Sherman cursed under his breath. Samuel had often experienced the frustration of a rigid chain of command and almost felt sorry for him. "Don't worry, we'll stall him. But make sure you show up. Walker still has sixty or seventy men with him. He outnumbers my tiny force three to one."

"I'll pull foot to the *Icarus*." Sherman extended his hand. "I wish you the joy of the hunt, and I'll do my utmost to follow as soon as possible." Months of living in damp conditions aboard ship had faded patches of his jacket to pink, and red dye stained his white breeches. His calf-length boots were scuffed and covered with mud, but the lieutenant was still every inch a soldier—tall, erect, and confident.

"I know. Because if you don't, we'll end up as the prey." Samuel drank some water, but it did little to slake his dry mouth.

The rosy sun had climbed out of the water by the time Chavez and a man of indeterminate age dressed in tattered shirt and trousers approached Samuel and Padraig, who were smoking in the shade of a palm tree outside the fort. "Marco has hunted in the hills around here for years."

"Sí, señor, I know every path and mountain trail." Marco's sunken face was dark and leathery from the sun. He extended a calloused hand. "This man said you'll pay me well? One piece of silver now, and another each day I'm on the hunt."

Samuel shot a glance at Chavez. He was handsomely generous with Samuel's money. "And he told you what we're looking for?"

Marco ran his hand through the fringe of silver hair around his shiny scalp. "I saw them last night when they sneaked through the village."

Samuel perked up. "How many?"

The wrinkles on Marco's forehead scrunched together. He spread his fingers and closed his fists six times, hesitated, and splayed his fingers again.

"He can't count," Chavez said, "but I guess that means seventy."

"That many!" Padraig flicked the stub of his cigarette onto the sparse grass. "We'll be hard pressed to slow them down."

Samuel opened his mouth to speak but hesitated. Walker had far more men; it was rash to pursue him with the Euronicas alone. He glanced at the steam frigates, with their masts and funnels casting long shadows across the water. The longboat bobbed alongside the *Icarus*, but there was no sign of Lieutenant Sherman. He twisted the ring on his finger. Army, navy, they were all the same; no one could ever make a quick decision. "Did you see which way they went?"

Marco's dark eyes lit up. "Sí, señor. North, up the coast trail."

Chavez, usually calmest man in the company, rubbed his hands together. "So we chase them, Capitán?"

Sunlight twinkled on the silver coin Samuel flicked to Marco. "Any idea what time they left?"

"Midnight."

Samuel pinched his lips together and took out his watch. "Six thirty. Quite a head start; we'd better push on. Tell the men we're leaving, and make sure they pack plenty of water. We're not stopping until we find Walker."

For five years—far too long—Samuel and Nicaragua had lived alongside the threat of William Walker, and he could stand it no longer. He would end it now.

He would save Sofia.

The rain pounded relentlessly on the jungle canopy, cascading through the leafy boughs arching overhead and soaking the Euronicas plodding the muddy trail. It was scarcely four in the evening, but twilight had already descended, dark and low as Samuel's spirit. He was running out of time. Sofia was running out of time; it was already the twenty-seventh of August, and Guardiola would murder her on the third of September. It was their fifth day in the jungle, and Walker seemed to have lost his way. The filibusters had backtracked several times, and Marco reckoned Samuel's party was only thirty miles from the coast. Jimenez had checked their back trail for Sherman and his marines but found no sign of them. The Euronicas were on their own.

Thank goodness they had a guide who knew the trails. The old hunter strode tirelessly at Samuel's shoulder as if he were simply crossing a field. Chavez and Cortez roamed farther ahead, serving as their eyes and ears.

The humidity clung to his chest, filling his lungs and weighing him down. He tried to disregard the sting of chafed feet in his sodden boots and Padraig muttering a stream of complaints to Filipe behind them. He scrunched his face at the rain streaming inside the collar of his oilskin.

Padraig caught up with him. "This bloody humidity. I feel I'm marching in a horse's mouth. Think he's far ahead?"

Samuel adjusted the Henry's sling over his shoulder. Even the rifle was heavy after lugging it so far. "I don't know, but I'm sure we're catching up. The Euronicas are used to trekking in the endless rain, but Walker's Americans won't be. I dare say few of them have been in the tropics before, and if they're hurting like I am, they'll be going slower."

"Probably shitting themselves." Padraig brushed a wet branch aside, showering Samuel with rainwater. "Many of Walker's recruits are townies. This place will terrify them."

"Not all of them. Last time we clashed, he had some tough country boys and war veterans, even a couple of Texas Rangers."

"I'd prefer city boys this time." Padraig jumped a puddle and landed short, splattering mud on Samuel. "Blooming deluge. I'll never complain about the rain back home. This place makes Ireland look like the desert."

Filipe trudged behind them. "City boys, country boys, choir boys—it doesn't matter. Even if they outnumber us four to one, I'll killed the cursed invaders."

The distant sound of musketry made Samuel shuffle back and bump into Filipe. "Chavez and Cortez?"

Padraig cocked an ear. "That gunfire's over a mile away. Many guns."

Samuel unslung the Henry. "We need to see what's happening ahead. Hide in the undergrowth if I give the word. Quietly, now."

The rumble and pop of muskets and rifles rose and fell in crescendos as Samuel picked his way ahead while his heart pounded. Over the next five minutes, it died off to a dribble of infrequent shots.

"Sounds like a running battle," Padraig whispered.

But who was fighting? Samuel prayed that Cortez and Chavez were safe. "Don't talk, lis—"

A figure materialized from the shadowed undergrowth.

Samuel startled, aimed the Henry, and relaxed. "Christ, Cortez, I could've shot you."

Cortez pointed at the path ahead of them. "Hondurans, Capitán, hundreds, and Walker walked right into them."

Chavez stepped out of the dusk. "Walker's retreating to the coast, señor."

Hundreds of Hondurans! Samuel's mind whirled with the ramifications. "Has to be General Alvarez. If he captures Walker, Guardiola will execute Sofia. He wants *me* to bring Walker in. We must get to him before Alvarez."

Padraig sucked in his cheeks.

"Alvarez?" Chavez raised his eyebrows. "Why does it matter who captures Walker?"

"Alvarez is Guardiola's political rival." Samuel whipped off his damp hat and scraped a hand through his greasy hair. "Guardiola believes Alvarez will use Walker's capture to advance his popularity in the next election, I guess, but who knows."

"The butcher warned us he'd execute Sofia if Alvarez captures Walker. We must bring the wretch back." Padraig flipped up his holster flap, drew his Colt, and checked his charges. Dry. Thank God for these oilskins."

"Blast it." Samuel kicked over a termite nest. "I should have moved on the fort sooner."

Behind Padraig, Filipe's grubby hand flew to his mouth as Chavez stepped back from Samuel's anger.

"Sorry, Chavez." Samuel placed a hand on his muscled shoulder. "I'm not shouting at you. I should have told you about Alvarez earlier. But with all that's—"

"I didn't mention it either." Padraig flushed and clutched his Sharps rifle to his chest. "I figured it unlikely we'd bump into Alvarez in this big wilderness."

Chavez pressed a cap onto the nipple of his rifle. "Understandable, Captain. There was much to consider. So let's catch Walker before General Alvarez does. By the sign back there, Walker stung the Hondurans in that skirmish. The Americans' rifles are deadly compared to their muskets, and the Hondurans are hanging back, reluctant to pursue, but they—"

"Then there's hope. We must apprehend Walker before they do." Samuel beckoned the old guide back, who was sipping water from his chipped jicara. "Marco, is there another way onto that trail? Where does it lead?"

"Río Negro, señor. And the coast."

"Walker's going to try for a boat. With General Alvarez behind him and the British waiting in Trujillo, that's his only chance. How far is Río Negro from Trujillo?"

Marco contemplated the jungle canopy as he made some calculation. "Nine, ten hours walk."

"Can we cut him off?"

"No, señor. The jungle is too dense."

Jimenez's stolen map had more blank space than details—the Royal Navy—had obviously not surveyed inland, Samuel would have to rely on Marco.

Padraig removed his slouch hat and dragged his forearm across his wet eyes. "And how will we avoid the Hondurans on the trail?"

"Shush!" Samuel touched his lips with his forefinger. "We must sneak past them tonight. Warn the men. No noise, no smoking. Cold tortillas for supper, I'm afraid." He peered through the rain. "Jimenez, come here. You're our fastest runner. Pull foot back to Trujillo and update Commander Salmon. Offer my suggestion that the *Icarus* hurry to Río Negro. Tell him that we'll drive Walker toward him."

"Capitán." Jimenez gathered his rifle and padded off into the gloom.

The rest of them settled beneath the thickest cover they could find to rest their weary legs. Samuel handed his coat to

Marco. As smooth as he was in the jungle, the poor man would have a hard time keeping up with the Euronicas tonight.

Samuel woke four hours later. The rain had stopped, and the forest reeked like a greenhouse salted with animal scat. He'd dozed off. The time? He rested against the scabby trunk of the enormous tree and pulled out his watch. The whirr of insects almost drowned the snores of the men on the small patch of ground they had cleared and trampled. It was too dark to tell the time. He rose and headed for a ribbon of moonlight lancing through the jungle canopy, his muscles aching as he picked his way past the men.

Miguel Quintero materialized from the shadows. "All is well, Capitán. Only the monkeys are out tonight. How much longer?" His dark face was prematurely leathered from sea and sun; he could've been any age from twenty-five to ten years older.

"Good night to you, Quintero." Water had condensed inside his watch. Lord, was any watch made that could keep out the tropical humidity and rain? "Ten. We've another hour. How are you holding up?"

"Good. Happy to see the end in sight. Once we capture Walker, we can go home to peace and perhaps on to Ireland. I'd prefer that we killed him, though."

Samuel gave a grim laugh. "You too? Go back to the others. I'll stand picket now. There's still time to rest."

The raindrops on the lush vegetation glittered like pearls where the moonlight touched them and trimmed the trail with a silver halo. Crickets chirped, and the warble of night birds filled the balmy air. At any other time, without the present danger, it would've been magical. Not now. With the threat to Sofia, the complication of seven hundred Hondurans loose in the jungle, and the dubious prospect of ending Walker once and for all, it was hell.

A branch crackled in the forest, and Samuel raised the Henry. Damn it, he should've heeded his duty post, now someone was sneaking up on them. He fingered the lever with a clammy hand.

A bulky shadow shuffled from the forest, and Samuel's breath hitched. He took a tentative step forward. White streaks striped the beast's dark fur, and it was at least six feet in length. A bear? It couldn't be a bear.

The beast snuffled and shuffled toward him, revealing a long tubular snout and tiny ears. What the devil?

Cortez's laugh made him jump. "A giant anteater, Captain. They're harmless." He spoke in English, as was his custom with Samuel and Padraig.

"Dear Lord, it scared the hell out of me, almost as much as your appearance did." Samuel rolled his tongue to wet his parched mouth. "Sure it's harmless?"

"Unless you're an ant or a termite."

The anteater lifted its long snout, sniffed the air, and scuttled back into the forest.

Samuel relaxed his grip on the Henry rifle. "Why are you up?"

"I couldn't sleep, so I thought I'd relieve Quintero of his watch."

"Relieve him of his watch?" Padraig emerged from the bushes shielding the clearing where the men were resting. "I thought Jimenez was the light-fingered one around here."

Cortez rubbed his chin. "Hmm?"

Samuel waved his arm. "Forget it, another of his stupid jokes. It seems nobody can sleep right now. Are you ready for this?"

"Me and the lads are raring to go, sir. We want to take Walker down for once and for all."

"Three to one odds." Padraig rubbed his hands together. "We can manage that."

"No. We won't confront them directly." Samuel swat at a mosquito on his neck. "We can't risk anything that could allow Walker to get away. We'll slip past the Hondurans and then drive the filibusters toward the marines—but, when the time comes, I'll take Walker. I want Walker myself."

"But what if they—"

"Jimenez will get a message through to the Icarus. They'll show up. Walker's end is nigh. Let's rouse the lads."

The faintest glimmers of fires marked the Honduran camp on the trail as Samuel squeezed through wet branches, bamboo, and tangled vines after Chavez. The rainforest wrapped around him like a verdant womb, lush and deadly, alive with strident bird-calls, the flapping of wings, and the hoots of monkeys. The air, smelling like rotting fruit, was as thick as warm stew in his lungs. It was baffling how Chavez picked his way through the under-growth with so little light to guide him.

Years ago, he'd trained the Euronicas in jungle warfare, and they'd been as good as the Burmese pathfinders he'd fought back in fifty-three. He glanced behind. Their muddy shirts and dark complexions blended into the night; shadows as imperceptible as the chameleons at the London Zoo. They moved silently, having secured their equipment to make sure nothing rattled.

A faint whiff of smoke tickled his nose. He halted, and Filipe bumped into him.

"Smoke." Samuel's voice was a parched whisper. "Can you smell it?"

Filipe shook his head.

"Hold on. I'll check." He crept ahead, testing the ground for loose twigs and roots that might trip him.

There it was again—the acrid scent of cheap tobacco. A sentry. The familiar tic started beneath his left eye. Chavez should've warned him. Where was he? He glanced back, but even Filipe was invisible. If he moved again, the sentry might hear him. He'd authorized Chavez to knock out any sentry as a last resort but not to kill him. With any luck, the Hondurans would blame it on Walker's filibusters.

A shadow emerged from the undergrowth. Chavez. "Capitán. A sentry, but I took care of him."

"You didn't harm him?"

"He'll have a headache, nothing more. And I dropped the American tobacco beside him as you asked."

"Good man." Padraig's tobacco might convince the Hondurans it was the filibusters. "Can we slip past them?"

"Yes, Capitán. Head directly west from here. I'll take the rear and cover our tracks. Have Soto give his macaw call when you're all clear."

He gave Chavez's sweaty shoulder a squeeze and padded along the animal trail, confident that Chavez would direct Zavala and the others after him. Somewhere to his left, a creature snuffled in the undergrowth, the sound faint against the constant whirr of insects in the dense jungle. The foliage closed in until he was almost doubled over. Time doled out seconds grain by grain. Wet leaves slapped him, and thorns scratched him as he crept forward. Sweat trickled down his torso, clammy and cold, and streamed down his forehead, stinging his eyes.

He waited for Filipe to catch up. "Stay close to me no matter what."

Filipe's eyes were black saucers in tiny white rings. "I will."

Someone hollered from behind, and a musket discharged.

"That's torn it," Padraig growled over Filipe's shoulder. "Carmona, who's behind you?"

"I don't know, señor."

Two more shots echoed in the jungle, and voices called out. They'd roused General Alvarez's Hondurans.

"Blessed Virgin, save us. I'll see for myself." Branches rustled as Padraig doubled back.

The last thing they needed was a confused battle with Alvarez's Hondurans. Samuel's stomach hardened as he peered into the darkness. They couldn't engage the Hondurans, no matter what. If they did, the Hondurans might accuse them of aiding Walker. And if he failed to slip past them and capture Walker, he'd be left empty-handed. With no bargaining chip to win Sofia back from Guardiola, she'd be doomed.

He held his breath and stood still. Judging by the shouts and noise, the jungle was alive with men.

When he could bear it no longer, he touched Filipe's shoulder. "Wait here. I must see for myself."

Two steps into the thick darkness, he stopped. What a foolish impulse. He'd only add to the confusion by thrashing around in the jungle. "Sorry, Filipe. I'd better wait here." He rested against the spiky bark of a tree and fought to control his breathing so he could listen.

More men yelled in the distance, and another gunshot made him jump. The undergrowth rustled, and Padraig appeared with Chavez, both panting hard.

Padraig came so close his breath tickled Samuel's cheek, stinking of the foul iguanas and plants they'd been eating since their food ran out. "We lost four men. I hope to God they're only behind the Hondurans and not—"

"Dear Lord." Samuel's heart clenched. "Who?"

"Delgado, Sanchez, Gutierrez, and Sergeant Zamora. He was at the rear. We—"

"Let's move on. We can do nothing for them." They had to continue the chase.

Padraig gaped at him.

Samuel plunged up the narrow trail brushing branches aside. "Zamora's smart, he'll keep clear of them."

"If they're still alive." Padraig adjusted his haversack and padded after him.

But Samuel hadn't the luxury of considering the fate of his missing men. He had to catch Walker and deliver him to Guardiola before the butcher murdered Sofia. The men understood that.

CHAPTER TWENTY-ONE

A day later, Samuel's weary legs burned as he climbed the overgrown path twisting through a leafy tunnel up yet another hill. It was already the twenty-ninth of August, and only five days remained in which to accomplish—well, everything. Actually, four days, because it would take the *Icarus* ten full hours to make the passage from Trujillo back to Tela. With their rifles handy, his Euronicas padded behind quietly without the subdued chatter of the old days when they'd conversed more than a similar patrol of British soldiers. They understood the importance of this mission. Cortez, the rear marker, halted every few paces to scan behind him.

Samuel paused and sagged against a gnarled tree. It was another steaming day, with low rain clouds pressing on the forest, trapping the morning heat like the lid of a kettle. If his lungs burned from his labors, the company had to be in the same poor condition.

The men shuffled to a stop behind him.

"Chavez, five minutes' rest. Make sure they drink water."

No sooner had they settled in a loose group, smoking, and talking with their rifles close at hand, then gunfire erupted on the hilltop. Bullets splatted into the mud around them. One notched the bark above Samuel's head, pelting his hat with splinters.

Soto clutched his side and doubled over.

"Ambush!" Samuel swung the Henry around and fired at the wisps of smoke on the ridge, working the lever as fast as he could. Spent cartridges *pinged* into the air.

"Rifles, must be the bloody filibusters. The Hondurans have muskets." Padraig fired up hill and reloaded in seconds to fire again.

"Has to be the yanquis, the Hondurans are behind us." Filipe ported Samuel's Sharps rifle and dashed off, jinking from tree to tree. He vanished into the curtain of vines hanging from the towering trees.

Stupid boy would get himself killed. Samuel rose to follow Filipe, but bullets pecked the trees around him, forcing him back to cover. "Jesus, Filipe. Get down and stay down." Bile roiled in his gut.

Then the gunfire lulled.

To hell with this. They had caught up to Walker. He couldn't cower here while the bastard escaped. Not with time running out on Sofia, not after the pain the filibuster had inflicted on his family. He'd kill him. He charged up the hill, and rifles barked behind him as the Euronicas lashed the hilltop with withering fire. The Henry's hammer dropped with an empty click. He ducked into the undergrowth, the rifle's hot foregrip burning his palm and stinking of hot gun oil. After wrapping his handkerchief around his hand, he reloaded, shells clunking down the steaming barrel as he gulped for breath and prayed Filipe had stayed undercover. He couldn't lose the boy too. By the time he released the sleeve's feeder and sighted on the hilltop, the gunfire was desultory, but the pungent stench of gun smoke clung to the wet air.

He threw up a hand. "Cease fire. Hold your fire."

The gunfire petered out and scattered curses replaced it as the men reloaded. Samuel coughed on the acrid gun smoke and peered at the hillcrest with watering eyes. Nothing. "I think they moved on. Cover me, I'll check."

He wriggled uphill through the mud and wild grass and paused ten yards from the ridgetop to listen. Silence. He pushed to his feet with a grunt and jinked from tree to tree, with his men's feet pounding behind him. They were vulnerable if the filibusters were still there. He jogged past three bodies along the trail. Another was propped against a tree, eyes closed as if he'd gone to sleep, but his shirt was soaked through with blood. Dead, like the other three. Samuel scanned the trail ahead; the filibusters had fled.

"It's only me." Filipe emerged from the trees. "They're gone."

"Young fool. Don't dash off like that again." Samuel lowered his rifle, panting. They'd got clean away. "What happened to Lopez? He should've warned us."

Filipe motioned to the undergrowth where he'd been hiding. "Back there. God, they . . . they cut his throat."

Not Lopez, too. How had the filibusters caught him? Lopez was an experienced scout.

Samuel trudged over. Lopez's eyes were staring at nothing, and the wound on his neck was a gory smile. Bright red blood, already blackening, soaked his muddy green shirt.

"He was a good one." Padraig's face crumpled as he winced. "I don't love music, but I liked the sound of his flute."

Poor bugger. All the way from a hut in Chinandega to die in the jungle in a foreign land because he believed in liberty. Samuel closed Lopez's staring eyes and jerked stiffly to his feet. "A pox on Walker. How many more of us will die before we end his tyranny?"

The undergrowth rustled, and branches parted as Chavez appeared like a wraith. "They hit Castro in the leg, and Soto took a bullet too, clean through his side. Nothing fatal."

Samuel flexed his fingers around the rifle. Damned Walker. Two injured men would slow them down, but they couldn't leave them out here in the jungle. "Let me look at them, then we'll bury poor Lopez. Chavez, have Cortez stand guard at the next bend. Lopez would want you to pray the last rites."

They were ready to move out again in less than an hour, but Samuel's spirits were dragging. Besides himself, Padraig, and Filipe, he had eight able-bodied men left. There was no way of knowing how many Walker had lost in his skirmish with the Hondurans a couple of days ago; Chavez reckoned from their tracks that Walker still had forty filibusters. He clenched his jaw and resisted the urge to press the men for a faster pace. He couldn't afford to exhaust them further. Now the odds were four to one—and worse, he was out of time.

Before they left, he pulled Marco aside. The guide gave him an answer that jangled his nerves: They were seven days' march from the Royal Navy frigates at Trujillo. If Jimenez hadn't delivered his message or if Salmon had failed to sail to meet them— even if he caught Walker first—Alvarez would take him from them, snatching Samuel's vengeance and Sofia's life from his bloody, exhausted hands.

"Río Sico." Marco, knee deep in the narrow river, splashed muddy water on his face before pointing east. "We're one hour from the coast."

Samuel's stomach churned, as much from hunger as anxiety. It was the last day of August. Only three days remained to deliver Walker to Guardiola, three days to save Sofia. He closed his eyes and choked back a hard sigh. No, he couldn't show weakness now, not when the men were exhausted and looking to him for strength, for leadership. The window to save Sofia was closing. If he flagged, she was finished. Carrying the wounded had slowed them down—they still hadn't caught the filibusters— and their meager supplies had run out. Even Padraig had lost pounds, his skin sunburned and muddy, the corners of his eyes wrinkled from squinting into the sun.

Nobody was talking now, no banter, no jests, not even a complaint. The men's faces were drawn and lined as they stumbled along the narrow path.

Filipe tripped over a gnarled root and fell with a curse. "This is hopeless. We're never going to catch Walker. They're going to kill Sofia."

"Rubbish. We're almost there." Samuel's legs ached as he stooped to help him up. Christ, Filipe's arms were thin now; the men were wasting away. "We've trapped him against the ocean. All we need to do is grab him."

He must sound more confident than he was. He nudged Filipe ahead. "Come on, best foot forward. We're going to save her, I promise, but I need your help to do it."

"I'm going to kill Walker for leading us on this chase." Padraig stepped to Filipe's other side.

"Not if I get the *maldito* first." Filipe strode faster and passed by Padraig. Mud spattered his expensive trousers, which were ripped at one knee. His shirt, stiff with sweat, hung out of his loose waistband, and he'd lost his oilskin coat.

The rest of the men were equally gaunt and ragged. Soto was pale and wincing with every step, and Castro was sweating, breathing shallowly in the makeshift litter. Fortunately, the men had killed iguanas and a sloth to supplement the mangos and plants Chavez foraged. Samuel tilted his face to the scorching afternoon sun. Chavez hadn't reported back for over two hours, come to think of it, not even about reaching the river.

Kawukawuk! The hoarse honk drew Samuel's attention to a bird with green and blue plumage and a ring of intense blue separating its black crown from its head. It was a cry some of the Euronicas used as a signal. The Bobo ticked its racket-shaped tail like a pendulum as it scolded the soldiers from its perch. At the riverbank, Filipe plunged his head under the water and flipped it back in a shower of droplets, closing his eyes as the rivulets trickled down his face. He filled his canteen, took it to the wounded men, and helped them drink.

The underbrush rustled, and Chavez emerged, dripping with sweat, his dark face flushed purple. Samuel stood so quickly that his head spun. Chavez almost vibrated, darting glances over his shoulder. He must've found something.

"They're in a farmhouse . . . up ahead on the bank . . ." Chavez doubled over with his hands on his knees and panted. "I saw—"

"How many of them? Did you see Walker?" Saliva flooded Samuel's mouth, and he swallowed hard. They had them. They had them!

Chavez accepted the canteen from Filipe and drank deeply.

Samuel shifted impatiently as Padraig caught his eye. *Easy, give the man a chance to catch his breath.* He folded his hands and watched as Chavez gulped. Walker. They had Walker.

Water dribbled down Chavez's flat chin. "Thirty or so. Yes, Walker's there. In the farmhouse. They look as played out as us, maybe a dozen of them wounded. The Hondurans mauled them."

Thirty! Samuel's face slackened. "My God, those are long odds."

Chavez inclined his head grimly.

Samuel placed a hand on Chavez's sweating shoulder. "Can you show me this farmhouse? The layout?"

"Yes."

Padraig picked up his rifle. "I'm coming too."

Samuel crooked a finger at Cortez. "We need to know if the *Icarus* has come for us, if Jimenez even got through to the coast. Hurry ahead to the bay and see if the boats are there, tell them to wait, that we're coming."

He would miss Cortez when they attacked the filibusters, but he was out of time, out of options. And he had to be sure Commander Salmon was waiting for them, if *Icarus* was even there.

Cortez saluted and jogged off without ado, leaving the rest of the men to recover at the river while Samuel and Padraig followed Chavez to the farmhouse.

The wood-framed farmhouse with its rotting palm-thatched roof wouldn't have merited service even as an outhouse back in West Cork, yet it was typical of most country cottages in Nicaragua. The farmer had cleared and tilled a couple of acres up the forested hillside. A dozen filibusters dozed in the shade of the lean-to, and two more sat at a small fire outside the cottage.

Samuel scanned the area with his spyglass. They had to act quickly.

Padraig snorted. "Look at the bugger, you'd—"

"Shush." He swatted Padraig's hand and signaled the others to withdraw. He'd seen enough. His brain was grinding so hard it ached.

Once clear of the farmhouse, Padraig halted his trudging steps. "Too many of them. It's hopeless. Perhaps we should wait for the marines."

"No!" Samuel's chest fluttered. Walker was his trading chip. If they waited, he would slip away or the Hondurans would catch up. They must capture Walker themselves or die on this hillside trying.

Padraig's eyes widened. "Samuel?"

Samuel exhaled and spoke in a calmer voice. "We can't risk waiting,"

"Well, what choice have we?"

"We must do this without the marines." Samuel locked eyes with his friend.

Padraig's features softened, and he stepped closer to Samuel. He was with him.

Samuel scratched his itchy chest and set off at a trot. "Come on, back to the lads. Here's what we must do."

That same night, concealed in the trees on the densely wooded hillside, the Euronicas were invisible to Samuel but well positioned to rain bullets on the farmhouse below. He plucked off his slouch hat—it stank of stale sweat and mildew—and wrinkled his nose as he dropped it on the wild grass beside him and picked up the Henry. It was the thirty-first already; he had three days to save Sofia. His nerves twinged, and he squirmed in the prickly grass. He'd made the right choice, regardless of the impossible odds. He hadn't time to wait for the marines. He didn't even know if they were still coming.

A spark flashed behind the farmhouse, and a tiny flame flickered on the roof as a shadow raced back through the field of yucca to the forest. A young Costa Rican named Juan Santamaria had once used fire to force Walker and his filibusters from a building, paying for it with his life, but Walker and his men had escaped. This time Carmona had to pull it off and survive.

Samuel's nerves jangled as Padraig disappeared into the trees, calling softly to the wounded Soto and Castro with their rifles close by. "Steady, lads. Wait for the signal."

As flames crept over the thatch and flickered higher, Samuel lifted the Henry to his cheek, exhaled fully, and squeezed the trigger. Time for shock and terror.

Rifles erupted along the hillside, vomiting flames from the undergrowth and flaying the flimsy farmhouse with minié balls. Birds burst from the leafy canopy overhead as the hillside echoed gunfire and flames lapped over the farmhouse roof. Shielding himself behind a tree close by, Filipe fired the Sharps as fast as he could stuff fresh rounds into the breech. Samuel began with sixteen rounds in the tube and another under the hammer, and in the minute it took him to empty the Henry, each Euronica had fired four rounds.

The gunfire stopped as abruptly as it began, but thunder still rumbled overhead.

"*Yanquis*, this is Major Chavez of the Honduran army. Two hundred men surround you. Surrender or you die." Chavez sounded commanding, even arrogant. Several shouting filibusters burst from the burning farmhouse and raised their arms. "Face down on the ground. The rest of you have one minute to throw out your weapons and join these wretches in the clearing or we . . . will . . . slaughter you."

A bolt of lightning forked across the sky. A dozen more filibusters trickled from the lean-to and lowered themselves to the ground. The first raindrops pattered on the canopy and sizzled on the Henry's barrel as Samuel reloaded. Thirty seconds later, more filibusters staggered, spluttering, from the smoking farmhouse.

He levered the action and broke cover. He didn't want Walker slipping away in the smoke and confusion. "Hold your fire. They've surrendered."

The heat from the burning roof warmed his face, and his men's boots sloshed the mud behind him as he raced toward the house.

Gunfire blazed out ahead, and bullets thwacked into the soft earth near his feet. Samuel raced on for a couple of heartbeats, then a hammer blow whacked his left arm, spinning him around. He hit the ground on his shoulder, and the air whooshed from his lips. Nauseated, he rolled onto his belly and tried to rise, but his arm wouldn't move. He struggled to his feet, his arm dangling limp and impotent.

More men scrambled from the burning house, firing revolvers and roaring. Samuel lost the Henry in the yucca plants, but he couldn't fire it with one hand anyway. A filibuster charged and bowled him over as he drew his Colt. He shot the man as he fell, and pain stabbed up his injured arm. Thunder boomed overhead, and lightning illuminated a shimmering vignette of filibusters prone with hands over their heads or firing guns. He swiped the rain from his eyes and fired. His bullets thumped into two men, and they collapsed in the mud as he staggered to his feet. "Surrender! You've no hope."

Samuel pivoted to shoot a filibuster firing at the charging

Euronicas. After spitting the copper taste of blood from his mouth—where was that from?—he swung to fire at another filibuster.

"I surrender," croaked the filibuster, dropping his gun and kneeling before lying down.

"I give up. God's sake, I surrender." Another dropped his rifle and threw up his arms.

"On your knees, then." Padraig's voice issued, harsh and commanding, from the darkness and driving rain. "Drop your weapons and you'll live."

The filibusters let their guns fall, and Samuel staggered among them, searching their smoke-blackened faces. Where was Walker? Where?

Walker wasn't among them.

Heat stung his eyes as he flinched back to the blazing shack. "Filipe, Rivera, secure the prisoners. Padraig, where the hell is Walker?"

Lightning pulsed across the sky and glittered on the Euronicas' bayonets as Walker stepped through the doorway of the farmhouse in a billow of smoke. Ash dusted his tattered frock coat, and his face was entirely black, but Samuel would've recognized him anywhere.

Walker peered through the rain and hailed them with a lift of his sword. "Kingston! It had to be you. The plague of my life. I'll die before I surrender, upstart, and I'll take you with me."

Samuel aimed his Colt and thumbed back the hammer. "Don't be a fool, Walker. It's over. Surrender or we'll cut you down."

"Ridiculous! I won't yield to face execution. I'm the president of Nicaragua, for God's sake."

"Horseshit," Padraig bellowed. "I say shoot the bugger."

Walker tipped his head back. "You're afraid of me, Kingston. You're as bad as these darkies. Your own kind would not marry you, so you married one of them. Deplorable. Typical of you to hide behind these—these people. Are you too afraid to fight me on your own?"

The farmhouse was fully ablaze now. Orange and yellow light danced behind the blackened doorway as flame, smoke, and embers erupted through the thatch.

Padraig pointed to Samuel's dangling arm. "You know the bastard trained with master swordsmen in Europe—you can't fight him like that." He drew his saber. "A bad cess to you. I'll fight you, Walker."

"Pah. Typical, letting a peasant fight your battle." Walker's lip curled, and he hefted his sword. "I'll kill him, and you'll be next. But I'll be damned if I'll face a Honduran firing squad. I'll die first."

The rain stopped with the abruptness of the tropics.

Samuel fixed Walker with a fevered glower, the need to kill swirling in his pain-twisted mind. The filibuster's arrogance was boundless. Men like Walker sowed the seeds of discontent and destruction wherever they went. But Walker wouldn't crawl away this time. This time Samuel was going to hack him to pieces.

"Padraig, stand down." He holstered his Colt and used his good hand to tuck the injured one in his waistband. "I want you for myself, Walker. I can trade you dead or alive for Sofia."

He drew his saber. This wretch had caused Father's death, Colonel Valle's death, the deaths of thousands. No, it wasn't enough to hand Walker over to Guardiola.

He would destroy him.

CHAPTER TWENTY-TWO

Walker's blade sang through the air, glittering in the flames from the burning farmhouse as he advanced. "It's always you, Kingston, thwarting me, spoiling my plans. You're a fool. You can't stop human progress, my purpose. I'm the elected president of Nicaragua. God intended that I civilize that woeful country."

The audacity of this churl, calling the misery he'd inflicted on Nicaragua progress. "What progress is that?" Samuel took a step toward his opponent, and the pain in his wounded arm made him stagger. The mud was slick as ice. If he fell, he'd be at Walker's mercy. Nevertheless, he had three days to hand Walker over, three days to save Sofia's life. He shook his head at the pounding pain and advanced again.

Walker's thinning hair hung over his eyes, and he whisked the back of his hand across his prominent forehead. "These darkies are barbarians, and whenever barbarism and civilization meet face to face, the result must be war. It's been like that since mankind stood to walk on hind legs." He advanced, right leg leading, flicking out snappy cuts from a middle-guard position with the economy of movement and poise of a master.

Pain seared Samuel's useless arm as he guarded and bile

burned his throat. He'd been mad to think he could fight with an injured arm. He grimaced, and Walker's eyes flashed; he could see Samuel's pain. He had to end this quickly. He thrust for Walker's chest.

Walker warded his blade easily, bringing Samuel to a slithering halt. "Is that all you have?"

"You're nothing but a tin-pot tyrant." Samuel struck Walker's blade again. "Thousands are dead because of you."

Walker rotated his blade under Samuel's and lunged for his chest. Samuel beat the blade aside and stepped back, his wounded arm flapping awkwardly like a bird's wing. His heartbeat throbbed in his throat. He was a fool. Even trained with sabers and himself a veteran, his injury would prevent him from defeating Walker.

Walker laughed and placed his free hand behind his back. "You've been the bane of my enterprise from the beginning. I'm going to take my time carving you up."

Heat flushed through Samuel. "Try. I'm not a helpless prisoner, not like my father, not like Colonel Valle, both kind and honorable men who you murdered. And for what?" He lunged with the saber, but Walker dodged, thrust, and grazed Samuel's side. Samuel skipped back, stumbled, and pain shot up his arm.

Walker's gray eyes fixed on Samuel, cold as the steel he flicked toward Samuel's face. "De Burg . . . Greenfell, whatever his real name was, killed . . . your father . . . and I killed Valle for being a fool. The words drummed out to the rhythm of clashing steel as he drove Samuel back through the trampled yucca. "Had Valle accepted the natural equilibrium of the races, our superiority, he'd still be alive."

The scum's bigoted diatribe fueled Samuel's hatred, swelling it. Walker pressed him toward the trees, his blade whirling like a flaming lash in the firelight, his feet never still, beating the muddy ground as though he danced on water. "It's natural, inevitable. There'll always be those who rule and those who serve."

Warm blood dripped into Samuel's trousers, but he squared his shoulders and pressed forward. This could not be. It would not be. He wouldn't permit this evil to corrupt the world.

"We're not like the darkies here." Walker jabbed out his blade and advanced. "We're better. They will soon be extinct when I plant these lands with American settlers."

How could he sound so reasonable when attacking Samuel and everything he'd ever stood for? Samuel disengaged his blade with a rasp and staggered backward to the edge of the yucca patch, snatching breath into his heaving lungs. It was a struggle not to gray out from the searing pain in his left arm, even as his right arm ached from warding Walker's lightning lunges.

"I'm not defeated. I'll never be defeated." Walker bared his teeth as he advanced, beating down Samuel's guard. "America wants me here, and no court will convict me. I'll kill you now, but even if your peasants return me to the States, it will not be in ignominy. I'll be back."

Blood roared in Samuel's ears. Walker and his cronies had killed too many of the Euronicas in the last five years. Father. Colonel Valle. Lopez. The villain had spawned a cholera epidemic that killed thousands. He couldn't let the man survive.

Samuel planted his feet and heaved out a guttural roar. "Not while I still breathe."

Walker's blade flicked out like a serpent's tongue, and pain burned Samuel's wounded arm as he scarcely brushed the blade aside. Walker sneered and drew his sword back for the kill. Samuel lunged recklessly, too close to his enemy to maneuver, and grazed Walker in the belly before slamming into him and driving him back.

"You're tiring, bleeding like a pig." Walker angled his body, daring Samuel to strike again.

Samuel retreated into the jungle, seeking a reprieve.

"Coward. Stand and fight." Walker's blade swished through the air.

Samuel backed into a branch, which bent under his weight, digging into his sweating back.

When Walker lunged again, Samuel ducked. The branch sprang forward and hit Walker in the face.

Samuel swung the hilt of his saber down on Walker's recoiling head. Ignoring the pain in his arm, he drew back to strike again. "This is for Father"—his breath exploded in a grunt as he swung, staggering with the momentum—"and Colonel Valle, and my wife . . . and all your victims scattered the length and breadth of Nicaragua."

The second blow of the saber's hilt drove Walker to his knees.

Samuel wound back for downward strike to cleave his head open. "You're a dead man."

This wasn't right. It wasn't enough. He halted his killing stroke, breath choking in his chest as he stumbled back. It wasn't enough that Walker die quietly in the wilderness. This filibuster was a hero in the American press, their "gray-eyed man of destiny," and they still encouraged others to join his murderous quest. The press needed to see him punished. The world needed to see him punished as a warning to others. Guardiola, the butchering bastard, would make an example of Walker America would never forget.

He seized Walker by his lank hair and shoved his face into the mud. "But no, I'm not going to kill you here in the dark wilderness. The Hondurans can execute you in the daylight, a warning to the world, to bullies who believe they can enslave nations."

A faint moan escaped from Walker, and his head twisted enough to permit a breath above the mire. Samuel swayed on his feet. The rain started again as it always did, an endless gray curtain that somehow blended the past and the present together here with the future.

The future—his future. Sofia.

Padraig ran up and took him by the elbow. "Sit down, and I'll dress your arm." He lifted Samuel's sodden shirt and released a gusty breath. "Whew, he only grazed your side, you mad bastard."

Samuel shrugged him off. "My arm's not bleeding anymore. Bullet went clean through. Filipe? Filipe, find my rifle. I dropped it in the yucca patch.

Chavez and Carmona jogged over and peeled Walker out of the mud.

Padraig steered Samuel away. "Samuel, you need to sit down and—"

"We must leave immediately. The gunfire will have drawn the Hondurans. We need to hurry. Sofia's out of time." Samuel slid his saber into its scabbard.

"Hell's bells. Just stay still for a minute." Padraig blocked Samuel and ripped his sleeve to check the bullet wound. "You're right, it went clean through the muscle. I'll patch it up in a jiffy. So where to? The coast—"

"Señor." Marco was shuffling across the yucca field. "The army's coming."

"Damn it." Padraig made another hitch in the bandanna he was binding around Samuel's arm.

"Not surprising, after the racket we made. How far away?" Samuel drew himself up to full height. He had to keep going. They were so close. Sofia's life depended on it.

Marco pointed this thumb behind him. "Thirty minutes back, hundreds of them."

"You said we're an hour from the coast?" Could Marco be lost himself? The brown river winding through the valley seemed to run on forever.

Marco bobbed his head, confident, as his eyes met Samuel's.

The roof of the farmhouse groaned and collapsed in an explosion of charred beams, flames, and flying embers. Walker swayed on his feet, propped up between Chavez and Carmona.

"Then we make a run for it and pray Jimenez brought the Royal Navy."

"And the prisoners?" Filipe used his head to gesture past Walker to the filibusters sitting under the Euronicas' guns.

"Walker's the only one who matters." Samuel scooped up his rifle. "Have the lads take the better weapons for themselves and throw the rest in the river. If these men have any sense, they'll make no trouble. Their alternative is to wait here, when Alvarez's Hondurans will slaughter them."

They were ready to move out five minutes later. Samuel ordered Walker's deputy, Colonel Rudler, to join him, Chavez, and Padraig for last instructions. Rudler had proven eager to join the race to the coast; he'd served with Walker since the beginning and knew how the Central Americans treated prisoners.

The farmhouse was a black pile of carbonized wood, and the air reeked of smoke and wet ashes. Poor farmer. What had happened to him? Samuel pushed away that thought; he had to get back and save Sofia.

"Padraig, you and Chavez lead. I'll take the rear guard with Filipe. Colonel Rudler, have your healthy men help the wounded filibusters along. Some are weak, but Chavez says they'll make it. Your filibusters must carry my man Castro. And no matter what happens behind you, keep going. Your lives depend on it, you don't want to fall into Honduran hands. My Euronicas will follow to ensure there's no funny business."

After twelve days in the jungle, Rudler was sunburned and gaunt like the rest of his men. His bloodshot blue eyes blinked furiously. "There'll be no funny stuff, Captain. We know the mess we're in. All we want is to return to the States."

"Earragh, I'm not too sure about that." Padraig stooped to a bucket Filipe had fetched to washed Samuel's blood from his hands. "You came down with Walker in fifty-five, and still you were stupid enough to—"

"Sufficient, Padraig. The man's not a fool." Samuel rolled his shoulders and glanced at the pink slash of dawn reminding him of his deadline—time was about to run out. "We need to go. Move out." He had two and a half days to deliver Walker to Guardiola in Tela—an impossible task unless Salmon had sailed up the coast to meet them.

The healthy filibusters jostled and shoved in their haste to get clear of the Hondurans, leaving others to stagger behind with the help of comrades.

Filipe prodded Walker with his boot. "On your feet, you wretch. Give me a reason to shoot you."

Walker rose stiffly, brushing at his pants where Filipe's boot had touched him. "No need to get personal, young man."

"It *is* personal. You murdered my papa." Filipe spat a gob of spittle between Walker's feet and shoved him.

Thundered rumbled in the distance. Walker wiped the rain from his eyes awkwardly with his forearm and regarded his bound wrists. A lump the size of a goose egg rose on his temple, and his hair was sticky with blood where Samuel whacked him a second time.

"Filipe," Samuel called, a note of warning in his voice.

Filipe scoffed at Walker. "Look at him—and he was going to conquer us."

"He'll cause no trouble. He's a beaten man." Samuel waved Filipe ahead.

Filipe spun Walker around by the elbow, and the filibuster shuffled away with his chin on his chest. He might appear subdued, but he was unpredictable, and there was no doubting his courage. Samuel would keep a close eye on that man.

CHAPTER TWENTY-THREE

They found Río Sico an hour later where it flowed east scarcely above sea level between bamboo thickets and jungle. Ribbons of tilled ground appeared, scattered along the riverbanks, dotted with impoverished farmhouses and hovels. The unexpected aroma of fried plantains made Samuel's shrunken stomach summersault as they passed the settlement. Three bronzed children splashed from the water on the far side of the river and hid in the undergrowth. Soto, Quintero, and the men carrying Castro waited at a small farmhouse on the edge of the ribbon of tilled land, looking as spent as Samuel. His head was reeling, pain wracked his arm, and his wheezing lungs burned. He had to stop . . . for a second . . . to catch his breath.

A moment later, he pushed through the men to where Padraig squatted by the bamboo stretcher, checking on Castro. "How are you holding up, soldier?"

Castro's youthful face was pale and drawn, but the corners of his lips twitched up. "I'm fine, Capitán. Carried by a couple of yanque porters like a chieftain, why wouldn't I be?"

"That's the spirit." Samuel patted Castro's shoulder. "*Icarus's* surgeon is one of the best. He'll fix you up as good as new."

"Good health just means I'll take longer to die, Capitán. Castro laughed along with Samuel and Padraig and then winced.

"He'll be fine. I've suffered worse injuries falling down drunk." Padraig stood and rubbed his belly. "Smell that food. I'm bloody starving."

Everyone was hungry. But this poor farm wouldn't have enough to feed fifty men. Besides, they didn't have time to linger. Samuel beckoned Marco over. "How much farther to the ocean?"

Marco scratched his ear, and his eyes wandered down river. "Fifteen minutes or so."

"And Río Negro?"

"It joins the coast another mile west of this river's mouth."

How would the *Icarus* know which river was which? It was impossible. He'd never get back in time to save Sofia. Cursed Walker. He glared at his enemy seated on a tree stump with his shoulders back and his chest puffed out. Bastard.

Samuel let out a heavy sigh.

Two paces away, Filipe craned around to stare at him. "What's the matter?"

Should he share his worry with Filipe? Yes, he was a man now and deserved to know. "It's the thirty-first. Guardiola said he'd execute Sofia if we failed to deliver Walker to Tela by the third. We have to find the *Icarus*." But it was hopeless, the frigate could be anywhere up and down the coast.

Filipe blanched. "He won't dare."

Saying it made the possibility of Sofia's death so real. Exhausted, Samuel glanced behind him up the river. Still no sign of Alvarez's Hondurans. He resisted the urge to clench his fists. Surely, Guardiola wanted Walker captured more than he wished Sofia dead. For all his faults, Honduras's president was an experienced general. He had to know that things went wrong in the field. *Dear God, make him wait. A few more days, that's all I ask of you.*

He jutted out his chin and squared his shoulders. He would keep going, and he would find that woebegone boat. He would save Sofia. He beckoned the two filibusters nearby. "Let's go. Pick Castro up. We're almost at the coast."

As the men moved off, Walker hung back and held up his bound hands. "Is this really necessary? I can't even ward off the mosquitoes."

The cheek of the wretch. Samuel's fingers curled. "You should've considered such snags before starting this mischief."

"This is a waste of time. Commander Salmon has already given his word to return us to New Orleans. He'll do anything to avoid more bloodshed, especially as he believes the courts will punish me for breaching the Neutrality Act." Walker sneered. "We both know that will never happen. Americans love me too much."

Samuel bit his cheek. Walker was lying. Salmon knew Guardiola would spare Sofia only if they handed Walker over, and he was too much of a gentleman to risk a woman's life. He glanced sideways at the pompous ass striding beside him. He was stirring trouble, seeking to divide them.

He turned his gaze to the leaf-dappled sunlight playing on the murky river.

"You know I'm right." Walker snorted and tilted his head back.

Salmon would never risk a woman. Samuel jammed his good hand in his pocket. But what if . . . ? "Shut up and march or I'll —" He seized Walker by the collar and shunted him ahead. "Shut your mouth."

Samuel stalked along in silence after that.

Filipe looked at him and raised his eyebrows. "What's the—"

"Hold your tongue. I don't want to talk about it." Samuel's savage rebuff caused Rivera and Perez, marching ahead of Filipe to falter, momentarily slowing the march.

Not long after, the line of men fidgeted ahead, murmuring and calling to each other. Something was happening. Samuel followed them around the bend in the river and glimpsed a flash of blue through a gap in the dense foliage. The ocean. It was almost over. He inhaled deeply.

Frantic shouts and cries sounded from—wait, the commotion was behind him now. He spun around. A dozen black-clad soldiers spilled around the river crook a quarter mile back, followed by dozens of conscripts in ragged white shirts and rolled-up trousers.

Hondurans!

Blood pounded in Samuel's ears. "General Alvarez! Make haste, men." But he knew they couldn't go much faster, not the men carrying the stretcher, and he would never desert poor Castro. None of them would. They'd endured too much together.

"Filipe, watch Walker." Samuel pushed ahead, urging his soldiers and the filibusters forward.

Moments later, he could make out the narrow beach and a strip of ocean—but not a single boat. The Hondurans surged toward them, only three hundred yards behind now, wiry men with sun-blackened faces, leaning into the chase and gesturing wildly.

Walker stumbled, but Filipe grabbed him before he fell and propelled him forward. The Hondurans wouldn't differentiate the filibusters from their Euronica captors. They would attack them all, and if Alvarez captured Walker, Guardiola would execute Sofia. Samuel sped up. "Push on."

A whoop from the distant ridge on his right drew Samuel's attention. Dozens more Hondurans were scrambling down the wooded hillside. Escaping that direction was out of the question, and the sea trapped them on the left. Where was the Royal Navy?

A whistle blasted: the *Icarus*'s steam-powered tender towed three longboats around the craggy headland, each with a sailor at the tiller and two red-coated marines in their distinctive bell-top shakos.

Samuel's nerves strummed, and he pushed the nearest filibuster ahead. "Pick up the pace, boys. We may yet make it." He was bloody well going to make it. Muskets erupted behind them, but he didn't spare the Hondurans a glance. Their weapons were ineffective at over sixty yards. The vegetation underfoot gave way to sand. "Keep going, into the water. Don't stop."

The tender's engine slowed to a rhythmic huff. Was that Jimenez, gesturing wildly in the bow?

"Keep going, señor," Jimenez called across the water. "Almost there."

The first of the filibusters waded into the shallows, urged on by Padraig and Chavez, as marines dropped into the water and pushed the tethered tenders closer to the shore. The sand hardened underfoot before Samuel splashed into the lukewarm water, where men heaved the wounded and the weak over the dipping gunwales. The salt stung his chafed, skin as he caught the arm of an injured filibuster and dragged him to the steamboat.

"You're cutting this one close." Lieutenant Sherman dropped a sodden filibuster inboard and held out a hand to Samuel. "Come now, everyone is on board."

And they were. Samuel clasped Sherman's hand, and the marine wrenched him from the water. He landed like a dropped cloak in the wet bilge, pain lancing throughout his wounded arm.

"Full speed, Davies," Sherman ordered. "Don't worry about the Hondurans. They won't dare fire on a boat flying the Royal Navy's ensign."

The engine roared, the propeller churned the sea, and the steam tender surged away from the beach, shuddering and yawing as the towing hawser took the weight of the longboats. Water splashed over the low gunwale, and Samuel pushed himself up among the others packed into the crowded boat. The tender jolted a couple more times as it jerked the other boats into line and forged away from the shoreline.

Behind them, the Hondurans milled on the beach, shouting, gesturing, and brandishing their muskets aloft. Samuel pulled out his spyglass. They could've been Nicaraguans: the same white or faded black uniforms, the same sun-darkened faces, the same—

"Hey, lads!" His heart soared. "They're alive! It's Sergeant Zamora and the others. They're on the beach."

The Nicaraguans on the steamboat gave a ragged cheer as he whipped off his hat and waved it at Zamora and the three other missing Euronicas. The other boats took up the cheer as the news passed between them. On the beach, Zamora lifted his hand to acknowledge them, and Samuel's exhausted muscles tightened. He would get them back no matter what it took. Them, and Sofia.

Samuel squeezed through the chattering men, struggling to balance on the rolling boat. Lieutenant Sherman better explain why he failed to follow them into the jungle days ago. He might have news, even news of Sofia. He stumbled in distraction, swaying against Soto, who yelped.

"Sorry, Soto—my word, I'm sorry."

The wound in Soto's side had reopened, and blood seeped through the makeshift bandage. Soto was sweating profusely, and his pale skin was taut across his face. "It wasn't you, Capitán. It opened when I climbed into the boat."

Samuel sniffed the wound, and it didn't smell putrefied. "It doesn't seem infected."

A hand clasped his shoulder—Filipe. "I'll take care of him. You're going to talk to the marine lieutenant, right?" He helped Samuel rise, and they locked eyes over Soto. "I'm eager to hear word of her as well."

Sherman flushed as Samuel drew near. "I'm sorry, Captain. The commander forbade me from joining the pursuit. He feared causing an international incident."

"Yes, yes, Lieutenant, but I need to know—"

"Of course. Your wife."

The wind whipped a tendril of hair into Samuel's face,

momentarily blinding him and stinging him with tears that streamed from the corners of both eyes.

"Guardiola moved her to the fort at Trujillo."

The men around Samuel fell silent as his churning gut and wind buffeted him from every side. "When did they mo— why . . . is Guardiola in Trujillo?"

Sherman caught his hat as the wind tugged it. "The commander thinks it's a political maneuver to show up General Alvarez. Trujillo is a bigger town, and it will enhance Guardiola's reputation to parade Walker there. That's where matters stood when your lad brought us word you were headed for the coast."

Safe. Sofia was safe. He covered his mouth with his hand and slumped to his knees. "Thank God." He craned around to catch Filipe's eye. "She's safe. She's safe."

"For now." Sherman scratched his chin. "Were those Alverez's troops back there?"

"Yes. And they captured four of my men. We'll have to get them back after we deliver Walker to Guardiola in Trujillo, perhaps. That's closer and we'll get there sooner, and . . ."

Sherman thumbed his ear. "The US consul in Trujillo is demanding we return Walker and his filibusters to New Orleans to face a fair trial by an American court."

"Fair trial. Fair?" The corners of Samuel's mouth twitched. "What about my wife? Confound it, they won't convict him in America. He's escaped conviction before. They think he's a hero expanding the Union."

"Commander Salmon believes it's not Britain's business what the American courts—"

"To hell with the courts . . . my wife. Commander Salmon can't allow Guardiola to . . . to sentence . . . to order . . . Salmon would never allow a woman to die for Walker."

A flush crept across Sherman's cheeks. "There's a lot of political pressure. Rumor has it the consul is a freemason, like Walker, and he's pressing us hard, and . . ."

The world went gray, and the nervous whispers of the men

receded around him. Samuel gripped the gunwale, his will to continue draining away. He raised his eyes to nothing but endless horizon.

". . . No, no he won't," Sherman was saying. "He's not that kind of man. No, she's safe."

Samuel picked blood, dried like rust, from his wounded arm. Could he trust the commander? Would he lose her again? Salmon would do the honorable thing. Surely he would.

"Here, mate." Padraig slid a knotted red handkerchief around Samuel's neck and helped him cradle his arm into the sling. "It's going to be all right. You'll see."

It was all the assurance he was going to get, for now.

CHAPTER TWENTY-FOUR

The sapphire sea showered glittering drops into the tender's bow spray as she sliced through the wavelets with the longboats strung out behind her. High clouds glowed white and pink in the setting sun, and the salty breeze was a welcome relief after the humidity of the jungle. Samuel's arm ached in the makeshift sling. He was exhausted, but his mind raced as he inclined forward, willing the steam tender to speed faster toward the *Icarus*, stationed a mile offshore. They still had two days, and they could reach Trujillo in time. Surely Salmon would not let Sofia die. No British officer would. But if he had orders . . . He tightened his grip on the gunwale. He wouldn't permit this. Somehow, he had to convince Salmon to Guardiola to save Sofia's life.

An angular frigate bird glided artistically overhead, and the sunlight shimmered on its white breast as it dove at a tern, forcing the smaller bird to drop its catch. It reminded him of Walker's way of harassing the weak.

The sun glinted off the *Icarus's* portholes and polished brass rails crowded with cheering sailors as the longboats swept into her lee. Walker sat amidships, talking with two filibusters. He met Samuel's eyes and glared back. The wretch truly seemed convinced he would be cleared of any charges again. Samuel fired his glare away to the shimmering ocean. Could Walker be right? No, Commander Salmon was a good man, he'd never leave a woman to die. Samuel wouldn't allow it.

He slumped against the gunwale with a slow smile as the steamboat bumped alongside the frigate and sailors caught the bow and stern lines. Soon he'd be back with Sofia, well and whole, and they'd return to Clonakilty to bury Father's remains and see the children. His insides vibrated: home. He'd hold his children again. How John must have grown these past few months—Maria, too.

A marine climbed up the ladder first, followed by Jimenez, and the tender rocked uneasily as its occupants stirred. Some stood unsteadily.

"Slow down, you bloody landlubbers," the weather-chiseled boson growled, "or you'll land the lot of us in the drink."

Castro's wounded leg was no longer bleeding as sailors hauled him up to the *Icarus* in a bosun's chair. The tender rocked and pitched, bumping the *Icarus*'s hull as the filibusters climbed the rope ladder eagerly, one by one. They'd think twice before signing up for another invasion.

A sailor tapped Samuel's shoulder. "Let's go."

Pain stabbed his arm as he stood. "How long to Trujillo from here?"

"Ten hours." The sailor gripped Samuel's belt to steady him as he stood in the rocking boat.

Samuel winced. Ten hours was forever with the clock running out.

The *Icarus*'s sailors gave a final cheer as the last of the men climbed aboard, but Salmon's face was tense when he shook Samuel's hand as marines marched Walker and his filibusters to the brig. "Well done, Captain. You've served your country proudly once again."

"Thank you for rescuing us, Commander."

Salmon licked his lips. "Might I have a word with you in private? In my cabin."

This was not the reception Samuel expected. he shot a glance at Padraig, but Padraig was chattering with Chavez and Filipe at the entry port. "Ah yes, of course, Commander. Lead the way."

Despite the brass windows thrown open to the sea breeze, the semi-circular saloon was stuffy, smelling of varnish, wood, and the coal-soaked air that permeated the frigate. The cabin was uncluttered, a bunk, a polished desk, and a small washbasin with a mirror and shaving gear on the wooden surround.

Boots scuffed the deck outside the cabin, and men spoke in low voices. *Must be the sentries changing guard.*

Salmon sat behind the desk and waved to the spindly chair before him. "Please, take a seat."

His formality quickened Samuel's pulse. Something was wrong, something dreadful. "What is it, Commander?"

"I, ah . . ." Salmon tugged at his collar and swallowed. "The US counsel in Trujillo has demanded I return Walker to New Orleans. Under no circumstances am I to hand him over to the Hondurans."

Samuel's stomach clenched. It was true. This was happening. "I don't understand. You can't . . . I must've misunderstood you."

Salmon averted his eyes and touched the parchment on his desk. "It's not my decision. You know I'd—Well, Britain can't risk a confrontation with America. In Barbados, the admiral ordered me to do all I could to mollify the American authorities in the filibuster matter. My job was to stop Walk—"

"I stopped him, Commander, not you. What about my wife? Guardiola will murder her."

"I'm sure I can talk to President Guardiola, and the American consul should have influence."

Blood pounded in Samuel's ears. "You were present when Guardiola threatened me. He will kill Sofia. Do you want that on your conscience? You can't do this. It's inhumane!"

Salmon broke eye contact and studied the turquoise sea

beyond the open window. "I'm sorry. While negotiating with Walker when he held the fort, I promised him safe passage back to New Orleans."

Heat flushed through Samuel and he sprang to his feet. "You're sorry? You keep your word to a—a murdering pirate and condemn my wife to die? And I thought you an honorable man, but you're worse than the aristocrats who call themselves soldiers and plagued my life. You can't leave my wife to Guardiola."

Boards creaked beneath his feet as he spun and paced the width of the small cabin. "This is a freemason plot, isn't it? Walker's a freemason. The US counsel is one, and you must be another."

The young commander regarded his hands. How could he be so cold?

"Walker is *my* prisoner. I demand you hand him to the Hondurans."

Salmon rose and moved to the window, still silent.

Samuel balled his fists at his side. "You, sir, are a liar and a coward."

"How dare you." Salmon speared him with a venomous glance. "You've gone too far. Get out."

Samuel's hand flew to his holster. "You won't do this. I won't permit it."

The cabin door banged open, boots thumped the deck, and a marine pinned Samuel's good arm to his side. A second marine grabbed his other shoulder, and agony from his wounded arm melded his feet in place.

"Calm yourself, Captain." Salmon still lacked the guts to look him in the eye. "Take the captain on deck and watch him until he comes to his senses."

Beyond feeling now, he wrenched himself free and hurled himself at Salmon. He punched the traitor in the face and was wrapping his one hand around his neck when a blow to the back of his head drove him into grayness and the deck.

~

Sitting against the gunwale, Samuel squirmed in agony and a pool of sweat. The *Icarus* had been steaming north toward New Orleans for twenty hours, the sea rushing past her keel like the sands of time running out for Sofia. If the frigate didn't turn back soon, it would be too late. But could he risk the men's lives in an assault on the ship's crew? His breath caught in his chest. Could he ask them to die? How many would fall?

". . . away with it." Padraig shook Samuel's shoulder, and pain screamed through his reeling head. "Samuel, shape up, for God's sake. Every revolution of the propellor takes us farther from Sofia. Christ, it's already the first of September; she dies the day after tomorrow unless we force Salmon to exchange Walker for Sofia."

His jumbled thoughts clunked into place. Could he ask them to die? He touched the neat bandage the surgeon had wrapped around his wounded arm. Could his battered, exhausted men even rise up? Could he?

As if he read his mind, Chavez touched the hilt of the knife at his waist. "We won't let them harm Señora Sofia. The lads are ready to fight. The marines are watching us, but we're also watching them."

Padraig pointed to the four marines leaning on their rifles at the gunwales amidships. "Salmon hasn't said it, but it's obvious they don't trust us."

The *Icarus* surfed down a wave and her engine roared louder, vibrating the deck.

Chavez glanced at Padraig for permission and received a nod in return. "Don Filipe and four of the lads are waiting close to the mess, ready to disarm the off-duty marines. Jimenez and the others are scattered about the ship, marking the rest of the redcoats. We'll strike at one in the morning, when they least expect it."

"I'll take the commander." Padraig grimaced, a wicked twist

of his lips that roiled Samuel's stomach. "If we have him and capture the marines, the sailors will buckle."

Eyes widening, Samuel touched the bump on his head. They were right. He'd rather die rescuing Sofia than stand by while Salmon abandoned her. But the Euronicas, Filipe . . . How many of them would die in this assault? Even if they succeeded, they would never be able to return to Britain.

He sat up, which made his head pound, and grabbed Padraig's arm. "I appreciate everything you're saying, but we cannot do this."

"No, no, I think we can. I'm sure we can."

"You'd never see your parents again, nor Ireland."

"It's worth it to save Sofia."

"The Royal Navy will hunt us mercilessly. Remember the *HMS Bounty*? They caught most of the mutineers and hanged several, and the natives killed those who escaped."

Padraig's cheeky grin lit his face. "This isn't mutiny—it's piracy. Anyway, I'll have a fine excuse to spend time in Nicaragua with Nelly Valle."

Samuel glanced around nervously. Sunburned marines still lounged in the shade of the closest tender as if taking their ease, but their alert eyes and the rifles beside them belied their pretense at leisure. Lieutenant Sherman was talking to his sergeant beside the companionway.

"I know." Padraig bobbed his head toward the marines. "They didn't dare disarm us earlier. The lads became belligerent, but it's a stalemate. They're watching us closely right now. That's why we'll wait until later when they drop their guard. We can take them in the middle of the night."

Saliva filled Samuel's mouth. He pulled himself up the guardrail with a groan and spat over the gunwale. Perhaps they could take the ship, but men would die on both sides. There had to be another way. "That must be a last resort. I'll talk to Salmon again and try to reason with him."

The frigate shuddered down a wave as he shuffled aft.

"Not another step, please, Captain." Lieutenant Sherman's voice was pleading.

Fiery pain shot up Samuel's arm as he lurched to balance on the slewing deck. "Lieutenant, I must speak to the commander. I promise there'll be no violence, not if I reason with him."

Sherman scanned the hostile faces of the Nicaraguans around the deck. "I don't agree with this either, Captain, but—"

"For mercy's sake, Lieutenant, my wife . . . I beg you, let me see the commander."

"Very well. But no tricks or—"

"My word on it. But quickly, please."

Salmon was at his customary station on the quarterdeck, glassing the horizon. Samuel coughed to catch his attention. Tensing, the commander lowered his lens. "Look here, Kingston, I don't—"

"Commander, please, a word. I beg you."

Salmon opened the ship's log as if to shut him out.

Samuel stepped around to face him. "Please listen to me. I promise you, no more aggression."

Salmon sighed hard. "All right, but there's nothing I can do. You must understand that. Orders. You, of all people, must comprehend orders."

"I do, Commander. And I've learned to question orders from incompetent men, not blindly follow them. I was there when idiotic generals ordered the Light Brigade to charge the Don Cossack guns, and they sent men and horses, flesh and blood, against a ring of steel. Hundreds died because no officer questioned that insane order. History is full of such examples. Don't let this be another." The words spilled out in a rush before Salmon could cut him off. "Return William Walker to New Orleans, and he'll mobilize another army and return. Everything we sacrificed, all the men who died, Sofia's death, all will have been in vain. The US has no truck with Walker; he's a Central American problem, a problem that the local governments should resolve. Why should he live and my wife die? It was he who sinned against humanity."

Salmon's face tightened, and he glanced away to the frigate's wake foaming aft through the blue-green sea.

"You told me earlier about your own sweetheart, Commander?"

"Amelia, yes. My fiancée."

"And what if the roles were reversed, with your Amelia a captive facing death and her salvation rested in the hands of another?"

"I can't. I wouldn't." Salmon tugged at his navy coat.

"This action will haunt you the rest of your life, Commander, your decision to send an innocent woman—a wife, a mother—to her death. All for a bigoted tyrant hell-bent on destroying nations to feed his naked ambition. You're too fine a man for that."

"What choice have I?"

"You can do the right thing. Hand Walker over to set Sofia free, Commander." He clutched his belly. Was Salmon wavering?

"I'd face a reprimand for it. Court-mart—"

"Or the world will praise you, Commander, as the man who captured William Walker and handed him to the nation he attacked, as the man who had the courage to save a young mother. The navy wouldn't dare punish you."

The *Icarus*'s mighty engine vibrated the hull, and the deck pitched and rolled as she burrowed into the waves, carrying Samuel farther away from Sofia. He held his breath while Salmon fidgeted, his eyes downcast.

Salmon threw up his hands. "Blast it, I've never been comfortable with this."

Samuel's hope soared. "And?"

"And you're right, Captain. We must save your wife—to the devil with Walker. I'll have the sailing master plot a course for Trujillo." He plucked off his hat and ran a hand through his hair. "Though I'll be damned if I know what to tell the admiral."

Samuel's hand flew to his mouth. "Thank you, Commander. You won't regret this."

"I know I won't." Salmon nodded and smiled slowly. "And I'll sleep easier at night."

"Thank you, sir." Samuel retreated from the quarterdeck as Salmon beckoned his first lieutenant. Sofia would soon be free; he and his men need not revolt. He pictured Sofia's flawless face, her skin the color of honey, her eyes glowing like twin flames, vivid and feisty, and his neck flushed as he willed the *Icarus* to speed faster. They had one day to reach Trujillo in time to save Sofia.

CHAPTER TWENTY-FIVE

The *Icarus* anchored in Trujillo the next day, on the second of September, and Salmon handed Walker over. Samuel realized he was drumming his foot on the *Icarus*'s deck and stopped as he squinted at the ancient walls of the Fortaleza de Santa Bárbara, backlit in pink by the sinking sun. They had met Guardiola's terms, and the Hondurans should've brought Sofia down by now. It was taking too long. He should've gone ashore himself. To hell with Commander Salmon's advice. He knew nothing about General Mariano Alvarez. Would he even release Zamora and the others? But Salmon said Alvarez was an honorable man, and unlike President Guardiola, held no grudge against Samuel. If the commander was right, Sofia should be coming any minute, and Sergeant Zamora, Delgado, Gutierrez, and Sanchez with her.

Seagulls glided above the purple sea and white sands of the bay, where the *Icarus*'s steam-driven tender rocked on the fingering wavelets with her bow touching the beach. On learning that Walker's brig, the *John C. Taylor*, was chartered in Frank Brogan's name and financed by Samuel, Salmon had permitted it to return to its home port. He'd also deported the surviving members of Walker's army back to New Orleans on *HMS Gladi-*

ator after making them swear never to return to Central America.

"They're coming," Filipe yelled down from the yardarm on the mainmast. The Euronicas crowding the gunwales stirred. "And she's with them. Sofia's with them!"

Thank God. Lightness floated Samuel's lungs as he glassed the group emerging from the trees. Sofia walked between Commander Salmon and the surgeon's assistant. An Amazon warrior with her slender neck, angular chin, and high cheekbones like they were carved out of gold-colored marble. She was slender, so slender now in her sweat-dampened shirt and riding breeches that clung to her curves, but it was the winsome smile on her bow-shaped lips that stirred Samuel most. Soon she'd be in his arms, and he'd never let her out of his sight again.

And there, behind her, strode Zamora, Delgado, Gutierrez, and Sanchez. General Alvarez had handed them over.

Samuel slapped Padraig on the back. "They're all there. Come, let's meet her at the entry port."

"She looks fine and healthy, thank the Lord." Padraig blinked at smoke tickling his right eye and took the cigarette from his mouth.

Filipe scrambled down the ratlines, shouting like an excited child. Time stood still as the boat launched from the beach with its precious cargo, her funnel belching smoke into the blue sky. Samuel's tongue was tacky by the time the helmsman laid the cutter alongside and Salmon handed Sofia to the ladder.

Padraig stretched a hand down, caught her elbow, and helped her aboard—into Samuel's one good arm.

"I knew you'd come." Her warm lips, fat as bees, tasted like coffee.

"Thank God you're safe." He nuzzled her neck, basking in her scent, a heady bouquet reminiscent of apples and fresh sweat. Her lithe arm muscles rippled, taut as harp strings, as she slid her hands down and wrapped them around his waist. His pulse raced. "The wound, it's healed? Are you in pain?"

She shook her head ever so slightly, their noses brushing. "Not much. Rob, the surgeon's assistant, took good care of me." He kissed her again before she drew back and scanned the smiling faces surrounding him. "How are you all? Has anyone been injured or . . ."

"Guido Lopez." Samuel's eyelids went gummy. The memory of the loss blunted his joy.

She took a step back. "Guido, oh no."

"He was point man when Walker ambushed us." Samuel drew back to his breast.

Padraig spat on the deck. "Blasted Walker. He has the blood of many on his hands. The rest of the lads have scrapes and cuts, Sofia, nothing more." Noticing the boson standing in the shade if an air scoop, he covered the gob with his boot.

Sofia shuddered, and her amber eyes glistened. "Guido was such a lovely man, and the music he played on his flute . . . We must care for his family. Filipe, you'll do that, won't you? He has a mother and two sisters, as I recall."

Filipe advanced, flush from his scramble down the ratlines, and wrapped his arms around her. "I plan to, of course. Dear Sofia, I was so worried about you. Thank God you're safe."

Samuel inclined his head to Commander Salmon. "Commander, thank you. I'm indebted. You—"

"Think nothing of it, Captain." Salmon's eyebrows wormed together. "I almost made a terrible mistake. 'Tis I who should thank you."

The Euronicas sidled up to Sofia in twos and threes and greeted her shyly.

Samuel saluted Salmon, reaching reflexively for Sofia's hand. "And Walker?" He already had a jolly good idea what would become of Walker.

"He'll face a military tribunal, charged with piracy and murder. He killed Hondurans in the bloody fight to capture the fort and more in the jungle. I believe they'll convict him quickly and execute him." Salmon tipped back his cocked hat. "Timothy

Clinton, the US consul, is furious at me. Guardiola was so happy to get his hands on Walker, he made no bones about freeing Sofia and ordering Alvarez to release your men. I know not how my superiors or history will judge my action, but thanks to you, my conscience is clear. Guardiola's the clear winner in Honduras, and he's even opened peace negotiations with José Cabañas. Old Cabañas must know he's no chance of winning without Walker's American riflemen. Central America has a real shot at peace."

It was over. Walker would never threaten his family or Central America again. What a terrible waste. Walker had so much talent—if only he'd applied his genius to a worthy cause. Samuel sighed heavily. "Walker's fate was inevitable. He wouldn't stop."

"Come, Samuel." Sofia tugged his elbow. "I need to rest. Do you have a cabin?" The twinkle in her eye hinted she wasn't tired at all.

Who was Samuel to object? "The navy calls it a cabin, but it's more the size of a wardrobe, if you ask me."

"A tight squeeze. Even better."

Commander Salmon flushed. "Well . . . ah . . . Anyway, Captain, I've a ship to make ready. We sail for Greytown in one hour."

Three weeks later, the melodious songs of many birds woke Samuel at dawn in the first guestroom of the Valle mansion in Chinandega, and he beheld Sofia sleeping beside him. Her skin was golden in the nascent light, unblemished except for the purple scar puckering on her side. He winced. He'd almost lost her. He'd be stricter if she ever tried to wade into danger again.

Now that she'd recovered, they would leave Chinandega for Panama on a chartered boat that morning. It was time to rouse her for breakfast, but she slept so peacefully, figurine perfect. It was a pity to wake her. On the other hand, it was always a pleasure to watch life return to her shapely limbs.

He shook her gently. "Sofia, darling, it's time to get up. The boat leaves on the tide, and it's a half-hour journey to El Realejo."

"Mmm." She was beguiling even as she awakened, with her black hair tousled and her amber eyes heavy from sleep. He wished they had time to do once more what they'd been doing most of the night. "Come along, darling. We're leaving."

She stretched like a cat and slid her hand down his arm. The soft pads of her fingers made his skin shiver. "The only thing I want more than to lie here with you is to be on my way home to the children. But Lord, it's tempting to pull you down here."

"You'll get no objection from me." He kissed her lips.

She pushed him away with a beguiling smirk. "We'll have plenty of time on the boat, as we had on the *Icarus*. Who knew the tiny cabin of a warship could be such fun?"

Twenty minutes later, the sound of laughter greeted them as they descended the sweeping marble staircase on their way to the dining room. Even with the windows and French doors open, the cherry velvet drapes stirring in the humid breeze, the room was smoky and smelled of men. Padraig, Jimenez, Cortez, Quintero, and Chavez, all seated at the long, spindly-legged table, sprang to their feet, followed by Filipe a second later. Samuel grinned; younger brothers seldom gave their sisters the respect they deserved.

"Breakfast. I'm starving." Samuel guided Sofia to the two empty chairs beside Padraig. "What have we? Rice and beans, beans and rice, rice and—"

"Plantains, rice, and beans." The room filled with laughter as the soldiers joined in Padraig's and Samuel's old complaint about the sameness of food in Nicaragua."

Padraig laid down his greasy knife and fork, and they clinked on his empty plate. "Better than that. We've eggs and delicious ham with the rice and beans. All the same, I'm looking forward to the bags o' mystery back home."

"Bags o' mystery?" Filipe craned around toward Padraig.

"Sausages, Filipe. Sausages. Did you learn nothing on your trip to Ireland?" Padraig wiped his mouth with his napkin. "Called that because only the bugger who made them knows what he put inside them. It could be bow-wow mutton for all we know."

Filipe groaned and glanced at Samuel.

"Dog meat, Filipe. Bow-wow mutton." Samuel pulled out a chair for Sofia. "For goodness sake, drop the slang. You're confusing the lad."

Teresa and Nelly Valle broke their huddle at the other end of the room and hugged Sofia. Nelly had stayed at the house ever since Samuel brought Sofia home three weeks ago, although she spent most of her time in Padraig's company—chaperoned by Sofia, of course, much to Padraig's frustration.

"You look gorgeous, cousin." Nelly pecked Sofia's cheek. "You'll have sailors hanging off the mast to catch a glimpse of you all the way across the Atlantic. Aren't you excited? Going home to little John and baby Maria. Oh . . . they must be so cute. I wish I were going with you."

"You do?" Padraig dropped his jaw, faking surprise. "And here I am, staying on a while to enjoy the pleasure of your company."

Samuel whispered into his ear. "And panting like a prize boar now that the chaperone is leaving. Be careful, Tio Hernan has a blunderbuss loaded and ready."

"Earragh, go on with you." Padraig shoved Samuel. "Eat your breakfast quickly. The tide waits for no one, not even for the man who captured William Walker."

"I did? We all captured him, the credit goes to all the Euronicas." Samuel picked up his napkin.

Emanuel Chavez poured coffee into Samuel's and Sofia's china cups. "Speaking of Walker, you won't yet have read the paper delivered from León."

Samuel's silver teaspoon clattered on the china saucer. "What happened?" In truth, he'd been too preoccupied with Sofia and helping Hernan's men and the Euronicas scour the department for any remaining rebels, filibusters, or bandits to follow up on Walker's demise.

Chavez set down the coffeepot and picked up the paper. "Blah, blah, blah. Ah . . . Here's the good part. 'A Honduran military court convicted William Walker, the scourge of Central America, of piracy and murder, rejecting the filibuster's defense that he was defending the inalienable rights of the people of Honduras and protecting them from tyranny.'"

"Tyranny!" Filipe gave a forced laugh. "If the wretch wanted to protect them, he should've stayed—"

"Shush, Filipe." Samuel scooted to the edge of his seat. "Let him read. Carry on, Emanuel, please."

Filipe grinned and picked up a tortilla.

"'On September twelfth, the man who was once president of Nicaragua faced a three-man firing squad behind the Fortaleza de Santa Bárbara in Trujillo. The first volley of shots did not kill him, but the coup de grâce blew away his face, and the Honduran authorities buried him in Trujillo's cemetery.'"

"So it's over." Sofia exhaled a sharp breath. "Now we can get on with our lives without fear."

She beamed at Jimenez and Cortez, who perched uneasily at the edge of their seats; neither man was used to visiting a fine house. "Carlos, Pedro, did you finish packing?"

"Si, señor." Cortez flashed a gap-toothed smile. Poor devils had little to pack: a change of clothes and their only footwear, the boots Filipe had bought them to work on the hacienda.

Sofia sipped her coffee, and the cup rattled as she returned it to the saucer. "We'll pick up warm clothes and shoes in New York on the way to Ireland. It'll be winter soon in Cork, and you've seen nothing like it here."

Filipe rolled his eyes and snorted. "You're both *loco*. I don't know why you're crossing an ocean to work with Samuel. You have a place here with me. And besides, I need veterans in my new squadron."

Sofia frowned at Samuel. "I don't approve of this at all. Tio Hernan should never have asked Filipe to police the department. He's too young."

After the explosion on the *Wheeler* had killed the corrupt Colonel Garcia, the government had appointed Hernan Valle as director of the Chinandega Department, and Hernan had recruited Filipe. Samuel swallowed his forkful of fried egg. "Hernan knew he was getting the Euronicas in the package, that's why. Besides, Filipe has wised up these last few years. He can handle himself."

Jimenez backhanded Cortez's arm and spoke around a mouthful of beans. "I'm glad I'm off to Ireland so I won't be crawling through the jungle after Don Filipe with Soto jabbing me up the backside with the point of his bayonet."

Even Sofia couldn't maintain her glower in the explosion of laughter. She dabbed her mouth with her napkin. "But the hacienda? Who's going—"

"Chavez and Teresa, of course. They're managing it now." Filipe glanced at his manager and raised his thick eyebrows.

"And making a fine job of it," Samuel added, as Chavez and his gentle partner blushed. "Chavez showed me the accounts the other day."

Although Filipe was only nineteen, he was keen to do his duty to make Nicaragua a better place. Samuel should do the same in Ireland. Men like Chester Inwood and Peter Norton wanted to level the field for all Irishmen. Thanks to intercepting the shipment of gold intended to fund Walker's war in fifty-five, Samuel was a wealthy man, and the threat of William Walker was no more. It was time he followed Father's lead and fought for justice at home. If it weren't too late, he would seriously consider Inwood's and Deasy's offer to stand for election; it was possible he could affect real change working in the British parliament. He'd discuss it with Sofia on the way home.

Sofia relaxed back in her chair. "Papa would have been so proud of you, Filipe."

"Speaking of fathers." Samuel wiped his lips and laid down his napkin. "Where's the wagon with Father's remains."

"All is ready. The wagon's loaded and waiting in the south barn. It's cooler in there. And the lads will have packed your bags in by now—not that Sis brought much. You've made a tomboy of my sister, Samuel."

Laughter rang around the table.

Padraig nudged Nelly with a grin. "To be fair, it's hard to fight filibusters in a whalebone corset and petticoats."

Nelly pinched him. "Shame on you, Padraig Kerr."

Samuel exchanged glances with Sofia. Was it possible another Valle woman would grace West Cork? Well, he was taking Father home, fulfilling his promise, and that lifted a weight from his shoulders. "Excuse me, darling. I need a word alone with Father before we leave."

Her features softened, and she offered a small smile. "Of course. Take all the time you need."

"Five minutes, more like it. We need to get on the road." Padraig reached for his cup with a grin.

When Samuel shouldered the heavy wooden door open, sunlight beamed into the barn to gild the dancing dust motes and glitter on the burnished brass handles of the coffin resting on the wagon. He removed his felt hat and touched the polished hardwood as memories flashed by. Father teaching him to wash his hair as a youngster. *You were always obsessed with hygiene, no wonder you never joined the army. You'd have hated these last few weeks we spent in the field, Father. It didn't enamor me either, but we got the job done. There's still much to do before there's true justice here, before all humans are treated equally regardless of race, religion, or social class, but that's true the world over. I leave Nicaragua hopeful that people like Filipe, Tereasa, and the Euronicas will continue the fight for justice here, and I will join the same fight back in Ireland, a fight you fought all your life. I wish you were here to see what we've achieved already and to meet my wonderful Sofia and the children. Little John not only has your name, he's also gifted with your generous nature. If only . . .* Samuel swallowed. No. He couldn't have saved Father no matter how much sooner he'd caught up with Louis Greenfell. That weak heart was going to kill him no matter where he was.

He stroked the smooth polished wood and spoke aloud. "You're going home to rest beside mother and our ancestors. Thank you for showing me the way by your example, although I was too stubborn to understand your lessons of humility and service. Back home, you can watch me make amends."

Footsteps and bantering voices sounded outside the yard, drawing closer. It was time to leave. Samuel kissed the coffin, smelling the wax and polish as his lips brushed the warm wood. "I love you, Father."

The Euronicas formed a color guard on the wagon, plain green uniforms clean and pressed, parading as straight as British lancers on horses Filipe had supplied for his new squadron. Filipe had spared no expense, and his Nicaraguans had not spared their appreciation. God, how he loved these people and this wild and beautiful country.

But it was the common folk lining the driveway and scattered along the road to El Realejo's tiny harbor that made tears well behind Samuel's eyelids. Men, women, and children had congregated in their ragged finest to thank the men who'd ended the threat of William Walker.

"*Viva los irlandeses!*"

"Gracias, Capitán."

"Viva *El Rubio.*" This hail to blond Padraig, repeated by several dark-eyed girls in colorful ankle-length dresses, earned him pokes from Nelly riding beside him.

They rode westward, threading their way through the small town and past acres of cane fields and cornfields that were a fraction of the vast Valle estate. High in the Maya-blue sky, the sun baked the mud on the rutted trail. A yellow-breasted bird scolded her unseen partner, and its shrill cries rang from the canopy of an ancient Guanacaste tree. The quiet air smelled of freshly cut vegetation spiced with sulfur from the distant volcano.

As they topped the next rise, the vast blue expanse of the Pacific opened before Samuel, glistening in the morning sun. Their chartered brig rode at anchor twenty yards off the ramshackle jetty.

Padraig urged his horse alongside Samuel and Sofia. "Tell Dad and Mam I'll be home before spring. Dad shouldn't worry about my fishing boats. Martin O'Sullivan will keep the crews in line. Dad can keep the books and pay them."

Sofia peered around Samuel, one eyebrow cocked. "And will you be coming alone?"

Padraig flashed his old cheeky grin. "That depends on your cousin."

Thank goodness Nelly didn't speak English; she might've poked Padraig again. Samuel was going to miss him. But he was sailing home, home to the children. His pulse beat faster as he unconsciously relaxed the reins, allowing his mare to surge ahead.

They were going home to Clonakilty.

CHAPTER TWENTY-SIX

The wind rocked the coach as it crossed Patrick's Bridge over the River Lee, chilling Samuel to the core. A couple of months in the tropics, and he'd forgotten how cold October could be in Ireland. He plucked up the collar of his frock coat and checked his watch again. Ten thirty already. They had to leave Cork soon or it would be dark before they arrived in Clonakilty. They'd disembarked in Queenstown at four this morning, but Whitaker Transport had taken forever to provide a coach, forcing him to return to the company's stable in Camden Place and make a fuss. Father's body and the luggage would be delivered to Clonakilty the following day, so all that remained was to collect the others at the Imperial Hotel in Grand Parade and get on the road.

And then, home. At last, they'd see the children, after five of the longest months of his life. Samuel's chest lightened. They must be so big now. He couldn't wait to go riding with John, to cuddle little Maria and smell the peach scent of her hair. She must be talking up a storm, the little chatterbox. He slid forward on the leather seat and rapped on the coach's door. "Hurry along, please? I need to get home."

"Sure, amn't I going as fast as I can, sir? Streets are crowded."

He stuck his head out the window, and the wind slapped his

face. Despite the inclement weather, the city was bustling: carts, coaches, and omnibuses trundling over the arched stone bridge, their wheels feathering plumes of muddy water, besmirching the pedestrians sloshing through puddles in threadbare clothing. The curses of carters and the cries of hawkers ricocheted above the soft patter of rain on the coach's roof as it labored down St. Patrick Street.

The memory of heads turning in the Imperial Hotel dining room that morning at breakfast made Samuel chuckle, all eyes on Jimenez in a sack coat and trousers of somber hue over a crimson cravat, and Cortez in a blue frock coat, flowery waistcoat, and striped trousers. Cortez had been quite adventurous when Samuel and Sofia had kitted them out at the finest tailor in New York. If the Nicaraguans made this much of a stir in Cork, they would undoubtedly shock little Clonakilty.

The coach lurched left on South Mall and soon clattered into the courtyard of the Imperial Hotel.

Samuel stepped out onto the cobblestones. "Wait here while I get the others, please."

The Imperial was almost as ornate as the finest New York hotel; stained glass, brass lamps, red velvet, and marble statues enfolded guests in a luxuriously inviting ambiance. The scent of roasting meat and cigar smoke met Samuel in the restaurant. The place was packed: aristocrats, businessmen, and the people who trailed them around. Sofia mesmerized him, wearing a flattering blue satin dress from New York with a dramatically spreading skirt made of infinite folds of flaring silk. The buzz of conversation muted as he joined Sofia, Jimenez, and Cortez at their table. No doubt the haughty buggers nearby were wondering what sort of woebegone would leave a beautiful woman in the company of colored men—or worse, even dare to bring them into the hotel.

"Coach is outside." He kissed her rosy cheek. "Are you ready?"

"Dying to be off, darling." She pushed away her china teacup and beamed at the others. "Ready, *muchachos*? Or would you like to eat some more?"

"No, Señora Sofia, I can't eat another bite." Cortez's eyes cut around the room as he laid down the napkin he'd wrung into a knot. "That last rasher—I think that's what you called it—it filled me up. Gracias."

Samuel's throat tightened as he drew out a chair for Sofia. Poor Cortez. Sitting amidst this bunch of gawkers must have been uncomfortable.

Jimenez burped and crossed his arms. The upper class would not intimidate him so easily. "Beats the hell out of your charred iguana, Cortez. Gracias, Señora Sofia."

Samuel hid his smile.

"Mistress Sofia, was everything to your satisfaction?" Breda arrived in a blaze of freckles and fiery red curls. Once a barmaid on the steamer from Queenstown to Southampton, Breda had helped Samuel and Padraig five years ago when they were evading the law, and Padraig had later found her employment here at the Imperial. A refugee who'd emigrated after the rest of her family starved in the famine, she'd seized the opportunity to return to Ireland. She seemed to be faring well as a waitress; indeed, the way she flushed when Cortez flashed her his gap-toothed smile . . .

Cortez scraped a hand through his tight black curls. "Thank you, Señorita Breda."

Samuel brightened as he offered Sofia his arm. Perhaps the Nicaraguans wouldn't find it too difficult to integrate after all.

"It was perfect, Breda, thank you." Sofia fluffed out her skirt. "You must visit us again in Clonakilty."

"Thank you, Mistress. We only get a few days off, but I'll come." Breda attempted an awkward curtsy while glancing sideways at Cortez.

"What is that? Come here." Sofia hugged the woman who'd helped Samuel speak to Father for the last time. "You must visit us." She flicked her eyes to Cortez, who was grinning at Breda like an idiot. "Perhaps Padraig can speak to his cousin, since she's still the manager here, and get you some time off."

They made their goodbyes. Samuel escorted Sofia past the tables, scorning the peering eyes and pecking lips. "How do you know she likes him, or that Cortez favors her?"

Sofia patted his hand. "Women's intuition, darling."

A small lump rose in his throat. Sofia was incredible. He was a fortunate man.

It had stopped raining but the sky was sullen, and the wind whirled rust-red and gold leaves around the courtyard. Typical autumn weather. As Jimenez swung the canvas bag containing rifles into the coach's luggage trunk, four constables in navy-blue frock coats burst in from the street and surrounded them, tapping truncheons against their palms.

"He's the one. Seize him!" Joseph Le Claire cried breathlessly, with sweat streaming down his jowly face. His paunch bulged the expensively cut waistcoat beneath his somber frock coat. "He's the one who assaulted me, an officer of the Crown."

Jimenez and Cortez crouched and each one thrust a hand inside his coat. They were going to draw knives. Samuel's heart lurched, and he pulled them back. "*Halto.* Don't do it."

He switched to English and strode forward. "Joseph, what is the meaning of this?"

Le Claire swept his arms in the air. "I've waited months to get you. You humiliated me and stole my weapon. Wasn't it enough that your family infected the peasants with notions of land rights? Now you dare to bring back these, these . . . *monkeys.*"

The insulting churl. The fat bigot. Samuel's muscles quivered, and he battled the urge to punch this gibface. The pigeon-livered captain of the disgraced Royal Irish Dragoons obviously hadn't learned his lesson in Lough Hyne last spring. But Jimenez and Cortez didn't understand where the lines were in this new place. If he struck, they would tackle the constables with intent to do them bodily harm—or worse. "How dare *I*, Le Claire? How dare *you*? You're the pro—"

"Joseph! Stop it this instant." Lord Le Claire stormed from the hotel's lobby and thrust himself between Samuel and his son.

Samuel was fifteen the last time he'd seen Lord Le Claire, when the powerful aristocrat had ejected him ignominiously from the Christmas ball at his manor, all because Father had objected to the abuse of peasants during the famine. Lord Le Claire's hair was iron gray now, but he was still lean and ramrod straight, his veins beating a visible pulse beneath the crinkled skin of his neck.

Joseph Le Claire stepped back jerkily. "But Father, he's t—"

"Shut up, you foolish boy, and get into the hotel." Lord Le Claire chopped a hand at the blinking constables. "What are you staring at? Get out of here before I call the sheriff. Get out!"

The red-faced constables shuffled their feet, wringing their truncheons with white knuckles, and flicked hooded glances at Joseph Le Claire.

The younger Le Claire's shoulders curled over his chest, and he waved a hand listlessly. "You heard His Lordship. Clear off." He stomped into the hotel.

Lord Le Claire wet his lips and drew Samuel aside. "I'm sorry. I told Joseph to steer clear of you, but he's envious. Despite your common birth, your father's ill-advised charity, your reckless career, and your inappropriate relationships, you're known as the unsung hero of Balaklava, and the wealthiest man in the county. It was all too much for Joseph."

Samuel was speechless. Too much for Joseph? The years of scorn and belittlement the Le Claires had wrought upon the Kingstons, and it was too much for Joseph?

But Le Claire pressed his elbows to his sides, seeming to shrink. "Look, I know the power you hold over those who were involved in Baltimore's slavery consortium. I promise you, this is the end of it. I'll keep Joseph in line."

Was the man actually fawning? "Lord Le Claire . . ."

"But I implore you not to publish the Baltimore letters. News of my involvement with slavers would ruin the family." The powerful aristocrat seemed old, almost pathetic. The smell of Le Claire's cold sweat wrinkled Samuel's nose, and he drew back. How had he ever yearned as a boy for the acceptance of this ruling class? His stomach roiled.

"Fine. But keep the wretch in line."

"You are so kind," Le Claire burbled. "I'm sorry he troubled you this morning."

This ascendency class needed to go. Ireland needed to change; it needed to be free.

Samuel locked eyes with the lord. "But one more thing."

"Sir?"

"I'm considering a run for parliament, and when I do, I expect your support." The implied threat hung in the cold air between them.

Le Claire glared down at his feet. "Absolutely, you have the full support of the Le Claires. But please . . . Bury those papers."

Rain drizzled on the funeral procession winding uphill past the stone walls and dormant fields of Springbough estate to the weathered crypt. The green copper roof stood out from the multicolored tapestry of deciduous trees clinging to their last red and gold leaves, while dark green conifers stood among them like guardsmen. Two black horses with red plumes on their heads hauled the gleaming black hearse through the sticky mud, dark drapes fluttering in the sea breeze. Jason and his wife, Ingrid, walked ahead of Samuel, followed by the mourners: relatives and gentry in black finery, and the tenants from Springbough and Las Peñitas in their Sunday best of faded coats, patched suits, and dresses frequently mended.

Heedless of the dogged rain seeping through his cloak, Samuel reined in four-year-old John from frolicking through the puddles. He inclined his head at Chester Inwood, who'd traveled down from Cork, and reverted to plodding beside Sofia, with bitter and sweet emotions swaying his heart like a pendulum. Memories of Father's gentle ways—melancholy sighs when Samuel departed for boarding school and war, joy when they rode together, moist eyes whenever he'd mentioned Samuel's mother—filled Samuel with heaviness, bringing tears. But a lightness swiftly swept sadness aside, a buoyancy where his heart was heavy and a brightness where it was dim: Father would rest at home after all these years.

Samuel had kept his promise.

If only Father could see how happy he was now with his growing family, his wonderful wife, his—

"John, stop splashing mud." Sofia yanked John closer to her. "You've soiled Aunt Ingrid's dress."

"I'll carry him." Samuel picked the boy up. He'd grown much in the months they'd been overseas. "Behave yourself, John. You can play once we bid Grandfather goodbye."

"You said this was a celebration," John piped. "Why's everyone so sad and quiet?"

Sofia tucked a strand of hair under her black bonnet. "They're not sad, they're praying. We said our goodbyes to Grandfather five years ago, and now we're welcoming him home. Of course it's a celebration."

The horses threw up their sleek black heads, rippling the red plumes on their headstalls, and the hearse creaked to a stop at the moss-speckled gate posts. Atop the crypt, stone angels perched with hands clasped in devotion and blank eyes cast toward the heavens, frozen in eternal prayer.

"I never even knew him," John said. "And Grandfather Valle's dead, too. I want a grandfather." He wriggled. "Put me down, Father, I want to go in."

The breeze swirled flaming red and burnt orange leaves around Sofia as she caught John's hand. "That's heartbreaking."

"You may not have grandfathers, John, but you've Uncle Jerry. He can be your grandfather."

"He's teaching me to fight like you. When's Uncle Padraig coming home?"

"Soon. Now stay with your mother while I help carry the coffin."

Samuel saluted Jimenez and Cortez, who stood out from the crowd with their dark complexions, good looks, and military bearing. As Mickey Spillane had said, *Sure the county's never seen the likes of them before, but I pity the man who'd cross them. Dangerous-looking buggers, they are.* Few knew that this pair had fought beside him for Father's liberty, although it had been in vain in the end.

A crow flapped off the crypt roof and circled high above the hearse, croaking at the mourners.

The coffin was light for a great man, reminding Samuel that only Father's bones lay inside. They maneuvered between the pillars and stepped down into the cool chamber, shiny shoes rapping on the stone flags. This dark space was a friendly place; Mother had waited twenty-seven years here for this reunion. He helped lower the coffin into the tomb as the Church of Ireland vicar from Kilgarrife, Reverend Mills, helped Father Mulcahy down inside, their footsteps echoing off the stone and their shadows folding across the walls in the flickering lantern light.

The reverend clutched his Bible to his breast like a love letter and approached the tomb. He read from the Book of Proverbs in a clear voice as the mourners waited patiently.

"Amen." Reverend mills closed his Bible and ushered Father Mulcahy forward. "Come, Father, you and Mr. Kingston were close friends. Would you like to say a prayer?"

It was uplifting to see these clerics were promoting harmony between their flocks. Perhaps this was a sign that Samuel too could unite Irishmen of all creeds in a common cause: justice. "Please, Father, I know he'd wish this."

The old parish priest's mouth had fallen open. "Me? Well,

I've never been to a Protestant funeral before. Sure, I've nothing prepared."

"Speak from your heart, Father. He respected how you gave everything you possessed to feed the hungry during the famine, and it gave him great joy to join in helping you."

The priest fingered the chipped wooden cross hanging from his neck. "I'm honored." He swallowed. "I'd the good fortune to know John Kingston most of his adult life, and in a time when this nation was most divided—rich against poor, Catholic against Protestant, Anglo-Irishman against Irishman—he never judged a man by the church he attended or the quality of his clothes. He fed the starving and dressed the shivering, unlike other landowners. Sure an' the man was a saint, and we'll need more of his kind if the country's ever going to mend. May he rest in peace with his beloved Victoria. Amen."

"Amen." The voices echoed around the musty chamber.

Tears welled behind Samuel's eyelids. He'd once scorned Father's acts of charity, which had alienated the family from their own Anglo-Irish class, but he regretted that behavior today. Now, with Nicaragua safe from Walker, he would redeem himself. He'd continue Father's fight for religious equality and justice in Ireland. He had plans. Big plans.

Jason muttered a last farewell and stepped back from the tomb. It was Samuel's turn.

The coffin lid was sealed, but Samuel imagined Father's compassionate face. *Finally you're home, Father. I regret it took so long. I'm sorry I was such a pompous ass, so focused on titles and privilege instead of justice and service, but I assure you I've changed. I hope you can see that from on high. I will strive for justice for all of Ireland. I will make you proud.*

"Farewell, Father."

Sofia slipped a gloved hand around his shoulder, cold where it brushed his neck. "He'd be so proud of you, darling."

Not yet. But he would be.

The clouds had parted when he stepped from the crypt with

tear-stung eyes. Sunlight fringed the green hills gold, the hedgerows glinted copper, and the sea shimmered steel blue in Clonakilty Bay.

John tugged his hand. "I want to be a grandfather when I grow up, so Father Mulcahy will say nice things about me."

"You and me both, son. You and me both."

"May I go hunting with Pedro now? He promised to teach me how to make a rabbit snare."

Cortez held up a ball of string where he stood behind the mourners. The Carib had become John's unofficial bodyguard since their arrival in a land so different from their own.

Sofia patted John's shoulder. "Certainly, run along. We'll be here awhile with the visitors."

Cheerily, cheer-up, cheer-up, cheerily, cheer-up. The steady, tuneful whistle drew Samuel's eyes to the red-breasted robin perched in the hedgerow. The tiny bird's promise buoyed him. He knew what he had to do with the rest of his life: to continue Father's fight for justice in Ireland. And there was no better time to begin, with the past now laid to rest and Father's final blessing freshly upon him.

THE END

HISTORICAL NOTES

The Seventeenth Lancers led the Light Brigade on their fateful charge up the North Valley in the Battle of Balaklava during the Crimean War. Major-General George Charles Bingham, Third Earl of Lucan, commanded the British Cavalry in Crimea, albeit timidly and poorly.

For all his faults, William Walker was a remarkable man. He attended the University of Nashville when he was twelve years old, got his first degree at fourteen, graduated as a doctor when he was eighteen, and then became a lawyer. He did oppose slavery in early years, and it must have been ambition that drove him to impose it on Nicaragua. Walker was the only American to assume the presidency of another country. After his removal from Nicaragua in 1857, he made two more attempts to seize control of Nicaragua, and the last led to his execution by the Hondurans in 1860.

Nowell Salmon saw action during the Crimean War as midshipman on the second-rate HMS *James Watt*. He served in the naval brigade and took part in the Siege of Lucknow in November 1857 during the Indian Mutiny and distinguished himself as a member of the force defending the Residency when he volunteered to climb a tree near the wall of the Shah Nujeff mosque to observe the fall of shot, despite being under fire himself and wounded in the thigh, for which he was awarded the Victoria Cross.

It was never clear why the young Commander Salmon turned the Icarus around and returned to hand William Walker over to the Hondurans. I figured saving the Sofia's life was as good a reason as any.

Salmon had a distinguished career first promoted to Commander-in-Chief, Cape of Good Hope and West Coast of Africa Station, then Commander-in-Chief, China Station, and finally Commander-in-Chief, Portsmouth as Admiral of the Fleet.

General José Santos Guardiola Bustillo served two terms as President of Honduras. The Honduran Congress first elected him president after the overthrow of Trinidad Cabañas, who later rebelled against him. Between those terms, he commanded one of the Legitimist forces fighting William Walker and the Democrat army in Nicaragua. His cruel treatment of his enemies earned him the nickname "Butcher," but his administration was one of the most liberal in Honduran history. His government allowed freedom of press, suffrage and respected individual freedom. His good relations with the British helped facilitate the return of the Bay Islands and the La Mosquitia region to Honduras. In 1862, during his second term, his personal guard assassinated him.

Cornelius Vanderbilt left school at the age of eleven to labor on vessels plying the East River, but was notoriously street-smart. He was reputed to keep everything in his head and always know his income and expenditures to the last cent. He started his first ferry service in New York Harbor at age sixteen and built his massive fortune first on steamboats and ocean steamers plying North American rivers and the world's oceans, and on his ever-expanding network of North American railroads after the American Civil War. When William Walker had his puppet president, Patricio Rivas, hand Vanderbilt's lucrative charters of both the Accessory Transit Company and the Atlantic and Pacific Ship Canal Company to his enemies, Morgan and Garrison, Vanderbilt swore to destroy Walker. He sent arms to the Central American countries fighting Walker and handsomely rewarded Sylvanus Spencer and Clifford for their successful scheme to capture the San Juan River from Walker. One cannot fault the Nicaraguan government for revoking Vanderbilt's charter and seizing all Accessory Transit Company assets in the country because, while Vanderbilt was making millions on the Nicaraguan business, Nicaragua did not see a penny of the agreed ten percent of profit. Vanderbilt claimed there was no profit. He slyly billed everything possible to the Accessory Transit Company—the cost of Colonel Childs's canal survey, the cost of the trip Vanderbilt and Joseph White made to England seeking canal financing, even the mortgage payments of ships he had put on the Nicaragua run.

After Walker was removed from power in Nicaragua, Vanderbilt wrested back the charter for the Accessory Transit Company, but he used the charter to block others from the Nicaraguan Transit Route and monopolized the Atlantic run to Panama with his new Atlantic and Pacific Steamship Company. I used this as the excuse why he did not cooperate with Samuel in Book 3 as he had in Book 2. Soon Vanderbilt forgot all about Nicaragua and focused on beating competitors on the transatlantic route.

I used the following books for reference:

Dando-Collins, Stephen. Tycoon's War. Hachette Books. Kindle Edition.

Doubleday, Charles William. Reminiscences of the "Filibuster" War in Nicaragua (1886). Kindle Edition.

Walker, William. The War in Nicaragua (1860). Kindle Edition.

www.ingramcontent.com/pod-product-compliance
Lightning Source LLC
Chambersburg PA
CBHW061309190726
48288CB00002B/427